The
Czar's Madman

The Czar's Madman

A NOVEL

JAAN KROSS

Translated by Anselm Hollo

PANTHEON BOOKS   NEW YORK

Library of Congress Cataloging-in-Publication Data

Kross, Jaan.
[Keisri hull. English]
The czar's madman : a novel/Jaan Kross; translated by Anselm Hollo.
p. cm.
ISBN 0-394-58437-6
1. Estonia—History—19th century—Fiction. I. Title.
PH666.21.R6K413 1993
894'.54532—dc20   92–50464

Book Design by Glen Edelstein
Manufactured in the United States of America
First American Edition

EDITOR'S PREFACE

AFTER THE FIRST OF MY WORKS dealing with historical subjects had attracted some attention among friends of that genre—a relatively dependable, if small, circle of readers—I found myself in a position to regard with kindly condescension those colleagues of mine who suffered from a chronic hunger for material and were always casting about for new subject matter: from persons known and unknown, I began to receive an ever-increasing number of letters containing suggestions, recommendations, even bibliographies regarding suitable historical persons and events. In many cases they referred me not only to what was publicly available, but also to material that previously had been completely unknown, or to new points of view on past lives already known in their main outlines.

The present manuscript was brought to me by an enthusiastic student of Estonia's early modern history, a resident of Tartu into whose possession it had come during the Siege of Leningrad in the Great Patriotic War. He had found it among the belongings of a deceased roommate by the name of Ignatyev. Due to a gap in his memory, of the kind that typically afflicts Estonians, the discoverer of the manuscript could not recall Ignatyev's first name or patronymic. At the time of the siege, this Ignatyev had been an old man; in his working life, he had probably been a clerk. All my efforts to establish his identity in order to find clues for further research proved futile. A conscientious historian would never make any claim about the origin of a manuscript that was based solely on its contents. Such conjecture is anathema to the conscientious historian, and only an author of historical romances, who has to rely on his imagination, would attempt to link this manuscript's cast of characters to that Ignatyev by hypothesizing that since the manuscript is the journal of Jakob Mättik, an uncle of Rear-Admiral Georg von Bock, its later possessor may have been a descendant of the admiral's wife, Anna Ignatyeva.

A few words on the editorial process. The reader will immediately notice that this text was not composed at the beginning of the last century. The original was written partly in a patois of Estonian and French, with a significant admixture of German; I have translated it into modern Estonian, standardizing all those linguistic layers into a form more or less comprehensible to the contemporary reader. It is to be hoped that a scholarly edition of Jakob Mättik's original journal, which is of considerable linguistic interest, will soon join the rapidly widening stream of publications from our historical treasure trove of epistolary and documentary literature (but only, of course, after we have acceptable editions of Russow's chronicle, Müller's sermons, Masing's letters, Faehlmann's works, and much else). True, the journal would have caused a much greater stir in Rosenplänter's *Beiträge*★ than it will in the periodical *Keel ja Kirjandus*. (In Rosenplänter's day, we did not, unfortunately, have a periodical in which it could have been published as historically valuable material.) But even in the ninth decade of our own century, its publication might be valuable in at least one respect: it could be one more reminder, to those who are not yet aware of this, that *manuscripts*, be they scholarly or fictional, do not age as well as *cognacs* or *military officers*, who automatically accumulate stars around their necks even when left in their barrels or reserves.

J.K.

★ See the Notes, which begin on p. 359, for discussions of foreign languages and unusual terms.—Translator.

Voisiku, Thursday, the twenty-sixth of May, 1827

First, let me record the occasion that impels me to begin this journal. *To begin*, I say, because I have no way of knowing if I'll go on with it. It seems rather doubtful that I will: neither the times, nor the country, nor even our family seem right for such an undertaking.

If I do go on, it will have to be a secret journal, and since it has to be secret, I might as well state the reason for its existence right here at the beginning. So: I have decided to keep a journal because I have found myself entangled in affairs so unusual that any thoughtful person, compelled to witness them by circumstance, would feel an urge to record his observations. It may well be that this particular witness is not thoughtful enough: were he more deeply reflective, he'd probably refrain from setting pen to paper. God alone knows.

Looking back, I have to admit that my involvement in these events is not a recent one but dates back at least ten years—even longer than that. In the course of those years, I myself have been transformed into an oddity. What other peasant boy from Holstre Manor could have learned and seen, during those years since 1814, all the things that were revealed to me in a sequence of events that most resembled the quick scene changes of Italian operas?

Well, then. Two weeks ago to the day, in a torrential spring rain, we arrived back here in Voisiku from our journey to St. Petersburg. "We" consisted of Eeva, nine-year-old Jüri, whom she had taken along against my advice, Timo, Käsper the servant, Liiso the lady's maid, and myself. Not to forget our coachman, Juhan—and our escort, consisting of a guard and three gendarmes.

Once again, bowing to Eeva's wish, we did not stay with Timo's relatives but—as usual—by the Moika, with the widow of Lehrberg the Academician. A few months ago, Timo had been transferred from Schlüsselburg to the Fortress of Peter and Paul. When at last, on the evening of the tenth of May, they brought him from the fortress to Mrs. Lehrberg's apartment, the guard stayed behind to keep an eye on him. He had to be lodged in the apartment overnight. Eeva told me to take the guard to Mrs. Lehrberg's kitchen and get him good and drunk. This turned out to be easier than I had expected, thanks to Mrs. Lehrberg's powerful cherry schnapps. She provided two bottles of it and gave me a wink: *"Um Gottes willen nicht sparen!"*

While the guard lounged in the kitchen, ate borscht and drank schnapps, whistled a tune, nodded off, and finally started snoring, four or five gentlemen, their faces hidden by the turned-up collars of their coats, entered the Lehrberg drawing room, greeted Timo with emphatic whispers, blew their noses. Who they were I do not know, since I only caught a glimpse of them through a crack in the door. Only one candle had been lit in the foyer, and the gentlemen's faces were concealed by those collars as well as by mufflers. I heard Timo address one of them as Vassili Andreyevich, and since this Andreyevich seemed to be even more excited than the others, it occurred to me that he might be the poet Zhukovski, whom I had once met five or six years before that night. It had been said that friendship with such a suspect creature as Timo would be considered doubly grave in the case of Zhukovski, who was the Czarina's tutor. To tell the truth, it surprised me to see so many friends appear during those few hours to greet us and express their sympathy; except for Zhukovski, practically nobody had stayed in touch with us during the nine years of Timo's absence.

At six o'clock in the morning, the guard roused himself and was joined by three gendarmes. Eeva put them to work immediately: they carried our valises outside and secured them to the roof of the coach. In the staircase, I heard one neighbor say to another, "What a woman, this Baroness von Bock . . . Not only has she managed to get her husband back . . . but they've even sent this little detachment to carry her baggage . . ."

The real purpose of these "porters," who were supervised by the guard, was, of course, to keep an eye on us on the journey from St. Petersburg to Voisiku. To make sure we wouldn't stray from the prescribed route—abroad, for instance: this was the greatest fear—or anywhere else. And also to make sure we didn't send off letters or bulletins or engage in discussions with outsiders about matters dangerous to the state . . .

After we were on our way, I had my first chance in nine years to take a close look at Timo. I had heard rumors that he'd become incredibly obese. This was not so. True enough, when they arrested him, he was a slender young man, dazzlingly handsome, looking much younger than his thirty years. Now he looked like fifty, perhaps even older on account of his lack of teeth. But to my mind, the most alarming thing about him was the gray coloration of his face, not the silver in his hair or the surplus weight he'd soon lose by exercising his horsemanship. As it turned out, he didn't waste any time: he opened the coach window and beckoned the guard closer, said something to him, then told the coachman to stop.

"Kitty, I want to ride a bit. I haven't had any exercise for ages."

He got out. One of the gendarmes gave him his horse and joined Käsper on top of the coach. Timo swung into the saddle and cantered off, the guard and two gendarmes following him at the respectful distance of fifty paces.

Inside the coach, I looked around. Little Jüri, tanned, button-nosed, lay curled up and fast asleep on the back seat under his checkered travel plaid; in the front seat, flaxen-haired Liiso was slumbering. I bent toward Eeva and asked her quietly, in the vernacular (later I realized that this had been a premonition of days to come when we could speak of these things only in Estonian):

"Eeva, what did they do to his teeth?"

She whispered back, "They knocked them out, one at a time."

She closed her eyes. Two small creases appeared beside her nose. Then she whispered:

"Because of some difficult matter. Timo told me what it was, but I didn't quite get it."

I stared at her pain-contorted face. Her eyes remained closed. The coach rumbled on, and the shadows of the birch trees by the roadside slid over her face. I thought:

I do not love my sister. I don't. She had been only too eager to leap into the unknown as soon as the young lord of the manor beckoned; she had entered a situation beyond all natural boundaries, and she had dragged me into it. Yes, indeed. Even if it had only involved the marriage of a peasant girl to a baron, her story would have been scandalous . . . No, I do not love my tempestuous, stubborn, incomprehensible sister—and she knows it . . . Yet she trusts me. Whom else could she trust? And I suppose I trust her, too. To express my appreciation of that trust, I took her hand which lay between the folds of her muslin gown and the upholstered coach seat and squeezed it. She squeezed back. I wanted to ask her a thousand things, first and foremost among them: *Eeva, tell me this—Timo has been certified as a madman, but is he truly mad? Or does he act the madman on occasion, so they won't throw him back into the casemate?* And something else, even more important: *Tell me, Eeva, why have they done this to him?* But I didn't ask her anything. I did not want her to retreat into herself and fob me off with a lie as though I were a stranger. I didn't ask her anything. I only looked at her and thought: I don't understand where my sister gets her impetuous nature. Just think about her hair, and what she did with it . . .

Ibidem, Friday, the twenty-seventh

Last night I was interrupted, or thought I was, and tried to put to the test if I'd be able to hide my journal quickly enough, without having taken the precaution of locking the door. I almost succeeded.

When I purchased the small black notebook, two weeks before

our last journey to St. Petersburg, in Schade's stationery shop in Viljandi, I didn't really think of it as a journal but rather as a commonplace book for aphorisms I might come across in my reading. Not in order to impress people in conversations, as the half-educated (such as myself!) often attempt to do (and as the truly cultured seem to be able to do without effort). I just wanted to note them down for myself. Aphorisms which in a line or two reproduce the content of tomes of two and three hundred pages. But after we returned from St. Petersburg, and Timo was among us once again, I began to think about our lives. The empty notebook caught my eye, and I conceived of the idea to keep a journal. And I discovered, here in my room, a hiding place where I could conceal it quickly if the need arose.

★   ★   ★

This room is still mine to use, even though Timo has returned: it is a garret at the end of the right wing, the same one that Timo had converted into a small study ten years ago. I moved into it after his departure. The room, six or seven square fathoms in size, has a door opening onto a hallway and two windows facing each other on the side walls. One of the windows is set into the façade of the building, the other has a view of the large, untended orchard. The building dates from the beginning of the last century. It is said that Timo's father couldn't afford a new manor because he had spent his money on the compilation and printing of all the plans, projects, and proposals he and Lehrberg had sent out for the opening of the University of Tartu. Hence, our so-called new manor is really quite old; its huge chimney stacks are tapered in the manner of their time. One of these colossal chimneys runs right through the middle of my chamber, attached to a Dutch blue-tile stove and a white-tile fireplace; these divide the room into two halves. Behind the stove, in the oriel facing the orchard, stands my tiny desk, the one at which I'm sitting right now and writing this. Here, too, is the hiding place that has tempted and encouraged me to keep a journal in a household like ours. The white wooden ceiling above my head is very low: one day, when I stood in front of my desk and happened to reach up and push against the ceiling, a board on the right side gave way and opened like the lid of a small casket. When I let go, it closed again with a quiet snap. I wasn't able to open it again, and it took me a while to find out how it worked. The board to the right moved only when I exerted pressure on the one to the left at the same time— the boards were joined by a hidden mechanism consisting of two small wooden blocks and a spring. I put my hand into the narrow opening and discovered that it led into a wooden box, two cubits long and two or three spans wide. It seemed to contain nothing but cobwebs and dust, and I knew immediately that this was the ideal hiding place for my journal.

I notice that I left off yesterday in the midst of a discussion of my sister's character—and hair . . . Yes, nature blessed Eeva with truly beautiful hair, even though it was nothing out of the ordinary in the villages around Holstre, where many have that coloration —those with pretensions to a vocabulary call it "Titian blond." Now, however, I suspect few people would take my word for it—because, as I well remember, on the first anniversary of Timo's arrest, the nineteenth of May, 1819, we hardly recognized Eeva when she came out of her bedroom and joined us at the breakfast table: she had dyed her hair the night before, and now it looked pitch-black. I remember that when Jüri, eight months old at the time, was taken to his mother, he emitted a powerful scream. It had a disturbing effect on all of us. I asked her why she had done it, and Eeva replied:

"So that I, and all of us, won't forget what they've done to me."

"All of us" referred to Dr. Robst, Käsper, Liiso, and me: no one else was left at the estate. Timo's brother Georg was with his regiment, Karl was in St. Petersburg, his sister Elisabeth had married four years before, and we hadn't seen her in over a year. I had heard a rumor that her husband, Peter Zoege von Mannteuffel of Vana-Harm in Estonia, had forbidden his wife to associate with the family of his brother-in-law, a man accused of treason—not to mention the fact that this traitor's wife was that incomprehensible, impossible, offensive thing: a girl of the peasant class . . .

For eight years, Eeva's hair remained a pitch-black banner of sorrow. She wore it proudly, defiantly, demonstratively—and I sympathized with her, although it is my opinion that only women can afford such striking gestures. Even so, those gestures make me feel uncomfortable. On the eve of the day on which Timo was to be delivered to Mrs. Lehrberg's apartment, Eeva asked for some strong vinegar, added some herbs to it, and washed the black dye out of her hair. Although Timo had seen her black hair when she visited him in the Fortress of Peter and Paul, she now wanted to welcome him to liberty looking the way she had before his arrest—if what lay ahead of her, and him, and of all of us, can be called liberty . . . But it was obvious that something had been irretrievably lost: even though she wasn't yet thirty, her hair had gone gray at the temples.

Voisiku, Tuesday, May thirty-first

The hypothetical reader of these notes won't be able to understand the unusual events of our lives without knowing something about their prehistory. I shall try to present that here, as briefly as possible.

We—Eeva, myself, and our younger siblings, a sister and a brother who succumbed to the croup while still very young, and at the same time—were born in the district of Viljandi on the modest farmstead known as Kannuka, which was tilled by our father, Peeter, in the village of Tömbi, which belongs to a crown estate, Holstre Manor, whose owner is a General von Berg. Eeva first saw the light in 1799; I was born in 1790. I was still a boy when our father was employed for several years as the coachman of the estate. This did not leave him much time to work on his farm, and he managed to persuade General von Berg to release him from his duties as a coachman but keep him on as the tenant of Kannuka Farm.

Until the spring of 1813, we lived the customary life of peasant children and village youth. The only advantage we enjoyed, one not shared by all children of peasants, was that our father taught us to read early on, and to write the letters of the alphabet with pieces of coal on birchbark until we were deemed fit to use paper and goose quill—at which point we could have copied entire pages from our catechism and book of sermons, had we been given enough paper. As a child, I was small and skinny, but according to my father, my "rage" to work made me grow up into a strong young man, well able to take care of a house and a farm—and this was a subject he brought up with increasing frequency.

In the spring of 1813, Sabine von Berg, the twenty-year-old daughter of the general, summoned Eeva to visit her and offered her a position as chambermaid. Mother regarded the offer with equanimity, but Father voiced violent opposition. True enough, the old general was in his seventies and rarely visited the estate, and thus posed no threat as a potential seducer. True, his son was in the field, had been fighting Bonaparte for more than two years. But there were all these stories about maids on big estates whose lives had been ruined in that certain way . . . Yet even back then Eeva knew how to get what she wanted, and our parents' conflicting views made it even easier for her to do so.

She said, "Nothing will happen to me against my will." And she accepted the offer. I have to concede that she was right, even though the most implausible things then did happen to her . . .

In the fall of 1813, Paul von Berg was granted leave from his regiment and came to Holstre Manor, accompanied by his regimental comrade, Colonel Timotheus von Bock. The latter, it was said, was a personal friend of the emperor's.

I have never asked Eeva what happened or didn't happen there on the estate. There certainly was a great deal of talk. Rumor had it that Miss Sabine had chosen her brother's friend for her fiancé, and that her papa and mama had regarded this as a done thing. However, one bright September morning, that selfsame Timotheus von Bock rode over to Kannuka Farm. I remember it as if it happened yesterday—because our Eeva was with him, riding sidesaddle on the hindquarters of the horse.

Baron von Bock jumped down and lifted Eeva off the horse. Instead of his uniform, with its decorations, he wore a plain white linen coat and trousers of the same material. But his riding boots were those of an officer.

"Is Father here?" asked Eeva, and I replied, "Yes, he's here." I hung the horse collar on a nail beside the stable door and followed them into the house.

Baron von Bock spoke Estonian, and really quite well, although his pronunciation had that hard and abrupt German tone that can still make me wince. Father had stood up behind the table, Mother was over by the stove, holding the lid of a butter churn in front of her like a shield. Baron von Bock asked Father, "Are you Peeter, the tenant of Kannuka?"

"I am he."

"I am Timotheus von Bock, from Voisiku Estate, right in the Viljandi District, by Poltsamaa."

Across the table he proffered his hand to our father, who did not respond. I don't think this was because he didn't want to, it was just that it was so sudden and astounding to be offered a handshake by a baron.

"Peeter, your daughter Eeva and I have pledged our troth. I want to marry her. But only with your permission."

Mother's face turned as white as birchbark. Father's bluish fingernails dug into the edge of the dining table, and I saw a flush rise on his neck. Eeva stared at the table. Father said:

"The gentleman must not be fully conversant with this language of ours. The gentleman meant to say he wants my daughter for his whore. One need not ask a father's permission for that."

"No-o!" shouted Mr. Bock and looked straight at Father with friendly, light-gray eyes. "Sit down!"

He seated himself astraddle the long bench, thus compelling father to follow suit and sit down.

"Please listen. I'll explain everything."

And so he did. He really wanted to marry Eeva. This was part of the grand plan he had drawn up for his life. By this marriage, he would prove the equality of all human beings before God, nature, and his ideals. He had watched Eeva for three weeks and had grown fond of her, as had she of him. He turned to her: "Eeva, is that not so?" And Eeva said, "Yes, it is." This did not concern anyone but her and him and their parents—and since his father and mother were no longer among the living, *her* parents, Peeter of Kannuka and his Anne. Now he wanted to send Eeva to his fatherly friend, Pastor Masing of Viru-Nigula, one of the wisest men in Estonia or Livonia; there, the pastor, and the nanny and the tutor of the pastor's children, would instruct Eeva in good manners, foreign languages, and book learning. The wisdom of

Eeva's heart was greater than most people imagined. This would not be a visit for a fortnight or a couple of months: she would stay there for five years, and then he would come and lead Eeva to the altar to make her his wife before God and man.

Our father had been listening, eyes closed. Now he looked up and stared at Mr. Bock. I could tell that the hoarseness of his voice was no longer due to anger but to confused emotion:

"I'm too old to believe in such crazy talk . . ."

"But it's the truth, and nothing but the truth!" shouted Mr. Bock. "Should I . . ."—he snapped his fingers, looking for the right word—"how do you say it—*schwören?* Swear an oath?"

He rose to his feet.

"I've never done this in my whole life—my word has been accepted without oaths. But if you think it is necessary . . ."

He took Eeva's right hand into his left and raised two fingers of his right hand toward the low ceiling of our house. He looked at us with his radiant light-gray eyes and said:

"I swear that every word I have spoken here is the truth—in the name of our Lord, and by my honor."

And he kept his word. Without delay, a tremendous machinery was set in motion. He arranged our purchase through the Inspector of Crown Estates, at double our official price. We received our certificates of emancipation, after which we no longer had any business at Holstre Manor. He found a farmstead for us in the village of Kaavere, on Voisiku land, and had all of us moved there with our belongings. As I write "us," I realize that isn't quite right: on the third day after our arrival, Eeva was taken to Viljandi and outfitted with a city wardrobe, and then she was told to pack her things. Käsper, the servant, was to take her in a coach from Kaavere to Viru-Nigula. Timotheus came to Kaavere for the occasion. When he arrived, Eeva was standing next to the coach in the yard. In her city clothes and shoes she already looked as if she belonged to a different world. Farewells had already been said. Mother stood with tearful eyes on the threshold of our new and as yet unfamiliar house. Father patted Eeva's shoulder and said, "You must know what you are doing . . ." Even I said goodbye to her. At that moment, Timotheus looked at Eeva and said:

"Eeva, are you sad?"

And she replied, "Of course I am."

With a beseeching expression, Timotheus looked at all of us in turn, until his eyes, now almost irritatingly bright, came to rest on me. He said:

"Eeva, would this be easier for you if your brother Jakob went with you?" I noticed how his eyes became even brighter at this thought. I had already noticed that he was able to forge momentous plans with lightning speed, and to follow through on them like wildfire. "If he went with you to Pastor Masing and stayed there? And studied things with you, and stood by your side as your brother, servant, helper? And became an educated person, just like you?"

The matter was decided, but Eeva's departure was not postponed by one minute for my benefit: no such allowances were made in Timotheus's grand life plan. I said goodbye to Father and Mother and joined Eeva in the coach. Timotheus rode alongside of us. At Voisiku Manor I was provided with some cleaner clothes, and after an hour, Eeva, the servant Käsper, the coachman, and I were on our way to Virumaa. Timotheus stood by the orchard gate to wave us goodbye—from my window I can see the spot by that whitewashed brick pillar. Later I heard that Timotheus left the next morning to join his regiment in Prussia, at Barclay's headquarters, to which he was attached at the time. As for me, I have to say that despite my dismay and reluctance, my feeling that I had been violated (no one had bothered to ask me for my consent), despite everything that had undermined my mood when we left, I could hear a ringing in my head, as of church bells—two churchbells, to be exact, one of them deep and slow, ding-dong, *treas-on, treason* against everything Eeva was sacrificing by her rise in the world; the other, high and quick, ding-ding-ding, *what a gift, what a gift, what a gift!* Yes, a strange gift had descended upon me from heaven: I was to become an educated person . . .

Ibidem, still, Saturday, June the fourth

While I was composing my last-but-one journal entry, I had imagined what it would be like if I were disturbed, and had tried to see if I could convey my notebook into its hiding place in the ceiling quickly enough. On Sunday, that experiment stood me in good stead: at ten o'clock in the evening, after an almost inaudible, perfunctory knock, Mr. Alexander Laming, the steward of our estate, entered my room so quickly I just barely managed to hide the notebook and open up Schiller's *Wallenstein*—to give the impression that I was being interrupted in my perusal of act three.

Mr. Laming, his daughter, and a maid live in "The Foundation," the smaller manor house, situated between the park and the orchard and behind the larger house. The left wing of The Foundation is occupied by the aforementioned Dr. Robst.

Mr. Laming apologized politely for the intrusion. He is the quietest and most courteous person of the manor. It is said that his excessively gentle nature led him to give up his original profession, that of a master builder, because he found himself unable to deal with foremen or construction workers or suppliers. Yet I doubt that overseers, grain storekeepers, workers, and peasants are any more likely to give of their best when they receive their orders so quietly. But when our former steward, Klarfeldt, had decided to give notice after Timo's arrest, Mr. Laming mustered the courage to apply for the position, and Eeva took him on. She had based the decision on three separate considerations. First of all, she had thought of the dangers of mismanagement likely to occur on an estate of this size—over thirty jugers—in the absence of a steward (and, in our case, also of a squire). Secondly, there was the sympathy Mr. Laming's courage evoked in her—a courage that was downright touching when compared to all the dismay and timidity we encountered all around us at that time; and thirdly, she must have been impressed favorably by his even temper.

Laming is a small man with a large head, bristly whitish-blond hair, and a good-natured, angular face. When walking, he seems to favor one side of his body in a way that looks both awkward and agile. And although there is no such thing as a cordial relationship between peasants and their overseers, I've never heard the former say a bad word about him. This Sunday evening he sat down in the wicker chair facing me and spoke to me (more or less) as follows:

"Forgive me, Mr. Mättik, for this late hour . . . But I was downstairs, talking with the squire about what needs to be done this spring—as you know, he's been taking an interest in such matters—and I told him and Madame all kinds of news from Riga. I just got back from there on Saturday. And after I left them—and after Madame had offered me some of the raspberry liqueur from two years ago—I noticed that there was smoke rising from the chimney, and since there'd been no fire in the downstairs fireplace, I realized it had to be coming from your room, and that you were probably still poring over your books. And, you see, there's something on my mind after my visit to Riga—and I think you could help me—you see, it's to do with—don't be surprised —it's to do with my Iette . . ."

For some years now I have known that I have a certain knack: I'll be talking to someone, I'll listen to what he has to say—and suddenly I know that in a moment his conversation will take an entirely unexpected turn, yet I know exactly what it is he'll say, five or ten seconds in advance. It never fails.

Nor did it last night. All of a sudden, ten seconds before Mr. Laming uttered the words, I knew he would say that it was something to do with his Iette. I was so certain, that the inevitability of his words must have brought a blush to my cheeks.

Iette is Laming's eighteen-year-old daughter Henriette. An elegant young woman, almost citified. Winters she spends in Riga, summers with her father. Round face, straight white neck, small pink mouth. She wears gowns with a fashionably high waistline, and ties her black shoe-ribbons around her calves, all the way up to the backs of her knees (I really don't know how I know this . . .). I have talked to her a few times in the past few weeks, in the park, in the yard, by the gate of the steward's house. I can't remember her saying anything particularly remarkable, but she has a sweet and enticing way of giggling . . .

Her papa continued:

"In the winter, Iette lives with my sister in Riga and goes to Miss Friebe's School for Young Ladies. At the end of the last school year, when I brought Miss Friebe a few victuals—a couple of hams, a jar of pickled mushrooms, that sort of thing—she told me, plaintively, that Iette hadn't been doing so well this year. Well now, it's not that she isn't an attentive and lively girl, you must have noticed that yourself. But she has no head for numbers, none at all, and she's not doing all that well in the history of the Russian Empire, either. Before she can begin her eighth year, this autumn, she'll have to study those subjects really hard, preferably with a good tutor . . . And so, as I was about to start out for home, it occurred to me—perhaps Mr. Mättik would be willing to help her? I know you didn't go to the university in Tartu or study in Germany—but you do have a much better education than most of the gentlemen with diplomas. And I imagine you could afford to spend a few hours away from your books. If you won't disdain a humble steward's silver, I'd like to pay you handsomely. And Iette would be most grateful to you."

Why should I have refused? It was an opportunity to earn a little money for which I wouldn't be obliged to Eeva, and Iette would be grateful . . . I asked him:

"Have you put this to Dr. Robst? I think he'd be more qualified. He studied in Germany, has worked as a teacher . . ."

"No doubt, no doubt. I'm sure he is a competent physician," said Mr. Laming, "and he may be able to teach little Jüri some French, and so forth—but as the tutor of a grown-up young lady, he just won't do. As you must have noticed, he is an eccentric, flighty person—he doesn't walk, he scurries along on tiptoe, he doesn't talk, he warbles . . . No, no, a teacher mustn't seem ridiculous to his pupil. A student must be able to look up to her teacher, the way Iette does to you. I know she does."

So I said, "All right, then. Let's give it a try." This afternoon, here, at six o'clock, Iette will start reviewing her subjects with me.

An hour later

Nothing to report in the meantime. I've tidied up my room a bit, and Miss Iette won't be here for another two hours, so I have decided to devote this time to my journal.

Eeva and I arrived at Viru-Nigula and stayed with old Pastor Masing for four years. We were like bottles being filled with a funnel and learned as much as we possibly could. From the very first day, practically, we were only allowed to speak German in the Masing household. Six months later, we had to start conversing with the governess and the tutor exclusively in French from morning until noon. Old Masing himself taught us the elements of Latin and would have proceeded to ancient Greek and Hebrew had not the governess, who was later to become his wife, put her foot down, saying that this would be overdoing it.

As it turned out, Timo had sent along two or three crates of books for us. These were a selection of the books he had studied as a child and contained many notes and underlinings in Lehrberg's hand. (For many years Lehrberg had been tutor and mentor to Timo, and to his sister and brothers, and I knew that Timo revered him deeply. I never set eyes on Lehrberg, but heard that he had been an orphan, the son of a simple craftsman from Tartu, and, it was said, of peasant stock. It was also said that he was so extraordinarily knowledgeable that he had been elected to the Academy in St. Petersburg when still quite young, and despite his uncommonly principled character . . . Regrettably, he died soon thereafter of a terrible rheumatic illness, even before we began our studies at Viru-Nigula. In the Masing household, his name was spoken with great respect. His widow even visited Viru-Nigula a couple of times—Pastor Masing's first wife had been Mrs. Lehrberg's sister, thus the widow was the aunt of Masing's children.)

Ours and those children's guide through Timo's old books—enriched as they were with Lehrberg's spiritual legacy—was Mr. Gruhner, the tutor, a pleasant fellow from Hanover. He was patient with us, but made us proceed at a gallop. All I can say is that even though there were times when Eeva and I had to hang on for dear life to the slippery rump of that fiery steed, *we never fell off*. In addition, old Masing took time to explain the rudiments of draftsmanship and surveying to me. I had to spend three weeks, staying up half the night, working on a map of the garden of the Viru-Nigula parsonage, before he declared himself satisfied. And so on. Meanwhile, Masing's future spouse and her maids kept Eeva busy learning the culinary and domestic arts.

One incredibly windy evening in September of 1817, Timo paid a surprise visit to Äksi, where we and the whole Masing household had moved from Viru-Nigula the previous year. I can still see the old oil lamp's quivering flame in the pastor's study, a large room cluttered with all sorts of things—books, manuscripts, pieces of cardboard and paper with notes on them, notebooks, engravings, flasks, retorts, tools for working wood and metal. Old Masing was striding back and forth, hands behind his back; Eeva and Timo sat on a tiny sofa between stacks of books; I stood beside the sofa. Then Masing stopped in the middle of the room, turned toward Eeva and Timo, and said, in his rather shrill voice:

"My friends, if I don't do it, no one else will. But I can't do it. I already have some charges pending against me. They claim that I have been marrying couples against the rules of the church and the laws of the state. And even though the people in question were just peasants, it's thought of as a scandal, from Riga all the way to St. Petersburg. Let me tell you this: any pastor in Livonia, Estonia, or Courland who dares to marry you will be chased from the pulpit forever! Timo, if you think I'm exaggerating, you don't know your own peers!"

Timo replied, "I do know them, Pastor Masing. And I don't think you're exaggerating."

"And that is why, my friends," said old Masing, now facing Eeva, "this is the first, and, I hope, the last time I or any other Lutheran clergyman gives you—or anyone—this bit of advice." He put one hand on Eeva's shoulder and raised her chin with the other. "That is why I advise you, my child, to turn your back to this unfortunate Lutheran church of Livonia. Convert to the Russian Orthodox faith! That is what you have to do, I can see no other way. Love has led people to do worse things. God will help you serve him, no matter where. Go to St. Petersburg, with a letter from me to one of my friends. He'll find a priest for you, and never mind if he's a greater drunkard or a greater humanist than one of our own would be. Then you come back, and everything will be almost *comme il faut*. At least no one will be able to fault you in that respect."

He stepped back from the sofa, rubbed his stubbly gray chin and looked at the two of them.

"But, as you well know, they will declare open season on you. I can well imagine the malicious gossip that will get underway as soon as it becomes known that you have really carried out your mad plan . . . The wolves will howl, the sly foxes bark, the snakes in the grass will hiss—*sssssss* . . ." Masing seemed to be enjoying the image he conjured up. But then he said, in an entirely different tone of voice, "Nothing is stronger than love. I know it is love that gives you strength, Eeva; I have seen that. And you, too, Timo—love is the ground you stand on, but there is something else, I don't exactly know what: philosophy, most likely. Well, people have died at the stake for that, too. And I know—to use the peasant vernacular—that you *don't give a turd* for the sidelong glances and poisonous whisperings of your fellow nobles." He laughed. "As long as you put your trust in one another. Not just generally speaking, but in absolutely everything. That trust will be your refuge from all the brouhaha—like a perfectly formed oyster to protect your pearl. The worst storm can't touch it— maybe just rock it gently . . ."

As for the hissing of malicious snakes, I had already heard it. Inevitably, Eeva and Timo's marriage plans had become public knowledge. In St. Petersburg, friends had whispered into Timo's ear—taking care to phrase it so it couldn't be taken as cause for a duel—that Eeva had become so bored that she had welcomed the embraces of young von Adlerberg of Uue-Varstu, or those of the handsome parish clerk at Viru-Nigula, one Johannson, of peasant stock. And a pair of well-informed ladies who paid visits to the Masing household made sure that Eeva overheard their story, according to which Baron von Bock had asked for the hand of none other than Miss Naryshkina, the very same in whom the emperor himself expressed a fatherly interest. However, the em- peror's personal benevolence toward Baron von Bock had not extended far enough for him to advise the young lady to accept the proposal. Oh no. She had turned him down! Hence, it wasn't so surprising that von Bock had remembered his Cinderella again. The ladies giggled.

Before the month of September came to an end, Timo and Eeva returned from St. Petersburg. They had been married by a Russian Orthodox priest. According to the document, Eeva was now Katharina—Katharina von Bock. At first, I thought and felt that she had become an utter stranger to me, an impression reinforced by the way Eeva's eyes now looked either more veiled or more radiant than before, and the way her gestures had acquired a proud grace that even seemed a little inappropriate.

Nevertheless, when Eeva told me that she and Timo were leaving for Voisiku right away, to live there for the time being, and that I would of course join them, I felt there was nothing else I could do.

In four years I had acquired the book learning of a lyceum graduate, and since I had done this at a fairly advanced, yet still receptive, age—I was now twenty-seven—I had also acquired a good deal of worldly wisdom and judgment of character. I did not, however, know how to apply any of it, except for the notion that I might, after gaining some practical experience, best serve Eeva and Timo by assuming the management of Voisiku, replacing Klarfeldt, whom Timo had long suspected of improving his own finances at his squire's expense—a practice few salaried stewards were able to resist.

Thus, the four us (Käsper the servant had been sent to fetch us from Äksi) rode home through the lovely sunny autumn colors, by way of Puurmann and Poltsamaa. I spent the entire journey in the company of Timo and Eeva—or, rather, Timo and Kitty, to use the name by which my brother-in-law now called her, in the English manner.

★ ★ ★

Until that time, I had only spent a few hours at Voisiku, on that day in the autumn of 1813 when Eeva and I were sent off in a coach, on our way to our new life.

I knew that the estate did not rank among the most splendid in Livonia, but it was one of the more prominent estates in the northern part of Viljandi Province, if not by virtue of the splendor of its manor, then by the number of its buildings, the age of its park, the size of the orchard, and, above all, by the size of its holdings, which extended all the way to the valleys of the Pedja and Ema rivers.

The so-called new manor, already a century old, was a stone building with a main floor and an attic. Even though my peasant standards had already been elevated by our sojourn at Masing's two parsonages, the luxuriousness of the place stunned me at first. Now I understood: if I had had to move there four years ago, I would have felt timid and awkward, just like any other young peasant. Now I found the luxury disturbing, and the more I thought about it, the more I had to admit that it evoked a feeling of impatience in me . . .

On the main floor there were sixteen rooms and a kitchen. The attic floor had four rooms for servants and for visitors of minor importance. I asked Eeva for one of these, even though it had been her original intention to let me occupy two rooms on the ground floor. I liked it better up there under the roof, and I would have the place to myself. So it was agreed for me to move into the garret facing the orchard in the left wing of the manor. By the way: although Timo had two studies at his disposal on the ground floor, he also chose one of the garret rooms in the right wing as yet another study to read and write in. For the same reason—greater privacy. I didn't even have to use the main entrance and make my way past all the von Bocks and von Rautenfeldts, in their wigs and once fashionable coiffures, staring down into the great hall from their gilt picture frames. The staircase to the upper floor could be reached from the door on the orchard side, and I used it from the very first day I spent here.

Timo and Eeva insisted that I at least take dinner with them every day. I didn't object to that, since no one appeared at their dinner table except for themselves and Dr. Robst. Timo's younger brothers, Georg and Karl, were both away, and their sister Elisabeth, who got married four years ago (I think I mentioned this before), now lived in Estonia. Elisabeth did not make any efforts to visit her favorite brother and his young wife, something I would have thought the normal thing to do. But we were not a normal case, and we found that out soon enough, in a number of ways. As soon as Eeva and Timo had arrived at Voisiku, they sent out the customary invitations to their neighbors—at least to those neighbors of whom it might be assumed that they weren't actively denouncing this marriage as Jacobin swinishness or canine rutting. None of those invited, however, deigned to appear. Some were traveling abroad, others had taken to their beds due to a cold occasioned by the autumn weather, or they had some other excuse. Consequently, we did not take our meals in the dining room, which, anyway, was close to the kitchen and hence afflicted by the odors of cooking—Timo couldn't stand them—but in the green tea salon next to the drawing room. The table, however, was set with the von Bock family's heavy silver. I had heard that old Baron von Bock had died a poor man, through no fault but his own (in the summer of 1812, as a captain in charge of military hospitals during Bonaparte's offensive, of "hospital fever"). Hence, Timo had to be a poor man as well . . . But it wasn't only the family silver that made me realize what a curious thing it is, this poverty of the wealthy.

At dinner, Dr. Robst faced me across the table. He cared for the health of the inhabitants of the estate and also attended the leaseholder of Poltsamaa, von Wahl, and the owners of the castle, the Bobruiskis, whenever they appeared in Poltsamaa between their stays in St. Petersburg and Paris. In addition, Dr. Robst collected butterflies and occasionally directed artisans' children in performances of excerpts from Lessing's or Kotzebue's plays. He always arrived at the table quite red in the face from the exertion of walking the two hundred paces from the old main building, the one known as The Foundation, to the manor. Even before we were seated, and also between bites of dinner, he recited quotations from Rousseau in a theatrical voice, or gave lectures on the song-birds of the region, punctuating these by whistling examples of their songs. He provided the scientific background to each one of these and always, with a bow, begged Madame to excuse the whistling. Across the table, I looked at his emaciated frame, which always seemed to be about to float up into the air, at his good-natured face, his sad eyes under brows that reminded one of the tails of terriers . . . I was glad to be able to gaze at him and thus avoid the glances of my sister and brother-in-law: they sent such uninhibited rays of their great love across the table that it wouldn't have been surprising to see the silver gravy boats of the von Bock service vibrate and ring like bells. Timo did not permit Käsper or the kitchen maid to serve at table. Eeva or he himself would get up to serve or fetch things from the kitchen. Every time Timo returned to the table and walked past Eeva, he bent down and kissed the nape of her neck—or, what seemed even more im-proper: when Eeva passed by him, she ran her hand through his lively shock of brown hair. Quite as if neither Dr. Robst nor I had been there. But love has always—

June the fourth, late at night

That Iette arrived so quietly and knocked on the door so suddenly that I was hard put to hide my journal.

As for her book learning, she is more ignorant than I had expected. In order to test her, I gave her an arithmetic problem, choosing a subject I assumed might interest a young woman: a cloth merchant has received twenty-four rubles for a sale of two kinds of muslin. One kind costs two rubles a yard, the other, four. He received eight rubles more for the cheaper than for the more expensive kind. How many yards of each kind did he sell?

In her even and rapid hand, Iette wrote out the problem, stared at it for a while, and when she found herself unable to figure out the answer on the spot, she simply started laughing.

"But dear Mr. Mettich, I won't be selling fabrics. The only time I go to a cloth merchant is when I want to buy something. And I wouldn't be buying muslin, in any case—it's been out of fashion for years." Then she looked at me with smiling eyes and red lips, as if expecting me to join in her merriment. Her slightly protuberant eyes are gray and have a kind of veiled sparkle.

Then, when I took a sheet of paper and drew a line twenty-four inches long (the small oval table at which we were sitting in our wicker chairs was covered with sheets of paper), when I drew this line, marked its middle, and asked her in my best schoolmasterly voice to think again, she immediately subtracted four inches from the second half, added them to the first, and then added the two-inch lengths of the first half to the four-inch lengths of the other half—demonstrating that she was well-endowed with plain old common sense. After a little thought and practice, she did quite well with the calculation of percentages, and was so pleased with her success that she indulged in a few more peals of laughter. But she had no idea whatever of the reforms instituted by Peter the Great, and I don't think my lecture on them was much use to her. I noticed that her mind wandered, and she played absentmindedly with a narrow golden ring on her finger. (It can't very well be an engagement ring—if she wants to continue her education, surely she isn't engaged to anyone.) However, there were some questions concerning the Russian Empire that aroused her interest. After I had discussed Peter's reforms, she asked me:

"Mr. Mettich—you're such an incredibly knowledgeable person—and at Miss Friebe's, we couldn't find out anything about this matter—tell me, what really happened there in St. Petersburg, in December the year before last?"

After a moment's silence, I said, "Didn't they tell you at school?"

"Oh no. There were just all these rumors. That there had been a rebellion. And that the emperor had been attacked. And some of the older girls cried. It was said that a group of handsome and well-born young officers had been put to death. Or received some terrible punishment. But no one understood *why* it all happened, and what the rebellion had been *about*. At least, I didn't. Maybe that was because our teachers didn't really know, either. And because I was still such a child, the year before last. But now I'm sure I could understand. If only some wise person like yourself could explain it to me . . ."

The young lady is full of surprises, I thought to myself. I am not so sure myself what really happened there. A handful of noble youngbloods had wanted to set the world on a new course. In the right direction, no doubt. But in a precipitous and arrogant fashion. That's what I suspected. Even though their intentions had been good . . . *Limitations on monarchy* and *constitution* were words that had reached my ears even before that December the year before last . . . From, among others, Major (then Colonel) Tenner, with whose surveying detail I trudged all over Courland and Grodno province, between '22 and '26. But to Iette I said:

"Listen, let's talk about that on Tuesday when you come to see me again."

Why should I reveal my own thoughts to some girl about matters on which the whole empire observes silence? Why indeed. On the other hand, I couldn't tell her I didn't know anything about the affair. A teacher has to know things. Well, by Tuesday the little scatterbrain will have forgotten her question.

She got up to leave, then suddenly stopped right in front of me and said:

"You are a kinsman of our lord . . . Well—you are and you aren't . . . Tell me: *is he really mad—like the government claims—or isn't he, really . . . ?*"

Once again, I didn't say anything for a moment.

"What do you mean, isn't he really?" I then said. "It's not just the government that says that, but the emperor himself. So it just has to be true!"

"I see," she said quietly. "I thought that maybe he just *pretends* to be mad." Iette looked at me with her glittering light gray eyes. "Because it's so very sad to think . . ."

She left. I stepped over to my desk and looked out the window. As she was walking across the garden, past the brilliant apple trees, toward The Foundation, she must have felt my gaze; she turned to look over her shoulder, and her eyes met mine. She gave me a friendly smile, raised her hand next to her head, and waved— the little coquette! I turned away from the window and noticed that the room was permeated by the exciting scent of a young girl's sweat and perfume.

The *question*, however, which she had left in my room along with her scent, had long been a matter of interest to me, and certainly more so than it was to her. During the three weeks we have spent under the same roof, I have hardly seen my sister and brother-in-law. I have not been invited to share their meals the way I did nine years ago. Eeva told me she would, at first, take her meals alone with Timo in his study or in the bedroom, to give Timo time to convalesce and become used to his home again. The table has been set for me and Dr. Robst in the dining room, and the two of us have been eating there for the past three weeks. (The doctor had been living in Poltsamaa for years, but before Timo's return Eeva had asked him to move back to Voisiku. Being an unencumbered bachelor, the doctor agreed to move from the township to the manor, certain that his patients would manage to come and see him here, only five versts away from town.)

I have seen even less of Timo than I have of Eeva. From my window I have seen him take walks in the park. Once I saw him standing in the orchard under an apple tree, smelling the flowers for a long time, five or six minutes, if not even longer. And I've often seen Käsper lead the saddled gray from the stables to the door facing the orchard, and then seen Timo jump into the saddle and ride away. He has struck me as a person who has become curiously silent, but I truly haven't noticed any signs of madness.

I have asked Dr. Robst for his opinion, firmly assuming that he must have one—he has, after all, moved here to look after Timo. His replies have left me none the wiser, since he responds to my enquiries with a sibilant torrent of medical Latin, and even what he states parenthetically, in comprehensible German and Estonian, remains a mystery to me. In emotional tones, he counters my perfectly lucid questions with absurd and silly questions of his own.

"Doctor Robst—by now, you must have formed a clear opinion of my brother-in-law's condition. Are you *sure* that he—er, well, that he's lost his sanity in prison?"

"But, Mr. *Mettich*—wasn't that *the precise reason* why he was released, by the grace of Our Imperial Majesty?"

"Ahem . . . Yes, but wasn't he, or so I've heard tell, imprisoned by order of our previous emperor because he was *already* insane?"

"And that gives rise to some kind of *question* in your mind?"

"It does. If that was the case, how could he lose his mind *after* he was imprisoned?"

"You're asking *me?*"

"Of course I am. What's your guess?"

"But, Mr. Mettich, don't you think that—that a *doctor*, if no one else, should refrain from any kind of *guesswork* in such cases?"

"So you are saying that he is now quite normal?"

Dr. Robst pursed his mouth, spread his fingers, and raised his hands up to eye level like two airy goblets:

"Dear God—what does *normal* mean?"

★ ★ ★

In any case, I won't interfere in the lives of my sister and her husband. I've spent the past weeks reading, taking walks, riding. I have visited Mr. Amelung's mirror works in Roika, where the manager made me a gift of a large handsome looking glass with a frame carved out of birch burl—a favor based on the fact that I, too, am a member of the *gentry* of Voisiku . . . But I'm keeping my distance from the family, no matter how Eeva may feel about it. Even ten years ago I felt strange and ill at ease in their company—and much more so now that their life has become quite incomprehensible to me.

And yet, in spite of this incomprehension, I went downstairs after Iette's departure and knocked on the door of Timo's study next to the yellow drawing room.

The study is a smallish, high-ceilinged room, in size perhaps one-sixth of the yellow drawing room. The ceiling is white-washed, the wallpaper light gray with gold stripes. The room is furnished with a mahogany writing desk, bookshelves, a drafting table with a huge globe on it, armchairs, a sofa, and a coffee table. The fireplace is to the right of the drawing room door.

Timo and Eeva were sitting on the sofa, behind the small round table, below two Claude Lorrain engravings. The day before yesterday a letter had arrived from the Tallinn art dealer, Arranzo. He wanted to know when he could expect the amount owed to him for those engravings these past nine years—an indication that people in Tallinn already knew of Timo's liberation, if one can call it that.

Beneath the table, Timo's legs were covered with a tartan blanket. Eeva was just pouring coffee into his cup of blue Poltsamaa porcelain.

Both of them acknowledged my presence with a nod. Eeva said, "Have a seat. Let me pour you a cup."

I sat down in an armchair facing them. Eeva went to the china cabinet and took out a third blue cup. Until that moment, I hadn't really noticed how girlishly slim and provocatively agile she still was, in her elegant gray silk dress that matched the two gray streaks at her temples and made them look like an intentionally modest diadem. The chief arbiters of adornment among the noble ladies of our land would have been forced to admit that the small cameo brooch on the front of her dress had been most skillfully chosen to compliment her still youthful face and the color of her hair.

Timo was wearing a soft dark-green smoking jacket. He had nicked his chin while shaving and applied iodine to the cut; the iodine stain looked like a yellow fingerprint on his pale skin. He looked at me with a clear and calm gaze.

I asked, "*Nun—wie fühlen Sie sich?*"

He raised his eyebrows, which had turned a mottled gray. I noticed that the coloration of his face had become much more normal during the past three weeks, and thanks to the twenty pounds he seemed to have lost horseback riding, his features could be considered almost youthful but for the almost completely gray (well-trimmed) mustache. In a tone of reproachful irony, he said, in Estonian:

"Jakob—with the Czar's colonel you used to be on a first-name footing. Are you afraid to address the Czar's madman in a familiar manner?"

I started to laugh, took a sip of coffee, gathered up my courage—and yet I was unable to ask him a straight question about his presumed madness.

The longer we talked, the more certain I became of the complete clarity of his mind. He said to Eeva who was leaving for Tartu the next day and would only return in a week:

"And don't forget, Kitty—go to Anders at the university library and get More's *Utopia* for me. But don't get the Latin or English edition, get the German one, so you can read it, too."

Eeva stepped behind him and ran her hand through her husband's hair. I couldn't see her face, but watching her hand I sensed (wincing a little in my mind) a strange anguished passion in the way it moved from her husband's neck to his forehead, hesitating and advancing, pushing the hair away and then again smoothing it back toward herself—just like nine years ago; but now her husband's hair was gray.

"I won't forget, dear," Eeva said. Timo turned to me:

"I'm sure you know this already—I have been *planted* here. I'm not allowed to leave Voisiku, except with the Governor General's permission. Emperor's orders. Quite brilliant, too, since they're based on the certain knowledge that I won't ever ask Mr. Paulucci (*sic!*) for anything."

"What if you just took off without permission?"

"I can't do that."

"You mean, it is a matter of . . . your *honor?*" I asked.

"Oh no, they can't touch that," Timo said as matter-of-factly as if he'd been discussing the most mundane measures and things. "But they did get Kitty's signature in St. Petersburg. I am her responsibility."

I said, "Well, that settles it. The only thing you can do is run away. Abroad. And together."

I didn't notice the change in Timo's expression, but Eeva raised a finger to her lips and said, "Shush!"

For at that instant there was a knock on the door; someone was waiting there to be asked to enter.

"Who is it?" Eeva asked.

The door opened, and Mr. Laming stuck his eager, smiling, flat pink face into the room. The rest of him followed immediately.

"Forgive me, madame, sir—I just wanted to—"

"*Who is that?*"

It wasn't just Timo's question that was strange. I noticed that his voice had changed, become unpleasantly hoarse.

"Timo," Eeva said, seeming a little taken aback, "you know, it's our Mr.—"

"Right!" Timo shouted with unexpected enthusiasm. "Come in, come in, come in! I didn't recognize you at first. Haven't seen you for a long time."

Mr. Laming took a crablike step forward, a little hesitantly. He looked at the three of us while Timo went on:

"And what's more, you've been dead all these years. Right? Soon it'll be three years. Three years in a casemate is long enough to distort a person's face. Three times three will distort it even more. Not to mention death. It changes a person's face completely. Even that of our friend and master. Goodness, how small and modest you've become! No, no, don't worry, I won't start telling you lies. I've always told you the truth. But nowadays I keep the truth to myself. The truth, you see, I tell you *straight*, and under four eyes. As always. You were peeved with me that time when I called you a *mortal*. Well, I won't do that again. Now I won't call you mortal, I'll call you *dead—Alexandre, le mort*. But let me tell you, straight, it is a pity that you . . . A pity that you employ those little snoopers. But, go with God. You're all dead, the lot of you."

"Please leave, Mr. Laming," Eeva said in a metallic voice. "My husband is not feeling well today."

Mr. Laming retreated, mumbling apologies, and Timo's eyes followed him out with a curiously empty stare. It seemed to me that his cheeks had, from some inner exertion, taken on a blush that showed through their otherwise grayish pallor; in any case, there were small droplets of perspiration on his forehead. Eeva took a white handkerchief out of the breast pocket of his green jacket. Timo closed his eyes tight, and Eeva wiped his brow.

I said, "I'll take my leave, too. Good night."

Eeva said, "Yes, that's probably best. Good night."

Timo did not say anything.

Monday, June the sixth

I still don't know what to think about the events of the night before last. Eeva left yesterday, accompanied by little Jüri, Käsper the servant, and Liiso the chambermaid. I did not have a chance to ask Eeva if Timo had frequent episodes like that, and what she thought of them. But the more attentively I review that scene with Laming, the more it strikes me that I truly cannot tell with any certainty whether Timo is mad or in his right mind.

Furthermore, as I look back over these pages, I begin to see the necessity for recording not only matters of yesterday and tomorrow, but numerous earlier events as well. Events without which matters of today and tomorrow may strike an outsider as even more confusing than they are beginning to seem to myself.

Well, then: the whole autumn and early winter of 1817, the three of us lived in Voisiku, or more exactly, in Voisiku and Tartu, since Eeva and Timo took many trips to Tartu and often spent several weeks there. Once or twice I accompanied them there.

Parenthetically, my plan to offer my services as the steward of the estate came to naught. When I told Timo about it, he laughed and said he'd noticed a long time ago that Klarfeldt was quietly cheating us; but didn't the Bible say that it wasn't right to bind the mouth of the bull that threshes your grain? And Klarfeldt was a competent fellow in all other respects. For *me*, Timo said, he had other tasks in mind:

"Jakob, I have noticed how you've perfected your handwriting since the days of your lessons with Masing—it's so marvelously regular and clear. I'm sure that's a matter of character, to some extent. And you have studied my old school notebooks for years, so you have no trouble at all deciphering my flea-sized scratchings. And so, I can't think of another person more suited to be the copyist of my manuscripts."

I asked, "What kinds of manuscripts do you have?"

He paced back and forth for a moment. I recall that this took place in the same room where he conversed with our dead emperor the other night; but at that time, he had just left his post as an adjutant to the living emperor, and was a strikingly handsome young man with beautiful posture. Snow was whirling in the air outside the large windows. Timo paced from one window, one snow scene, to another, stopped by the drafting table, spun the globe. I remember thinking: Look at that, he thinks he can spin the world according to his whim . . . He said:

"Well, for instance, a biography of my teacher, Lehrberg. Who was your teacher as well, to some extent, if posthumously. Once I've knocked that into some kind of shape, I'd like to ask you to make a fair copy of it. That way, it would be easier for me to read—what's more, I've found that I'm more likely to notice the flaws in a text written by another hand than in one that I have penned myself."

Thus, retired Colonel von Bock was contemplating a move from the military to the literary realm, with me as his scribe. But that plan was destined to bear even less fruit than my own of becoming the steward of Voisiku.

In Tartu, we stayed in a house on University Street, formerly owned by Timo's father. I don't know who its owner was back then, ten years ago; apparently some relatives, members of the Livonian aristocracy, had acquired the house after old Georg von Bock's bankruptcy and demise, and they were kind enough to put four or five second-story rooms at our disposal. While we stayed there, Timo would go to the new main building of the university, the one that looked like a Greek temple, to attend Professor Ewers's history lectures. In half a winter, he took such meticulous notes that he filled dozens of blue notebooks. I browsed through them. It was a course in medieval history, and I noticed how often Ewers had discussed *chivalry* as the ideal of the period. In his notes, Timo had carefully underlined those passages, which I found a little amusing, especially after one evening when I heard Timo voice very different opinions.

In the evenings, Timo's friends would congregate either on University Street in his and Eeva's quarters, or elsewhere. Mostly the group consisted of young aristocrats and literati, with a sprinkling of older gentlemen and university professors and their spouses. None of them showed any disdain for Eeva or acted as if they thought themselves superior to her. On the contrary: it seemed to me that they were trying to be especially amiable, which, on the other hand, sometimes seemed a little ridiculous— as when they would interrupt their conversations in French as soon as Eeva entered the room, and proceed to address her in their often very stiff Estonian. And when she replied, with an almost imperceptible smile, "*Mesdames et messieurs, continuez donc en français, pour moi c'est moins difficile que pour vous l'estonien*"—some of them went slack-jawed with amazement ("So, the pretty peasant girl that crazy Bock married really *did* get an education, just like people had been saying . . ."); others became instantly more talkative and inquisitive, although they would keep their curiosity about Eeva within the bounds appropriate to cultured society. Once in a while, this resulted in a comical effect, especially when they noticed that Eeva was not the only anomaly among them— that she was accompanied by me, a French-speaking Estonian villager in German trousers . . . I remember one ruddy, bug-eyed old gent, who, after he had exchanged five sentences with the two of us, suddenly realized what was going on and exclaimed:

"I realize that *it is possible* to encounter divine exceptions among *any* otherwise undistinguished group . . . But now—after this—do we have to conclude that if our yokels were given the *chance, all of them* would be able to speak French and support Voltaire . . . ?! *Est-ce qu'il nous faut conclure . . . ?*"

After which Professor Parrot looked at Eeva and me with a memorable expression of regretful amusement and said, "*Oui, mon cher Bruininck, c'est ça qu'il faut conclure!*"

From those few evenings I still remember, if a little hazily, Professor Ewers, and Monsieur La Trobe, with his flowing mane, who would improvise on piano or harmonium or clavichord— him I had even met once at Voisiku, he was from our part of the country. Interestingly, he was not only an enthusiastic music lover but also the district judge at Poltsamaa. And I do, of course, remember Professor Moier and his pretty wife.

For some reason, the Moiers' house has remained particularly vivid in my memory. A modest wooden building with yellow stucco and a red tile roof, it stood in the snowy fields, really outside the city limits, on a corner where the road to Karlova met a little alley leading to the Ema River. It had six or seven spacious but low-ceilinged rooms on the ground floor, a few more upstairs. I recall that the doors were so low that if Timo went through them without bending his neck, his dark blond hair brushed the lintel. In those rooms, all kinds of people bustled around the florid-faced host and his sibylline wife; in retrospect, I'm surprised that some-one actually whispered to me (I remember this clearly, though I despise such remarks): "Just look at that—our hostess has taken her husband's arm, but what is she is holding in her other hand? A book, right? But whose book? Well, Zhukovski's poems, of course! Their author has been in love with her for years . . ."

I had heard Zhukovski's name mentioned before in our house-hold, and in our library I had seen collections of his poems in-scribed to Timo "in sacred brotherhood." In any case, it seemed that the fellow wasn't just some third-rate versifier who had gained a bit more notoriety than one would expect, but a poet to be taken seriously (to the extent that such an occupation can be so taken). I was told that Zhukovski had received an honorary doctorate from the University of Tartu, the year before last, and had just been appointed to a post as the Russian tutor of the fiancée of Grand Duke Nikolai Pavlovich. This was why he did not put in an appearance that evening at the Moiers', where he had been a frequent visitor and had even spent some time as a house guest, up there under the rooftiles. I also knew that Timo's friendship with him had begun under that same roof.

On the evening so clearly etched into my memory, everything proceeded according to social convention. The ladies sat in the rooms on the street side, in their fashionable, light-colored dresses, their hair worn up and curled at the temples, eating soft-centered chocolate confections and prattling about Mesmerism and an opera based on Fouqué's *Undine*, which had premiered last year in Berlin.

(Although only a few of the ladies had seen and heard the opera, it was a safe bet that all of them had read the novel.)

The gentlemen sat in the rooms facing the river, the windows open to the snowy garden to let out the dense smoke of cigars and pipes. There were punch glasses on the smoking table, on the floor, in the gentlemen's hands. Now and again, one of them stepped into the large parlor and refilled his glass with a silver ladle from a large glass bowl; but if voices were occasionally raised in argument, this was not due not to the punch but to the subjects under discussion. Speaking of the punch, that English beverage had been introduced to us the year before last, together with many other English fashions, after our Livonian officers had helped defeat Bonaparte and celebrated the victory in Paris with their English allies.

The subjects, however, that occasionally made the gentlemen gathered at the Moiers' raise their voices all had to do with the peasant question of our own country. The Moiers' social circle did not include anyone who rejected the idea of reform out of hand, but even among those who favored reform, personal opinions varied wildly. As for Professor Ewers's ideal of medieval chivalry, it was precisely here that I heard Timo explain his views on it, to Ewers himself and even more so to the other gentlemen:

"*Chevalerie*—yes, it is undoubtedly the most elevated spiritual achievement of the Middle Ages. And our Baltic nobility really doesn't have to feel the least bit ashamed because it has stood up for that spirit with great purity, and for a long time after other ideals superseded it in the rest of Europe . . ."

I remember well what I felt as I listened to him: that as a scion of one of the most illustrious noble families, Timo was obliged to say these things—and I also felt that his words were *alien* to my way of thinking, and that there was something fundamentally and essentially *false* about them . . . As these thoughts were passing through my mind, he continued:

"And yet, gentlemen, and yet—let us, for once, open our eyes. This splendid *chevalerie* of ours was, and is, a completely *internal* affair! It applies only among *ourselves*, among those whom we regard as our equals! To those *below*, we have done—and are still doing—*the most disgusting things!*"

And I remember how I felt: the mainspring of my protest, wound tight inside me by his words, was suddenly released. My knees felt weak, and I began to fear for myself and for Eeva and for him . . . At that moment, Eeva walked into the room, and everyone fell silent. Shocked as I was, I had some difficulty keeping a straight face as I observed the eagerness with which the gentlemen tried to demonstrate that *they* certainly mustn't be counted among those who are unkind to their inferiors . . . As it happened, Eeva turned to the aforementioned Bruininck and addressed some vacuous pleasantry to him. In unison with the others, Bruininck had sprung to his feet, and since he was momentarily too confused to locate an ashtray, he tossed his cigar through the open window into the snow, so as not to make the impression of a boor who would converse with a lady while holding a cigar. Some of the gentlemen tried to disperse the smoke clouds by waving their hands. Eeva was offered three chairs at once and showered with compliments from seven directions. But Timo didn't allow any of this to interrupt him (a fateful trait, from the start). He left the group of men and walked over to Eeva, put his arm around her shoulders, then turned back to his audience.

"To this very day! The most disgusting things! Now, the teachings of Christ are the only thing with which we can justify our presence in this country. We are the descendants of those who brought those teachings here. It isn't much of a justification, because we know that Christianity would have triumphed here even without our ancestors. But that's the only argument we have. All the more reason to ask: *How have we treated Christ here?* The more highly strung among us are now trying to cleanse themselves in floods of tears at prayer meetings, à la Mrs. von Krüdener. Nothing wrong with that, she has her own sins on her conscience. But what about the other sanctimonious members of our nobility— and their numbers are increasing every day—what is the burden of sin that has begun to afflict them so? Let me tell you. What they are feeling, not clearly or consciously as yet, but by force of nature, is the guilt of all the educated classes of this land, and that of the German nobility in particular. Because we are, *in corpore*, grinding Christ's face into the dirt every day, every moment, every minute. By what we are doing to our peasantry. I'm thinking

about what Christ said: whatever you do to one of my lesser
brethren, you also do to me. Look at my wife here—she could
have served Praxiteles as a model for his Aphrodite! And, er"—
I noted, with reluctant approval, that Timo couldn't resist adding
a drop of the sweetened vinegar of irony to his preachy lecture—
"and, well, Kitty hasn't read any less of the writings of Immanuel
Kant than any of our other ladies. But, as you all know, I *bought*
her a few years ago. According to the laws of this land, for the
price of four English hunting dogs. But if Christ happens to be
old and sick and covered in wounds, he isn't worth even *one*
hunting dog. Consider that, gentlemen, and tell me if it is wrong
of me to ask: What, then, is the value of all our Christianity and
all our *chevalerie?* Should we not strip ourselves naked and put on
the rags of a peasant and retire—oh, I don't know, to islands in
the marshes, huts built out of peat—to meditate—upon our honor
and upon God?"

I saw clearly how uncomfortable Eeva felt during this speech.
She stared at the floor with a bewildered and apologetic smile.
Toward the end, however, she leaned the back of her head and
neck and shoulders against Timo in a truly charming fashion, then
turned and looked at him with a puzzled yet reassuring expression
and said, quietly, as soon as Timo had finished, "Timo, it is not
your friends' fault—"

Timo turned her around to face him, looked over her head, and
said with characteristic, somewhat merciless, consistency, "Not
directly. But I wouldn't be their true friend if I didn't remind them
that it is, indirectly, *all* our fault. Now, even yours."

Eeva's ability to control the situation, and to do it so smoothly,
really amazed me. Taking Timo's hand, she said, with an almost
radiant smile, "And now you have fulfilled your obligation for
today." She turned to the others: "Gentlemen—*Monsieur* La Trobe
would like to present a new piece of his in the drawing room—
and you know how he is—he didn't want to come here himself,
to disrupt your talk with this invitation."

And so, everybody headed to the drawing room to listen to
Monsieur La Trobe. With the probable exception of Timo, the
gentlemen seemed positively thankful to see the dubious topic
shunted aside—as it had been, in such salons, for many a year.

I had time to ponder Timo's words while we were riding back to Voisiku through the snow. When old Baron von Bock had died, Timo had inherited a couple of hundred souls. As soon as Timo had been able, during the great campaigns of the 1813, to return home for a brief visit to attend to his affairs, he had promptly set these people free. But on the subject of the freeing of the serfs, Timo had some opinions that were all his own. To his mind, the serfs should not be freed by *imperial* edict. If the Czar were to act as their liberator, Timo felt, this would cause a complete moral rift between them and their overlords . . . (A childish notion, of course—as if the chasm between masters and serfs could possibly become wider than it already was!) Therefore, Timo thought, the Czar should concentrate on dealing justly with his own peasants in Russia—on, for instance, compensating those at Oranienbaum, whose crops were trampled into the mud every year during the army's autumn maneuvers. It was Timo's firm conviction that the serfs of Livonia should be freed by *the Livonian squires themselves*. And that wasn't all: by means of relentless kindness and unfailing justice (a total impossibility, in my opinion!), the squires should forge strong bonds between themselves and their peasants, to further the achievement of I still don't really know what common goals . . . Maybe, I thought, the idea was that *all* the barons would go off their rockers and marry their maids, while their daughters would rush into matrimony with their farmhands; what other goals could they otherwise have in common . . . ?!

Monday, June the sixth, 1827
at night

My idea of the night before last—that Timo should go abroad—had not occurred to me out of the blue.

This afternoon, I wrote that the three of us had spent the entire autumn and early winter of 1817 at Voisiku, or more exactly, at Voisiku and Tartu. This is true—but with at least one exception. Two weeks after our arrival at Voisiku, we went on a journey. To this day I hardly know anything about the events that led up to it—but in a certain sense, everything that happened to Timo and us later, and is happening today, can be seen as aftereffects of that journey.

One October morning in 1817, as the three of us and Dr. Robst were sitting around the table with Käsper serving us, Timo said:

"Dear friends—today, Kitty, myself, and Jakob, will be traveling to Riga. To visit my mother's relatives, the von Rautenfeldts. There are quite a few of them there, but we'll try to get back in a week. We won't need the coachman, or you, Käsper—we'll manage, Jakob and I, with Kitty along to gladden our hearts and eyes."

I have mentioned before how averse Timo was to dawdling: two hours later, we were on our way to Riga in a brougham. To the curious folk along the way who enquired after our destination—there always are some, loitering at the post stations along main imperial highways—Timo gave the same reply: to Riga. To visit relatives.

Timo and I took turns on the coachman's seat. When it began to rain, as it often does in October, we raised the bottom of the front window a little and took the reins inside. As I recall, we were already somewhere between Rencen and Volmar. Yellow leaves stuck to the rain-streaked windows. The backs of the horses were black from rain, their legs red halfway up to their knees from the wet clay. As the rain drummed on the carriage roof, Eeva served us hot coffee from a traveling jug, and Timo started talking, holding the reins in one hand, a coffee cup in the other:

"Dear friends, allow me to announce that we are actually traveling farther than Riga. We won't even stop in Riga, or maybe on the way back. We are going to Mitau—or Jelgava, as the Latvians call it. The capital of Courland."

Eeva asked, "And whom shall we see there?"

"Count Peter von Pahlen," Timo said. "He was a friend of my father's. He's not a Livonian, though; he is from Estonia. I want to consult with him on a matter of great importance to all of us. Do you know who this Count von Pahlen is? Or rather, who he *was*? He was the military governor of St. Petersburg in the time of Czar Paul. A member of the highest imperial council. The man actually in charge of the empire's foreign policy. And, to mention

what Mad Paul considered his most venerable attribute: Grand
Chancellor of the Russian Priorate of the Order of the Knights of
Malta—thus, second in line to the Czar himself. More impor-
tantly, he was the only man who had the courage to make any
decisions in Russia during the reign of Mad Paul. Even the most
difficult decisions. It was he who persuaded Alexander to agree
that Alexander's unworthy father had to be dethroned. He did it!
At a time when no one said a word. Or simply groveled and
groaned. And Alexander whispered to him, ". . . Let's do it!"
Paul's murder was never part of Pahlen's plan. The intention was
to arrest Paul (and why should we not arrest an emperor when
he does unworthy deeds?) and to assign him quarters in Mikhai-
lovskoye Castle—complete with a riding academy and a theater
and a company of soldiers for his make-believe parades . . . Well,
you know what happened. Paul refused to give up the crown and
raised the alarm. Pahlen wasn't there when Paul was killed. Pahlen
didn't participate. Maybe he had a foreboding, but then Alexander
may have had one, too! And yet: a week later, when it was all
over, when Alexander had ascended to the throne and all of Russia
celebrated its relief, the selfsame Alexander exiled Pahlen to Mitau,
where he has been living for more than seventeen years. And one
might say that Pahlen's fall from grace was the first clear indication, to a discerning eye, of the double-edged nature of Alexander's
notions of honor."

We arrived in Mitau late on the second day.

I remember the stuccoed walls and the small, lit-up windows.
The long bridge across the dark Lielupe River. The ride down
streets of low stone buildings. Finally we turned into some kind
of park. Timo was driving, and it seemed to me that he knew the
road well. We stopped and Timo tied the reins to a tree. We waded
through piles of wet chestnut leaves and entered a low-slung building that looked like a country manor on the edge of town. An
old retainer asked us to wait, then reappeared and led us inside.

Count von Pahlen was sitting in his study. Four large wax
candles cast light on his graceful rococo desk. When he saw that
there was a lady among his visitors, he sprang from behind the
desk and hurried toward us; considering his age, he was almost
comically agile. His attire, as I recall it, consisted of an old-

fashioned—but obviously quite new—formal tailcoat and knee breeches with white stockings, and his left calf was much thicker than the right.

Our arrival did not seem to surprise him, nor did he seem to find it burdensome. Timo introduced Eeva and me. The old gentleman kissed Eeva's hand, embraced Timo with the light touch of a man of the world, and, in passing, extended to me his cool, speckled, very smooth hand. Then he took a theatrical step backward, scrutinized Eeva from top to toe, and spoke, in a cracked falsetto voice:

"Madame—ich muss gestehen: selten sind Gerüchte so absolut begründet wie das Gerücht über Ihren ausserordentlichen Zauber!"

He motioned us to seat ourselves by a glowing fireplace. Then the old gentleman rang for bitter oranges, nuts, and wine. For a quarter of an hour, while we were chatting about this and that, with Eeva contributing a couple of sentences in response to his questions and me probably not saying anything at all, I subjected this former potentate of Russia to careful scrutiny.

I clearly remember my impression that the old gent really consisted of two separate persons. There was the exterior one, far from senile yet rather like a worn-out wind-up doll designed by Droz, an affected rascal in a powdered wig. Then there was the interior man, much smaller yet very energetic, who peered out of the eyeholes of the exterior one as though from inside a suit of paper armor with surprisingly sharp eyes—although their gaze was a little arrogant in its omniscience, and also a little sad.

Suddenly Pahlen turned to Timo and asked, *"Mais voilà—quels sont tes problèmes?"*

Their conversation proceeded in French. It was clear that the Count thought that Eeva and I (or at least I) could be excluded from it by this shift. Timo, apparently, didn't feel it was necessary to conduct the conversation in private. Eeva's presence may have seemed quite normal or even important to him, not only because of the content of the conversation, but also, I believe, because Timo was eager to prove to himself and others that his wife was fully his equal. That eagerness may have included me, as well, so that my presence seemed natural to him. Who knows? In any case, my curiosity joined forces, as it were, with my awkwardness, and probably my vanity as well, to prevent me from rising to my feet and saying, Gentlemen, do you wish me to retire? . . . And so, I stayed and heard their entire conversation. Timo, in his typical straightforward way, said:

"Count—I need your fatherly advice. And your opinion on a decision I have—more or less—made. I am, finally, disappointed in our emperor Alexander. I only regret that it has taken me so long. I believed in him for many years. I won't try to excuse my naïveté by listing my reasons for that, nor need I explain to you the reasons for my disappointment. In any case, I am now convinced that I can no longer render any honorable service to my fatherland. Every individual's honorable deeds are now drowned in general shamefulness. And that is why I have decided to leave the country. I must leave Russia. And I would like you to approve my decision."

Pahlen did not remain silent for too long, nor did he reply too quickly. He toyed with his white silk handkerchief and spoke quietly, in a slightly hoarse voice; if there was an ironic tinge to his words, this was, it seemed to me, caused not so much by Timo's youth but by an awareness of the ways history has of repeating itself.

"Timothée, believe me: I am familiar with all of this. But I cannot approve your decision. I would understand it—if you were in more or less the same position that I find myself in. As you know, I am subject to an imperial order that forbids me to cross the borders of Courland. But what you don't know is this: over the years, all my actions have been subject to every possible kind of surveillance. My visitors, my conversations, my letters . . . It depressed me so much that I stopped keeping track of it. Thus, I don't even know, at this moment, if it is still going on or if they have given up, at last . . ."

(Here, I will add: there is no evidence that Pahlen was still under surveillance at the time of our visit. Still, it appears that the Czar got wind of it. After Pahlen's death last year, Budberg, our Civilian Governor, mentioned to acquaintances—and it reached our ears—that when the Czar issued the order for Timo's arrest, he also issued one for the secret surveillance of Pahlen. He had, in other words, *reinstated* Pahlen's surveillance.)

Pahlen continued:

"Nevertheless, I haven't fled abroad. In practical terms, it would have been easy. The only obstacle has been my own lack of initiative, my indolence, if you wish"—he smiled with an old man's comical coquetry—"and, perhaps, also my affection for these Seville oranges. They ripen very slowly here, in the greenhouse. You'll notice how tart they are to the tongue and the palate, and even to your fingertips. And yet, as far as I know, they are the northernmost Seville oranges grown in all of Europe . . ."

He used his silk handkerchief to wipe the juice off his fingers. Then he said, in a curiously mild tone but in a voice that still reflected the resolve of a man who was used to making decisions:

"But a free man, like yourself, can find—must find—an application that is right for him. Let's say, the writing of his memoirs. That is something I can't afford to do—because I would have to hide my manuscript so well that I couldn't even find it myself. But what could keep you from it? And, generally speaking, only those who seek revenge go abroad. Who seeks something more important stays at home."

After this, Pahlen reverted to German and to commonplace subjects. Soon we were called to the dinner, which was by no means as plain as what we were used to at Voisiku (as far as the menu was concerned), yet it was surprisingly frugal. We spent the night in upstairs guest rooms under light goose-down comforters manufactured in the German fashion and now heavy with dampness in the Livonian fashion. At the crack of dawn, we started out on our return journey, heading toward Riga.

We spent only one day in Riga visiting the elderly Rautenfeldt sisters, Timo's aunts. They were very pleasant ladies, members of the city bourgeoisie rather than the landed gentry. Timo asked us not to mention our trip to Mitau to these aunts nor to anyone at home, where we returned after several days' absence.

And since Timo and Eeva stayed within their homeland, and Timo never mentioned the idea of going abroad again before his arrest, I consider all the things that were to happen a consequence of this journey. It seems clear to me that Pahlen's words were the main reason for Timo's decision to stay.

Tuesday, June the seventh, late at night

I simply have to say this: I can't make up my mind whether Iette is an unbelievably depraved young whore—or an unfortunate child whose fate it is to fall in love with me.

Today, around five o'clock, she arrived for her lesson. The weather had been cloudy since the morning, and during the day we had heavy showers, which was unseasonal for June. She, however, had managed to stay more or less dry, except for some water stains from the dripping trees on her puffed sleeves and on the hem of her skirt which was damp from the grass. As we sat down on the wicker sofa by the table, she raised the damp hem a full hand's breadth above her delicate ankles, which were encircled by black shoe-ribbons.

We bought and sold wheat, filled and emptied ponds dug in the shape of perfect rectangles, calculated the interest on loans. I don't think we had time to discuss Peter II and Menshikov before it was seven o'clock and time for Iette to leave. Now, however, the rain had become heavy again. Since she would have to run through it from the manor to The Foundation wearing only a thin crepe dress, I took my own light travel duster off its peg and draped it over her shoulders.

"You can bring it back on Saturday."

I walked her downstairs and followed her to the door that leads to the garden. Now it seemed to me that it was really raining too hard, and besides, my duster only protected her skirt halfway. We stood by the door. The rain was pouring down on a hundred and twenty apple trees, whose tops, outlined against the dark sky, looked surprisingly light, as if lit from within; and the raindrops that spattered into my face seemed to smell of appleblossom. I took Iette's arm and pulled her inside the door. And everything that followed was due to two things: first of all, ten inches inside the doorway the scent of appleblossom changed to the scent of lilac perfume on her rain-wet face; and, secondly, she didn't resist my grasp in the least. Or she *did*, but only just enough to allow it to happen. That scent of hers—and that sense of giving-in-after-all—gave rise to my decision to *see just how far she would let me go* . . .

Oh, hell! These pages will make some sense only if (and even then, just barely!) I am as candid about myself as I intend to be about her . . . As we stood there in the vestibule, old—and, in fact, rare—escapades from my days as a noncommissioned officer flashed through my mind. With country girls from Grodno and Courland. Naturally, these are embarrassing memories—in some cases because those affairs had been so crude and vacuous, in others because the tomfoolery had tended to take a serious turn. My old tricks. *And my old hunger.* There may have been a third reason for my action: a desire to take revenge, *on someone for something,* by some degraded act in this house of Eeva and Timo's much-praised love. I don't really know whom I wanted to punish, or for what, and right now I'm not calm enough to figure it out. I spoke, and my voice sounded hoarser than I would have wanted it to sound:

"Let's go back upstairs and wait there for the rain to stop."

I held on to her arm and guided her back up the stairs. I took my duster off her shoulders and tossed it on the back of a chair. She sat down on her former place on the wicker sofa and said, for some reason almost in a whisper, and as if she had read my thoughts:

"All right, then. Today you were going to tell me about that revolt in the capital, the year before last . . ."

I said, "We'll get to that later. Today, I'd like to talk about something altogether different . . ."

I had kept the water kettle warm on the stove. I poured tea and brought it to the table with Eeva's raspberry liqueur bottle and two small goblets.

"Well, let's warm ourselves up a little. Such weather!"

She shook her head, but I drained my goblet. Now I wouldn't be at a loss for eloquence, nor for a desire to employ it—I don't feel that way very often. But I did now, because I wanted to find out how far she'd allow me to go.

Hang it all—this *is* embarrassing to record, even on pages no one else but me will read during my lifetime. Truly embarrassing . . .

"Miss Iette, have you noticed the picture in the oval frame that hangs between the windows of the small drawing room? It's a painting by a famous French painter—Greuze. His favorite subjects were young, fragile girls with slightly puzzled expressions. They also had to be—how should I say this—amazingly fresh and pretty, in a peachlike sort of way. Iette: I've been watching you for a month now. Greuze would have considered himself lucky if he could have seen you. But he died a long time ago. So, now I'm the lucky man. But I couldn't paint your portrait. I wouldn't know how to do that. But I know how to *see* you. How pristine you are. How womanly and childlike at the same time—and I really want to find out *how* those qualities are combined in you." And so forth . . . So that the speaker himself, if he happens to listen in to his words, begins to feel a little ashamed, and then goes on with even greater intensity, because he notices the impression his words make and feels both the intoxication and the sadness of conquest; they alternate and mingle in his mind as he sees how the girl's neck and face begin to glow, how the frightened expression of her mouth finally can't help changing into a smile of pleasure, and how she can't resist enjoying her own fright. Until the speaker has taken her hand between his own. Until she finds herself between the man's palms. And until her mouth is no longer able to give a reply to the fevered and evanescent question she has been asking herself all the while: Oh, Lord—how far will I let him go . . . ?

I don't know how urgently Iette asked herself that question. In any case, she let me go all the way.

When I became conscious of the surrounding world again, the rain was still beating on the window by my desk. We lay on a rumpled gray blanket on my iron-frame bed, turned away from one another. I thought that Ovid was right, after all, when he said that *afterward, all animals are sad* . . . Even though I feel that the opposite should be the case . . . Then, suddenly, I realized that Iette had pressed her face into a pillow, and that her bare shoulders were shaken by sobbing.

It took me only a moment to realize that it was my duty to console her; and also, that this was a boring and unnecessary task . . . I reached out, stroked her copper-colored hair, and gently tried to turn her face toward me, thinking: Just look at that, it's raining even harder now, and now this business has become my responsibility, one way or another . . . I asked her (the way one always does in this situation):

"Iette, why are you crying? *Why?*" I shifted something aside in myself—some curtain pinned up between things (and felt a pin prick me!)—and said, "*Dearest*—there's no need to . . ."

She went on crying even more emphatically, as always in this situation, but then suddenly turned toward me, as if fully opening herself to me only now—turned her damp and mottled face to me and looked at me in a way that shook me out of my torpor. She said:

"But it's so awful . . . The *way* you took me . . ."

"How so . . . how do you mean?"

"You don't even notice . . . you don't even care!"

"What don't I notice? What don't I care about?"

I really didn't understand what she was talking about. To tell the truth, I didn't really give a damn what it was—until she answered, because this is what she said:

"That I wasn't a virgin."

I was quiet for a minute. Maybe even longer.

Good grief. Well, a girl may be a virgin, or she may not be.

That may or may not surprise a fellow. And he may pretend surprise, or may not do so. But when a girl tells you something like that, she gets closer than close to you . . . Just because—it seems—a human word has been added to all the dumb tricks that all of creation's dumb creatures engage in with each other . . . Oh, I don't know. I said:

"But Iette, please understand—I didn't want to insult you with my curiosity . . . What I thought was . . . that if you wanted to tell me about it, you would . . ."

All right . . . This was partially true, at least until she had told me about it. To be candid, I *had* had the passing thought: A girl who can be taken this easily must have been taken at least ten times before. So why should I feign surprise and ask questions? She wouldn't believe my pretense, or perhaps she would *pretend* to believe it and try to concoct some story about having fallen out of a tree when she was a little girl . . . But now, after her *own* admission, I said (although I *still* felt that I wasn't being truly honest):

"Iette, to tell you the truth, I would really like to know."

I took her hands in mine, and she sat up and told me her tale, staring down at her lap. The man had been the nephew of the headmistress of her school, a law student at the University of Tartu and a member of the *Curonus* fraternity. He had promised marriage, from the spring of last year, through the summer (during which Iette had stayed in Riga), and until the autumn: but in September the young gentleman went back to Tartu, and in October he became engaged to the daughter of a local squire. That was why Iette had made so little headway with arithmetic problems or Peter the Great's reforms—especially after word had reached Riga that *her* Peter had been married around Christmastime . . .

I had to console her, of course. It seemed to me that her story, whether all of it was true or not, was true enough.

So then I talked to her the way one always talks in this situation: Dear little Iette, this isn't the first time innocence has been betrayed and abused. Believe me, the stain of betrayal does not adhere to the victim, but to the betrayer. I said, Please believe me! Believe me! *Darling*, I said. I started kissing her bare arms again. And when I happened to take another detached look at myself, I no longer felt embarrassed at all. But then she suddenly drew back from me and said, sounding frightened:

"Jakob! We've forgotten that Father may show up here any minute to look for me!"

Which was, of course, true. We hurried to make ourselves presentable, and I sent her off in my duster (the rain had almost ended). We agreed to meet tomorrow at noon behind the manor park, at a spot bounded on one side by a field of rye, on the other by a copse of alders that extends all the way to the northeastern corner of the park.

I really don't know why. Nor do I know what will become of it. Does it matter? We shall see.

Thursday, June 9th

Soon after breakfast, around half past nine, pistol shots started ringing out in the park: Timo practicing his marksmanship, just as he used to do regularly in former times. A couple of weeks ago he'd fired a few rounds in the park—then, too, on a day when Eeva was away. That time, I think, she had gone to Poltsamaa to take care of some official business with the district judge. This morning it occurred to me that Timo perhaps thought the noise got on Eeva's nerves and had decided to get a little practice in while his wife was not at home.

I heard him fire four shots at approximately one-minute intervals, then stopping to load his four pistols, which took five minutes. Now and again he took a break of fifteen minutes or so.

At half past ten I went downstairs. My plan was to make a little detour to my rendezvous with Iette, so as not to attract attention. No need for our walks to be noticed in the manor. But maybe I was just too restless to linger in my room reading a book.

I walked through the apple orchard to the northern edge of the park, then proceeded down a bridle path on the far side of the acacia hedge in the direction of Timo's pistol shots. I thought I'd bid him good morning and ask permission to watch his target practice for a while. It seems to me I even pondered the right approach; his alleged madness always made addressing him a slightly confusing experience. Each time, I felt as if I had to step over some small obstacle.

I could see through the acacia bushes, which were still wet with yesterday's rain. Timo stood some ten paces from the hedge in his green smoking jacket, holding a pistol in his extended right hand, taking aim. At a distance of forty paces, at an appropriate height, a long, narrow strip of wood had been attached to two old linden trees like a crossbar. Vertical holes had been drilled into the crossbar to accommodate a row of green fir cones at intervals of half a span. The cones on the left third of the crossbar had already been shot down. A shot rang out, and the cone on the far right exploded. Timo turned and walked back between the trees, in the direction of the hedge. Right where I stood, on the other side of the hedge, there were a couple of yellow garden chairs and a table on which lay three long-barreled Kuchenreiter pistols, a cardboard box full of bullets and cartridges, and a powder box. I didn't call out to Timo through the hedge but turned and walked ten paces over to the gate in order to reach the table. But then I stopped. Through the wet hedge I saw Mr. Laming appear among the trees, walking to join Timo and to proceed with him toward the table with the pistols. At that moment, I decided not to enter the park. I had no desire to meet Laming. Nevertheless, I couldn't help overhearing their conversation—against my will, in the sense that I hadn't meant to stay to listen to it. Yet I have to admit that I was quite eager to eavesdrop—Timo's strange, recent conversation with Laming had aroused my curiosity. I heard the steward ask Timo:

"And how are you today, sir?"

"I am fine," Timo said, putting his pistol on the table next to the other three. "But those equibs are bothering me."

"They are—again . . . ?" Laming asked with a sorrowful look.

"Yes, now and again, but just a bit. Have a seat."

Timo sat on the edge of the table and started loading one of the Kuchenreiters. Mr. Laming (to tell the truth, I wouldn't have thought he had it in him) lowered himself carefully into one of the garden chairs.

"Well, what's on your mind?" Timo asked, blowing soot off the pistol's lock and glancing at Laming from the corner of his eye. I have to admit that I was a little puzzled by the casual tone in which Timo addressed Laming, after the peculiar tension I had heard in his voice on Saturday. Laming puzzled me even more. Did the steward really believe that his master wasn't crazy at all? It would take a good deal of courage to start a conversation with a madman who is busy firing four pistols—considering that this madman had been clearly hostile to him only last Saturday. Or did this mean that something really compelled Laming to talk to Timo . . . ? The steward pursed his mouth for a moment, squinted at Timo—I couldn't tell whether this was an indication of mirth or fatigue—and said, rather strangely:

"The last time we spoke, sir, you promised to tell me the truth. When we were alone."

"And so?"

"Well, we are alone now."

Now I understood what made Laming's voice sound so peculiar to me: he was being both aggressive and anxious at the same time.

Timo finished loading his pistol and asked, much more quietly than I would have expected:

"Well, sir, what is it you want to ask me?"

Mr. Laming said, slowly, "When I was your master, you weren't too happy with me, were you?"

"No, I wasn't."

"So then we might say that you really don't have any objections to my death. Am I right?"

"You are."

"It's so good that you are candid with me. But now I would like to know—what do you think of my brother?"

"Oh, I see," said Timo slowly. "But isn't he supposed to be dead, too?"

"You mean you think Nicholas is dead, too?"

"Nicholas? What do you mean?" Timo sprang to his feet, faced Laming, and placed the muzzle of his long-barreled Kuchenreiter straight on Laming's blue coat at the level of his heart.

"Now listen to me, Laming: enough of this nonsense! You had only one brother, Johann. Half of Riga knew that drunkard. And he has been dead for ten years. Who is this Nicholas you're babbling about? Eh?"

"Oh my goodness, Baron von Bock, you didn't hear me right," Laming exclaimed, a little frightened but calmer than one might have expected. He tried to nudge the pistol away from his chest. "I never even mentioned the name Nicholas! God forbid! I didn't . . ."

"I see. Well, then," Timo said, sounding surprisingly indifferent. He stuck the pistol in his belt. "Yes, well. Then it must have been my own equibs that mentioned him."

"For sure, for sure," Mr. Laming said. He got up and slid his chair across the wet ground, away from Timo. "But those *equibs* of yours—what are they really like?"

"Oh, don't try to find out about them," Timo said gloomily. "Whoever finds out what they are like, is beset by them at once. And if you don't know the right formulae"—once again he pointed the pistol at Laming's chest—". . . well, it's really exactly the same as—*bang!*"

Mr. Laming retreated a little, smiled, and turned to go. Timo loaded the remaining three pistols, then took one of them and walked back to the line drawn in the dirt to resume his target practice. I wondered if there would ever be an appropriate time for me to speak to him about this truly strange encounter; it did seem far too embarrassing. Besides, I couldn't very well admit that I had witnessed it.

I stepped back from the acacia hedge, careful not to make it rustle, circled the field under cover of the alder grove, and, by my watch, arrived punctually at the appointed spot—but Iette was already there.

The pliant softness of her palms and arms and the wondrously silky glow of her cheeks was so *real* that the mad or half-mad business of a moment ago slipped my mind entirely. I took my canvas duster off Iette's shoulders and spread it out on the grass in the shade of the alders. I told her all sorts of things. From a hundred fathoms away, the slowly spaced reports of Timo's pistols sounded distant and muted. I consoled Iette in every way . . . but stopped short of promising to elope with her. After we had agreed that she'd come to me again on Tuesday for her tutorial, I felt like teasing her a little and asked her:

"It seems to me that the great December revolt no longer interests you at all?"

She looked at me with big eyes and wrapped her arms tight around my neck and pushed her nose against my sternum and shook her head. It felt like a swarm of small fluttering birds under my shirt collar . . . Oh, Lord—

★   ★   ★

I had better get back to my recollections of how Timo, Eeva, and myself got on with our lives here at the manor in the spring of '18. Inasmuch as we did get on with them.

At the end of February, after Timo and Eeva returned from their latest journey to Tartu, Timo became very busy in his attic

room—which is now mine—working on some literary project. I
assumed that it was the biography of Lehrberg that Timo had said
he intended to write, but didn't feel close enough to him to ask.
I didn't ask Eeva, either, although she visited him up here very
often and seemed to be quite informed about his doings. This
became apparent—or so it seems to me in hindsight—in that
Timo's change, his turning peculiar in certain ways, was sometimes reflected in her behavior; but it may well be that I didn't
really notice any of those things back then. Things like the way
Timo grew rather taciturn at the end of that winter (he was never
a talkative man except when intoxicated with some subject of
particular interest to himself). And the way he would sometimes
say things that sounded like tragic premonitions. The fact that the
gentry of our district, and even their own relatives, ignored them
(or should I say us?) may also—no, *must* have affected their moods.
And it wasn't just that we were ignored! It was much worse than
that. I'll relate an example.

In April, with the winter's last snows still on the ground, we
drove to the castle church at Poltsamaa to attend the Easter service
and old Temler's sermon, but mainly to hear the magnificent
organ. None of us was the churchgoing sort, but we did go on
major holidays. When the three of us and our coachman arrived
at the church, just in time for the organ voluntary, there were at
least a thousand people gathered there, from both the township
and the surrounding countryside. Our coachman slipped into a
pew at the rear, and we proceeded down the aisle and took our
places in the von Bock family pew directly below the pulpit.
Suddenly, the mistress of Lustivere Manor, Marie Samson von
Himmelstiern, stood up in the pew just behind us in the section
reserved for the nobility. Her face was rigid, she looked like a
furious statue carved in stone. Pulling her spouse, Reinhold, along
with her, she said in a shrill voice that could be heard across the
church:

*"Eher werde ich im Kuhstall mein Gebet sagen! Da weiss man wen-
igstens, wo man ist!"*

Single file, the husband at the wife's heels, they marched out
of the church. With alternating feelings of sarcasm and suffocation
I watched how the rest of them followed suit, first the ladies—

Mrs. Vietinghoff of Pajusi, Mrs. von Below of Pärsti, and the devil knows the rest of them and their names—and behind them, with lesser or greater alacrity, their husbands; and how, after the departure of the Samsons, it took only a few minutes for the pews around us to empty out. Only the leaseholder of Old Poltsamaa Castle, stour Mr. von Wahl, and his giggly wife, remained in their seats. It was said later that the wife had indeed tried to drag her husband away, but he had managed to fall asleep even before Temler's sermon, and thus she'd had to stay put as well. But as we found out later, that story wasn't entirely fair to old Mr. Wahl.

Naturally, Mrs. Samson's words were not lost on Eeva who remained motionless in her seat, turned pale, stared at the floor, and took a white lace handkerchief out of her otter-fur muff. Without the least intention of bursting into tears, she just twisted the handkerchief to relieve the tension of the moment. After the people had left, Timo looked around, shrugged, and, if I'm not mistaken, gave a brief contemptuous snort; then he turned back to contemplate the altarpiece. At that moment, Eeva's handkerchief fell from her lap to the floor. Too late, I realized that I could have picked it up. (To this day, I'm aware that good manners really haven't become second nature in my case.) Timo, however, didn't wait for me to move but performed a—how should I put it?—*grand little gesture*. It was an odd one, but it was also magnificent. He picked Eeva's little lace handkerchief off the floor and pressed it into her hand. Then he raised Eeva's hand to his lips— we were seated in plain view of everyone, and the Stackelbergs of Adavere Manor and some others behind our backs were still scrambling out of their pew—*and kissed Eeva's hand until there was no one left in the pews reserved for the nobility.*

That spring, Elisabeth must have been the only one of his relatives who deigned to pay us a visit—this was Timo's sister Elsy, the one married to Peter Zoege von Mannteuffel of Harjumaa. Elsy had managed to persuade her husband to come along. They spent only a few days at Voisiku, acting restrained and self-important in a rather revolting way that was obviously designed to make us realize what an unheard-of and amazing gesture their visit was. They didn't pay much attention to me, neither the freckled and constantly sniffling Elsy nor her rawboned, dark-haired but balding Peter, who was destined to become the malevolent and clever busybody one could discern in him even then. For Timo's (and appearances') sake, they treated Eeva with apparent tolerance, and I noticed that they were even a bit surprised when they met Eeva, talked with her, and got to know her a little. As for Timo, Elsy saw him as the regrettable—but also a tad admirable—victim of his own romantic weakness. She couldn't help feeling that speck of admiration for her older brother, of whom, until recently, the whole family had been so proud. Peter, on the other hand, simply regarded Timo as a fool capable of even crazier things than this marriage.

Come to think of it, Timo's younger brother Karl also visited us at Voisiku in the spring of '18. He was a very pleasant young gentleman, and out of respect for Timo he treated Eeva as though he were a gallant admirer. He came to us with the intention of staying at Voisiku for an extended period, but left abruptly after only a week.

Here, I would like to record some of the things Timo said that spring; they were soon to assume a greater significance than it seemed at first.

I remember the three of us sitting downstairs in Timo's study by the glowing fireplace. I think we had just talked about how the peasants in Courland had been emancipated, at last, while those in Livonia were still serfs, and how the Diet of Livonia wanted to take steps in that matter as soon as possible—when Timo suddenly said:

"Who knows how long I'll be able to dwell here with you . . ."

I remember how Eeva's face, though it had just seemed so animated in the glow of the fireplace, grew petrified.

I asked, "What do you mean?"

And Timo laughed and said, "There's no telling what might happen. One of these days, Napoleon may arrive on the shores of France again in a little sailboat, and the French may rise up, and we'll have to go and pacify them, in the name of the Holy Alliance . . . It looks more likely, every day."

I asked him precisely *what* looked more likely.

"That he who has come through sixty battles unscathed will become a casualty in his sixty-first."

Or another time, at breakfast, when spring had really arrived. The three of us were sitting around the table, and Timo had just told us about the Czar's notorious speech at the parliament in Warsaw a few weeks ago in which he had said that he would have to give Russia "what the Poles had already been granted"—in other words, a constitution. Timo looked at Eeva, over the first cowslips of the year, which stood in a vase on the table, and said:

"Kitty, whatever happens, but especially if we have a son— make sure that he receives the best possible education."

Eeva replied, and she seemed a little dispirited (or maybe I'm just imagining this in hindsight—God only knows):

"But Timo, that's something we'll make sure of *together*."

Whereupon Timo took the hard-boiled egg he was just about to peel, crunched it onto the table next to the silver eggcup, and said:

"Well, that's if the Czar really grants us a constitution. But he won't." He picked up the egg and began to peel it with special care.

He said, "But we shall see."

And I must admit: we, of course, never saw a constitution. But we were to see a multitude of other things, much sooner than we had anticipated.

Friday, the tenth of June, in the evening

A windy day. Iette was here in the morning. We find less and less time for arithmetic problems . . . No, I haven't promised to marry her. I am not entirely certain I will, but I am seriously considering the matter. It is true that I have promised Eeva that I'll stay here at Voisiku and help her in her troubles—but it seems to me that she doesn't really need me. And besides: if she were to ask me to stay, I could stay here as Laming's son-in-law. I intend to speak to Eeva about it. She returned from Tartu yesterday and brought with her a physician, at Dr. Robst's request, to consult with him not about the state of Timo's mental health but, as I understand, about some nervous disorder that has caused a painful rash on his neck and chest. I saw the doctor from Tartu only briefly this morning, but I made haste to tell Eeva that I had happened to overhear Timo conversing with Laming about Laming's impersonation of the dead. I wanted Eeva to know about this in case she should also discuss Timo's mental state with the doctor. This I told Eeva in a hurry, half whispering in the foyer beneath the family portraits of Bocks and Rautenfeldts, and it seemed to me that Eeva looked a little frightened by my news.

Then she asked, "Anything else?"

I shook my head, and she said, "Jakob, I want to speak to you. As soon as I can."

At the dining table, Eeva did not say anything. She appeared there only out of courtesy, took a couple of mouthfuls with the two doctors and me, and went back to Timo. The physicians must have discussed the state of Timo's health among themselves, but in my presence they did not touch upon the subject. The doctor from Tartu was in his thirties, a narrow-boned man with a large head and an angular face whose slightly ironic matter-of-factness was the exact opposite of Dr. Robst's lyrical eccentricity. After our meal, I invited the doctor from Tartu to a game of chess in my quarters. His name was Faehlmann. At first, young Jüri watched us play (for an eight-year-old, the little beggar plays an outrageously good game and is always interested in the strategies of his elders), and I wasn't able to speak freely to the doctor; but as soon as the boy got bored and left, I brought the conversation around to my question—what did Dr. Faehlmann think of Mr. Bock's *mental* health?

Dr. Faehlmann looked straight at me with his aggravatingly large, dark-gray eyes.

"I have been told that Mr. Bock was released from prison for the very reason that he had lost his sanity."

"So they say."

"So it follows that if he hadn't gone mad, he would still be locked up in Schlüsselburg."

"Maybe so."

"Given that, if the government were to notice that Mr. Bock is *not* insane, the consequence—not an inevitable but a *possible* one—might be that he would be locked up at Schlüsselburg again."

"And so . . . ?"

Dr. Faehlmann pursed his firm and stubborn-looking mouth in a curious way.

"You, sir, are the brother of our dear and scandalous Mrs. Bock?"

"I am."

"Well, you see, I do not know what the state of Mr. Bock's health may have been at any given time at Schlüsselburg. *Now*, as far as I can see, he is fatigued and nervous, but he has, in any case, managed to survive his nine years in the casemate quite well—with the exception of the loss of his teeth—and is of absolutely sound mind. Allow me to repeat that: *as far as I can see.* But I am not a healer of the mad. Formally, I'm not even a physician yet, only a student. Mrs. Bock wanted to invite Professor Erdmann here, but Professor Erdmann was unable to leave and sent me instead."

After that he said, "*Gardez!*" and four or five moves later I conceded the game.

At six o'clock in the evening, Juhan the coachman took Dr. Faehlmann back to Tartu, and I waited for Eeva, hoping she'd come to tell me what she wanted to tell me—and hear what I wanted to tell her. But she has not come, and it is already nine o'clock.

Our fifty cows and fifty heifers are coming home from pasture. Sitting here at my desk, I can't see their arrival, but from behind the barns over to the left, their hundred-throated mooing sounds not so much like the noise of twice fifty cattle as that of twice fifty *Yelizaveta*s—the name of the steamship I saw plying the route between St. Petersburg and Kronstadt, blowing its foghorn, the time Eeva and I went to the capital with Pastor Masing in the spring of 1817. But I haven't as yet written down *half* of what happened *in the spring of 1818.*

★ ★ ★

One bright May morning (I remember: it was Sunday, the nineteenth) I got up at my usual time, around seven. I went to the open window and stood there for a moment to breathe the fresh morning air. I recall that I heard Timo, another early riser, playing the piano in the small drawing room. He was an excellent pianist. I also noticed that he was playing a piece I had heard him play before: a passage, he had told me, from Schubert's Fourth Symphony, which had been published last year and had become famous so quickly. He stopped playing in the middle of a bar, and I remember wondering as I got dressed why he had stopped so abruptly. I went to the window again, to contemplate my program for the day (read fifty pages of Eichendorff's book *Ahnung und Gegenwart*; turn over forty square fathoms for vegetables) and to look at the garden. *Then I saw an armed soldier standing among the apple trees, behind the currant bushes.* I remembered that there had been a time, in Timo's grandfather's day, when armed guards were posted in that orchard—but only in the autumn when the trees were laden with ripe apples; and even then, the guards had not been *soldiers* . . . And I recall how some recent events that I had hardly noticed at all now cohered in my mind into dark foreboding and fright, as if my body had been pierced by an almost painless and imperceptible but nevertheless paralyzing lance . . . I went downstairs.

I walked through the study to the vacant billiards room, heard voices from the small drawing room, and entered it through a door flanked by two blue-uniformed gendarmes. Timo sat in a small armchair beneath the Greuze portrait and Eeva stood behind him, her hands on his shoulders. In another armchair, facing them, sat a small squint-eyed man in a general's uniform with a collar embroidered with golden oak leaves and a considerable number of medals and crosses on his chest. Next to this general stood a colonel with a braided cord around the left shoulder seam of his uniform. The door to Timo's study was open and I saw a number of gendarmes going through his desk drawers. As I entered the room, Timo said to the general:

"This is my wife's brother. I don't suppose the Marquis has any gracious imperial orders concerning him concealed in the hilt of that dagger."

The general replied, in an irritated tone of voice, "Mr. Bock, I tell you again: I am under the emperor's express orders not to cause your spouse and family any discomfort."

Eeva said, "Jakob, may I present Marquis Paulucci, our Governor General. He has come to us under the emperor's personal orders, to arrest Timo and to spare his family any discomfort. Quite an honor, don't you think?"

Two gendarmes came out of the study carrying armloads of papers. They set these down on the carpet by the general's feet.

The Marquis leaned forward, picked up a few papers, held them right in front of his face. He was obviously myopic.

"Whose letters are these?"

Timo glanced at the letters. "They are from General Dumouriez."

"The revolutionary émigré?"

"If you say so."

"These are letters from him to *you?*"

"Yes, that's what they are."

"Where does he know you from?"

"We met in England."

"When?"

"In 1813."

"What were you doing there?"

"Ask the emperor."

"Ahem."

The Governor General picked another piece of paper from the stack. "What is this?"

"It is a poem."

"I can see that. *'An Herrn Obristleutnant von Bock. Den 22. Oktober 1813 . . .'* Who wrote this to you?"

"Goethe."

"Come, now . . ."

"Take a closer look. It is in his own hand, and it is signed by him."

The Marquis eyed the sheet of paper, then looked at Timo. "Tell me, why did you say such terrible things about me to the emperor?"

"Such as?"

"Well—*ce plat aventurier italien, cet homme à six serments, dont chaque croix rappelle une bassesse!*"

Since it was Paulucci whom the Czar had sent here to arrest Timo, it couldn't have come as a surprise to Timo that the man would know what he had said to the Czar—although this wasn't quite as clear to me then as it is now. Timo did not act surprised but paused for a moment before he replied.

"I just told the emperor what I thought."

Marquis Paulucci's prominent lips suddenly seemed even more so, and I realized that he had turned pale. With a slight tremor of suspense, I waited for what would happen next, for I knew that after such words had passed between gentlemen of their rank, matters could be resolved only by means of a duel. But one of the gentlemen had just been arrested! I had no idea what would happen. Well, nothing did. The gendarmes brought further arm-loads of papers from both the downstairs study and the study up in the attic and stacked them before the Governor General. He picked some up and dropped them back onto the large pile. The clock in the drawing room began to strike eight, and Eeva said:

"*Monsieur le Marquis*, perhaps our noble ladies would invite you to breakfast even in a situation such as this one; but, as you know, I'm not really one of them. And I am not inviting you. So, you may send your gendarmes to watch us. My husband and I wish to have breakfast. Come, Jakob."

She led Timo out of the room and proceeded through the billiard room and the gallery to the tea salon. The Marquis did nothing to stop them. I turned to follow, and then Paulucci got up and joined us. When he had nearly caught up with her, he said to Eeva, with a sour smile:

"Madame, I do not aspire to your hospitality. But I must be present at your conversations, because I would be loath to demand from you a promise that you will not speak to each other."

We arrived in the salon and sat down at the round breakfast table. The Marquis seated himself off to one side, on the sofa beneath the mirror. Käsper came in with the hot water for tea, followed by Liiso with smoked ham and raspberry preserves. Käsper's face had lost all its color, tears glistened in Liiso's eyes. I noticed a slight tremor in Timo's hands when he used the silver tongs to put sugar cubes in his tea. He exchanged a few words in French with Eeva—the entire conversation up to that point had been in French. Then Eeva suddenly asked him in Estonian:

"Tell me what I should do."

Timo gave her a bewildered look. Then he understood. He took her hand in his and said, in his still rather awkward Estonian—and for the first time I forgave him that awkwardness:

"Raise our child. Remember me. And, if you possibly can, don't condemn me. You must know already: it is all you can do."

"To whom could I appeal for mercy for you?"

"No use to appeal for it from anyone but the emperor. But I beg you: do not plead with him!"

From the sofa came the Governor General's voice:

"Je dois vous prier de parler une langue compréhensible."

There had been a couple of times that morning when I had already marveled at Eeva's behavior, both with approval and with disapproval. In my inner turmoil of fear and excitement, I had thought: This sister of mine is still a girl, only twenty years old, and three months with child—a situation that does not tend to increase a woman's self-confidence. Where does she, at a time like this, find such boldness and courage? And at the same time I had winced a little and thought: Damn it all, she's being too impudent! As far as I could understand, all of us were at the mercy of this cross-eyed governor . . . Can Eeva really afford to lash him with her tongue . . . ? And now her response startled me even more —my wild sister turned her beautiful angry child's face to the Governor General and said, in polite French:

"Monsieur le Marquis, you are under the emperor's orders not to cause me any discomfort. Thus, you should be the first to obey that order. Do not cause me discomfort!"

The Marquis decided to be gallant about it. He smiled and said to Timo:

"Mr. Bock, I count myself among those who resolutely condemn the political steps you have taken, but not among those who do not understand your marriage."

Timo said, "Marquis, you are at liberty to count yourself among whomever you please."

Timo summoned Käsper, told him to bring writing materials, and there at the breakfast table wrote an order specifying that in his absence Eeva would be paid an annuity of three thousand rubles from Voisiku's accounts.

To Eeva he said, "Now, Monsieur Paulucci might of course say that I wrote this document while already under arrest, and therefore contest its validity."

"For Heaven's sake, madame," Paulucci said, "surely you don't believe I would do such a thing . . ."

And then the two of them stood there, Eeva and Timo, by the front steps of the manor, next to a small windowless carriage that

stood waiting there with two mounted gendarmes as its escort.
Timo and Eeva stood there holding each other for a minute or
even longer, their faces close together. And Marquis Paulucci, let
it be said, showed that he was a man of honor by not ordering
the gendarmes to separate them. Then Timo waved to those who
had come to see him off and got into the carriage, and a guard
with a Tatar mustache locked the carriage door and climbed up
into the driver's seat.

"Where are you taking him?" Eeva asked. She was as white as
a sheet and her eyes glittered, but she wasn't crying.

"My orders are not to tell," the guard replied, proud to be
entrusted with a state secret. And the carriage rolled out the front
gate. I remember thinking—or maybe I only thought this later,
when I recalled how Timo was taken away from us in a windowless carriage:

Everything in this life is really terrifyingly simple. Nothing is
simpler than the way a new and initially strange situation becomes
mundane; and the destruction of that new and, as it turns out,
frightfully fragile everyday state of affairs is even simpler than
that. The fate of a human being, and perhaps even the fate of the
whole world (should that exist separately from human fate), all
of it depends on small motions in space—on a stroke of the pen,
a resounding word, a turn of the key, the swoosh of an axe blade,
the flight of a bullet—

Midnight

Eeva came at ten.

Thank God I didn't start our conversation by telling her about
my own concerns, that is to say, my plans for Iette, but let her
speak first. As always, she looked well-groomed in her dark-gray
silk dress. And determined, as always. But I noticed one thing:
after she had sat down, she stroked the armrest of the old wicker
sofa in a way that struck me as a little peculiar.

I asked her, "What has happened?"

"Jakob, yesterday I saw Monsieur La Trobe at Poltsamaa. He
had asked me to come to see him. And he had such news to tell

me that I sent that doctor from Tartu ahead in our carriage and stayed to hear what Monsieur La Trobe had to say. I only got home a couple of hours ago, in his carriage. Jakob, an order has come from the Governor General. That is to say, an imperial order. Voisiku has been placed under guardianship, and the head of the board is Monsieur La Trobe. The other two guardians are Mr. Lilienfeldt and Elsy's husband, Peter."

"Well, something like that was to be expected," I said. To tell the truth, I felt a touch of malicious glee about the extent to which this development seemed to affect Eeva, the lady of the manor, while it really didn't mean much to an untrammeled idler like myself. At least, that was the way I tried to see it.

"But what it means is that there will be great changes here," Eeva said. "Monsieur La Trobe will move here with his wife and son."

"Let them move in, God bless 'em," I said. "We have more than twenty rooms here. You'll receive your three thousand a year in any case, won't you? And your son will enter the lyceum next autumn. I'm not wed to Voisiku. I've been wanting to talk to you about my plans for the future. Mr. Laming . . ." I hesitated, trying to figure out how to proceed from the father to the daughter.

Eeva said, "Mr. Laming will be dismissed from Voisiku."

"What are you saying?"

I felt no particular affection for Laming, true enough. But on the other hand, there wasn't all that much wrong with him, either. His dismissal did not please me at all. And his departure would ruin my ripening plan.

"Why will he be dismissed?"

Eeva gave me a strange, tense look. Then she closed her eyes and spoke, rubbing her temples with her fingertips:

"Jakob . . . I'm telling you this because you have to know. And because, oh—once in a while I feel that all of this is simply over-whelming . . . You see, Laming has been the government's ear in our household, for eight years. Klarfeldt was dismissed by a secret order from the Governor, and Laming was installed in his place. For many years, I never realized that, and I only understood it fully just a little while ago. But now that Timo has come back, and Laming is no longer sufficiently cunning as a spy . . ."

In other words, Mr. Laming is . . . *the one*. Well, then. Of course they have to exist, those people. How else would the government find out what is said and thought in households that are considered suspect? Still, it doesn't feel too good to think about it. It's rather like coming home and realizing that the front door has been open all this time, and the room has grown cold, and there are strange muddy footprints all over the floor . . . Perhaps Iette, too, is somehow involved in her father's business . . . Of course she is! But, no . . . Well, I don't know. I'll think about it later when I have some time to myself.

I asked Eeva, "But what was the significance of Laming's and Timo's talk about telling the truth? And about Laming's being *dead?*"

Eeva told me the whole story. The story she had formerly refused to discuss. Timo had told it to her in confidence.

It all went back to St. Petersburg, at the Winter Palace, in '14 or '15, when Timo had been the Czar's aide-de-camp. One evening the Czar had summoned him and said, "Timotheus von Bock, I have been watching you for quite some time. And I have come to the conclusion that you are one of the sort of men I need. The kind from whom I expect much more than from others. You are one of those few. Come!" He had taken Timo by the arm and led him to a chapel adjoining his apartments. A Bible lay on the altar between lit candles. And the Czar had said, "Timotheus von Bock"—then even corrected himself: "*Timothée, mon ami*—place your hand on the holy book and swear to me that you will always and in all things tell me the whole truth, that is, what you hold to be true in your inmost heart. And not only when I ask you for it, but also when you yourself find it necessary."

And Timo had sworn that oath to the Czar.

"But that Laming," Eeva said, "he also knows about it. God knows how—well, it's obvious, of course: the secret police told him. And being such a blockhead, he tries to play these idiotic games with Timo, now and again—pretending to be Czar Alexander, so that Timo has to reveal his thoughts to him . . ."

"What about Timo—is he taken in by that?"

Outwardly calm, I waited for Eeva's answer with considerable excitement: one way or another, it would tell me what Timo really was in Eeva's opinion—mad or sane.

But Eeva just looked at me for a moment and said, "You saw and heard it yourself."

And I understood that she had seen through my anticipation and declined to give me a straight answer.

I asked:

"So who will be assigned to spy on us now?"

"God only knows," said Eeva. "Maybe some new and even more taciturn candidate will show up on Monsieur La Trobe's doorstep to offer his services as a steward . . ."

Before Eeva left, she paced a few times from one window to the other, and I thought she had more to tell me—but all she said was:

"You won't talk about this to anyone?"

"Of course I won't."

She was already at the door to the stairs. She smiled and held out her hand.

"Will you give me your word? Just like Timo gave his to Alexander?"

I squeezed her hand and said, "Of course. I'm not crazy enough to give anyone a vow as to what I'll ever *say*, but I do give you my vow of *silence*."

Now I sit here at my desk. It is long past midnight. The sky is turning violet, I could blow out the candle and see well enough to go on writing. I have managed to record everything—and in such detail, I suppose, because, while not really aware of it myself, I wanted to gain time before answering a certain question:

How do I feel about Iette after what I have been told about her father?

Pacing back and forth in my room tonight, I have given this question a great deal of consideration. I admit that it would, of course, be better if Iette's father were a person I could respect. But I am wooing the daughter, not the father. True, the Bible says that the sins of the fathers are visited upon the third and fourth generation; but I have arrived at the conclusion that I can, and should, be more tolerant than Jehovah of the Old Testament. While doing so, I have seriously asked myself *what it is* that makes me so tolerant. Have I, in my thirty-eighth year as a confirmed bachelor, finally encountered what they call *a great love?* I reply to myself: No! I'm not that great a fool! But, to make no bones

about it, I am tired of my solitude, and this warm and soft slip
of a girl pleases me. When she came to me this morning, hugged
me, and then unwrapped a white piece of cloth to present me with
half an almond cake (which she had baked herself and smuggled
out under her father's eyes), I felt more delighted than I can remember ever feeling. So, let Mr. Laming remove himself and his
tarnished reputation from our estate—it is not a blow, it is a
solution! Let him go where he wants! Let him go on spying, I'll
stay here with Iette. I'll marry her, set her heart at ease. I'll read
my books. I'll tend my vegetable garden. Whatever else may
change here, on an estate this size I can always find a garden plot.
We'll live here, in my room and a half in the attic. I'll have someone
whispering endearments in my ear. And when we slip into bed,
not even the dogs will have a right to bark at us! Another thing
that's really excellent: we stand on the same rung of the social
ladder. She is the daughter of a man who has been a failure as a
master builder and has just been dismissed from his job as a
steward—and who is said to be a government spy. And me, I am
this old fellow who happened to fall off a manure wagon into the
family of a landed gentleman who has caused any number of
scandals . . . So maybe, at last, even this old bachelor . . .

 No. No, it won't do.

 It occurred to me an hour ago. Strange that I didn't think of it
sooner. (Damn, I've chewed my goose quill down to a stub.)
Well, I could certainly forgive Iette her student from Courland
and all the others who may have enjoyed her before him. However
many there may be—if any at all. God bless them all. I am no
infatuated schoolboy! And I could spit on her father's spying: let
it be. It doesn't have to taint his daughter . . . But it was at that
juncture that I recalled the girl's curious questions. I remembered
our first lesson and how she had questioned me about the December rebellion in St. Petersburg—how she had wanted to know if
Timo was really mad or if he had lucid moments . . . Her father
was a government spy: those would be questions at the top of his
list . . . And I sensed how *suspicion* invaded my mind. It was like
being drenched with cold water, soaked to the skin. I realized that
I could easily become dry again by simply imagining the warmth
this girl would bring into my life. And yet, I would not be able

to protect myself against renewed cold showers of suspicion . . .
Time and again, even after I would have asked her about it ten
times, and she would have sworn her innocence a hundred times
—time and again, night and day, suspicion would descend upon
me, so that no matter how carefully I'd lock my door, it would
still remain open, because it would be impossible to close, and my
floor would be covered by the muddy footprints left by a stranger
. . . my own wife. For she would have become my wife only in
order to gain access to the house through me, and would remain
in the house as the government's ear and eye, with her father as
the intermediary . . .

No. Never mind how much this is hurting me now—I do not
want to spend the rest of my life afflicted by a fever of suspicion,
or in fear of such fever attacks.

Enough!

Wednesday

Iette and her father left Voisiku the day before yesterday, on
the thirteenth. They had four wagon-loads of possessions. Our
horses were to haul these to Vonnu. I did not ask Laming where
they would go from there, and Iette didn't know. I heard, however, that Laming intended to go on to Riga in search of employment in the building trade (resorting to it once more to
replace, at least partially, his employment as an informer).

On Sunday morning, Iette came to see me. A difficult moment.

I said to her, "My dear child. It is so sad that you must leave.
But what can we do."

The first ice-sheet of parting was already between us. Iette tried
to break through it to reach me again.

She said, "But I'm not leaving . . ."

"How so?" I asked, pretending rather unsuccessfully that I didn't
understand. "Doesn't your father want you to go with him?"

"But if you did not want me to go . . ."

Now I had to tell her. I said, "Iette, I want you to go with your
father. As duty demands."

Just around the corner from my false fatherly pose, a repulsive little devil was grinning and enjoying his easy victory. Then Iette stepped on him. For she said, in a quiet voice, her straight and slender neck blushing with agitation:

"I know why you want to abandon me. It is because of what you have heard about my father."

I really don't know why I answered her like I did—whether I wanted to show her that she couldn't just bowl me over with her candor, or whether I wanted to say something *truthful*, after all (because I really had forgiven her her father). In any case, I said:

"No. It is not because of that . . ." Having said that, I believed I was safe from reproach. On what score could she still attack me? But she stood up from my wicker sofa and said, wringing her pretty hands, her voice a little hoarse with excitement:

"What you have heard . . . is . . . true. My father takes his orders from the Governor. But *I* am truly not to blame for that! I'll confess to you the only thing I feel guilty about in regard to you: when I came to see you that first time, it was because my father had told me to. And I asked you what he wanted to know. About the rebellion in St. Petersburg, and about Mr. Bock's health. That was all. After that I came only because of you." She gazed into my eyes. "So, now there is no shadow of doubt between us. And I believe"—her voice dropped almost to a whisper—"that you will save me . . . from having to leave here with Father."

But I had made my decision. The fear of future suspicions loomed too large in my mind. To put it bluntly, my love for Iette had been found wanting. After all, a *great love* is supposed to endure even death in the name of love. I took her cold hands in mine and said, without much emotion:

"Iette. Your father is waiting. Go now. I wish you the very best in your life."

I saw how her eyes suddenly went blank, her face froze. She tore her hands out of mine and ran from the room. I was standing on the hearthstone. I squeezed my eyes shut and turned toward the fireplace. When I opened my eyes again, I saw on the mantelpiece, between the candlesticks, a small round portrait made out of colored bits of stone—of Peter the Great, I seem to remember—in a thin brass frame. The bug-eyed Czar with his pointy mustachios. I don't know when it had been placed there, or by whom. I took it, just to grab hold of something, and squeezed it until my hand hurt. Then I threw it down onto the hearth and stepped on it with the steel-tapped heel of my boot. It didn't break. I stamped on it again, ground my heel into the imperial visage, heard metal grate against stone. I grabbed the mantel and pushed against it in order to give my boot more weight. I remember groaning: "Damn, damn—damned—*oppression* . . ." Then the image finally shattered and disintegrated into screechy gravel . . .

Early Monday morning I rode over to see the bookkeeper at the Roika mirrorworks. I never saw Iette again.

Saturday, the eighteenth of June

I still don't feel quite *collected* enough to go on recording last week's events, and prefer to return to matters of a decade ago. Turning back to see what I have written, I notice it seems to be my pattern to alternate passages dealing with the present and the past. So be it. From now on, I'll try to maintain this alternation rather than diverge from it, even though this might be confusing to an outsider, should such a person ever get to read this—I don't care . . . especially since it seems to me now that I myself have some difficulty distinguishing the present from the past in and around me.

After Timo had been taken away in the windowless carriage, Eeva came up the front steps, went to the Governor General, and addressed him:

"*Monsieur le Marquis*, how much longer must I endure the honor of your presence here?"

Inwardly, I shook my head at her tone, but this was not the moment to proffer advice to my proud sister. Marquis Paulucci replied, so drily it sounded almost menacing to me, "Only long enough, madame, for the officials accompanying me to collect your husband's papers, and for me to acquaint you with the emperor's letter concerning this case."

They went inside, to the door of Timo's study. The gendarmes had completed their task there and were now in the small drawing room stuffing bundles of papers into sacks made of sturdy gray cloth. The Marquis asked Eeva to precede him into Timo's study.

Eeva said, "*Monsieur le Marquis*, I would like to hear the emperor's letter in the presence of a witness. I wish my brother to be present."

"The letter is written in French," said the Marquis.

"He has no problem with that," Eeva replied.

"As you wish."

Eeva beckoned to me, and I followed them into the study, closing the door behind me. Eeva walked around the mahogany map table and stood on its far side, behind the globe. Paulucci and I stood on the other side. I clearly remember thinking: Oh, now this sister of mine has demonstratively placed the entire Arctic Ocean between herself and the man on whom she is now more dependent than on anyone except for the Czar himself. Such a stupid and thoughtless gesture!

My headstrong sister remained standing and did not offer the Governor General a chair. She said only, "I am listening."

Paulucci pulled a sealed letter out of a breast pocket beneath his decorations. Of course I don't remember it word for word, any more than I recall exactly what Paulucci added parenthetically while reading it to Eeva. But I daresay I remember it quite accurately. I noticed that as soon as the Marquis had taken out the letter and had started introducing its *spirit* to Eeva, his cool and until now somewhat playful tone of a man-about-town changed, no doubt inadvertently and unconsciously, to one so unctuous that I realized he himself must have been convinced that he was speaking words of sacred truth . . . It was a long introduction. Paulucci said he wanted Eeva to understand that the emperor's letter was a testimonial to His Imperial Majesty's most astounding and profound humanitarianism. Then he read the letter, but it seemed to me that he skipped a good deal. I recall that the Czar wrote that Mr. Bock had sent him a sealed bundle of papers some time ago. After reading it, the Czar had arrived at the conclusion that Mr. Bock must be mad—so confused, repulsive, and downright *shameless* were the thoughts expressed in those papers. In any orderly realm of state, such dangerous madmen had to be weeded out of society. The Czar wrote that he was sending these papers, or a part of them, to Paulucci for him to read, and to form his own opinion of them. Paulucci interrupted his reading of the letter to say that after perusing the papers he had found himself *entirely* in agreement with the emperor.

Eeva listened to this parenthetical remark with an impassive mien, and I certainly wasn't about to ask the Governor General whether, indeed, there *were* occasions on which he *did not* completely agree with the Czar . . .

Further, the Czar wrote that since this was the state of affairs, he was ordering the Governor General to undertake a personal journey to Voisiku (thus, I thought, giving the matter a disagreeable sense of importance) and there to arrest Mr. Bock and with all due dispatch transport him to his destination. Incidentally, if that destination was mentioned in the letter, Paulucci made sure not to reveal it, leaving us ignorant of it for years. In addition, the Czar ordered Paulucci to seal Mr. Bock's papers and to remove and examine them carefully, to make sure that there were no other like-minded people involved. It seemed to me that there was something skewed about the imperial logic in this instance, but I wasn't able to put my finger on it—until my irrepressible sister remarked with a smile:

"*Monsieur le Marquis*, what a great medical discovery—and one made by His Imperial Majesty himself!"

"*Pardon?*"

"That madness is contagious."

The Governor General swallowed and said:

"Madame, the emperor writes, verbatim: 'I do believe that this is the most charitable interpretation of Mr. Bock's behavior. During any previous reign, he would have been dealt with according to the full severity of the laws applicable to the case.' And I believe, madame, that your attitude will change altogether as soon as you hear the final paragraph of His Majesty's letter."

I do remember the final paragraph nearly verbatim—perhaps because Eeva and I later discussed it so many times. The Czar wrote:

. . . After this grave measure that I have decided to take, albeit with great and heartfelt pain, I feel obliged to con-

sider the fate of Mr. Bock's wife and their offspring—
because I have been informed that his wife has given
birth to a child. *(God knows who had told the Czar this:*
Timo and Eeva's child was not due for another five months!)
General, I entrust the fate of this family to your compas-
sionate heart. In disregard of the views of his peers,
Bock married an ordinary peasant girl, and his wife
must already have suffered all manner of hardship in society. Ensure the quality of her living conditions. Explain to her, with sympathy, the reasons for the grave
measures that have been taken in her husband's case.
Console her. Make sure that she is not bothered in any
way, and that no one begins to create difficulties for her.
Inform me if she finds herself in adversity. I will try to
assist her. Give me a detailed report on all of these
circumstances.

Alexander

At Perekop, the 8th of May 1818

"Well, then . . ." said the Governor General. "Madame, you
may not be able to appreciate this entirely, but I can tell you: one
can *count on one's fingers* the number of families in whose fate the
emperor has taken such a heartfelt interest!"

Eeva smiled her incredibly tight and arrogant smile, the same
smile she had already mastered as a girl of twelve, when she stood
with muddy toes by the stove in our house at Kannuka, next to
the chopping block, listening to Louka-Leenu from the manor
house, who would sit on that block warming herself, singing the
praises of the kind heart of the steward of Holstre Manor . . .
Only now, on the face of the grown woman, that smile was
infinitely more arrogant and effortless. I recall—some moments
of this kind remain with you for a lifetime—how I feared and
hoped, hoped and feared that this sister of mine, now a lady of
the manor, would at least formally ask the Marquis to convey her

thanks to the Czar . . . Because, never mind how strange it was to think this less than fifteen minutes after her husband had been taken away, Timo must have done *something*, that much was obvious, and even more obvious was the fact that one had to regard such imperial concern as miraculous . . . But my reckless sister let her smile fade and said mildly:

"Please inform the emperor that I shall appeal to him when my need for help is *so* great that I find it appropriate to do so. That is all—I believe."

Upon his nobleman's word of honor, Marquis Paulucci told Eeva that he did not know where the Czar had ordered Timo to be taken. Not that his word had to be considered binding in Eeva's case—she herself had told the Marquis that she did not count herself among the nobility. The house search, not the most thorough but fairly extensive due to the official importance of the case, lasted until two o'clock in the afternoon. Eeva did not ask the Marquis to stay for dinner, and so the guard of gendarmes surrounding the manor was called off at ten past two, and the Governor General rode away, accompanied by his aide, the colonel, and two dozen mounted gendarmes, whose horses carried the gray sacks containing Timo's papers and some of his books that had been deemed subversive.

Eeva did not appear at table that day. The perennially huffing and puffing Dr. Robst said the mistress of the house had told him that she wanted to go for a quiet walk by herself, and that we shouldn't worry about her. But when Eeva had not returned by six, eight, and finally ten o'clock that evening, Dr. Robst became feverish with panic. And although I consoled him ("Believe me, some lady of the gentlefolk might do something foolish to herself in such circumstances—but our lady? Never!"), I did not feel so sure about things by nightfall. I called at the Karlfeldts'. I visited the farmyard and asked the hands, who were just returning from spreading manure on the fields. I went to the dairy barn and the cowshed and the old infirmary. No one had seen the Baroness. I walked to the lake and the mill and the miller's house. No one there. I walked across the dam to the island and peered through the windows of the locked summerhouse. Empty chairs. Under cover of deepening dusk I managed to return to the manor without

Dr. Robst spotting me from his windows. Back in my attic room
in the left wing, on the orchard side, I noticed that my mouth
was dry from anxiety. Then I had an idea, bounded out of my
chair, and ran to the door of the room in which I am now writing
this. It was latched from the inside. The old door didn't fit its
frame too tightly anymore, and I raised the latch with the back
of my metal comb. I entered the room—and there she was, my
missing sister. The floor was littered with books that had been
removed from their shelves, opened one by one and shaken—in
the expectation that rice-paper lists of the names of Timo's co-
conspirators in madness would fall out of them . . . Eeva was
asleep, curled up on the wicker sofa. Her muddy shoes were on
the floor beneath the sofa. She had covered herself with an old
cloak of Timo's; one corner of it had slid to the floor, and Eeva's
feet in their white cotton stockings peeped out from under the
edge. I put my hand on her shoulder but had to shake her twice
before she raised her head. I saw that she had rolled up Timo's
green smoking jacket and used it as a pillow. Where her face had
rested, there was a dark stain from her tears.

"Where have you been?"

"In the woods."

"Tell me—what does it all mean? Why did they take Timo
away? What has he done?"

Eeva was silent for a moment. Then she looked me straight in
the eye, to make sure I understood.

"I don't know any more than you do."

And that was that.

Eeva said, "Let me go back to sleep now. I must have a clear
head again. As soon as possible."

Eeva pulled the edge of the cloak over her face, and I left her
on the sofa and went back to my bedroom. I can see myself sitting
there in an old armchair with creaky springs, listening to the
sounds of nightfall, the sleepy bark of the watchdog, the clank of
the well chains, the nightingale in the shrubbery behind the orchard. I was aware of the twofold nature of my feelings for my
reckless sister. What I felt now was respect, tinged with amazement, fear, and anxiety. Good Lord, was this an impossible situation for her! Our Eeva from Kannuka Farm, who had managed
to be lady of the manor for six months, and whom the entire

Livonian gentry (especially the women, of course) hated more vehemently than they hated the snakes in the yard. Who had endured all that venomous turmoil with the sole support of her strange husband . . . And who now, as of that morning, not only was deprived of that support but was also the wife of a criminal . . . (Oh, I could see it coming: until now, the manorial gossips had pitied poor Timo because he had taken a wife with whom he could only discuss the watering of calves. But now, of course, they would soon be blathering about how it was Eeva, that re-bellious daughter of the dungheap, who had put subversive ideas into her husband's head, and so he had been thrown into prison because of her . . .) Yes, indeed. Yesterday, Eeva was the wife of a respected nobleman—today, the spouse of a criminal against the state. And while noblemen were granted certain privileges even in prison, Eeva's title was nothing but a bleeding wound, the kind into which the world dearly loves to rub the salt of derision . . . In addition, she was a rarity among the wives of such criminals: she had been declared an object of the Czar's special mercy. (The devil knows what that's about!) But that wasn't all: in an unprec-edented fashion, she had proudly declined both that imperial mercy and its messenger ("How much longer must I endure the honor of your presence here?"). A mad girl . . . More and more, my own amazed and fearful respect for her became overshadowed by a feeling of censoriousness—did she *really* have to act that way? And, I have to admit, there was even a touch of spitefulness: Well, now you've got what you wanted, *Baroness* von Bock! I won't deny that I also felt a twinge of anxiety about my own fate. My sister's desire to ascend to God knows what heights in this world had brought both her *and* me close to the brink of the abyss . . . I didn't have the faintest notion what was to become of our lives.

Wednesday, the twenty-second of June

Laming's dismissal has left us without a steward, but Monsieur La Trobe has found a new one for us, old Timm of nearby Soosaar Farm. The dilapidated steward's house behind the barnyard is being repaired for him. I know him well, he is a dour and unaffected man. He is certainly not our new informer.

Early yesterday morning, after my swim, I passed the bleaching green on my way back from the lake. Six or seven maids were carrying bolts of linen cloth to the green and unrolling them. Most of them were young, their faces flushed with the exertion of straightening the heavy cloths. They greeted me in a proper fashion, and I returned their greetings and strode past them, feeling a little ill at ease. Fifteen years ago, the proximity of young country girls—all the possibilities—would have given me nothing but pleasure, but now I was no longer so sure whether to think of them as "women" at all, and if so, with what degree of familiarity . . . At that moment, one of them reached the end of her bolt right next to me and straightened her back—and I exclaimed:

"Eeva! What are you doing—playing Penelope?" (Nausicaa sprang to mind first, but then Penelope seemed more apposite; in fact, very much so.) Eeva laughed and said:

"I came here to help the girls . . . Do you mind?" She was quiet for a moment, catching her breath, and then said, "But listen, Timo and I agreed . . . to ask you to have supper with us tonight." She looked straight at me. "Well—do you *mind?*"

"Of course I don't," I said and walked on, thinking: This inability of mine, to feel a sense of belonging, does not afflict me only now, or only in regard to those maids, or only with women—it has afflicted me always and everywhere. It is the same with the farm laborers sitting at the edge of a field or by the kiln door in a tight group, eating their provisions, dusty, sweaty, caked with mud. As I walk past them, I greet them, as is customary, I say a few words (but instantly feel I have been too familiar, or too fatuous, or too supercilious, or inappropriate in some other way); and I know that although they treat me with deference to my face, behind my back it's "that half-a-squire" . . . (Well, they also call me "Manor House Jaakko," but I don't know which appellation they favor.) I feel even worse among the gentry, by whom I am mostly ignored and anticipate this by ignoring them all (or, to be more precise, by alternating between supercilious indifference and unintentional humility, occasionally lapsing into abrupt awkwardness). Only among the literati at Dean Masing's, or among Timo's friend in Tartu, have I occasionally met people with whom I have sensed what it might feel like to get off this perpetual seesaw of superiority and inferiority and just feel at ease. In such company, however, I have had to take care that the gaps in my knowledge and experience did not become too evident, because only some old informer like Laming would have the gall to flatter me by claiming that I was more learned by far than the gents who'd gone to university . . . Eeva is altogether different: she'll go and help the maids with the linen or the butter churn, she'll take medicine to the village women in childbed and joke with them as if she were one of them; and they tell her all their troubles, though she does not tell them hers. Even in the gentry's attitude toward her something has changed over the past ten years. It has, of course, always been rather strained, now even more so, after Timo's return; and yet she herself is quite free and easy in the midst of all that strain . . . Well, there are times when she herself seems strained, but not out of awkwardness, or apathy, or any sense of ineptitude (as is the case with me). She acts whenever she has decided to gather all her resources for a known purpose at a given moment. The devil only knows where she has learned the skill to be the way she is.

I should mention that Eeva and Timo really seem to be settling in again. They no longer confine themselves only to Timo's room facing the front yard, where they have also been sleeping until now, but have moved their sleeping quarters into the chambers behind the yellow drawing room and spend their days both in that drawing room and in Timo's study.

Last night Timo looked much healthier than he did two weeks ago. Several times (and I haven't asked whether he has permission to do so) he has ridden out as far as Vortsjärv for a swim, and that is a distance of more than twenty versts. The three of us supped at seven (very lightly, as is their habit: tea and thin open-faced sandwiches with Aberdamm cheese and celery salad). Then Timo crammed four new English words into little Jüri's head (*celery, celebrity, purpose,* and *persistence*), after which the boy went back to his room to continue reading about the adventures of Telemachus. And then Timo invited us to the drawing room, where he performed a brief, half-hour piano recital for our benefit.

I am certainly no expert, but I have heard that Monsieur La Trobe, a masterful pianist, thinks that Timo's playing is just as splendid as it was before. In any case, Timo's memory seems faultless: at the end, he began to play a piece that I couldn't name although it sounded familiar to me. He stopped after a few bars and asked Eeva:

"Do you recognize that?"

Eeva nodded, significantly somehow, and Timo said to me:

"That was the last piece I played on this piano, nine years ago. It's from Schubert's *Tragische Symphonie*—appropriate, wouldn't you say?"

We returned to his study. Eeva sat down and picked up her embroidery frame. Timo and I lit our pipes.

I asked, "What was it like for you, there at Schlüsselburg?"

I noticed that Eeva gave me a slightly apprehensive and reproachful look from behind her frame. But Timo picked up the bowl of his meerschaum pipe, blew a big cloud of smoke into the evening light that filtered into the study from the yard, and said, his eyes fixed on the smoke:

"It had its ups and downs. I played that Schubert there, as well."

"Oh, really? Where did you . . . ?"

"In my cell."

I had to giggle. "On the edge of your cot?"

"On the Czar's grand piano." I winced inwardly. I felt strange, the way one always does when the person with whom one is conversing lapses suddenly into irrational statements. Good God —when at long last, in the summer of '21, Eeva heard from Georg that Timo had been held in the Schlüsselburg fortress all those years and was still there, she began to gather information about the place, in order to get a picture of the conditions in which the prisoners lived there. True, she had received a few letters from Timo during those years, but the place and the *conditions* in which the writer of the letters lived were, of course, not mentioned at all. In the spring of '21, Eeva and I journeyed to the town of Schlüsselburg, because we thought (or rather, feared) that Timo was perhaps imprisoned behind those walls. As we did not have permission to visit the fortress, all the boatmen refused to row us from the town to the island (they were, apparently, forbidden to do so) where we might have tried to speak with Major-General Plutalov and enquire after Timo. Thus, we were none the wiser after that trip, but we had seen the island fortress and its massive towers with our own eyes and had tried to imagine what it would be like to be kept there—in a gigantic bowl of stone surrounded by ice and water. That summer, after Georg had obtained some reliable information for us, Eeva looked up General Plutalov in St. Petersburg. This pockmarked gentleman, however, turned out to be rather like a character in Fonvizin's plays—the name defined the man. What was Eeva told by him, or by his aide? That life for those imprisoned for crimes against the state was positively idyllic: there was sufficient light, plenty of room, not too much humidity, effective heating, and more than enough to eat. The prison regime, however, was, of course—»Режим, уважаемая госпожа, конечно тот, который они своими престпленилями заслужили.»

So that even according to General Plutalov, conditions in Schlüsselburg did not really permit piano soirées. Not content with her interview with the general, Eeva had sought out one of his retired prison guards. I understood him to be a gnarled old fellow who had grown cynical in his occupation but was willing to talk candidly if offered some cash for vodka. He gave a much more telling description: the two-hundred-year-old stone walls, one fathom thick, reached down to the groundwater of the low island and had become saturated with water like sponges. During the long winter, with the cold winds blowing across the water, those walls froze so thoroughly that they kept the interior cold all summer long. But of course, the old man cackled, an ice cellar keeps the meat from rotting . . . The cells were like low turnip cellars, furnished with a cot, a stool, a table, and a latrine bucket. The library consisted of a prayer book.

So it was that I didn't quite know how to react at first to Timo's talk about a piano. I cast a baffled glance at Eeva, then, lamely jocular, asked Timo:

"So the Czar sent his grand old friend a grand piano?"

"That's right," Timo nodded.

"How did that happen?"

"Nothing much to it. One day the guards dragged it into my

hutch. It was a really fine Schröder. Then Plutalov came by and told me that it was a personal favor from the emperor."

"I see. Pianos weren't all that common there, were they?"

"Plutalov said this was the first one."

"What made the Czar send it to you?"

"How should the Czar's poor madman know what caused his wise emperor to get such a crazy idea? I can only make *assumptions*."

"Such as?"

"Perhaps he thought that music would soften me up. One might suppose that such *imperial kindness* would make an impression in that closet of stone . . . Which it did, of course, I won't deny it. Just imagine: everything is gray, damp, heavy, silent—and suddenly there stands this shiny black resounding shape with its big wing . . . That alone—and then, the music . . . the worlds you can enter while playing . . . But you have condemned yourself to rot there, while your emperor waits, hopes, *begs you* to come to your senses and *beg him* for *mercy* . . ."

I asked, still not quite free of disbelief, but in order to express my admiration for Timo somehow—perhaps it was mere courtesy, or perhaps there was an element of boorish sycophancy in it, the devil only knows—

"But they didn't soften you up?"

"I don't believe they did."

Fair enough. If that hadn't been the case, I don't suppose they would have started knocking out his teeth, later. I don't exactly know what they used to do that, nor to this day do I know *why*. But I have promised myself not to ask him anything about the past, leaving it up to him to talk or not talk about it. Last night I realized that I had broken that promise by turning the conversation to Schlüsselburg.

I asked him, "But what are your plans for life *from now on*—yours and Eeva's?"

Timo, suddenly restless, got to his feet.

"Well, what kinds of plans can one make in our situation?"

Eeva said, "First of all, Timo has to get his strength back."

"And then?" I asked, perhaps a little too persistently; but the matter did concern me. It was a question of the future, and I hadn't promised anyone that I would refrain from *all* questions.

Timo walked over to Eeva and said, looking into her eyes (and I noticed, looking at my sister's profile, that she wasn't sure whether or not I should hear what Timo was about to tell me):

"Every day, Eeva talks to me about what you yourself suggested a couple of weeks ago. When we were having coffee together. Do you remember?"

"What did I say?"

"That our only chance is to flee abroad."

Yes, I thought, this means they will escape. And I'll be rid of them. Of them and of the government's informers along with them. I'll get out of Voisiku. I'll take the few hundred rubles I saved from when I worked for Tenner. I'll buy a cottage and a garden plot in Poltsamaa, or in the outskirts of Viljandi . . . But if that's how it's going to be—why could I not have taken Iette for my wife? But that decision has already been made.

★ ★ ★

And so, last night, the three of us pondered their chances of escape. Timo locked the door to his study, just in case, and even closed the window, even though it was still light outside and we could have seen anyone coming. I asked if they knew who our new spy might be.

Timo said, "God only knows. I don't trust anyone except for Kitty—and, of course, you. Her brother."

I felt how irrevocably those words drew me into their circle of conspiratorial trust. As for their actual plan of escape, it turned out that Eeva already had a broad outline for it; what's more, it was an outline you couldn't argue with. *If* one were to escape, this would be the way to do it. Eeva had realized that the least dangerous route out of the country would be by ship from Pärnu. They would have to ask permission from the Governor General ("No, you're right, Timo—not from Paulucci but from the emperor himself—and it would not be shameful to petition Czar Nicholas for it . . .")—for, say, a visit to a physician in Viljandi or Tartu. That permission would have to be secured, and if they were forced to take some watchdog along, a way would have to be found to get rid of him. Then, on the way to the announced destination, they would turn toward Pärnu at some suitable juncture and arrive at a prearranged time at a prearranged vessel.

It is also clear that none of this can happen before next summer, first of all because there won't be enough time this summer to make arrangements. Money is the main thing, and that is why we must first wait until the financial future of Voisiku has been clarified.

Timo said, "It turns out that Kitty has already put money aside for the escape itself. From the three thousand she received annually from Voisiku through the Livonian treasury, she managed—can you believe it?—to save a third. Eight thousand rubles. But, as Kitty says, we must have something to live on once we are abroad."

I asked where they were planning to go.

Eeva said, "Timo has to decide that. He's seen half the world. We'll disembark wherever the ship takes us, provided that it is a country that won't extradite us back to Russia. After that—we have talked about Switzerland. They say there are many refugees there, of all kinds. And Timo's brothers have some friends there."

We also arrived at the conclusion that although escape wasn't possible this year, it would be a good idea if one of us were to visit Pärnu before the autumn to see what the possibilities were —to find out what kinds of ships docked there, where they sailed, and how one might board one unobserved. We would, of course, consider only foreign vessels, since no captain sailing under the Russian flag would be willing to agree to such an undertaking.

Eeva continued, "We might even come to an agreement now, in principle, with some captain for next summer."

When Timo unlocked the door for me, he said, "Well, then. I suppose it goes without saying that tonight's conversation has been for our ears only."

I said, "Of course it does!" Then I walked upstairs to my room, where until midnight, both with pleasure and misgivings, I pondered the unexpectedly deep—and, I might add, reckless—trust that had arisen between them and me. I also pondered my observation that in this matter of flight abroad, Eeva had seemed even more eager than Timo; and that, for a woman, Eeva had thought it all out in a very clearsighted way.

Enough. From now on, I must hide this journal even *more* carefully than ever before. Wherever a house is forced to accept ears, so, also, the eyes that travel with them.

Thursday, the twenty-third of June

In my entry describing the nineteenth of May, 1818, I left Eeva in this room, on the wicker sofa, trying to sleep to clear her head from the shock she had experienced.

A clear head was, indeed, what my sister needed from that time onward. Dr. Robst, Klarfeldt, and all the others were simply paralyzed by Timo's arrest, and I won't try to deny that I was, too. They were even less able to explain it than I was: at least, I had heard the main points of the Czar's letter to Paulucci. On the other hand, this may have made my sense of paralysis even more disheartening than it was for the others: it was clear from the Czar's letter that there was, in fact, little one could expect or hope for in regard to Timo's case—neither justice nor mercy.

We could not console ourselves with the hope that Timo's arrest had been some kind of mistake—in their infallibility, the emperors of Russia are kin to the popes of Rome.

If anyone among us kept a clear head that first week, it was Eeva, even though she had suffered the hardest blow. Looking back, I can see that she had one advantage: she was better able to guess at the reasons for Timo's imprisonment than anyone else. And that, perhaps, also made it possible for her to feel some degree of hope.

After a week or two, Lieutenant-Colonel Georg von Bock, the older of Timo's two younger brothers, arrived at Voisiku; I no longer recall whether he came to us from St. Petersburg or from Poland. This was the first time I met him. As tall as Timo, and probably a jovial man under normal circumstances, he seemed grief-stricken, and his handsome Hussar mustachios seemed (and probably still seem) incongruous on his slightly morose face. He treated Eeva with respect and was civil to me. Altogether, as we were to find out, he was the most sensible person among Timo's relatives. Even though he was only a couple of years younger than Timo, Georg seemed to have grown up in unswerving admiration of his older brother. The influence of their late tutor, Lehrberg, may also have had something to do with this; in any case, that admiration was also reflected in his attitude toward Eeva.

Incidentally, it was Georg who, while visiting the Wahls of Poltsamaa and other families, set in motion this story: *Timo is supposed to have sent an offensive letter to the emperor? Well, maybe, but in spite of any free-thinking views, it surely must have been chivalrous in form and noble in content! From Mr. Timotheus von Bock, anything else would be simply unthinkable.* Eventually, this became the accepted view, first among the family and then, by and by, among increasing numbers of the Livonian nobility. As *they* saw it, their kinsman or fellow noble was simply incapable of less than chivalrous and noble actions, never mind that he'd been a complete blockhead in his choice of a spouse—and even in that folly, he was merely a victim of his own chivalry and magnanimity . . .

Baron Georg was still at Voisiku when clerks from the Livonian State Treasury arrived from Riga—another event that shook our world. It wasn't as stunning as Timo's arrest. Personally, I had nothing to my name at Voisiku, not even the couple of hundred rubles that are now gathering mold in my cupboard, nor did Eeva stand to lose anything except for the jewelry and clothes Timo had given her and a couple of dozen rubles in her purse. At this time, she had not yet received her annuity of three thousand rubles; not entirely certain that she would actually get it, she had been counting on it nonetheless, and that made this new crisis seem the more severe. With ink-stained fingers, the two polite but insistent treasury clerks, their bony frames garbed in threadbare tailcoats, opened their canvas briefcases and spread papers and abacuses on the green baize of our billiard table. Then they announced to us —that is, to Eeva, Georg, and, for some reason, me—the following: *The unpaid loans advanced to Col. (Ret.) Timotheus von Bock by various nobles and commoners, with or without the collateral of Voisiku Manor, by far exceed the worth of his property. Therefore, an imperial order has been issued to determine the net worth of Mr. Bock's fortune and the extent of his indebtedness. In order to ascertain all of his debts, notice has been given to all his creditors to register their claims . . .* Creditors had flocked to the main treasury office in Riga, registering claims ranging from less than a hundred to several thousand of rubles. Their number was incredible, at least to me. In such matters, my powers of comprehension were—and still are—limited by the view our father held throughout his life, as a peasant serf at Holstre, as a coachman, and as a freedman working for Pastor Rücker at Kolga-Jaan: "A real man doesn't ask for anything, a tailor asks for ten kopecks, a huckster at the fair asks for a ruble, and only a cheat or a rogue asks for more." But now, we—or the estate of Voisiku—suddenly owed a hundred thousand rubles . . . Eeva and I did not have the faintest idea how these debts had been incurred, nor where the money had gone. I must admit that there were moments when I was overcome by the inappropriate suspicion that Timo, in spite of his almost inhuman correctness, or underneath that surface, was some strange kind of adventurer . . . I did not tell Eeva this, and she neither asked my opinion nor told me what she herself thought of her husband's debts. Then events took an unexpected turn.

Eeva decided to go to Riga to speak with the chief treasurer, a Privy Councillor Cube, and I accompanied her. This was in August of '18. The weather was hot, the roads incredibly dusty, and Eeva was seven months pregnant. In that condition, ladies of rank no longer travel or exert themselves. When I mentioned this to Eeva, she said that if we waited for her to give birth, we wouldn't be able to call on Privy Councillor Cube before the following summer. Besides, she didn't think she was that much more delicate than other women of peasant stock—our own mother, for example. And so we went to the coach house, selected a small cabriolet with gentle springs, and traveled for three days.

I remember how we proceeded from our inn to Riga Castle on foot since the distance between the two was short, and we thought it might make the wrong impression if we drove up to the door. It also allowed us to speak of matters we had not wanted to discuss in our coachman's presence: Where would we go, what would become of us now? The estate would, of course, be sold to pay Timo's debts, and we would no longer have a place there. The cottage at Paluka that Timo had found for our parents could not support us. All we—or rather, Eeva—had was Timo's wedding gift to her: a necklace, a bracelet, and two rings, all gold, all together worth a few hundred rubles . . . Eeva said, "We may even have to sell those to satisfy some impatient creditor."

We entered the castle gate and asked the officer on duty for directions. We strode along cool stone hallways, and before we ascended a brick staircase, Eeva said to me, "Wait a moment . . ." Just as we walked into Privy Councillor Cube's stone-vaulted chambers, I noticed how pale she was and hastened to take her arm. The chief treasurer, a smooth-looking man with dark yellow hair, sprang from his seat behind the desk to offer a chair to a lady in such delicate condition. But Eeva clenched her teeth, sat down with the faintest of smiles, and said with an ease that amazed me:

"Ich bin Frau Katharina von Bock, aus Woiseck"—which for some reason caused Privy Councillor Cube to leap to his feet once again—"and this is my brother. We have come to you in order to gain full clarity in regard to the debts incurred by my unfortunate husband. And to find out what I can do on his behalf in this matter."

I fully expected the chief treasurer to put on a sour face, spread his white hands, and begin to explain how hopeless the matter of Mr. Bock's debts was, unfortunate, to be sure—but instead, he reemerged from behind his desk, smiled radiantly, took a seat on a leather chair opposite Eeva, and said, positively beaming:

"Madame, I haven't had a chance to express my delight in the fact that I am in a position to tell you some good news! Yes, indeed! It is truly miraculous. We have been able to balance your husband's debts. They no longer amount to a hundred thousand rubles, but to merely forty thousand—which is only a little more than half the value of your estate at Voisiku. If we include chattels and furnishings, even less. And we have ascertained that the estate does, after all, produce an income of five and a half thousand rubles a year. Thus, madame, I have the pleasure to inform you that there will be no insolvency, and you are guaranteed your three thousand rubles a year."

"I am, of course, truly delighted to hear that," Eeva said, and I noticed that she took a deep breath before continuing. "But allow me to be curious—what happened to the sixty thousand?"

"Ahem . . . You see, your husband's *main creditor* notified us that he is rescinding his claim. He has canceled Mr. Bock's debt."

"Of sixty thousand . . . ?" Eeva asked, almost in a whisper. I understood that she had to find out more about this in order to believe it.

"Yes, *precisely* that amount," Cube said, almost ingratiatingly.

"And who is this creditor?" Eeva asked.

"His name is . . ." The chief treasurer eyed the slightly soiled knee of his light-colored trousers, then suddenly looked up at Eeva (with an expression that seemed to say, 'Well, now, do you really not know who it is?'). "It is Count Stedingk."

"I see," said Eeva without acting particularly surprised—and as if such a gesture by some Count Stedingk seemed entirely comprehensible to her. She added, "Truly, it is most humane of him to waive that debt."

We took our leave, left the castle, and stepped into the bright sunshine of the street. As we were walking across the cobblestone square, I asked Eeva, "Sixty thousand rubles? Just now, when all the nobles are shunning us as if we were lepers . . . Who is this Count Stedingk?"

"I have no idea," Eeva said. "I have never heard that name before."

Thursday the thirtieth

I have not had a chance to take my journal out of its hiding place for a whole week. We are in the throes of another upheaval. It almost seems as if my writing about the shocks we suffered ten years ago had called forth new ones.

On Monday morning, Peter arrived—Timo's brother-in-law, Peter von Mannteuffel. At ten o'clock, Eeva asked me to come downstairs to be there "while Peter informs us about the new order of our lives," as she put it while we descended to the yellow drawing room.

Von Mannteuffel was sitting in the same armchair that Paulucci had occupied ten years ago, idly tapping his signet ring on the top of the coffee table. His swarthy, close-cropped head sat a little askew on his shoulders, and his gray silk bow tie looked slightly squashed under his heavy bluish chin. Timo also occupied the same chair as he had then, ten years ago, and Eeva stood behind him as she had stood then, her hands on his shoulders—just like then.

Peter said, "I'll be brief"—and before he could go on, Timo said, "Wait!" He turned to Eeva. "Have Jüri called in here. I want him to hear this."

"Nonsense!" von Mannteuffel exclaimed. *"Whatever for?"*

But Eeva strode into the billiard room and shouted for Jüri who was in the adjoining study room reviewing his French with Dr. Robst. The boy came to the drawing room and Timo beckoned him, put his hand on the boy's shoulder, and said:

"Now listen carefully. Uncle Peter is going to tell us how we will live here in the future. So—listen and learn!"

"Learn what?" the boy asked.

"Whom to love—and whom not to," said Timo.

Von Mannteuffel raised his dark brows from the document in front of him and measured us with reproachful glances.

"Tell me, why make such a *spectacle* of this?"

Timo replied mildly, "Because we're still free to do so, if nothing else."

"Oh, come, come—well, all right!" Von Mannteuffel dismissed Timo's words with a wave of his hand. Then he got down to business.

"I promised to be brief. The guardianship board (you know—myself, La Trobe, and Lilienfeldt) has received instructions from the highest level. In accordance with these, the board has decided that since the estate currently lacks a squire, the committee will *rent it out*, and the tenant will be Monsieur La Trobe, until I have settled my affairs at Harm and Elsy's proprietary rights to Voisiku have been confirmed in the appropriate manner. After that, I shall move here with Elsy and the children."

"And what do Georg and Karl have to say about this?" Timo asked.

Von Mannteuffel snorted contemptuously: "Matters have been settled with those two. They relinquish their shares to me, and I send each of them fifteen thousand rubles, to a bank in Geneva."

"And Elsy agrees to this?" Timo asked, very calmly.

"Of course Elsy agrees with my decisions."

"Your decisions, which coincide with those of the Governor General—and the Governor General's decisions, which coincide with yours?"

"Yes. Fortunately."

"And what have you and the higher powers-that-be decided in regard to us?" Timo waved his right hand in a small arc that contained the four of us around his chair.

"Your situation remains the same. You'll go on living here like God's own fowl in the air. Not in this house, of course."

"Where, then?" Timo asked, as calmly as before. It seemed to me that his face was as pale now as it had been when he returned from Petropavlovsk, and he was patting Jüri's little shoulder a bit more energetically than was necessary; and yet, God be my witness, the shadow of an impish smile hovered around the corners of his mouth.

"You'll move into The Foundation," von Mannteuffel said, a mite glibly.

"What fun!" Jüri exclaimed. "We'll have squirrels coming right inside, through the windows—I've seen them!"

"Monsieur La Trobe and his wife and son will move in here first—then, later, I and Elsy and the children. That's as it should be. And you'll have plenty of room in The Foundation—ten rooms for four persons. Dr. Robst has already been told that he'll share the steward's house with old Timm. So you'll have the whole building at your disposal. Get your things packed this week, and I'll send men to move your furniture on Monday."

"And Monsieur La Trobe knows all about this? And is willing to move into our place?" Eeva asked. It was her first question during this conversation.

"Yes, yes, of course!" von Mannteuffel exclaimed with an air of extreme impatience. I couldn't tell whether he was impatient with Eeva or with La Trobe.

"So you are sure that I am completely sane?" Timo asked unexpectedly but still calmly.

"What? In what sense?"

"In the sense that you're not afraid I'll get up and strangle you?"

"Oh . . . Well, come, come . . ."

But I saw that while von Mannteuffel was making slightly distracted noises, he was also inserting his right hand into his left breast pocket. Timo, as mildly as ever, said, "Thank God you're not trying to fool us. About your subtlety *or* your courage."

"What do you mean?"

"Well, you just showed us that you carry a pistol."

A sharp observation on Timo's part—but it did not improve our situation. Heaven knows, nothing too scandalous is happening to us. For Timo, of course, it is more of a tragedy; yet in some curious way even I sense something degrading in this. On the other hand, I am aware how absurd that feeling is when I recall our former cottage in Kannuka, or the coachman's quarters at Holstre, and compare them to The Foundation.

The Foundation is, after all, a house built for gentlefolk, even if it is a hundred and fifty years old. In Livonia, at least, most of the not so wealthy gentry do not inhabit better dwellings, by any means. It is true that few manor houses have thatched roofs anymore—most of them have been replaced by tiles. But otherwise, The Foundation is quite a building, fifteen fathoms long and five fathoms wide. The walls are made of solid old logs that rest on a stone foundation that rises almost as high as a regular room. There is a huge vaulted cellar with a good sauna to one side, complete with a large stove, a wash room, and a vestibule. In the house itself there are ten rooms and a kitchen, with closets and larders. A couple of rooms have fireplaces in addition to tall white Dutch tile stoves with ornamental facings. The building stands beneath the old willows of the manor park and is surrounded by a dense hedge of wild rose bushes that take your breath away this time of year with their powerful scent of roses.

Eeva has decided that I'll be given two rooms in the back of the house, facing those roses and the park. The larger room is about three fathoms by four and has two windows, both of them, regrettably, facing north. The other room, only half that size, its windows facing east, will be my bedroom. I'll be lodged quite a bit more splendidly than I was in the attic of the main building, especially considering that the ceilings in these rooms are a fathom and a half high.

And yet, and yet, we have been evicted from our home . . . Timo, in particular. He is now a cottager on his hereditary estate. So, of course, is Eeva, regardless of whether the manorial splendor she has enjoyed until now really suited her or not; she feels particularly bitter about the eviction because it goes without saying that the "unfortunate colonel"—or "mad Colonel," depending on the speaker's intentions—would have been allowed to remain in the manor, even by such an arrogant brother-in-law as Peter, *if* his wife had been some predictably appropriate lady with a maiden name like von Schoultz, or von Stackelberg, or von Schlippenbach . . . When I think of my sister's situation, I can understand that it must be triply painful for her: she must be aware that her humiliation also extends to her son . . .

In The Foundation,
late Tuesday night,
July the twelfth

Now we have settled in, at last, I on my own side of the house, Eeva and Timo and their son on the other. They have seven rooms at their disposal; the eighth one has been partitioned into two, one for Liiso, the kitchen maid, the other for old Käsper.

I should really be quite content and at peace in these quarters, but I don't feel like that at all. I just closed the windows and drew the thick linen curtains, shutting out the view of the wild rose garden. I locked the door. God knows that my behavior in these matters may be as exaggerated as Timo's—but here, on my desk, next to this journal, within a circle of light provided by two candles, lies the most surprising and exciting discovery to have resulted from our move.

The night before last, at dusk, I went back to the manor house. Those of Timo and Eeva's belongings that didn't fit into The Foundation had been stored in the chambers behind the drawing room. Even in the fading light, I could see the unfaded rectangles left on the wallpaper by the removed family portraits. In the tutorial room, pale plaster yawned where the blackboard had been. Now that blackboard hangs on the wall of Jüri's room in The Foundation. The manor echoed with emptiness as if a note from Timo's grand piano had still lingered on. I went upstairs to my former room. There was still enough light to see without a candle. I did not want to be noticed by anyone looking up at the window that had been stripped of its curtains. I stepped into the oriel where my desk used to stand and opened the ceiling board. I took out my journal, tucked it beneath my vest. The eye-level ceiling board had already swung shut, and I opened it once again, I don't even know why—perhaps because I knew that I was dealing with it for the last time. In any case, I pushed both hands into the hiding place and ran them over its interior. Nothing but dust. While I was probing that space, my journal slipped from inside my vest onto the floor. As I felt it slipping and started pulling my hand out of the opening, I accidentally pushed harder against a board on the far side of the box. The board turned, my hand slid between it and the ceiling boards, and my fingers encountered a bundle of papers.

Now those papers lie on my desk. I have spent two days reading and rereading them. No doubt about it, *this* is the secret of Timo's imprisonment! It is a sixty-page manuscript written in French and must be a copy of the memorandum Timo wrote in the spring of '18 and sent to the Czar—the reason for what happened to him thereafter.

I can say that I have read it with *care*. I even threw my own books out of their baskets and piled them on the floor in order to lay my hands on Legrand's large dictionary, to make sure I understood every word of Timo's memorandum.

God, how unsuspecting we have been, all these years!

We have always believed that Timo's imprisonment, and all that he suffered during it, was an incomprehensible and unprecedented injustice. That even if something similar had happened before to others (as, indeed, one gathered it had), none of these others—at least among those who lived in the Baltic provinces under Russian imperial rule—none of them had suffered *such* terrible and obvious injustice as Timo! Certainly those whose knowledge or suspicion about the causes of his incarceration was based only on hearsay (I among them) were convinced that this was so. Perhaps in our initial amazement we thought that Timo must really have committed some serious crime against the state. Otherwise, the crown could not possibly destroy a respectable nobleman, an officer with twenty decorations, a personal friend of the emperor, without any repercussions, and so silently that it seemed as though he had never existed—as though all who believed Timo actually *had been there* a short while ago had suffered from hallucinations . . . But soon, as I think I have mentioned, the conviction first expressed by Georg gained ground—that Timo's fateful letter to the Czar *could not have been* anything but what was proper for an officer and a nobleman. Of course, I don't know what Eeva thought about this in private, because I don't know how deeply initiated she had been into Timo's affairs. But I have felt certain all these years that she actually knew more about them than she told me—in other words, more than *I* knew. After our initial shocked suspicions, the rest of us—myself and Timo's acquaintances in Tartu, his relatives, and the rest of the gentry—quickly adopted this belief in his innocence: his friends because of friendship, his kinfolk because of kinship and aristocratic pride. And I . . . well, I adopted it because of the damned *family tie* that joins us. It was, apparently, beyond my power to admit that the only nobleman to whom I (or any Estonian) was legitimately related was either mad or a criminal . . . It was easier to accept that the Czar was, let us say, *small-minded*, and someone in his government brutally harsh, and one of his jailers simply a brute . . . Well, whoa there, it is certainly not my intention to justify the atrocity of smashing his teeth, nor the devilish trick of making him the gift of a grand piano in a stone-walled casemate! Nor anything else that was done to him that I don't even know about. But *something* surely had to be done—about one who had dared to write these pages that I am now reading behind a locked door, trembling with excitement . . .

I would not understand any of it half as well had I not found, in the packet of papers closely covered with writing, a separate page that seems to have been a draft for Timo's cover letter and reads as follows:

Your Majesty:
The manuscript that I am sending to You herewith was originally intended as the text for a speech at the Livonian Diet this past summer. In fact, I began it as such, but as I continued, the painful truth with which it concerns itself became so overwhelming that I soon arrived

at the conclusion that I could only present it directly to You. Nevertheless, I have retained the form of a parliamentary speech, because it seems to me that the concreteness of the ideas that I am presenting becomes more evident in this than in any other form. That form will enable You to perceive more acutely that the ideas in question already are everyday facts in the minds of the thinking segment of your subjects. Only their unfettered expression may seem rare, at first. I believe that my letter, in this form of a parliamentary speech, may compel You to ask: "But what if such a speech were actually made before such an assembly? And what if I, the Emperor, were compelled to admit (as I am compelled!) that every word in it is the *unalloyed truth?*" The very same *unalloyed truth,* fragments of which You have, on occasion, already heard from me, and which You have always and rightly expected from me.

March 1818   T.v.B.

Well. In the course of these years, I have observed, more than once, how the Czar is to be addressed in writing. It is always done in a manner almost impossible to translate into the common people's tongue:

> To Our Most Resplendent and Mighty Lord and Emperor Alexander Pavlovich, Absolute Ruler of all Russians, *and so forth and so forth and so forth.* His Most Gracious Lordship . . .

And the salutations at the end go something like this:

> With an attitude of utmost submission, Your Imperial Majesty's most loyal of subjects,
>
>   So-and-so . . .

Compared to that style, Timo's cover letter sounds presumptuous, to say the least, though it does not strike me as criminally insulting.

It does, however, give rise to grim premonitions of what it introduces. Now, as I turn the rough, yellowed pages of Timo's memorandum for a third time, I feel unable to tear my eyes away from its lunatic lines, and am sometimes at a loss where to look next . . .

> Gentlemen—a man is hostage to his fate, and I do not expect to end my days by the hearth of my home. This may, indeed, be the first and last time that I shall participate in this gathering . . . I ask for your attention both as a nobleman and as a man of honor. Be so kind as to follow certain lines of argument which will not be predicated on self-regard . . . Let us abandon conciliatory attitudes and admit that in matters of our fatherland, we must not spare ourselves or others, even if they are our own fathers and mothers . . . We live in a remarkable century. The whole world is in turmoil, in a ferment that extends from the polar regions to the Equator, from the shores of Peru to ancient and unchanged China behind its walls. One might think that God is revising His creation and putting a new face on everything, from the individual's most secret thoughts to the most important institutions of nations . . . How many drastic changes have we not seen in the realms of power, opinion, and knowledge! No longer can we remain mere bystanders. The crisis has affected us as well. With our own eyes we can all see how useless the old ways of life have become. New and better ways are coming— but at what cost, after what sacrifices and mistakes? That is the question the present generation must answer, and answer for, to its children . . .

Well and good, I can feel how the verve of a great preacher makes my small hairs tingle and stand on end, but through all that impressive din I perceive flashes of the brazen ideas of our decade . . . Skipping over his subversive historical digressions and allusions, I read, over and over, and in a state of terror, the most frightful passages of his essay:

. . . With his life, Emperor Paul paid for his oppression of the nobility's rights and humanity's rights in general . . .

Dear God, all the history books tell us that Czar Paul died of a stroke of apoplexy in his own bed . . . And *if* anyone suggests anything else, then that person also knows that whatever else happened, happened with the complicity of Alexander Pavlovich . . . Therefore, anyone who speaks of this to the Czar himself *must be* a madman, just as the Czar claimed that Timo was! But Timo goes on to say:

And even though traces of tyranny and slavery still remain from those times, the desire for a lawful and honorable way of life expresses itself with increasing vehemence, now that the people have discovered their unity and strength . . .

That may well be the case—but what this amounts to is nothing less than a *threat* to the Czar, and a most explicit one! And then, dear God, come these merciless personal slaps across the emperor's face:

. . . Our army does not want for praise—we can leave it to the French to testify to its qualities. But all that is reprehensible about it is the fault of our Emperor, for he harbors the illusion that he is a great warrior, as did his father and grandfather before him. They, too, always returned from their parades, at which they had played the martinet for foreign emissaries and their own aides, with the air of victorious heroes returning from battle . . .

Maddest of all madmen!

. . . Needless to say, all and sundry complimented them on the good posture of their Guardsmen, and sycophantically assured them that these parades provided a firm foundation for the entire social order and the nation's well-being, not to mention Christianity . . .

. . . What did the Emperor do in the year 1812? What did the Emperor do at the battle of Bautzen? He made a botch of it. And after it had been irrevocably botched, he removed himself from the scene as quickly as possible. At the same battle of Bautzen, Grand Duke Constantine ignored his own aide-de-camp's accusation of *cowardice* and took to his heels, commanding practically all of the cavalrymen held in reserve to follow him. After the battle, this same Grand Duke inspected the Hussars of the Guard, who had lost twenty-three of their officers. He gave them a dressing-down and dismissed them with the words, "All you stupid bulls are good for is brawling!" Gentlemen: one must have water running in one's veins to be able to tolerate such insults . . . Oh, gentlemen, have you ever heard tell of Speranski? Or Beck? Or certain professors? Not to mention the *thousands* who have been killed by our so-called tribunals? . . .

I ask you: Who are we, then? Are we the cattle of the Romanov family?

God Almighty—why use such expressions in regard to the imperial family? For what reason? *Abuse* . . . Well, you speak of water in your blue-blooded veins, you say that a Grand Duke had the gall to refer to noblemen as bulls . . . My dear brother-in-law—don't you know that "cattle" is what your own family calls your beloved Eeva's people, and has been doing so for six hundred years? Or should *we*, at long last, come to the conclusion that we have been abused? Then you bring up Speranski, as if to taunt the Czar with a red flag, and refer to our tribunals as "so-called," implying that they are nothing but engines of massacre . . . Although after all that's been whispered about those tribunals, especially after the December before last . . . God only knows . . .

. . . However, Gentlemen, should there be those amongst you who think that I am merely ranting when I ask these questions—who believe the greatest and most assured hap-

piness can be found in blind surrender to the boundless
mercy of the noble House of Romanov—I beg their permission to read to them an order issued by the Empress
Elizabeth Petrovna, published by the Senate on the 30th
of August, 1743. It concerns certain brazen rumors to
which some of the ladies at Court had lent their ears, as
well as persons who in confidential conversations had expressed regret about the exile of Münnich, Golovkin, and
Ostermann. No proof or documentation was provided.
Here are the provisions made in that order: ". . . in view
of the above, and after consideration of the matter in the
General Assembly of the Senate, in the presence of the
most prestigious dignitaries of the clergy, the military, and
the civil service, We hereby sentence all the aforementioned
defendants, for such Satanic and highly detrimental and
evil transgressions against Our Empire, to death in the
following manner: Stepan Lopukhin, his wife, his son, and
Anna Bestuzheva shall have their tongues torn from their
mouths and severed, after which they shall be torn in two
on the wheel, and their bodies left on the wheel; Ivan
Moshkov and Prince Putatin shall be drawn and quartered;
Alexander Zybin shall be decapitated, and the bodies of
the lattermost three shall be hung on the wheel, while
Sophie Lilienfeldt shall merely be decapitated. However,
in spite of the fact that all these persons have been found
deserving of such punishment by law, We, due to our
inherent gift of mercy and maternal spirit of pity, have
decided in favor of clemency: We shall not let them suffer
the penalty of death, but dispose instead that Stepan Lopukhin, his wife, his son, and Anna Bestuzheva shall be
flogged with the knout and have their tongues severed;
that Ivan Moshkov and Prince Putatin shall be flogged with
the knout, but Alexander Zybin merely scourged, and they
shall be exiled to a distant place, even as Sophie Lilienfeldt
shall be exiled and flogged with the knout after she has
been delivered of the child she is now carrying, and all her
chattels and property shall be confiscated . . ." Or have
you forgotten, Gentlemen, that even the father of our pres-

ent Emperor ordered that the tongue of one of his officers be severed—as punishment for an epigram? And that once, when he was petitioned to pardon an innocent man who had been sentenced to a flogging, that selfsame Emperor shouted, in the presence of his entire Court: "Are you saying that I can't have them flog anyone I please, and as hard as I please?"

This is certainly monstrous, and may well be true . . . (Of course it is true, and it is only a fraction of the truth!) But, for God's sake, why would someone with even a whit of sense start rubbing the Czar's face in the atrocities of his predecessors! They were, of course, committed by members of his family . . . The Czar did take it upon himself to publicly condemn the atrocities committed by his father—albeit laconically, and without any show of pleasure or outrage; but that was only natural, considering that this was a *son* dealing with his father's legacy. Inevitably, filial sentiments (especially considering that he himself had almost been guilty of parricide) restrained him from settling such accounts with greater severity . . .

But why, why, if Timo has the least smidgen of sense in his head, does he stir up matters like these? He must *not* have any sense—just consider what he goes on to say:

> . . . The governing principle of the Emperor's actions is his surrender to his own moods and passions. He can justify even the most scandalous behavior by the fact that it is *he* who says: "*I* desire!" or "*I* refuse!" He does not recognize any obligations toward his people, nor any authority higher than himself, one to whom he would be answerable. He even regards himself as a saint—after he has, to use Tartuffe's phrase, "made a bargain with the Lord" with the assistance of a friendly father-confessor.
>
> The Emperor loves to issue decrees concerning matters with pretty names. He desires to be praised as a Christian, a Solon, a hero and a liberator, a protector of the arts and sciences, a founder of the well-being of his nation. But when it is time to translate fine phrases into reality, he

designs uniforms and appoints committees. Naturally, he is the most important member of these committees. Because honorable and gifted persons might outshine His Majesty, the execution of decisions made in committee is left to sycophants and adventurers! As long as a Minister is a fool and a rogue, he can rest assured of his monarch's benevolence. If he shows character and talent, he finds himself on the wrong side of the door . . . Hence, Alexander's initiatives merely compound Paul's absurdities, and we have, in fact, reached a state of complete anarchy. The likes of Pahlen, Panin, and Rostoptchin have been exiled; the Kotchubeis, Czartoryskis, and Saltykovs have retired, while the noble Arakcheyev (who would so like to turn Alexander into a hypocritical and blood-stained Tiberius, if only he himself had the genius of Sejanus) acts the part of the Grand Vizier, the brothelkeeper Golitsyn is Minister of Clerical and Educational Affairs, the former pimp and headwaiter Volkonski is Minister of Defense, the honorable Kozadaviev is Minister of the Interior, and our Colbert, Guryev, Minister of Finance; the clown Lobanov, Minister of Justice, and Lopukhin, who sold his own daughter, is the Head of the Imperial Council of the Nation. Allow me a brief digression: when Lobanov was appointed Governor General of Riga, he began with the proclamation that his doors would be open to all who were oppressed, and that even the poorest of the poor would find a defender in him. The next day, the entire castle yard was full of peasants. Lobanov made a speech to them. In Russian. The peasants did not understand a word. And Lobanov, peeved because they had not managed to learn Russian in a hundred years, stuck his tongue out at them and ordered the guards to disperse them . . .

In a state of bewilderment I keep turning these rustling pages. Their exposure to alternating states of humidity and dryness has turned them stiff and brittle. I feel embarrassed, for Timo's sake . . . Good Lord, how can one use the word *sanity* in regard to a person who writes to the Czar and tells him that all the members of his government are whoremongers and scoundrels . . . No doubt about it, all of them may—they *do*—have their human flaws. Their human vices. Many of them may be truly evil; during the years I have spent associating with well-informed people, I have heard rumors about many of our statesmen, sometimes expressed in whispers, sometimes out loud . . . But no matter how justified they might be—to begin to proclaim them *publicly*, to write a letter that rubs the Czar's face in them—that can only be the work of a *madman* . . .

> Gentlemen—three questions and their answers. First, and once again: Why does the Emperor love a parade? Because a parade is a triumphal procession of vanity! Because in a parade, every soldier, in front of whom His Majesty would have to cast his eyes down in shame on the day of battle, is turned into a mannequin. There, the Emperor can imagine that he is the sole commander, that he is God . . .

I must admit, I even heard Major Tenner say something like that, back when I was working for him, trudging across the swamps of Grodno in the footsteps of his surveyors. Now, to call Tenner a man of few words is an understatement. The son of an estate steward, of peasant stock, he seems to assume that the more maps he draws of the various corners of the empire, the faster his rise through the ranks will be—and he is, of course, right about that. *He'll* never hasten to proclaim the truth to the Czar. He'll go on producing maps and getting himself promoted to colonel, general, member of the Imperial Academy. No doubt about that. And, like everyone else, he'll keep his mouth shut . . . (So, what am I saying—that he's a liar like the rest of them? Well . . . I don't know.) But he did open it once: I remember the occasion. He was poring over his maps, one early morning on the verandah of a Polish priest's house, his chin swarthy with stubble, his small piercing roach eyes bloodshot from lack of sleep. Newspapers from St. Petersburg lay on the table, next to the maps. Major Tenner glanced at *The Bee*; its front page sported a massive headline about the Imperial Parade at Tsarskoye. He pushed the paper

away with the back of his hand and muttered, "Ugh, that ridiculous *paradomania* . . ."

. . . Secondly: Gentlemen, how was it possible that a prostitute was able to give birth to a Holy Alliance with the
Emperor's assistance?

God Almighty. We all know, of course, how the Czar has been
kneeling and praying and shedding tears in the company of Mrs.
Krüdener. We all know how polite society keeps its mouth shut
about the lady's past (she is, after all, a noblewoman, a novelist,
an ambassador's spouse), except, perhaps, for the whispered comment that the lady's youth was rather adventurous . . . In any
case, she is the Czar's spiritual sister . . . But here, my harebrained
brother-in-law calls her a *prostitute* in a letter to the Czar, and says
that their Holy Alliance is the child of a whore . . .

Thirdly: How has the Emperor become a traitor to the
fatherland? By importing into it sixty thousand Polish set-
tlers, and by despising the idea of a fatherland as the highest
principle. All he wants to hear about is *provinces* whose
only reason for existing is he himself, and his yes or
no . . .

So, by God, there he goes and calls the Czar a traitor! And for
ten long years we have consoled ourselves by thinking that the
Czar was punishing him excessively for a few ill-considered
words.

. . . Therefore, gentlemen, we are fully within our rights
when we proclaim to His Majesty, never mind how dangerous and hurtful this may be (it is, after all, an onslaught
against the most important cornerstone of our society),
that an absolute monarch who allows himself to be swayed
by his sycophants and his passions compels his subjects to
remind him of his responsibilities and to show him *the truth*
stripped bare . . .

I've been pacing the wide, uneven floorboards of my new room for a long while. Something occurred to me: What if Timo was simply—simply such an *idiot*, such a *child*, that he wrote all this because the Czar had made him *swear* to never tell him anything but the truth? This possibility, ridiculous as it seemed, made me so overwrought that I jumped up and paced back and forth, hoping for some kind of answer to emerge from the creaking floorboards. But they did not provide me with one, and I have sat down at the table again to write this: BUT WHAT DIFFERENCE DOES THAT MAKE? ACTING LIKE DOLTS GETS US WHIPPED IN SCHOOL—WHY SHOULDN'T IT HAVE THE SAME REPERCUSSIONS IN THE CZAR'S COURT? See what he goes on to say:

> . . . We did not shed our blood, we did not sacrifice our wealth for six long years in order to make His Majesty the head of some Holy Alliance. We fought because we could not abandon our pride and our honor. The people of Russia saved both Europe and Russia in spite of His Majesty, for the people were willing, the nobility were their leaders, and that His Majesty could not prevent . . . Sword in hand, we won the air we breathe, at the cost of our blood, our slain brothers, our burned towns and villages. We cannot tolerate that His Majesty, who owes everything, including his daily bread, to the magnanimity of the people, treats that people the same way his father used to treat individuals . . . Therefore, the nobility calls for a national legislative assembly. In that assembly, the aristocracy will, together with the other estates of our society, pass the laws we do not have. *Decrees*—proclaimed by tyrants and madmen, by favored household servants and actresses, by Turkish barbers, by dog handlers from Courland, by Arakcheyevs and Rosenkampfs—are not *laws,* any more than the decrees by which Japan or Algeria are ruled. Such a system is nothing but anarchy, where might is right, where no moral obligation exists, and where life is lived according to the principle "Better kill than be killed" . . . Therefore, we need true laws to end our scandalous and insupportable

situation and to prevent worse from happening in the future. Now we shall see whether Emperor Alexander is a usurper or a true son of the fatherland willing to make the greatest sacrifice. Here, then, are the laws which, in my opinion, we need—

Enough! My head is spinning from my perusal of these ravings and from all the commotion of the last few days. I can't go on to his legislative ambitions. Tomorrow, when the sounds of life will be heard once again from all sides, I'll get a saw and a hammer and construct a hiding place for these documents and my own journal in this room. I already have a plan.

Saturday, July the sixteenth

Well, the hiding place is done. Its location was, in fact, inspired by my garret in the main building. The ceilings here are too high for an exact replica, but the doors are relatively low. I removed the lintel board above the door between my rooms, on the bedroom side, and fixed it so that it can be pushed aside, to the left, by half its length—rather like the lid of a pencil box. Then I cut about a foot and a half out of the beam underneath and stowed my dangerous papers in that space. And that's where they'll remain, at least for today, because I have a great deal to report on the day's events. (It occurred to me that it might be wiser to leave them unreported; but then I considered everything I have already recorded here and realized that I have gone far beyond the point where *caution* could provide a reason for silence.)

Last week, the La Trobe family's belongings were brought here from Poltsamaa. Monsieur—or, God knows, should I write Herr, or Mister?—Jean Frédéric, or John Frederick, or Johann Friedrich had paid a quick visit to Timo and Eeva on Wednesday, but as I was in Viljandi that day, I did not meet him.

Today, all three La Trobes arrived, the gentleman, his spouse, Alwine, and their twelve-year-old son. I have to put down a few facts about them, or at least about Monsieur La Trobe, especially considering the outcome of the story.

This gentleman, born in the same year as Bonaparte, hence fifty-eight years old, carries his years well, cuts what the people here call *eine stattliche Figur.* By birth, he is a Frenchman, related to the counts of Bonneval in Languedoc. Nevertheless, in the Livonian church register he is listed as an Englishman, regardless of the fact that he came here thirty years ago from Germany. His ancestors were sectarian refugees in England, and it is said that his father had become the superintendent of the Congregations of the Brotherhood. The son, our John, had been sent to Germany, the land of origin of those congregations, to the famous schools of Niesky and Barby. Due to some controversy, he had left those schools, as well as the congregation, and gone to the university at Jena to study medicine. There, it was said, he had associated with Hufeland and other famous people, and Goethe himself had held him in high regard. *But, but . . .* I have to smile, as it occurs to me what self-serving creatures human beings are, myself included. After all, Goethe once dedicated a poem to our own Timo—I have mentioned this before in this journal but haven't described the circumstances—that fact has always raised my esteem for Timo, which must mean that I have always harbored a secret hope that my brother-in-law might gain greater esteem in the world's eyes. I've been saying to myself, "That all may be so, but Goethe wouldn't have written a poem for just anyone . . ." But just now, as I began to recall what I have heard about Monsieur La Trobe's kudos from Goethe, I wanted to write: *But, but—a rumor that Goethe once approved of someone does not instantly make him a member of a greater race of men . . .* To go on with the story: while in Jena, Monsieur La Trobe had supported himself by giving English lessons. One of his pupils had been an eager boy from Tartu. When Monsieur La Trobe finished his studies, he found he couldn't afford to pay for his graduation, and that boy—who was, by the way, Lehrberg, Timo's future tutor—had encouraged him to apply for a position as a tutor in Livonia, where he could earn the required sum. Monsieur La Trobe followed this advice, went to Livonia, and stayed. He never received a licence to practice medicine but worked as a *Hofmeister* for the Siverses of Heimtal and for the

Lilienfeldts of Old Poltsamaa. He was an officer of the Home Guard during the Napoleonic War, then served as the notary of Viljandi, as district judge of Poltsamaa, and held leases on several estates. In time, he even acquired a passable command of Estonian. Everything he does, he does with care and with some success. I say *some*—because his main interest lies in composing music. And he is, as I remember Timo once telling me, "a pleasant, ineffectual, unpretentious, and straightforward person, an aristocrat in his thinking, a follower of Zinzendorf at heart, a cosmopolitan by vocation, and a provincial by fate . . ."

Monsieur La Trobe married a number of years ago: after many years as a bachelor, he courted and won Alwine, who is the daughter of the great love of his youth, Sophie von Stackelberg. The slender lady has brilliant green eyes and ash-blond hair. She is thirty years younger than her husband, and sometimes her shrugs and glances seem to say, well, yes, maybe my husband is an Englishman or whatever he is, and maybe he is the greatest composer in Livonia today—for someone who is a *geborene von Stackelberg* he may be good enough in the eyes of God, but not really quite good enough in the eyes of society; but I'll be able to overcome that discrepancy, thanks to my obedience to the Lord's commandments, my education as a faithful sister of the Brotherhood . . .

The La Trobes came to visit us at The Foundation, just in time for a late afternoon cup of coffee. I imagine his first words upon entering last week (when I wasn't here) must have been the same he uttered today:

"My dear friends . . . This is so embarrassing . . ."

And I'm sure Timo interrupted him in exactly the same manner:

"But my dear Monsieur La Trobe, *someone* has to be the leaseholder of Voisiku—emperor's orders! And my wife, myself, and to be sure, my brother-in-law, are *delighted* that you agreed to undertake that task. Is that not so?" Timo looked at Eeva and me.

"It is undoubtedly the best solution," Eeva said with conviction. I nodded, and Timo continued:

"Peter Mannteuffel told us that your stay might be temporary; that he may replace you after some time. Now, I am, as we know, a lunatic, and therefore I can tell you the truth: I much prefer you to Peter." Suddenly Timo smiled, and this gave him a relaxed and almost childlike expression. "Maybe that is because all he can do is blow his hunting horn, whereas you are such a magnificent pianist. May I prevail upon you to take a seat and some coffee with us—and then, perhaps, play a little?"

"What would you like me to play?" Monsieur La Trobe said with unexpected alacrity.

"Well, that old organ minuet of yours? I remember it from 1817. We don't have an organ here, but I'm sure you can perform it on the piano."

Monsieur La Trobe accepted a cup of coffee and drank it down quickly. Eeva and Madame Alwine sat on the sofa next to each other and discussed children and chicken pox. From her experience with Jüri's affliction, Eeva advised Madame Alwine what medicaments she should use on her youngster's scabs, and Madame Alwine interjected many questions to indicate her eagerness to learn. It seemed to me that this eagerness (after all, her own husband had studied medicine at Jena) was meant to express, consciously or not, her *humility in the Lord's eyes* . . . In any case, Madame Alwine had long been one of those noblewomen who, over the last decade, had begun to acknowledge Eeva, with some of them taking a little longer than others. In fact, Alwine had been practically *compelled* to do so by her Johann, who was one of the first men in the district to exclaim, ten years ago: "My dear Ladies and Gentlemen—who does not respect Baroness von Bock is a damn fool! Or at least, a fool!"

Monsieur La Trobe finished his coffee, sat down at the piano, and let the strains of his minuet ring out under the small windows of the old drawing room of The Foundation. Even the stiff family portraits that had been hung here in a row upon the walls of vertically striped wallpaper looked like they wouldn't mind dancing to this music. Monsieur La Trobe went on to play other compositions of his own, then some Boccherini, some Mozart, and then his own pieces again, with such enthusiasm that once Käsper had lit the candles on both sides of the music rest we could see the perspiration glisten on the maestro's forehead. He played for an hour, then wiped his bony face with a silk handkerchief, kissed Eeva's hand, offered his arm to Alwine, and left, but only after repeating his apologies.

After they had gone, Eeva opened the front windows of the

drawing room which had become a trifle stuffy. The air outside did not seem any fresher. The three of us stood by the window, looking at the purplish-gray thundercloud that had risen above the woods in the direction of the brewery building.

Eeva said, "What do you think was bothering Monsieur La Trobe?"

It seems that women are more observant in such matters—I hadn't noticed anything special.

Staring at the thundercloud, Timo said, "Nothing. What should have? Except that he doesn't feel all that happy about his enforced role as a leaseholder."

"I don't know," Eeva said. "It seemed to me there was something else weighing on his mind . . ."

The three of us chatted for a while longer. When the thunder rumbled closer and the first lightning bolts split the darkening sky, Timo rose and closed the drawing room windows. I thought: Look at that—could it really be that he who had looked death in the eye in sixty battles was afraid of thunderstorms? And, as if he were reading my thoughts, he said:

"I wonder about that myself . . . I've had my share of standing in the midst of whining bullets and exploding grapeshot. And I've always felt a kind of, let's say—slight intoxication, and a bit of painful curiosity: Will I get hit or won't I? But a simple thunderstorm can make me feel so oppressed and miserable that one could almost call it *fear* . . ."

We listened to the first raindrops splashing down, followed by the full rush of a downpour and the footsteps of someone running toward the house and banging on the front door. Käsper opened the door, and we turned to look. It was Monsieur La Trobe, his gray hair in a wet twist, the shoulders of his coat drenched. He spoke in a scratchy voice:

"Pray forgive me! It's really coming down now . . . I put Alwine to bed. She's worn out by the move . . . Listen to that: the Good Lord is playing Beethoven!"—a reference to the thunder rolling over the house. "Well, you see—I'd like to have a word with you." He looked at Timo and Eeva.

"Go ahead," said Timo. "The three of us keep no secrets from each other."

I was pleased with that remark, yet annoyed by it at the same time, and thus decided to stay put. I also had the impression that Timo's words were intended to annoy Monsieur La Trobe a little, as well. But if Monsieur La Trobe had insisted that he wanted to talk only with Timo, or Timo and Eeva, I am sure Timo would have agreed. However, Monsieur La Trobe merely glanced at me with his nearsighted eyes, then said, with a catch in this voice, "Fine by me. No problem."

He sat down on the edge of a chair. The candles lit his face, which was wet from the rain and perhaps perspiration. When he finally spoke, it was with surprising vehemence.

"You see, I agreed to do it! You must understand, I'm not really a member of the aristocracy. I'm just a foreigner who can be deported if he doesn't do as he's told . . . And now that I have responsibilities to my wife and children—I say children, because we have another one on the way . . . Well, I *agreed!* But only on one condition—"

"I know," Timo said. "Only on the condition that you will be Livonia's most irreproachable leaseholder."

"I am not referring to the estate. I'm referring to *you!*" Monsieur La Trobe shouted, at a volume that came close to being impolite. "I agreed to write reports on you. Do you understand? Twice a month. To the Governor General, or someone, I don't know exactly. I suppose they have some sort of third department now, under Benckendorff. *But only on one condition!*"

Timo sounding a little puzzled, asked, "And they agreed to your condition?"

"No, good God, no—I didn't tell *them* about it! It's a condition I set only for myself."

"And now you have decided to tell us what it was?"

"Right! Exactly! Absolutely!"

"Well?"

"The condition is that *you* must read my first drafts of all those reports. And delete everything you don't want, and add anything you want to add. You see, I realized that they would get *someone* to write those things, no matter what. And which would you prefer?" Monsieur La Trobe turned to Eeva. "Tell me, madame, which method would benefit your husband more?"

Eeva bit her lip for a moment; I saw her eyebrows rise and her eyes become shiny. She spoke slowly.

"I think that would be an excellent way to do it . . . But I imagine that . . . It's just that—"

"It's just that I can't do it," Timo said, very quietly.

"You—you can't?" Monsieur La Trobe looked shocked.

"I say that with regret," Timo said. "Monsieur La Trobe: first of all, if I did it, it would indicate that I don't trust you. And secondly—and I won't deny that I find this of equal importance —it would involve both assisting and deceiving an institution I do not wish to assist or deceive."

"But . . . how can I . . . ?" Monsieur La Trobe sounded almost childlike in his sincerity. It wasn't clear to me what he was referring to.

Timo said, gently, "You just write what your conscience dictates. When one follows the dictates of one's conscience, no moral problems arise. And we can rest assured that our interests are cared for by an honorable man."

"No, no, no . . . Baron . . . Oh, dear . . . You make it sound so simple—but it is much more complicated. Believe me! *You* ought to know, after all you have been through." Monsieur La Trobe got up, went over to Timo, stood in front of him, raised his clasped hands in front of his gray-and-white-striped bow tie. He spoke in a loud hoarse whisper:

"Baron von Bock—I *implore* you . . . Or else Madame Eeva, could you . . . ?"

"No! She can't, nor can I!" Timo exclaimed in a surprisingly metallic and vehement tone, softening it as he added, "Monsieur La Trobe, you mustn't worry so much about this. We are convinced that your reports will be as favorable to us as is humanly possible. But if I—if I should undertake to help you . . ." The way he lowered his voice and almost stammered indicated that he was looking for a persuasive argument. He found it: "You must realize that it would be detrimental to my health if I had to weigh what can and what cannot be said, with all its implications for the present and the future and the past. It could be *fatal*. Surely you, as a physician—"

"Oh, dear God—Mr. Bock, what a fool I have been! I never thought of that at all . . ."

Monsieur La Trobe left again, after further profuse apologies. For about five minutes we sat there in silence. The thunderstorm had passed. In the north-facing windows of the drawing room, purple lightning bolts still flashed through the soaked wild rose hedge, but the thunder was now rumbling at a distance, somewhere beyond Poltsamaa.

Eeva said, "I think Jakob should go to Pärnu at the end of this month, to find out about those ships."

Monday, July the twenty-fifth, 1827

During the month that had passed since our journey to Riga, in August of 1818, Georg had obtained leave from his regiment and joined us at Voisiku, perhaps—at least to some extent—to be of some assistance when his sister-in-law gave birth to her first child. It was the end of September, and I remember well our conversation about the mysterious Count Stedingk, the person who had so graciously made a gift of sixty thousand rubles to Timo—wherever *he* now was.

We sat at the breakfast table in the dining room of the main manor, and Eeva asked Georg (in French, so the help wouldn't understand) who this Count Stedingk was. I expected Georg to tell us about some old friend of the family, albeit one I had never heard of, but he said, to my surprise:

"*Count* Stedingk? Nonsense."

"How so?" Eeva asked.

"The only *count* of that name was the supreme commander of the Swedish army, in '13. Timo has never had anything to do with him. The Stedingks are a Swedish family, and the rest of them are mere *friherrar*—and in Russian that translates as baron, no more, no less. Count Stedingk was the Swedish ambassador to St. Petersburg during Czar Paul's reign, and it was to him that Paul uttered those famous words: 'In Russia, a great man is one to whom I am speaking, and only for as long as I am speaking to him.' But of course, there may be some Stedingks left in Russia, even if there is no *Count* Stedingk."

I gave Georg a brief summary of the treasurer's remarks. Then

I said, "That means the name is just a pseudonym—but for whom?"

Georg poured himself and me a fresh tankard of good strong St. Michael's Day ale, took a drink, and wiped his dark mustache with the back of his hand. I don't know his motives for telling us what he did, but it seems to me that he wanted to reinforce our conviction that his brother was, in spite of his strange marriage and criminal reputation, a very special person. Georg also had a tendency to clarify his own thoughts by voicing them out loud. God alone knows. In any case, he gulped down his beer like a good officer, asked the servant to fill the tankard, waited until the servant left the dining room, and then told us the following, in French:

"Madame—surely you have heard the stories with which the gossips of St. Petersburg at one time tried to disturb your peace of mind? Like all such stories, they arose out of jealousy and professional inquisitiveness. According to them, Timo had asked Marina Naryshkina to marry him but she declined the offer. You've heard that, haven't you?"

"Yes, certainly," Eeva said and smiled across the baby stocking she was knitting. "That must have been in '15, or thereabouts . . ."

"Very well," Georg said. "And you did, of course, understand that that talk was based on nothing but malicious fantasy. You knew that Timo was completely sincere when he sent you to the Masings to get an education—typically, making no bones about it."

"Yes, that was my consolation," Eeva said.

"And yet, madame, a hair of truth had been stirred into that concoction. Not enough, though, to change the fact that the story was completely false," Georg said, obviously enjoying his insight into the matter. "Well, now: both of you must have heard whose daughter this Marina Naryshkina is?"

"We have heard things," Eeva said.

"Her mother is the Emperor's *de facto* wife. The devil alone knows if Naryshkin is her father. In any case, according to all informed sources, her younger sisters—one died around '15, the other is now twelve years old—they are not Naryshkin's but the *emperor's* daughters. Thus, this Marina, now the wife of Count Guryev, as perhaps you have heard, may well be considered a member of the imperial family. And that's not all. Our Czars have always been rather intolerant of their legitimate offspring, but for this, shall we say, "stepdaughter," the emperor had as paternal and caring a regard as if she had been a child particularly dear to his heart . . ."

We were sitting at the breakfast table in the dining room, and I stared out past Eeva and Georg and the samovar, through the misty window, to the orchard in its autumn colors where young girls were picking the last bright red apples and putting them into birchbark baskets. Bending over her knitting, Eeva asked:

"Well, and what is that hair of truth you mentioned?"

"Ah, yes," said Georg. "It is that there really *was* a plan at that time for a marriage between Timo and Marina."

Eeva looked straight at Georg. In her pale and still childlike face, whose features had grown more definite over the years, her eyes looked curiously dark. She did not comment but waited for Georg to explain.

"So," Georg said after a little pause (he was, after all, a lieutenant-colonel of the Imperial Guards, and he had just played a good card—and was about to top it with an even better one). "There was a plan, but it wasn't Timo's plan. It was the emperor's. And it wasn't Marina who refused to go along with it, but Timo, as soon as he got wind of the emperor's intention. Because he had already chosen *you*. And, allow me to say, in all sincerity—his choice can be seen in more ways than one. Especially if you consider it in principle. There was a chasm between your social standing and his. But facts are facts. Timo bridged that chasm. So the aristocracy chose to interpret events as a refusal on Mademoiselle Naryshkina's part. What else could they have done? Otherwise, they would have had to admit that the emperor's aide-de-camp, Colonel von Bock, had refused to marry the emperor's stepdaughter—in favor of whom? Well . . . And the people who drew that conclusion had never set eyes on you, my dear. But what becomes apparent from all this, and what I really wanted to say, is that the Emperor at one time was *so very fond* of your husband that he wanted to make him a member of his family!"

Eeva remained silent, concentrated on her knitting.

I said, "As far as Timo's choice is concerned, it does have an imperial precedent."

"How so?" Georg asked.

"Well, for instance, Peter the Great. He, too—"

Georg exclaimed, "Jakob, man, you surprise me more and more! *That* was Timo's most powerful argument! Being an officer, he had to ask the emperor for permission to marry your sister, and he wrote: 'I believe that Your Majesty cannot object to this marriage, mismatched though it may seem in many respects, considering that Your Majesty's most illustrious ancestor himself preferred a maiden from the common folk . . .' Permission was granted, of course. But word of this insolent bit of reasoning spread through the court like wildfire. And, among other things, it also sowed the seeds for the rumor that Timo was a lunatic."

Eeva said, "Mr. Georg, you're telling us all this in order for us to discover the identity of Count Stedingk?"

The ale from our own brewery was fairly strong stuff, and it may well be that it took the three tankards Georg had downed after breakfast to loosen his tongue sufficiently for him to tell us what he now told us, especially in those distant early days of our acquaintance. For a moment, he contorted the left side of his face and closed his left eye.

"If you ask me, *Count* Stedingk is none other than the emperor himself. Timo did, of course, have expenses while associating with the Naryshkins and other families of that level. The emperor knew that and has decided to assume his debts from that period."

"A strange kind of generosity . . . while at the same time locking Timo up God knows where . . ." I have to admit that those words escaped from my lips before I could stop myself; then as now, it is my usual practice to refrain from commenting out loud on what I hear.

"*Generosity?*" Georg repeated. "More like an attempt to alleviate the pangs of conscience. If not to buy absolution—for sixty thousand rubles . . ."

Eeva straightened out the blue and white stripe on the stocking between her knitting needles and examined it. Then she looked at Georg.

"Well, it makes me feel good to know that you regard Timo with—all your old respect . . ."

"Of course I do," Georg said. "And the same goes for you, madame. Or rather, I regard you with *newfound* respect." He added—and this addition, too, must have been fueled by the brew, for all its candor:

"Come to think of it, madame—I really do not know *how* to regard you . . . You do not conform to any of the accepted norms. In any case, I'm beginning to understand Timo's choice."

Coming from Georg, that was an uncommonly potent compliment. Especially during that time of angry and malicious gossip, whose echoes reached us now and again from the district and from farther away. Georg was still at Voisiku a week later when Eeva gave birth to a boy; he attended the christening in the yellow drawing room in full regalia and held the infant while Dean Rücker, from Kolga-Jaan, sprinkled water on the infant's ruddy head. The boy began to whine, and Uncle Georg, meaning to raise him up to the level of his own mustachios, accidentally scraped the infant's cheek against the St. George's Cross on his uniform, which of course made the boy raise his voice even more—as if he wanted to protest the fact that he was now named Georg, after this uncle and godfather, and his grandfather as well.

A few days later, Uncle Georg left for St. Petersburg, with a letter from Eeva to Timo. A letter about the birth of the boy, to be forwarded to his father, God knows where, through the good offices of Prince Volkonski, Chief of General Staff; or to be tucked away in God knows what secret drawer, to turn yellow over the years—labeled by the Chief of General Staff in accordance with an imperial order: NOT TO BE OPENED! Eeva had already sent Timo at least a dozen letters, addressing all of them, as she had been advised, to that same Prince Volkonski, to be forwarded to the criminal against the state. All of them had disappeared without a trace, without a sound, as if they had fallen into a bottomless well. This in spite of the fact that the missives, as far as I could judge from the few draft pages Eeva had shown me, were not only beautifully composed but so touching that I must admit they made me wipe the odd tear from the corner of my eye.

Dearest,

I know that you are doing everything in your power
to return to us. And you know that I would never expect you to take a single step your views do not allow
you to take. You must know that just as I shared all
your considerations during the months of our happiness,
so I am with you now and forever. Beloved, I am, of
course, a little afraid of the arrival of my difficult moment, as I'm sure every woman is who experiences it
for the first time. But I know that my life will soon be
that much easier—since you, even though you are far
away, will be with me in the shape of our child, and no
one can take you away from me . . .

I asked, "Eeva—do you think it is wise to write 'as I shared all
your considerations'? By saying that, you declare yourself his co-
conspirator! Do you see? You share the guilt of his insolence—*if*
that is what he is guilty of, as so many claim. You don't need to
do that."

Eeva replied, "You know, I gave that some thought. I don't
think there is any real danger that they'll take me to task for it.
Not as far as I can see. Anyway, never mind about me—Timo
needs me to say it. He needs to know that he still has *someone* who
does not reproach him. At least one human being . . ."

Tuesday, the twenty-sixth

I have reread what I wrote yesterday. Well, in the autumn of
'18, Eeva still wasn't the only one who refrained from reproaching
Timo.

I did not reproach him then, nor much later, nor even last
week—at least not the way I do *now*, after the pages that prove
his guilt have landed on my desk in such an incredible, yet inevitable, way.

Yes, here they are on my desk again: because what happened
that Friday evening the week before last (our conversation with

Monsieur La Trobe), and everything that happens to us every day, has its origin in these yellowed pages. Dear God, no one who had any knowledge of their contents could be surprised in the least by what is happening to us. One might perhaps marvel at the strange manner in which madness and lucidity became intermingled in my brother-in-law's mind and soul. And not only madness and lucidity: there is also a curious mixture of aristocratic prejudice and a broad humanistic view of the world. For he writes: "Slavery is an institution as senseless as it is despicable . . ."

Yes. Yes, indeed. But when he writes about his own ancestors, he does spare them somewhat:

> Six hundred years have passed since our forefathers first set foot on the shores of this land—as strong and sincere defenders of Christianity, in the spirit of their own century. In their day, no one had any notion of international law, and these warlike proselytizers thought that they were performing a sacred task when they bestowed their own eternal bliss upon the innocent aborigines, in exchange for these aborigines' earthly happiness and liberty . . .

Ahem. They really believed they were performing a sacred task . . . ? Merkel doesn't think so. Neither do I. I think that if my brother-in-law believes they believed that, he is more naïve than he ought to be.

> . . . at a time when, among themselves, the Knights were inspired by a spirit of honor and freedom rare in their time, the aborigines were forced into a most frightful state of slavery . . .

Yes, indeed. And he does not say that this happened because those natives were savages—which is what most of those few Germans believed who disapproved of the enslavement of the original inhabitants. Nevertheless, he goes on to say:

The Knights did not consider Estonians and Letts to be creatures like themselves. But then, the ancient Romans thought of their slaves as half-tamed beasts of the forest . . .

And so they did. *But*: here my sister's husband does not seem to be aware of how he manages to insinuate his ancestors into the moral company of the mighty ancient Romans—how he lets those forebears bask in reflected glory but neglects to ask: Is there, then, no fundamental moral difference between soulless pagans who lived by the law of the sword, and the Christian bringers of a doctrine of mercy?

Of himself, he writes:

> I do not belong to those who torment human beings. In my house there are no slaves. I regard even the lowliest serf as my neighbor, my brother, created by God, just like myself, to strive toward a more dignified life . . . I am not one of those whose nobility consists only of their crests, scoundrels who hide behind a mask of ridiculous insolence. All of you know whom I have chosen to be my wife . . .

But on the matter of the freeing of the serfs, the most burning question in Livonia ten years ago, he expresses such odd views that I was repelled at first:

> . . . Gentlemen, it may well be that the premature freeing of the serfs would not create any difficulties for ourselves; but I ask you to explain what the serfs would gain from finding themselves without the protection of their masters . . .

Good Lord! Did Timo really not understand that even though he himself, in all his quixotry, perhaps *was* some kind of a protector to his peasants (that is, so long as he himself was a free man), the other estate owners, ninety-nine out of a hundred—or ninety-five out of a hundred—were oppressors, exploiters, each in their own particular way, downright bloodsuckers and slave drivers? Did he not see that? It would seem not, because he writes:

Our good intentions have already taken us too far in the matter of the freeing of the serfs, and we shall not proceed one step further. It cannot be our intention to confuse them with the empty word *freedom*. We must lay a firm foundation for the entire nation's well-being, one where the tiller of the soil does not lose his proper place . . .

It is true that the freedom our peasant serfs were granted a decade ago mostly turned out to be an empty word. Yet I don't quite understand *what* my dear brother-in-law really wanted.

For this is what he goes on to say:

The Emperor will merely use the freeing of the serfs as an excuse to shatter the only class in our society that has, until now, demonstrated a will to resist the most extreme manifestations of tyranny . . . In the vanguard of our own peasants, we can, should the need arise, find ways to oppose oppression by force . . . (Lord, what a thought) All of us are descended from a long line of soldiers. We have a goodly number of courageous and experienced officers, and six years ago we gave a significant demonstration by training the peasants to act as protective units, which, in turn, grew into regiments. Naturally, our serfs are not on our side. We can expect their support only if we are able to gain their trust and respect and love as honest judges and fatherly masters. Or else, and I have said this before, we shall sooner or later become the Romanov family's cattle, led to the slaughter . . .

The very thought—that the aristocrats of Livonia could lead their troops into battle against the Emperor—is demented . . . Especially since it is voiced by a man who goes on to claim that he is no rebel at all, and that it is not his intention to start a revolution but to prevent the outbreak of an impending one . . . Well, it appears that the lords of the land feel oppressed by the government, even though it seems to me they are treated with kid gloves . . . And yet, I am not surprised by the demented nature of my brother-in-law's thoughts on resistance, merely by their ridiculous and tragic childishness. By the appalling flaws in his knowledge of the world. By the absurd belief, hard to reconcile with his education and experience, that the lord of an estate could somehow gain the *love* of his peasants . . . Regiments of Livonian peasants, commanded by their esteemed and beloved estate-owner officers . . . Just imagine: troops consisting of tirelessly strong semi-partisans drafted from the gray cottage folk, enthusiastically responding to orders emanating from their handsome officers' eyes and hastening to obey them almost before they have been spoken . . . Those handsome officers (honest judges, fatherly masters), their uniforms bedecked with decorations from 1812, secure in their membership in the allied knighthoods, commanding their army of courageous slaves from above, from the saddles of prancing steeds, conveying their orders through bailiffs and stewards: *"Chil-dren! Muskets . . ."* (The only weapons of these troops would be muskets left over from the Seven Years' War.) *"Take—aim! at the troops of the— usurper! Fire!"*

My dear Timo, I say unto you: if you expect love and trust between estate owner and peasant to provide your ilk with redemption (and, God knows, there may be no other way out for you in the course of history), then you are a band of men condemned to death. Men who condemned themselves to death a long time ago. The chasm between peasant and aristocrat has grown so wide in the last six hundred years that no heavenly or earthly power will ever bridge it—not even if some on one side, and some on the other truly attempt to build a bridge *with the help of reason*. Even if they would, in the daytime, push support beams across the chasm and strengthen them with struts to build the span—at night, in their sleep, like moonstruck men, they would rise on both sides of the chasm and under the compulsion of their darker nature tear down again what their own hands had built in the light of day . . .

And yet . . . In his own life, at least, my brother-in-law has managed to build a bridge across that chasm. True, he paid for it with the stigma of madness. But as far as I can tell, he did find happiness in it, and I must admit: if his political fate had not been what it is, my reckless sister would surely have been happy in her marriage to him, even in spite of all the vehement disapproval that surrounded the two of them. And despite their vulnerability upon which that enmity fed . . . my brother-in-law managed to build a bridge. And if I admit that this is true, I also have to admit that this achievement, however fragile (yet undeniable), is a seed of truth in the midst of all his fantasies . . . Laughable, of course, but in a certain way, *impossible to crush.*

Thursday, the twenty-eighth of July

I had a dream last night . . . I have tried to refrain from discussing overly personal matters in these pages—but this mad dream was, in more ways than one, a reflection of our strange lives.

In the dream I saw *Iette* visiting my bedroom here in The Foundation. I have tried not to think about her since she left, a month and a half ago, and have been unexpectedly successful in that endeavor. I have not written a word to her. (I don't even know where to write her.) She hasn't written to me, either, although she knows where I live. And it is better this way.

Last night, in the small hours, she came to my bedroom. She looked exactly like herself, the way she was in her happy moments. She was holding a white cloth bundle, and her blue-and-white polka-dot gown showed off her straight neck and round shoulders. With a sweet smile, she opened the bundle. But what she lifted out of it—and I was trembling with a fearful premonition—was not half an almond cake. It was Czar Alexander's head, very pale, almost white, perhaps made out of plaster of Paris—but dripping blood from its neck . . .

Iette said, "Look, Jakob, my father is dead now. So there is nothing to keep you from . . ."

She placed the emperor's, or her father's, head on the oval table in front of my wicker sofa, and I thought: Now she is staining my table with blood, and if they find out about it, God knows what repercussions it'll have . . . But when I turned to her to utter a reprimand, I was struck dumb by a glad surprise. For at that moment, Iette stepped out of the pile of clothes she had let fall at her feet. She was dazzlingly naked and held the white cloth up in the air between us so that I couldn't see her face, and she came and straddled me, quite without shame . . . Oh, madness!

Friday, the twenty-ninth

It was a very different dream I had meant to record here yesterday—not mine but one that Timo told me about the day before, after Eeva had summoned me to their quarters after dinner to discuss the question of my reconnaissance trip to the coast, and after we had pondered it this way and that and arrived at the conclusion that I should go to Pärnu in the latter part of August.

This discussion of our joint and very secret plan again brought me closer to them, for the second time in two and a half months. And just as on that other occasion, when we had talked about the same subject, I once again failed to satisfy my curiosity. I didn't dare to come out with the obvious question: *Timo, tell me, why did they do this to you?* Because, dammit, I don't care if he's a lord, a madman, a criminal, or my brother-in-law, *in some curious way* it has become impossible for me to be anything but candid with him, after all that has happened to him! Well, more or less candid . . . Now that I have discovered, by means that may be ethically questionable, *the reason* for the punishment meted out to him, I can no longer pretend ignorance or ask him things I already know. I picked up our conversation where he had felt comfortable with it the last time. After we had filled and lit our pipes for the third time, I said:

"That story about the grand piano you were telling us—remember? I've been thinking about it—it really is strange . . . Did you experience any other . . . imperial eccentricities while you were in Schlüsselburg?"

Timo's face seemed to grow a shade paler. I tried to avoid Eeva's predictably reproachful eyes. Timo got up and paced back and forth in his cloud of smoke. He closed the orchard-side door of the drawing room and came back to us. Then he answered:

"Yes, I did. Only I can't be entirely sure whether it really happened, or if I just imagined it—due to my derangement, you see . . ."

Then he proceeded to tell us about his life during the first couple of years at Schlüsselburg, by way of introduction to that dream of his. Because I refuse to believe that it could have been anything but a dream. Nevertheless, there was something so intriguing about his tale that I'll try to record it just as he told it:

"Well, you know, it was ordinary prison life . . . in an ordinary casemate. Its windows plastered shut so you couldn't see the sky. Low vaulted ceilings, gray with black spots, water dripping. Rats scurrying across the floor. The usual . . . A peephole in the door, and behind it, a guard . . . You could hear every wheeze and cough . . . Nothing unusual in that . . . The air—expectably foul, like a rotting floor rag . . . The food—after a while I realized it wasn't the most meager fare, but at first it was hard to get down even one morsel. Of course I had been prepared for absolutely anything, once I had sent my memorandum . . ."

Eeva got up and closed the other door. I kept my eyes averted from her—and felt that I wouldn't have been able to meet her gaze now. I looked down at the floor and asked:

"But what was the memorandum about?" I recall reassuring myself with the thought that I really didn't know his own view of the document.

"It was—how to put it—a portrait of Czar Alexander. Framed by the conditions of the empire. Assembled from parts that had long been on the minds of all thinking men . . . By 1818, I had seen too much, and in too much detail. I was no longer the Czar's friend. I say no longer, because I had been his friend. But I had decided to act honorably, come what may. And that was when I began to realize: if I know what everyone around me is thinking, and if I myself think likewise but remain silent in front of the Czar—if I pretend that I don't have the faintest idea of what people are thinking all around me, and by my own silence give the impression that I agree with the sycophants at court—how can I call myself a man of honor? I'll be nothing but a *scoundrel!* Even worse, considering my *special obligations* to the Czar . . ." I assumed that Timo was referring to the oath Eeva had told me about. "So I wrote his portrait. And sent it to him, via Vyazmitinov. And with it, a very preliminary outline of a constitution for Russia—yes, one might call it that. It had fifty-four points . . . After I had done that, I was, of course, prepared for anything . . .'' Here Timo suddenly screwed up his face as if in pain, or as if dazzled by the sun, so that his upper lip rose and for a moment bared his gums and their shattered stumps. Then the pain seemed to pass and he went on, affecting a lively manner. "I remember saying in my memorandum that I could be trusted in at least one respect: my motives were not selfish. I have had time to reconsider that, and now I appreciate that I was mistaken. In actual fact, my step was a relentlessly selfish attempt to rid myself of guilt."

Eeva, in a strangled and intense voice, said, "Timo, please don't blame yourself. You know that I have never blamed you for anything . . ."

"I know, I know. You haven't," Timo said, "neither have I— of course, I was extremely mortified because I had caused pain to the person I love most in the world—but I did not *blame* myself. Because at first, as I said, I did not understand that I was selfish. And later, when I began to see it, it didn't strike me blind—what I mean is, it didn't keep me from seeing the *other* side of the matter. Because I am still convinced that whatever one may think of my action, subjectively, it also had its objective side. And objectively, it could have given the impetus for a rebirth of Russia. *If* the Czar had proven to be the man I mistakenly believed him to be. I was, of course, aware of the possibility of that mistake all along, and that was why I was ready for anything, from the very beginning."

I found the selfish smoothness of his arguments a little trying.

"Even for having your teeth smashed?" I asked him.

"Jakob!" Eeva cried out, in a strangely horrified tone. For a moment I thought (we human beings are prone to absurd notions) that a reminder concerning Timo's teeth might act as a kind of trigger to release his demented trains of thought, and that Eeva knew this. But Timo's reply was restrained, almost calm:

"Yes. Even for that . . . Or maybe not—really . . . Because I did *believe*, after all . . ."

To steer the conversation into calmer waters, I asked him, "And what was your life like then?"

Timo returned to his story:

"On the fourth day, early in the morning, I was taken in a boat from the town of Schlüsselburg to the island. They were really in a hurry to lock me up, they didn't even care to search me properly. Then, after I was in the hellhole assigned to me—later I found out that it was the Top Secret Department's casemate number six—I was visited by General Plutalov himself. At four in the morning. He was in full uniform, with all his decorations, and he read me all my restrictions. Conversations with the guards: prohibited. Receipt of letters: prohibited. Writing of letters: likewise. Paper, quills, pencils: prohibited. I was not allowed to draw pictures. Nor to take walks in the fortress yard. Nor to see a physician—this was not specified in the regulations, but it soon became apparent. The only person to whom I was permitted to address myself was General Plutalov, and I could request a meeting with him through the commander of the guard. As time went by, I realized how strange this was: the general always appeared in my casemate whenever I asked to see him, day or night. Over those years I must have requested his presence at least a dozen times. Perhaps more often, there were periods I can't remember clearly. Whenever he did not come to see me—and there were times when he didn't—he apologized later, explaining that he had been away on business or on leave. When I asked him why, in that case, I hadn't seen his deputy, he told me that his deputy was not authorized to talk to me . . . Well, you asked me about imperial eccentricities: I thought this was a rather eccentric imperial decision, to decree that not even the Deputy Governor of a prison was allowed to speak to a particular prisoner, while the Governor himself, on the other hand, is under orders to present himself to that prisoner at any hour of the day or night at the prisoner's request! Or how about this: I received regular prison rations. When my meals were brought in, I could see that the same meals were served, in the same wooden bowls, to the other cells, of which there were ten or eleven more in the 'secret building.' Oatmeal, rye porridge, boiled beef, sometimes fish, cabbage or beet or turnip soup, black bread. But from the very first day, I was also given chocolates and cigars. Plutalov said: by the emperor's special order. So—rot away, turn gray, be forgotten! Chew your black bread! But have a bite of chocolate for dessert, and consider your emperor's sweet thoughts . . ."

"Well, I'm sure your thoughts weren't any sweeter . . ."

"I never even *touched* his gifts. After a few days, they were taken away and replaced with new boxes . . . Later, when he sent me the grand piano, I *did* touch that. I couldn't resist the temptation. Whenever I played it, I started out with the Marseillaise, as a special treat for the Czar, before I went on to Bach or Handel . . . But the piano only arrived after I'd been there for two years. Up to that point, there wasn't a single interrogation, a single threat. No contact whatsoever. Just imagine what that feels like when a prisoner does not have the least interest in remaining silent, but very much desires to talk . . . when the prisoner is *bursting* with the desire to talk . . . My pride didn't allow me to approach the Czar through Plutalov. I had decided that if the Czar had chosen to imprison me, it was up to him to show any further interest. Not that I wasn't on his mind . . . As I now know, he avoided St. Petersburg in those first years, spending his time in Moscow, Kharkov, Warsaw, Troppau, Vienna, Ljubljana . . . As if he'd been running away from something . . . I don't mean to say that I was the only person or thing he was running away from. *But I was on his mind.* First, those ridiculous chocolates. Then, the grand piano. And soon thereafter, Count Lieven. That's right, the same Karl von Lieven whom I believe you met with me in Tartu in '17. Already then, he was the curator of the university. In the autumn of '19, he walked into my casemate, and I invited him to take a seat on my stool:

"Holà-là-Monsieur le Comte . . . D'où est-ce que cet honneur?"

"He was rigid with embarrassment and tried to wiggle out of it, in his slippery way. You know the type, a pious courtier who keeps a sachet of powdered orange flowers in his waistcoat pocket . . . so one and all can enjoy the scent of Paradise. He told me that Alexander Nikolayevich, Prince Golitsyn, had been told by the Czar to ask him to visit me . . . In addition to Paradise, he also smelled of salons, cigars, even fresh air . . . After a couple of visits, he sent Pastor Mortimer in his stead. Finally, Prince Golitsyn himself came . . ."

"And what did they want from you?"

"My permission for them to write to the Czar that I understood the error of my ways. Permission for them to tell him that I was begging his forgiveness for my insolence!"

"What did you say to that?"

"I said, 'Gentlemen, if it is your wish to provide this lonely man with cultured company, I shall always welcome you. But if it is your desire to make me retreat from my convictions, I find myself compelled to tell you: please do not waste your time! What's more, I am compelled to ask you to refrain from visiting me. Forgive me, but I find the role of the surrendering hero boring at best . . . You see, I consider this time in the casemate my sixty-first *battle*!"

I asked him, "Timo—who was your *adversary* in that sixty-first battle?"

He was standing by the south window of the drawing room holding a glowing pipe and looking out at the wild roses. They had already shed their petals but not yet ripened to rose hips. He turned, with a surprised expression.

"The Czar, of course. And the *tyranny* he represents."

I asked, "But, Timo . . . in that battle, could you—did you have the faintest hope of victory?"

"Of course I did. That hope was what I relied upon. And all the grand pianos and Mortimers and Lievens just reinforced it. Because I was hoping that he would not be able to endure it. *That the Czar wouldn't be able to endure it to the end.*"

"Endure—what?"

"That he was—because of a truth he could not bring himself to admit—*gradually killing his former friend.*"

"But he had better nerves than you thought?" I won't deny that there was a touch of malicious glee in my question. Timo paid no attention to that. He said, "They were not as strong as one might have thought. On the other hand, I can't say that my own nerves were made of steel. After two years I began to notice how frayed they had become. I broke out in spots, a horribly itchy rash. The stench of the latrine made me vomit. Sometimes it took me half a day to remember, let's say, old Lehrberg's first name. I began to be plagued by deranged and idiotic dreams. Sleep itself became so brittle and sporadic that I hardly slept at all anymore. And then, I believe it was in May '21—I had lost count many times—a *physician* came to see me. Among other things, he asked me about my sleep, and I told him I didn't sleep well at all. Then he asked, 'What about the last couple of nights?' I said, 'Goodness, yes—the last two nights I slept really well, better than in a long time.' I remember adding, 'Like in an ebony coffin.' Chuckles all around. Then he left, and my supper was brought in, with a tankard of ale. It occurred to me that I had never been served ale before—except for the last two nights . . . And maybe I had seen or heard something in that black coffin of mine, in my dreams or *through them*, I don't know . . . In any case, I became *suspicious* . . . I ate half of my supper, as was my custom, but poured the ale into the latrine. Then I stretched out on my cot, feigned sleep, and waited for things to come . . . The guard always changed at ten o'clock, without any commotion or audible reports. The guards were not allowed to converse within earshot of prisoners, nor were they allowed to talk to prisoners. I wasn't allowed to speak to them, either, and I never did, at least not that I can recall. I had decided to obey, since not to do so could have been inter- preted as a plea for mercy, to them or to the emperor. The guards, however, would exchange the odd word with each other, some- times even a few words—about the cabbage soup, the weather, a girl. The rebellion of Semyonov's regiment, in a loud whisper. Or else they giggled about something. Or—excuse me, Kitty— traded farts, when their officers weren't nearby. Most of them must have been young men, not that I ever saw them under normal circumstances . . . So, this time—I was lying on my cot, waiting. Nothing. Water dripped from the ceiling, and Venjamin Ivanovich scuttled across the floor. He was the chieftain of my water rats. Then, suddenly, I noticed that my guards outside the door were uncommonly quiet that evening. I also noticed that my insomnia had returned in full force. I wasn't the least bit tired. On the contrary, and as usual during all those years, my mind was work- ing feverishly. Streams, rivers, torrents of *arguments*—and, I thought, *perfect* ones—directed against all kinds of possible op- ponents. Long strings of quotations—Montesquieu, Kant, Marcus Aurelius, all in a jumble. Incredibly bad jokes (excuse me again, Kitty): *Gentlemen, are you aware that tyrants are stupid buggers? You didn't know that? Well, that must be why you put up with them!* And then, a sweet sudden tremor of memory—like a knife coated with sugar: good Lord, there is a world outside these walls! In which there is Kitty, and our child . . . Our child is two and a half now, *if* all has gone well . . . It *must* have gone well—it can't all be as horrible as this . . . If only I knew if it is a boy or a girl . . . Then, after midnight—I had learned to tell time without a clock—keys turned in the locks of the guard room. I heard the soldiers jump to attention. Next, my door was unlocked, but, as I noticed, very quietly, and two officers entered with candles in their hands. They took up positions on either side of the door and allowed a third person to enter the casemate. Peering out of the corner of my eye, I recognized him instantly: Prince Golitsyn. I scrutinized him through my eyelashes. His large, bald head, his sturdy but some-how deformed body, his small feet. He ordered the candles to be placed on the lid of the grand piano, walked over to my cot and looked at me from such a close distance that I felt his breath on my face and was afraid he'd notice a tremor in my eyelids . . . After that, he left the casemate again, followed by the officers. And then the Czar entered, by himself . . .''

I could not help asking (and at the same time encouraging Timo's critical faculties), "Timo—are you *really* sure it was the Czar?''

Timo said, "I wasn't sure at first. He was wearing a short black cloak with a hood covering his head. I couldn't open my eyes and look straight at him, because I wanted to know what was going to happen next. Then I recognized him with full certainty, in the light of the four candles, and also from what he proceeded to do. For a moment, he stood by my cot. I had to muster all my will-power to keep my breathing regular. As you may imagine, I felt incredibly torn: on one hand, I felt *triumphant.* He had come to me, after all! On the other, I was deeply disappointed—he hadn't come here to establish human contact, but to spy on me in an underhanded way, as if I were just some *creature* rendered blind and dumb by God knows what drug . . . Finally, he stepped back from my cot, and—just imagine this!—knelt down on the floor, which was covered with rat droppings—I watched him through my eyelashes—and began to pray—two feet away from my ear! I could hear every word he whispered.

" 'Lord, I pray to Thee for this blinded neighbor . . . and for myself . . . Lord, for this headstrong brother of mine—who rebels against *Thee*, O Lord, by proclaiming unprecedented obscenities against his Anointed Sovereign . . .' He stopped for a moment, as if to draw breath for a confession, and I forgot myself and opened my eyes. I looked straight at him. Yes—he was kneeling on the casemate floor! He had brushed back the hood of his cloak, and I could see that his forehead was wet with perspiration, all the way up to his bald pate. He had aged perceptibly since 1816, his features were both ruddier and less distinct, and there were pouches under his eyes. He was staring up at the ceiling, his eyes half-closed. And the expression of his face was—it was so oblivious, and reflected such a mingling of pleasure and pain, that I found myself both embarrassed and repelled by it . . . Then I heard him whisper: 'Lord, Thou seest all his thoughts, as Thou seest into my heart. Thou knowest that I know: he is not right about all of it—but there is a great deal, a great deal he is right about. I thank Thee, Lord, for letting me see that—for letting my anger and confusion ripen into understanding. And I thank Thee for the clarity Thou hast granted me in Thy divine wisdom—to see that I cannot admit that this headstrong brother and subject of mine is in the right! For if I admitted that, I would not, in the end, serve Thee, O Lord, but the Demon of Chaos . . . And I thank Thee for the burden Thou hast thus placed upon my shoulder, the heaviest among many others, as a touchstone for my worthiness as a Sovereign . . . But I must confess that this burden is weighing upon me more and more, every day, and it may overwhelm me . . . Therefore I beseech Thee, Lord, make this Timotheus von Bock see reason and make him apologize to his Sovereign for his unimaginable words—so that I might forgive him and become free of the burden it is to me to keep him imprisoned . . .' He closed his eyes and said, as if to himself: 'But if Thou hast decided otherwise, I say like Thy son said to Thee at Gethsemane: Father, I pray to Thee—but let Thy will be done, not mine.' And then, Jakob—then he lowered his head and opened his eyes, and looked straight into mine . . .

"Well. Two words was all we exchanged. He whispered:

" '. . . Timothée?!'

"And I said, '*Tartuffe!*'

"He covered his ears with his palms and ran out of the casemate,

in rather unimperial fashion. And I haven't seen him since." Timo
cleared his throat and added, sounding somewhat self-deprecating:
"At least not awake, that is . . ."

I said, "Timo, this story—surely it was only a dream?"

Timo had walked over to the far corner of the room where the
shadows cast by the sconce mirrors combined to create near-
darkness. He stood there, almost invisible; even the glow of the
pipe he was holding had gone out. Then he laughed and said:

"Well—whatever you think is best . . ."

Wednesday, the seventh of September

Yesterday—at last—I returned from my journey to Pärnu,
where I had to spend almost three weeks, but with good results.
For this I have to thank Eeva and her carefully thought-out plans.
In early August, I spent many evenings in the tavern near the
mirrorworks at Roika, chatting with workers and villagers who
spend their kopeks there on liquor and beer, to the enrichment of
the leaseholder of the tavern, which is owned by Amelung, the
proprietor of the works. While I was there, I heard some songs
about the war against the French and wrote them down:

> When the storm raged in Moscow,
> smoke covered the river,
> Napoleon took his rest
> behind the Kremlin walls.
> But when he woke up from his sleep
> he saw the flames . . .

And one that stuck in my memory for a long time:

> I saw that the men coming toward me
> were gravediggers.
> Oh, oh,
> gravediggers.

Well met, gravediggers,
whom are you burying?
Oh, oh,
whom are you burying?

This is the famed Bonaparte,
it's him we're burying.
Oh, oh,
it's him we're burying.

In mid-August, Eeva went to Tartu, where she saw old Masing
and confided our plan to him. He gave her a letter of introduction
to Pastor Rosenplänter at Pärnu. This Rosenplänter had gained
fame over the last twelve years with the newspaper he published,
Beiträge—laudable and well-deserved fame according to some, but
dubious notoriety according to others, and the latters' voices
tended to carry more authority. A few days later, I rode over to
Poltsamaa, left my horse in the stable, to be taken back to Voisiku,
and took the mail-coach to Pärnu.

Rosenplänter lives on Königstrasse in the rectory of Elizabeth
Parish and is a friendly, bright-eyed man in his mid-forties. His
black hair, cut in a fringe across his forehead, and his lively gestures
seem rather untypical for a man of the cloth. When I first saw
him, I thought: If I were the director of a theater company and
needed to cast a kind-hearted French revolutionary (well, there
must have been *some*), I would pick him for the role. Later I heard
that he had, indeed, taken part in local theatricals at Pärnu, even
acting in Estonian.

After I handed Masing's letter to him, he chased four or five
children of various ages out of his study and opened a desk drawer.

"Take a look here—this is where I keep Dean Masing's letters.
I already have more than a hundred here."

But after he had broken the seal and read the new letter, he gave
me a long stare, then looked out to the street for a while, then
again at me.

"Well, well," he said slowly. "Clearly, this is not a letter to be
preserved in this drawer." He excused himself for a moment.
When he returned, he said, "Natalie has put the coffee pot on in

your honor. And the coffee will be even hotter, thanks to that letter."

What Rosenplänter had to say was cool and deliberate, and the coffee in our cups grew cold many times over. But it became clear that he was really willing to help me—or rather, *them*—which was quite surprising, considering the subversive nature of the enterprise and his respectable position and solid character. But I could sense his deep respect for Masing, the irascible old firebrand who had provided me with that letter of introduction. Rosenplänter spread out my notes on folk songs across his desk, while I stayed in the glassed-in verandah on the garden side and read books. We agreed that it was not a good idea for me to be seen too much in town. In any town of Pärnu's diminutive size, a stranger was conspicuous, an object of curiosity. Nevertheless, I took a stroll to satisfy my own curiosity and to gain a sense of the place. I took a look at the commercial port by the wide Pärnu River, across from the mouth of the Sauga, and saw seven or eight sailing ships and a number of sloops. I also looked at the Customs House, the port guardhouse, and the two taverns by the river, where I would probably have to host a night of drinking with the port guards. But for the most part, I stayed with Rosenplänter on Königstrasse, read books, talked to his pleasant wife, whittled toy animals for his children . . . While attending to his pastoral duties, Rosenplänter also paid coffee-time visits to acquaintances among the town's merchants and shipowners. Then, early one evening toward the end of the week, he asked me to join him for a walk in his garden.

His name translates as "planter of roses." With the help of his confirmands, he has planted roses and young trees in at least half of the cemeteries of Pärnu, and his garden is a small outdoor exhibition of horticulture as well as a nursery. In an arbor surrounded by elder trees, beside a tankard of ale, sat a man with a coppery face and a steel-gray skipper's beard. Rosenplänter introduced me to him and walked away.

This was Captain Snyder, a Frisian from Cockdorp, a village on the island of Texel. During the last five years, he had had little opportunity to visit his home port: for almost that long, he had been sailing the same route twice a year for the Pärnu merchant firm of Jacke—from Pärnu to Oporto, in Portugal, with a cargo of Livonian flax, and from Oporto back to Pärnu with a cargo of that country's famous port wine for the connoisseurs of Livonia and St. Petersburg.

It took a couple of evenings of drinking ale in Rosenplänter's garden, and later, when it began to rain, sipping tea on the glass verandah, for Captain Snyder and me to overcome our initial mutual tendency to be men of few words and to reach some clarity in the matter. Yes, Captain Snyder was willing. Next May or September, let us say, he could quietly take aboard two or three passengers and conceal them in a prepared hiding place in the cargo. Naturally, he would have to let a few members of his crew in on the secret, but these were men who knew how to keep their mouths shut. The passengers would have to deal with the port guards, but Captain Snyder didn't anticipate any great expense . . . I expanded the idea: I would strike up an acquaintance with the commander of the guard. As a former noncommissioned officer, I could offer my services to him. I could befriend the guards. On the evening of Timo and Eeva's escape, I could buy the guards so many rounds that they would be lying in the back room of the tavern like dead men . . . In any case, Captain Snyder will contact Pastor Rosenplänter immediately when he, God willing, returns to Pärnu next year.

As for Captain Snyder's remuneration, we have not agreed on an exact sum. When I asked the captain about it, he replied, between gargling puffs on his pipe:

"You may not know this, but I have also transported a few people from Portugal to Amsterdam. The summer before last, the Portuguese had another big argument about a new *carta de lei*, or constitution. Some for, some against. Of course, true southerners that they are, they resorted to pistols. And then the English got in on the fracas. Those can be times when people need to travel without delay. But I can tell you this, with a clear conscience: the silver coffers of my passengers were not *all that much lighter* when we put them ashore in Amsterdam. So—my passengers needn't fear that they'll get robbed."

As soon as I got back last night, I reported to Timo and Eeva what had transpired in Pärnu. Timo said, "You deserve our gratitude. And it is excellent that we have at least until May."

Eeva said, "And it is excellent that it is now a sure thing—God willing."

Saturday, the tenth of September

The last two nights I have locked my door and once again spread out Timo's manuscript on my desk. I have decided to copy the most important points of his "constitution" in order to have them in my book and have them at hand when I will consider them, and perhaps write about them, or for when I refer to them in my writing about Timo and our lives. I don't want to struggle with this horrendously crackly and stiff bundle of papers every time I want to refer to them. So, then:

> The Christian faith must be the foundation of our social order . . . Accordingly, a spirit of the most complete tolerance must be created . . . But religion must stand apart from all secular ambitions and advantages . . . And both morality and respect for religion must be founded on love for the fatherland . . .

Here, he adds to the legal text his first parenthetical comments, and even though they refer specifically to the Russian government's wavering attitude toward Napoleon, they strike me as essential enough to include here:

> (If the Government obliges the Church to declare anathema a person who has nothing in common with the Church, and then obliges the Church to honor that same person as an ally, this erodes the people's respect for religion. When a Government orders its people to offer up daily prayers for persons whom the entire world clearly hates, this shows the Church in a light that makes one suspect it no longer is a church but merely a stage managed by the police . . .)
> The arts and sciences in all their dimensions are the main supporting pillars of education and faith and must be honored as such . . . Magnanimous benevolence must be the

highest law . . . Monarchy must be seen only as a means, not an end in itself . . . The fatherland must remain undivided and limited to its present size. It must have clearly defined borders . . . (By annexing Finland, Bessarabia, and Poland, Czar Alexander has incurred Europe's justified displeasure, and while we ourselves are subject to insufferable tyranny, we must now also live in fear of the repercussions that threaten the Usurper . . .)

Russia must be governed by a dynasty. Monarchy is preferable to anarchy, and a Bourbon is preferable to a Robespierre . . .

Well, it certainly wasn't this last statement that landed him in prison; although even it could be suspected of some hidden seditious intent—after all, the claim that the Bourbons are better than Robespierre can only be made *after* one no longer regards it as self-evident! On the other hand, any way of thinking that does *not* regard the superiority of the Bourbons as self-evident *is* seditious . . . Ha-ha, so there! What comes next must surely be counted among the deranged statements for which he was arrested—perhaps it was the very one that cost him his teeth:

The Sovereign must govern according to a law that stands above him. God's name must not be taken in vain . . . The Sovereign must be the nation's first servant, sacred in his person but responsible for his actions to the extent that he may be arrested if he falls victim to shameful passions, neglects his duties, and takes immoral steps . . . The fatherland shall be represented by spokesmen of the people . . . These shall congregate in regular general assemblies . . . The nation is divided into estates based on interests, but every citizen must have equal protection under the law and equal freedom as a citizen. No torturers, no shackles . . . In official appointments, the level of competence shall be the deciding factor . . .

Just a moment—the level of competence shall be the deciding factor in appointments? That—that is indeed a shocking thought—expressed with shocking concision . . . Not social class, not family, not recommendations, but *the level of competence?* Well, that, of course, is as impossible, or even more impossible, than everything else he has fantasized.

The Empire shall have a united, unified, and influential nobility. This nobility acts as liaison between the different parts of the State. It shall be the factor that prevents rulers from becoming despots, the trustee of the nation's honor . . . However, the nobility shall not be an end in itself, but a means to further the common good . . . The esteem in which each social class is held shall depend on its moral standards . . . The Empire's armed forces must defend the fatherland against aggression, but must not engage in aggression . . . No law shall be approved without the entire nation's consent . . . The same applies to taxation . . . The Sovereign has the right to propose legislation, and the nation must have the right to demand such proposals from him . . . All judges shall be elected by vote . . . Legal proceedings, both civil and criminal, shall be public without exception . . . Each and every secret action by the State shall be regarded as an act of tyranny . . . Every breach of the law shall be regarded as a crime against the State, and every citizen shall have the right to seek legal redress for it . . . No one may be declared guilty without a trial . . . Everyone shall have the right to do all things that do not cause public disorder . . . Everyone shall have the right to his opinions and the right to speak his mind. Legal sanctions will be applied only for lies, slander, and rioting. Citizens are what Russia needs. Slaves it has more than enough . . .

The devil take it—it almost sounds like the Magna Carta of the English translated into the idiom of the old stone tablets of Rome. Perhaps there is a place on earth where such things are truer than they are here; but here, in Livonia, Viljandi District, Voisiku Estate, one can only call my brother-in-law's fantasies splendid and himself mad as a hatter for proposing them.

The eighth of October, 1827, late at night

Haven't written a word in this journal for almost a month. This is probably due to the "journal fatigue" that sooner or later overtakes you—and maybe to the fact that there hasn't been anything extraordinary to record, except that autumn has come and winter draws near; the yellow forests are beginning to turn the same gray as the stubble fields.

Jüri celebrated his ninth birthday the day before yesterday. Liiso woke him up with a plum torte, and his parents gave him a large sketchbook, decorated with the family crest in gold, and bound in calf by a bookbinder in Tartu.

For his age, the boy is a good draftsman, and generally a bright and eager lad. In response to his parents' wishes, I have been teaching him some arithmetic and geometry. I have noticed that Timo has great expectations for the boy's future. Of course, it is hard to tell how fanciful such expectations might be for the son of this father, in our present circumstances . . . And yet, the "imperial mercy" that the late Alexander proclaimed to our family—and which the family did not stoop to accept—seems to have survived into the reign of Nicholas. While the father is kept a virtual prisoner on his own estate, and his every word and step are watched, the boy has been chosen, by imperial edict, to be one of the students to enter the lyceum at Tsarskoye Selo this autumn. We have known this since last spring. Yesterday, Jüri's mother accompanied him on his journey to a new life.

Thus, Jüri's birthday celebration two days ago was also an occasion of farewell—of course, not forever, nothing as dramatic as that; and yet, the parting felt more poignant than it might have been in other noble families, because it is obvious that this imperial concern for the boy's education also implies an imperial desire to remove the boy from the seditious atmosphere of his home at the earliest possible age. From the state's utilitarian point of view, it is simply a matter of detaching the boy from the oppressive proximity of a discredited father.

Knowing that he would have to leave the next day, Jüri looked—in spite of his enthusiasm for the celebration—more drawn and pale than usual. Gifted with a precocious intelligence, he may have had his own suspicions about the reasons for this change in his life—or, God knows, perhaps his mercilessly honest father had explained it to him in plain words: Well, Jüri, now the emperor takes you away from your parents so that you won't be so closely influenced by your father, who has been declared a lunatic. So that you'll grow up to be the kind of man our emperors believe the country needs. Your mother and I have given the matter some thought and come to the conclusion that if we were to prevent you from going, we would ruin any possible future career for you. So—go. Learn. Grow. And decide what is right and what is wrong . . .

Perhaps the boy already knew all this.

I made him a present of a small box with a black-and-white gaming board on the lid and small traveling chess pieces inside. After our arithmetic and geometry lessons, it has been our habit to play many games of chess, and in the summer after Iette's departure, when my thoughts tended to stray, the little rascal had managed to beat me two or three times . . .

The night before last, at eleven o'clock, there came a sudden knock at my door. I gathered up Timo's manuscript off the desk, stuffed it into its hiding place above the connecting door, and went to see who was there. It was Jüri, small and pale in his nightshirt, the traveling chess set under his arm.

"Uncle Jakob—let's play one more game!"

Since my room was rather cold, I told him to take my bed jacket off the back of a chair and wrap it around his shoulders. I've told Käsper I will attend to the heating of my quarters myself, but that night, being engrossed in my second reading of Timo's constitution, I had not bothered to light a fire. We set up the pieces. He palmed two pawns behind his back, then presented me with his small white-knuckled fists. I picked black, and he was obviously pleased.

He said, "You know what I decided? If I got black, I'd have a hard time at Tsarskoye. But I got white."

"Now why would you have a hard time there? In arithmetic,

you can figure rings around boys in the third form. The same goes for your French. And your German, of course."

"But I don't have any Russian. Papa started teaching me, but we did it only for a few months."

"You'll learn. Many others at the lyceum will be in the same position."

"You think so?"

"Of course. German-speaking Germans. French-speaking Russians."

After seven or eight moves I noticed that Jüri was taking longer and longer to ponder each move. At the ninth move, he said, "Uncle Jakob, I have a question . . ."

"One you want to ask me?"

"Yes . . . It's something I can't ask Mama or Papa. And the others—are strangers."

I had realized a long time ago that my nephew did not regard me as a "stranger," but I must admit it was good to hear it from him.

"Well, go ahead."

"Tell me . . . at the lyceum, do I have to become a friend of the emperor?"

The skinny nine-year-old fellow gave me an intense stare, his reddish-brown, already close-cropped hair standing straight up, his small mouth precociously serious, his dark-gray eyes almost black in the candlelight.

I asked him (and this, only to gain time), "Has someone told you that you *have to?*"

Juri nodded, his lips firmly pressed together.

"Who told you that?"

"Monsieur La Trobe, Madame La Trobe, Master Timm. And Dr. Robst."

"How about your father?"

"Of course not."

"Or your mother?"

He shook his head angrily.

I asked, "So—does that mean that *until now* you have *not* been the emperor's friend?"

He shook his head again.

"Why not?"

"Well, because of Papa. And everything . . . You know what I mean."

Why did he assume that I knew it all so well? He had left his queen unprotected from my knight. He hadn't noticed, being so intent on gazing at me. Even I registered his mistake only in a remote fashion—I was so taken up by thinking: Dear God, what can I tell him! I could, of course, respond with some misleading phrase or jest, the way we reply to most children's questions—and not only theirs. I couldn't very well tell him (as perhaps only his mad father could tell him, perhaps even his mother, since her husband was a madman): My dear boy, please remember that a boy with parents like yours should never ever try to gain the friendship of emperors such as ours!

But there are many reasons why I can't tell him that, mainly because I feel responsible for his future, even though he is not likely to give very much weight to an outsider's advice, as is often the case with children. But I fear that the lad will endow my answer, now and in the future, with a more fateful significance than I would care to give it . . . So, I feel responsible for his future. What right do I have to push him—the push may well be insignificant, yet, on the other hand, it might be decisive—why push him in a direction that would lead this lively boy-child, his parents' pride and joy, to spend the rest of his life, in spite of his gifts, as a shabby fool wandering around his fields, a country gentleman, a bitter wit at the Livonian gentry's card tables—of whom his fellow nobles, having themselves obtained government posts and general's rank, would whisper: "That fool Georg von Bock could have been a general or admiral, but he decided to avenge his father and became a member of the opposition . . ." What right do I have to inflict this upon him?

And then, even *fairness* compels me not to advise him to shun the friendship of the Czar, after all the undeniably horrifying statements his father did make to our previous sovereign . . . (I cast a frightened glance at the top of the doorframe—with a feeling that my secret is beginning to show through the pine board, that the board itself is crumbling to dust, that the fateful contents of my hiding place are spreading irretrievably all over the world . . .)

Lord, yes, just because there is no denying all those things, it would be selfish and exaggerated and downright immoderate on the boy's part to bear a grudge against our present Czar because of his father . . .

All that being so, should I not tell the boy, who is sitting there like a big skinny alert bird, wrapped in my bed-jacket: The very fact that you have been chosen for the lyceum shows that the Czar is giving you a chance to become his friend? But only if you want to be his friend. And believe me, because I know things that make it possible for me to state this unequivocally—*this is a very magnanimous gesture on the Czar's part.* Yes, indeed; more magnanimous than you can possibly comprehend at your age. Because it is— but I'm only telling this to myself—it is magnanimous *even* if the Czar is trying to estrange the boy from his parents. God, even in that kind of interest I can sense—not approval, by any means, but a kind of silent respect for the reckless tradition the boy represents by bearing his father's name. Thus, there is even a touch of chivalry in the imperial desire to estrange the boy . . . (Is there, truly? God knows, God alone . . .) And finally, Jüri's election to the lyceum is, at least as far as the family is concerned, a sign that Timo's monstrous words have been forgiven . . . (Have they, really? When Timo himself is still held prisoner here? So, maybe not . . .) Well, *for practical purposes*, the most sensible thing would be to assume that. (Would it?)

Damn it, there's nothing I can tell my nephew.

I say, "Jüri, you just moved your queen into the path of my knight. Take her back and make a sensible move."

It takes him a few moments to return his gaze from my face to the chessboard. He says, calm and seemingly unconcerned, "You can't change a move once it's made. I concede." Then he looks at me again and says, "But I'm still waiting for an answer."

And I tell him, "Jüri, you're asking me something that every-body has to decide for *himself.* You're still a young boy, you can't make that kind of decision yet. A good decision, one you wouldn't regret later. So I think you should postpone this decision until you're mature enough to make it. Give it ten years. Maybe only five—if you grow up as quickly as it now seems to me you will. Until then, don't be the emperor's foe but don't be his friend, either. Just be the most assiduous student of the Imperial Lyceum."

Yesterday they left, he and his mother. Jüri waved to me from the carriage window until they turned onto the Poltsamaa road. It will take Eeva two or three weeks to get back here.

The fourteenth of October

I am rereading last week's entry.

What I did not tell my nephew was: Answer your question yourself; but remember your father. From the state's point of view, your father is, of course, a madman. But when put to the test, he is the most honorable man you have ever seen and ever will see in your whole life. (Unless you happen to meet one of those men who, the year before last, were sent to the far reaches of Siberia to work in the mines, as punishment for their part in the December rebellion.) Yes: your father's madness lies in his sense of honor.

I did not tell him that. You can't tell a *child* such things. Or can you? Perhaps one *should* tell a child such things?

Saturday, the twenty-third of October

This morning Timo asked me to join him in the sauna. As on every Saturday, Käsper had heated the sauna we have here in the cellar of The Foundation. Eeva had not yet returned from St. Petersburg and Tsarskoye, and it occurred to Timo that this was our chance to take turns slapping each other with the sauna whisks.

Timo strode along next to me across the new snow, from the front door around the building to the cellar door. I noticed that he was wearing an old broken-down pair of shoes, with tattered uppers and wooden soles, and an old smock (in contrast to his usual habit of dressing rather elegantly, even at home). When his feet came into contact with the snow, he grumbled with pleasure: "Cold as a bear's arse . . ." And I thought: Well, now, does that expression, one Eeva would not have approved of, indicate that he's a little mad, or that his mind is sharp as a razor?

As we were sitting on the bench, ruddy from the application of our whisks, birch leaves sticking to our skin and the sweat pouring off us, I asked him:

"Did they let you take a sauna at Schlüsselburg?"

He said, "Once a month. My escort of guards sat behind the door and watched me through the peephole. And that was just a bath in a tubful of lukewarm water. But I did have a sauna, all by myself, every day . . ."

"How did you manage that?"

He swept his salt-and-pepper hair back from his forehead and laughed.

"By running. Which was also my history course. Course, derived from the Latin *cursus*." He laughed again. "Although they hadn't put me in shackles, I was still left without any opportunity for exercise. So I had the idea to run. The casemate was three fathoms long and two fathoms wide. It was furnished with my cot, a table, a stool, the latrine. When I put the table and the stool on the cot, that permitted me to run laps of a little more than nine fathoms around the room. Later, when I was given the grand piano, it stood right in the middle and was easy to get around. So I started running, every morning. Bare-chested. At first, the commander of the guard told me running was prohibited. Like everything else, to be on the safe side. I kept on running and shouted, 'Let me see General Plutalov about this!' They didn't call Plutalov, but they left me alone. I did ten laps around the casemate clockwise, then another ten anticlockwise. At first, I was out of breath and dripping with sweat after only a few dozen turns. After a while, my stamina improved, and I didn't sweat as much. Then I thought of *history*. As a way to restore my memory, and also as a source of moral inspiration. I decided to think about events. One lap, one year. Starting with the birth of Christ . . . Eight turns just to warm up, I can't think of anything . . . The dark spots on the whitewashed walls flash by, making me a little dizzy . . . I scrape my elbow against the wall, but my body warms up, my heart beats stronger . . . On the ninth lap: Arminius of the Cherusci shatters the forces of Publius Varus in the Teutoburg Forest . . .

Varus impales himself on his own sword. Just like his father, Philippos—must be a family weakness. Not one the Romanovs are afflicted by . . . Five more turns. The last years of old Augustus. On his deathbed, he has himself proclaimed a god. At least he waited until then . . . My body is tingling, my forehead is damp . . . Now Tiberius is emperor . . . The seventeenth lap: Germanicus has chastized the rebellious Etruscans. His triumphal procession winds through the roaring city of Rome, and they're dragging a captive woman—who is she? It is Arminius's wife, Thusnelda . . . and the boy—is their son, their two-year-old son, born in captivity . . . Groan . . . Keep going, keep going . . . The eighteenth lap: Ovid dies in exile . . . Keep going . . . Lap thirty-three: Christ is nailed to the cross . . . Keep going . . . Caligula. Claudius. Nero . . . Keep going . . . Lap sixty-five: Seneca kills himself, obeying the emperor; Lucanus kills himself, obeying the emperor; Petronius kills himself, obeying the emperor . . . Why are they so weak?! Why do they surrender?! Keep going . . . Lap sixty-eight: Nero kills himself—obeying whose order? So—*keep going* . . . Lap seventy-seven, -eight, -nine . . . Two thousand Pompeiians suffocate in the ashes raining down from Vesuvius, eighteen thousand flee, screaming . . . Against that screaming river goes one bald man with a sinewy neck—without a word, he struggles on, fights his way *upstream*. He is *summus dux*. He is an admiral. No one orders him about. He makes his own decisions . . . Pliny the Elder, correct. He has decided to find out how volcanoes erupt. He has decided to defy both the volcano and himself. He is buried by the cloud of ashes—and yet, he isn't . . . Keep going . . . Lap eighty, lap ninety . . . My eyes are stinging. Sweat is pouring off me. Red blotches dance among the gray blotches on the whitewash . . . The first time, I collapsed during the reign of Domitian . . . I was in really poor shape then. But as soon as I revived, I poured a bucket of cold water over my head and told myself—not that I'd be free when I was strong enough to run all the way to 1820 —no, I never surrender to that kind of self-deception—but I told myself that I wouldn't be released *before* I was able to run all the way from the birth of Christ to the present day, at one stretch . . . So I started over, each morning. At first, my thigh muscles were on fire and all my limbs felt like they'd been pumped full of lead. Slowly those sensations waned. After six months, I managed to get as far as the Huns. Every day I added a few laps. On some days I didn't do as well as on others. Some days I lay on the floor in the clutches of a fever and didn't run at all . . . In any case, on the last morning when my memory was still intact, I made it to the year 1793 . . ."

I asked, casually, "What happened to your memory?"

Timo started, awoken from his thoughts. He looked hard at me, as if in response to an unpleasant surprise. He picked the cold-water bucket off the steps (for a moment I thought he might hit me over the head with it), then poured its contents over his own head, and said, through the downrush of water:

"That's enough for today. Some other time."

Sunday, the thirteenth of November, 1827

This morning brought us a small and unexpected, albeit also very pleasing, event.

Around eight o'clock we sat at morning coffee, still by candle-light, munching the plum tortes Eeva bakes for birthday celebrations. It was Timo's fortieth birthday. During our desultory conversation I was aware, more keenly than was usual, of the limitations caution imposed on our choice of topics. Although there were only the three of us in the room—old Käsper would peek in now and again—it didn't seem right to talk about the celebrant's past, so heavy with blows of fate, nor did it seem right to talk about his future—he wasn't really supposed to have one . . . I decided in favor of the past, after all:

"Timo, tell me—when did you emancipate the peasants of Voi-siku? Was it as early as 1813?"

Timo said, "Yes, it was. I didn't have all that many to eman-cipate. I did it on a quick visit home to take care of my inheritance. But when Kitty and I came here in '17, the peasants still hadn't received definite confirmation of my decision. So I proclaimed them free, once again. But before confirmation arrived, I was dragged off to the casemate. So officially they became free only after the Emancipation Law of '19 was ratified."

Just as we were talking about the peasants, Käsper came in and told us, shrugging his shoulders, that three men from the village and the estate's blacksmith, Mihkel, were asking for an audience with Mr. Bock.

Timo raised his eyebrows.

"But don't they know that I have no authority anymore? Let them go and see Timm or La Trobe."

"But it is Mr. Bock they want to see," said Käsper. "They wish to congratulate him on his birthday."

"Oh . . . ," said Timo. "Well—if they . . . if they think that's important . . ." He laughed mirthlessly. "But do they have the Governor General's permission to do so?"

"That I don't know," Käsper replied, guilelessly.

"Well, since you don't know, let them in," Timo said and turned to the window to watch the falling snow.

Ushered in by Käsper, four men entered the dining room through the door from the kitchen. They wore short fur coats and felt boots and held snowy fur hats in their hands. I recognized Mihkel the blacksmith and another man who, I had been told, was employed by the mirrorworks as a forester, somewhere downriver. I recognized him because I knew he had lost an eye in the war against the French. The men stood by the door, mute at first, and formal in that peasant way that I have always found annoying. Timo spoke:

"Well, what did you want to tell me?"

The reply was surprisingly eloquent. The thinner and darker of the two bearded strangers standing next to Mihkel the blacksmith stepped forward and said:

"Sir—we come as representatives of the peasants of Voisiku, although we have not spoken to each and every one of them. But when we talked about it in the taverns at Nomavere and Luhavesk, everybody agreed. That the four us should come to wish you happiness, sir. And to welcome you, belatedly, on your return. And to honor your birthday, sir, which is today . . ."

Mihkel and the other bearded fellow began to unwrap a small bundle, and the spokesman continued:

"Blacksmith Mihkel's brother lives on Ko Estate land, on Käo Island by the Loopr River. There is a place there where they used to mine lead during the Swedish reign, and there still is some lead ore in the ground. So Mihkel's brother brought him a chunk, and we watched while Mihkel extracted the lead from it in his cauldron. And then, at the Luhavesk tavern, we came up with the notion of having Mihkel make a candlestick out of it, for a gift to you, sir. To thank you, sir, for setting us free six years sooner than the rest of the Livonian peasants—although you weren't able to be here to make sure that your order was obeyed, sir. And also as a homecoming and birthday present."

He took the unwrapped, dark-gray candlestick from Mihkel and proffered it to Timo.

"And so, sir, we beg you to accept this from us. True, it is lead and tarnishes easily. But it is lead from our own land. And we tested it: it can withstand even sulphuric acid."

Timo got up from his chair and received the gift. After a moment's thought, he asked Käsper to bring a candle. Käsper took a wax candle out of a sideboard drawer. Timo lit it from a candle already burning on the table and placed it in the candlestick he had been given. Then, holding the candlestick, he turned to the men.

"Well, then. I thank you. And I assure you that I shall use your candlestick. Although I don't know whether much benefit will accrue from that, to either you or myself."

He looked at Eeva as if to ask her what else he should say or do. Then he set the candlestick on the table, went over to the peasants and shook hands with each one of them, holding their hands between both of his own—a thing no estate owner in his right mind would have done, here or elsewhere. And he did more than that: he also demonstrated the reason for his impulsive gesture to us all. From the peasants, he walked back around the table to Eeva, stood behind her chair, turned her face toward himself, bent down, and kissed her on the mouth.

"Kitty—was it your idea?"

Eeva shook her head.

"No, it was their own. I had no inkling of it."

The men left the room. Timo lit his pipe, and I noticed from the slight tremor in his fingers that the scene had affected him more than I would have thought. I had never observed any particular warmth in his relations with peasants, not even ten years ago—in spite of the idea, expressed in his letter to the Czar, that the aristocracy had to win the hearts of the peasantry. These days he seemed to keep his distance from peasants, but, then, he kept his distance from everyone, except for the couple of people who were closest to him.

Tuesday, the twenty-ninth November, 1827

If memory serves, it happened eight years ago to the day—or at least very close to that, eight years ago.

In the evening, Eeva summoned me down from my garret to her bedroom. She was sitting in front of an oval mirror mounted on the wall, in the light of two candles, combing her pitch-black hair, the color of which still startled me. I remember how she got up and closed the door to the yellow drawing room behind me, even though neither one of us yet suspected that there were spies in our house. Then she sat down again in front of the mirror, pulled the comb through her hair, and asked, in a quiet voice (little Jüri was asleep in his crib at the end of the bed):

"Jakob, how well do you remember our last breakfast?"

I didn't quite get her drift.

"Breakfast? This morning?"

"No—back when Paulucci joined us and couldn't understand what we were saying in Estonian. In the tea salon."

"Well, yes, I think I remember it rather well."

"Do you remember when I asked Timo, 'Tell me to whom I could apply for mercy for you?' "

"Yes, I do."

"And do you remember what Timo said?"

"Yes. He said: 'No use to appeal for it from anyone but the emperor. But I beg you: do not plead with him!' "

"Right. But today I heard, from Madame La Trobe—Mrs. Wahl had told her, at Poltsamaa—that the emperor's mother is traveling from Riga to St. Petersburg and planning to stop for the night at Torma." She pulled the crackling tortoiseshell comb through a tangle and looked straight at me.

"And so?"

"Well, Timo told me not to plead with the emperor—but what do you think: Can't I plead for him with the emperor's mother?"

Eeva and I have always been candid with each other. We do not hide our thoughts but express them freely whenever we feel the need to do so, or when one of us asks the other. We have never treated each other with kid gloves. Well, here's something I wouldn't admit to anyone except this page: when my sister asks me, "Jakob, what do you think the weather will be like tomorrow?" I look out through the window, thinking to myself: Who knows, maybe it'll clear up—but then tell her, as often as not, "Well, what do you think, more of the same, rain rain rain . . ." Just to get her goat, just a little—and I don't really know why I do it. Maybe it's in revenge for her incredible and tragic rise in the world . . . so that, even then, I gave her this reply:

"Well, I don't think Maria Feodorovna will be able to set Timo free. All she can do is to ask her son. If she takes the trouble. She might. They say she is an ambitious woman; when Paul died, she would have liked to ascend to the throne instead of her son. So they say. And that son hasn't left her with much to occupy herself, except for charitable works—all she was permitted in Paul's day. So, perhaps she would try to do something for you. It's just that—"

"What?"

"That turning to her differs from turning directly to the emperor *only in form.*"

"So you think—I shouldn't?"

"You have to decide that for yourself."

Eeva sprang to her feet. But she didn't raise her voice, because little Jüri was lying there, practically right between us. She said:

"I believe that a woman must do everything she knows how to do to help her husband. With *maybe* the exception of those things her husband has explicitly forbidden her to do—if they should prove injurious to his honor. So, my mind is made up. Get ready, we're going to Torma tomorrow morning."

And to Torma we went. Or rushed: Eeva had ordered our coachman to drive our sleigh as fast as the horses could go. We had, of course, brought our snow shovels, and for such a long journey, mostly through wooded terrain (for some eighty versts) I had also brought my rifle. After we had passed Kaave Estate but before we crossed the Imperial Highway, we did see two wolves, and they started trotting abreast of our sleigh. The horses were about to bolt, and I told the coachman to rein them in. From the window of the covered sleigh, at about fifty paces, I shot one of the pale gray creatures. The other one fled into the brush. I wanted to hand the rifle to the coachman, but he said he had his hands full holding the horses. I looked at Eeva.

"Take this and use it if necessary."

Eeva said, "I will." But she didn't have to.

I ran back and dragged the dead wolf up to the back of the sleigh. I couldn't resist: it was a large handsome male with a coat that spoke of a good summer of sheep, and it weighed at least a hundred and fifty pounds. I had shot it in the chest, and a streak of blood ran between our tracks for many versts before the carcass froze. The horses remained skittish all the way to Laius. For my troubles, I now have this slightly moth-eaten wolf skin hanging on the log wall above my desk. To digress for a moment: I don't know how some stories get started, they all seem to originate in some form of logic, or illogic—but no one has ever thought of that wolf skin as *my* trophy. In spite of the fact that I—even back in target practice with Tenner's surveyors—was and am a superior marksman. For eight long years it has been said that the thing on the wall is the skin of *the wolf that Mrs. Bock shot on her visit to the emperor's mother* . . .

The truth is, Eeva didn't bag any wolves on this trip, neither real ones nor the metaphorical kind. We arrived at Laius Deanery at nightfall. I can still see old Dean Jannau—a large man with a shock of hair like a haystack above a face as gray as lead. (He went to join his Lord and Maker the following year.) He received us hospitably, sent the wolf I had shot to be skinned by the forester, and was still congratulating Eeva on her aim as we took our leave at dawn on the deanery steps.

We reached the Torma post station at noon. Our breakneck

speed had not been in vain. Postmaster Anderson, an energetic old fellow, knew that Her Imperial Highness was scheduled to arrive in the afternoon. However, Count Albedyll, her chamberlain, had already arrived, graced the station with an inspection, and then decided to reserve lodgings for Her Imperial Highness at Torma Manor.

Anderson had sent a young lad on horseback to watch the road in the direction of the Igavere station and to report back as soon as he spied Her Imperial Highness's retinue. Eeva decided that Juhan should harness our horses as soon as the boy galloped back to the station; we'd let the retinue pass, then follow it to Torma Manor in a dignified fashion. Once there, we would decide what to do.

Around four o'clock in the afternoon we saw five covered sleighs and a pack train of six or seven soldiers on horseback file past us in the direction of Ninas. Keeping a seemly distance, we followed them to the front entrance of Torma Manor, where a few sleigh-loads of ladies and gentlemen from neighboring estates had already gathered. We saw Maria Feodorovna, followed by her baggage, ascend the front steps, which had been swept clean of snow; Baron von Samson, the owner of the estate, who had hastened here from Tartu, met her halfway up the steps, bowing and kissing her hand. When the Czar's mother had disappeared into the house, the ruddy Baron came back out and led the local gentry, including us, inside to take our seats in the dusty but opulent guest parlors of the manor. An unexpected number of people assembled there. The more illustrious among the district's nobility obviously regarded it as a matter of both honor and profit to come and greet the Czar's mother on her way through their lands—as a sign of gratitude for the honor thus bestowed on them. While kissing her hand, it was these gentryfolk's custom on such occasions to let her know, with appropriately pious sighs, how fervently they prayed for the Lord's blessings upon her and her beloved son. Eeva conversed with some of them. I noticed how heads turned, eyebrows rose, and faces assumed a multitude of expressions, from anger and perplexity to unconcealed interest, as soon as people heard *who* she was . . .

I overheard only one conversation: in the course of it, a gray-haired old lady, the widow of Pastor Asverus of Torma, who had died the year before last, confessed that she hadn't really come here to pay her respects to the empress. With a smile, and in a half-whisper, she admitted that it had been her ten-year-old grandson who had insisted on seeing the Czar's mother. The snubnosed boy next to her, his brown protuberant eyes shining, playfully, chanted, "Wants to see, wants to see, wants to see what the Czar's mama looks like!"

Count Albedyll entered the guest room and began to ask for the names of people requesting an audience, and a secretary wrote them down. When he heard Eeva's name, he asked the secretary to stop and went back to the inner sanctum. A bewildered hubbub arose among the gentry.

Old Mrs. Asverus whispered to Eeva, "That Count Albedyll may look like he's swallowed a cane, but you're in luck, madame—I've heard that when the emperor was young, almost twenty years ago, Count Albedyll was the head of that commission that was trying to stop the torture and beatings of prisoners in Russia . . ."

I recall the absurd thought that occurred to me at that moment: perhaps the Count looks the way he does because he did *literally* swallow a cane, back then . . . And then I thought, alas, no—the cane is still in widespread use, even against free persons . . . The Count must not have started digesting it yet.

Then Eeva was called in to meet the Czar's mother and spent half an hour with her, during which many of those assembled walked up and asked me *why* her husband had been imprisoned. I told them that I didn't have the faintest idea—which, at that time, was no lie.

Count Albedyll's secretary reappeared and announced:

"*Son Altesse Impériale a le plaisir de prier Monsieur*"—he looked at his sheet of paper and continued—"*Monsieur Jacóp Mettic!*" It took me a moment to realize, with a start, that it was I who was being asked in.

The secretary led me to the Czar's mother's quarters, where an idyllic tableau met my eyes. In the glow of a fireplace, in what looked like Madame Samson's private guest room, my reckless sister and Maria Feodorovna sat on a sofa, prettily side by side— and I was secretly amused by the thought that they looked like old friends having a cordial reunion . . . I got a close look at Maria Feodorovna. Born Sophie Dorothea, Princess of Württemberg, she was sixty years old at the time (Czar Paul had wed her when she was sixteen) but her looks did not show that she had blessed her half-lunatic spouse with one emperor, three grand dukes, and three grand duchesses. She turned her rather sharp-featured face and cool but observant gaze to me and said:

"*Und Sie sind mir also das zweite Wunderexemplar, mein Herr?*"

I bowed in silence, and Maria Feodorovna continued:

"There are, of course, highly educated persons in Germany who have risen out of the peasant class, but they are few and far between. Well, I have met some in Russia, as well. The odd ones —musicians, actors. But that there are even Estonians who speak German and French and have risen into the aristocracy—that really is news to me . . ."

Her eyes held mine while she was saying this, and it seemed to me that an answer was required. It had to be one that didn't cause embarrassment . . . Something along the lines of Eeva's elegant phrases—sufficiently polite but also, in the best of cases, a little pointed . . . I said:

"Your Imperial Highness, I have the temerity to assume that this news is, nevertheless, *pleasing* to you . . ."

"But of course it is," Maria Feodorovna said with noncommittal benevolence. "And your sister pleases me enormously. She is truly a woman. And truly a lady. But the *reason* that has brought her here—it pleases me much less. I have heard about it. Who hasn't? And I haven't just heard about it, I have discussed it with Alexander Pavlovich. My dear child"—Maria Feodorovna took Eeva's hand—"I must disappoint you: if your husband has told you that his manner of addressing the emperor was *correct*, then his notion of correctness diverges, to put it mildly, greatly from the commonly accepted one."

"But, your Highness," Eeva said, "was it not natural that it *had to* diverge from the commonly accepted one?"

"How so?" Maria Feodorovna asked, looking surprised.

And Eeva replied, "Because the emperor had made my husband swear an oath."

"What kind of an oath?"

"That he would always tell the emperor his true opinion."

That stopped Maria Feodorovna for a moment. I noticed that she was debating with herself whether to let go of Eeva's hand or not. Then she said, stroking Eeva's hand:

"I know that Alexander Pavlovich had a few such confidants in his youth. But your husband is not the only one who has suffered misfortune because of that. No oath obliges you to be uncouth. Especially toward your sovereign."

"But *the truth*—" Eeva began.

"My dear, not even the truth. Or what calls itself the truth. Your husband may praise himself lucky that his behavior has been construed as madness. But I understand you. I do. Indeed, I admire you. And I assure you that I shall keep this matter in mind. But it is best not to indulge in any hopes."

And thus, we returned from Torma, no more hopeful than before. On the way back, I asked Eeva what Timo's oath to the Czar had consisted of, and how the Czar had made him swear it.

Eeva said, "Jakob, I don't want to talk about it anymore. And please, don't you talk about it with anyone, either."

It would take eight years for Eeva to tell me the details of Timo's oath, and I have recorded that occasion on a previous page.

The second day of Christmas, 1827

Yesterday, we had unexpected company at our modest Christmas dinner: Georg has come to Voisiku. I mean Georg senior, Timo's brother, the retired Colonel. We shared our meal in The Foundation's dining room, the one with the bumpy floorboards. Even though Monsieur La Trobe had come to plead in person that the guest should take lodgings in the main building, Georg had politely declined and decided to stay in The Foundation in his nephew's (and namesake's) now-vacant room, in which we had had to keep a fire going for six hours before the ice melted off the windows.

Georg had retired from the army with a colonel's rank a few years ago, and had taken up residence abroad. Before that, still in

St. Petersburg, he had married Teresa Lopushka, a Polish countess, and their union had been blessed with a daughter. The official reason for their move abroad was the state of the daughter's health. Georg had told Eeva and me the real reason before their departure back in the autumn of '21, speaking to us in a near-whisper in Timo's old study in the main building:

"You must understand—here in Russia I can't escape from Timo's shadow. And it doesn't matter whether it impedes my career, or whether, on the contrary, the emperor's pangs of conscience help speed that career up . . . The last few years, I have in fact suspected the latter to be the case: in only a year and a half, I was promoted from lieutenant-colonel to colonel. I must admit that this really seems even more repulsive to me than if I had been overlooked. It would be the normal thing to do, to put the brakes on my progress. But this premature furthering of my career strikes me as an imperial bribe, designed to console me for Timo . . . Well, we won't be living abroad in grand style. In the beginning, we'll have to rely solely on Teresa's modest dowry . . . I'll try to earn some money writing—even though my writing skills are poor, compared to Timo's . . . And maybe Mr. Cube can send us something from the Voisiku funds once in a while . . . I think we'll manage somehow. In any case, I'll be free of the pressures of my two-faced situation. Because I have at last realized that I can't do anything for Timo here at home."

On that same occasion, he told us about his adventure some time ago in St. Petersburg. At first, the circumstances had seemed most propitious. He had found out when, and along what route, the Czar deigned to take a walk in the park at Tsarskoye, and had waited for him to approach under the cover of some bush, his nerves and legs tense as those of a horse before a steeplechase. He had worn all his decorations, had prepared his speech: "Your Majesty—by your imperial order, my unfortunate brother has been languishing for more than two years in some location unknown to his family. The uncertainty is very taxing to that family . . . Your Majesty, my brother has an almost three-year-old son who has never seen his father! Nor has the father seen his son . . . Your Majesty, my unfortunate brother's scandalously low-born wife (whom you, so graciously, put under special protection from all hardship) has indeed suffered, during all these years, the worst kind of hardship of one kind and another . . . Your Majesty—"

Then the Czar had come striding down the sandy path between flowerbeds and shrubbery, and Georg had stepped out of hiding and positioned himself along his route. The Czar had advanced up to a distance of seven or eight paces—but before Georg had been able to get a word out, the Czar had recognized him and had immediately turned onto a side path, down which he then had proceeded *almost at a run* . . . An hour later, an officer of the gendarmes had intercepted Georg and had ordered him to present himself at the Castle to Court Secretary Volkonski (the man whom Timo in his manuscript calls a brothelkeeper and headwaiter). Volkonski had told Georg that he must never again try to bring up his brother's case with the Czar—that he must abandon entirely the notion that the Czar would ever deign to listen to what he might have to say about Timotheus's case! Presently, I have no difficulty understanding that command, but to this day Georg still considers it grossly unjust and arrogant.

Another man would have been completely downcast by such a turn of events. Not Georg: he is endowed with a good dose of his family's stubbornness. (Popular Livonian opinion, as I have heard it expressed more than once, states that even their *name* indicates that old fundamental trait.) Instead of admitting defeat, Georg decided to invest many thousands of rubles in a new attempt—I don't know the exact amount, nor do I know whose pockets it lined. In any case, he obtained the information which both Volkonski and the Czar's personal chancellery had refused to reveal to the family: he found out *where* Timo was imprisoned. He discovered that it was Schlüsselburg, a fortress with an even worse reputation than the fortress of Peter and Paul. And this was when he really embarked on what *I* call his daring escapade. He went to the appropriate authorities—I don't know exactly what office—and introduced himself as, let us say, Ivan Ivanovich Plutalov—in any case, the *nephew of the commandant of Schlüsselburg, Major-General Plutalov*. He had just returned from Poland (or somewhere) on leave from his regiment, had decided to pay his uncle a visit, and was now requesting the appropriate permit. His manner was perfectly consistent, and this, as well as his colonel's

uniform, decorations, and the lucky circumstance that no officers
of a higher rank were present, got him the permit to Schlüsselburg
without delay. In no time at all, he was in the saddle and on his
way, in a hurry to get to his destination before anyone discovered
the ruse.

He galloped into the town of Schlüsselburg, where Eeva and I
had stood staring at the island and its fortress towers, a diffuse
melancholy in our hearts—*perhaps* this was the place where Timo
was incarcerated . . . Since we had not been able to obtain a permit,
that was as far as we got. But Georg slapped his permit on the
port guard's desk, the officer in charge clicked his heels, and a boat
and crew were put at his disposal. He was taken to the island and
admitted into the fortress. Soon thereafter, he stood in a candle-
lit room with walls a fathom thick, facing the old pockmarked
Major-General Plutalov. The latter examined Georg's permit. Just
as he cleared his throat, raised his eyebrows, and parted his lips
to begin roaring at the intruder, Georg addressed him:

"General Plutalov, sir! Colonel Georg von Bock, at your service. This was the only way I was able to reach you. I am the
brother of your top secret prisoner, Timotheus von Bock. I implore you—not in your capacity as a general, or a prison governor,
but as a human being and a man of honor: allow me to see my
brother, in your presence."

Silent, General Plutalov stared at Georg for a moment. It may
have been the flickering candlelight that made Plutalov's pockmarked visage appear pale and ruddy by turns. Then, still not
saying a word, Plutalov began to pace back and forth in front of
Georg. It seemed to Georg—so he told us later—that the general
was doing this in order to conceal his emotions. When the general
finally came to a halt before his visitor—so close that the strong
odor of onion soup made Georg's eyes smart—his mien was
inscrutable.

He said, "Colonel, I can see that you *are* your brother's brother.
Do you know, sir, what I should do to you?"

"I believe so, sir," Georg replied. "You should arrest me and
await the emperor's orders. As a general and governor of this
fortress, that is what you ought to do. But as a man of honor,
you should comply with my request."

"Damn it all to hell!" Plutalov roared. "Don't push your luck! Thank your lucky stars that I am, indeed, a man of honor, and therefore willing to neglect my duty!" Then he said, in a quieter voice, "Come over here." He took a bottle from his desk drawer and poured Georg a teaglassful of vodka. "Sit down." He poured himself another glassful and sat down opposite Georg on the wooden bench.

"Your health, sir!" He knocked his drink back. "Now. What I ought to tell you is that I don't have the faintest idea of your brother's whereabouts, and that I don't know anything about his case. That he *certainly* isn't here. And so forth. Or, even better, I shouldn't tell you anything at all. By rights, Colonel, you should have been locked up half an hour ago. But I am talking to you now, and I won't deny that your brother is here. I am the only person he is allowed to see. By order of the emperor. Count Lieven has been authorized to admit other persons, but only after he has consulted with the emperor. I assume that you'll want to approach Count Lieven with your request—if you do so, I would appreciate it if you did not mention my name." He cleared his throat. "You want to know how your brother is. I will tell you: *he is the way it is possible to be here.* Nothing out of the ordinary. And it is my personal opinion *that he does not have to be here—but he has decided that this is where he has to be.* That is all. And now, get out of my sight! Let them row you back to town! Wait a minute—finish that drink, so you won't get chilled on the boat ride. *Adieu!* We've never met."

Georg continued his tale:

"After that, I did go to see Lieven, and what I saw and heard finally convinced me that there was nothing I could do for Timo. Like Timo, I knew the Count from our Tartu days, perhaps from even farther back. Our fathers had known each other from the Diet of Riga, and so forth. But I have to say that this Count Lieven—curator of the university, close confidant of the Czar, archangel of Bible study groups—Lieven behaved in a way that made the old owlish gendarme Plutalov seem like a knight in shining armor . . . At first, Lieven denied that he had anything to do with Timo's case. Even though he is, by birth, a most distinguished member of the aristocracy, with personal aspirations to sainthood, he had the gall to tell me that lie, a courtier's smile on his sallow horse-face . . . He pretended to rack his brains for some long-forgotten matter and then told me, to my face, 'Oh yes, yes, I did hear, many years ago, something about an ill-considered step Timotheus had taken . . . And I heard that the emperor was offended, *deeply* offended. But that is all I know about the matter, believe me. You must understand, my dear Colonel, that I would be most reluctant to meddle in such business, to interest myself in it . . . So—well, how is your daughter doing? And how does Madame Teresa like it in St. Petersburg?' "

Georg went on:

"I left those questions unanswered. With the right of an old acquaintance, I walked up to his desk and told him, 'Count Lieven, I know with absolute certainty that Timotheus is being held in a casemate of the Secret House at Schlüsselburg. I also know that *you* are the person authorized to decide who can visit him.' And, you know—when I saw how he started to spread his waxy hands for yet another denial, how he didn't hesitate to sink *that low* in front of me, being a good von Bock—a family with a decided theatrical streak—I pulled a pistol out of my pocket! Not to threaten *him* with it—God forbid. No, I pointed it at my own temple and I said to him:

" 'Count Lieven! As it says in the good book: who speaks false-hood allows his mouth to destroy his soul. Now, speak the truth! Or I'll pull the trigger, and in ten seconds I'll be standing in front of Our Lord—and even if he sends me to Purgatory for my deed, I'll have time to tell him: Lord, I know that my soul shall rise from Purgatory, because it *lives!* But that Lieven back there, lord-ing it over Russia—he has *killed* his soul with his lies! He is nothing but a soulless cadaver! I'll be there in ten seconds—' And I began to count: 'One, two, three, four, five . . .' I was about to say 'six' when he shouted 'Stop!' " Georg laughed. "Which is not to say that he *broke down*—that wouldn't be right word, but he did *give* a little, the foolish old hypocrite, and pulled himself together and started piping a different tune. Yes, indeed. He jumped up, made me sit down on the sofa, sat next to me. He placed his hands on my knees and explained, with a serious mien: 'Oh, my dear Colo-nel, with the wisdom of a Solomon you have returned me to the *truth* . . . I thank you for it . . . Now, listen to me . . . The story of your unfortunate brother is more than tragic. You can't imagine *how* energetically I have fought to save his life. But he won't budge from his fateful skepticism! It is frightful to see how he has changed! He has become a complete atheist! And it is exactly for *that* reason that the emperor refuses to forgive him! And because of that, any thought of a pardon is hopeless . . .' Pale with grief, he gazed at me with his equine visage, and I saw tears roll down that yellow mask . . . Yet I knew better—just a short while before this, Timo's first letters had reached us, and he wrote: 'My dearest, we cannot trust in people. So let us trust in God, as I do, with certainty . . .' "

Georg concluded:

"I'm sure you understand—after *such* a profound lie from *such* a highly placed person I simply had to realize that I can't trust anyone anymore. So, the only thing to do is to leave, to live abroad, and that's what we're going to do. We have the emperor's permission . . . Well, God knows, other countries are just as riddled with lies, just as suffocating . . . No, no, they aren't! I have *felt* something, or surmised it, at least . . . And you know, even if I should be proven wrong, if my idea of life in, let's say, France or Switzerland were just an émigré's superficial impression—even then, it will be an enormous difference! Yes—an enormous difference, even if disgusting lies and oppression are rampant there: because I still would not have to feel, at every step I take, that I am personally responsible for all the horrors—do you understand? No, I don't think you can quite understand that . . . Because you've come up from *below*—or, as my fellow nobles would put it, forgive the expression, 'up from the dungheap' . . . You have acquired an education, a broader horizon, a view of the world. By chance, by a miracle. And that is why you have an even keener sense of the absurdity of the world. But you also have the holy birthright to call atrocities by their name—if not publicly, at least in your hearts. *I* do not have that right. I am a member of the imperial nobility, a pillar of law and order! I am that, I must be that, and—God knows—I want to be that! But what kind of order has fate ordained me to support? I have to invent elaborate excuses for the emperor's abominations, explain why they should be forgiven . . . I have to tell people that *evil* exists in the empire only because the good emperor does not yet know about it . . . *I've had enough of all that!*"

His voice had risen from a near-whisper to almost a shout. Then he said, in a gentler tone:

"And I am not the only one who has understood that. There are honorable and thoughtful men in the officer corps. I know there are. Perhaps we can expect some action from them, perhaps even sooner than we think. They have asked me to join them. But, and I say this with regret, I can't allow myself the luxury of their friendship. Because I am absolutely sure, thanks to careful observations, that the Government has had its snoops on my case for four years . . . Any contact I made with—with some secret society would be the kiss of death to its members . . . And so, the only thing Teresa and I can do is to use our three-year-old daughter as an excuse (because that's what we are doing!) and slink away, to live abroad . . ."

A few days later, Teresa and their daughter joined Georg at Voisiku. Teresa was a brisk young woman with dark hair, of the type people hereabouts tend to think of as "Spanish." She was obviously quite intelligent, even though I found her attempts to appear worldly-wise rather transparent. Three-year-old Agnes impressed me as a very healthy little girl.

They spent a few days in Voisiku before setting out for Riga— if memory serves, this was September of '21. For years, we heard from them only occasionally; I recall a few lines from Cracow, a few more from Berlin. Not long after that, Timo's old friend Zhukovski visited Tartu for a few days and said he had met Georg in Berlin and introduced him there to his pupil, our present Czar's wife. After that we did not hear anything from or about Georg for years. Then we heard that he was in Germany and was doing business with people in Riga, and a few months later he appeared at our Christmas table, laughed his raucous laugh and told us, after Käsper had served the ham and left:

"Praise the Lord, now I can see it with my own eyes: Timo, you are exactly as mad and not a whit more than you were twelve years ago, when people first started calling you mad in St. Petersburg because you rejected the emperor's plans for you and Naryshkina and remained faithful to your Kitty. You know, when we heard, last summer, that you had been set free *because of mental derangement*, I was a little frightened at first. I thought: well, he's always had a mind of his own, that dear brother of mine—so, perhaps something in his head really snapped out of joint during the years he was confined within those hard walls of Schlüsselburg . . . Which makes it an even greater joy to see you now and find out *how* very well you are."

Timo said nothing to that. I noticed a slight twitch in his left eyelid. He looked down at his plate and cut his rather leathery slice of ham into little pieces, to be better able to eat it with his toothless mouth. And it occurred to me that Georg's enthusiasm for Timo's state of health was perhaps not *completely* sincere, after all . . .

The third day of Christmas

Today, around ten o'clock, Käsper knocked on my door and said that Timo wanted to see me. When I entered the drawing room, the three of them—Eeva, Timo, and Georg—were sitting in old creaky armchairs in front of the fireplace, their backs turned to the grayish snowy light from the windows, their faces reflecting the glow from the fire. Georg had a tankard of ale in front of him on the fireside table; in front of Eeva lay some document. Timo spoke:

"Jakob, you may be a little acerbic at times, but you're always fair. Tell us who is in the right in this matter. In the spring of '18, I borrowed sixteen hundred rubles from Georg. With interest due, I now owe him twenty-five hundred rubles. Georg and his family back in Germany are in dire need of cash. Georg would like to petition the Governor General to have the debt paid back to him out of the income generated by Voisiku. But in Kitty's opinion, an honorable man would not make such a request . . ."

"Dearest—perhaps I was unfair to Georg," said Eeva, stroking Timo's hand. "And the document Georg wanted, I wrote it two months ago . . ."

"What documents do *you* have to write in a matter like that?"
I asked, with genuine surprise.

"Well, you see, I am mad," Timo said. "A debenture signed
by me would be invalid." He pushed the document toward me,
and I read:

I, the undersigned Katharina von Bock, wife of Colonel
(Ret.) and Knight Timofey von Bock, hereby state in accordance with the best of my knowledge and belief:

As I have been aware, thanks to several both oral and
written statements made by my husband in full command
of all his physical and mental faculties, he is indebted to
his brother, Colonel (Ret.) and Knight Georg von Bock,
for several cash loans to the total amount of one thousand
six hundred and sixty-six rubles and eighty kopecks sterling, to which shall be added legal interest accrued from
the seventeenth of April 1818 onward.

During the legal inventory of my husband's debts, Col.
(Ret.) Georg von Bock did not register as one of his creditors at the appointed time, partly because he was unable
to present the customary document as proof of the debt,
but partly also due to fraternal charity, so as not to appear
as a complainant against his own unfortunate brother, since
he believed that the latter would soon be released and could
then fulfill his obligation in due course. As the years passed,
these expectations proved to be vain, and when my husband was returned to me after nine years by order of His
Most Illustrious Majesty, the ordeal he had undergone had
caused his mental state to become such that he was no
longer able to discharge this debt by his own signature.

As long as my very restricted income does not permit
me to meet my husband's brother's justified request on his
behalf, I beg his brother to use the enclosed document as
a mortgage for the entire amount of the regrettably still
unpaid debt, two thousand five hundred and sixty-six rubles and eighty-seven kopecks sterling. Should I depart
this world before paying this debt, which I am most de-
sirous to discharge, I expect and trust that my dear, presently still underage son Georg von Bock, now a student

at the Tsarskoye Selo boarding academy, will without delay, as soon as he achieves maturity, discharge this obligation that his father has not been able to discharge, all
the more eagerly since his uncle's friendship and truly fraternal concern, during long years in which that uncle often
found himself in great financial difficulties, gives him a
well-founded right to his brother's, that is, my husband's,
and hence also my and our son's gratitude.

At Voisku
in the district of Viljandi
in the province of Livonia
the 26th of October 1827

Katharina von Bock

I looked at them nonplussed; I asked what they thought *I* could
tell them in this matter. It was clear that Georg thought that the
idea to invite me in as an arbiter was a bad joke (I thought so
myself). He sipped his ale and didn't say a word. But Timo said,
"Tell us if you think that Georg has a right—and I'm sure you'll
understand that we're not debating legal rights, those are beyond
suspicion—but does he have a *moral* right to try to get his money
back?"

I asked, "So Eeva thinks he doesn't?"

Eeva equivocated, and I understood from her melancholic glance
at Timo that she wanted to speak the truth but also wanted to
alleviate Timo's curious agitation:

"I *did* think so . . . But considering our circumstances . . . But
I have already told you that I may have been wrong . . ."

I asked, "Well, and to go by what you have written here about
your gratitude to Georg, it is obviously the right thing to do—as
far as I can see?"

"That is true . . ." Eeva said.

"But what ever made you think he didn't have a right?"

". . . I felt that no matter how great his need is, he is,
nevertheless—well, he is free to come and go and to attend to his
affairs. That was why it seemed to me that he should not, after
all, make use of this document."

Timo got up and, with a curiously strained expression, paced
back and forth between the grand piano and the fireplace. Then

he came to a halt again by the side of the mantel, paler than usual but with the right side of his face glowing in the firelight. He said:

"My dear friends . . . who cares about those twenty-five hundred! I, of course, am nobody anymore. I am just the shadow of a former name. And I own nothing. Nevertheless, I say: the hell with the twenty-five hundred! It is something else that frightens me: *How can I believe that the creation of a just society is possible when the two souls closest to my own interpret morality in such different ways! And when it is impossible to decide who is right!*"

That I had been invited to act as a judge by these three—two aristocrats (never mind that both were penniless and one a certified madman) and a third who also, I noticed, signed her letter with a *von*, even though she had come up from the dungheap and was my sister—I have to admit that this invitation quite tickled me, in spite of everything . . . And besides, the answer that occurred to me felt *right*. It was also likely to dispel Timo's slightly ridiculous sorrow. I said:

"Listen, what's so frightening about our inability to resolve this question? It is not a matter of principle, or, as Timo would have it, philosophy. As far as I can see, it hinges simply on knowledge, or lack thereof. Both legally and morally, Georg is in the right—provided that his distress is greater than ours."

Timo crossed his arms over his chest and gave me a delighted look.

"Jakob—truly, your name should be Solomon!"

I continued: "But what we lack is a measuring stick for distress. We have only two sets of feelings here. And both sides feel that their distress is greater."

"Absolutely true!" Timo exclaimed. "And do you know what we'll do? We'll resolve this dilemma! We'll resolve it by *ordeal!*"

The rest of us looked at him, perplexed. It seemed to me that he rather enjoyed our perplexity. He said:

"In the course of history, this has been done in many different ways. Four hundred years ago, they would have buried Georg up to his waist, and then they would have given him and Kitty swords. Or they would have been put to an ordeal by water or fire. Which is not to say that the way we'll use didn't exist then—"

He left the drawing room, and the three of us staring at each other. Georg sipped his ale and asked, not without a tinge of irritation, "Kitty, what is he up to now?"

Eeva rose to follow Timo but he returned at that instant, holding two black-eyed ivory dice in his palm. He handed one to Eeva and the other to Georg and said, in a cheerful, matter-of-fact tone:

"First Kitty, then you . . . Agreed? If the first roll is a draw, you continue until one of you rolls the higher score. If Georg gets the higher score first, he'll collect his debt; if Kitty wins, Georg waives it." He turned to me: "Don't you think that's fair?"

What could I say to that? Even if Timo hadn't been standing next to me, I could not have asked the other two if they deemed his suggestion crazy or not . . . But the proposal itself was as unexpected as it was . . . what should I call it? Crazy? Mad? Strange? Eccentric? Or was it, after all, and even by normal standards, an *acceptable* solution? Even logical, somehow? Or perhaps the *only* logical solution—in these circumstances, where it was quite impossible to decide which was greater, the distress of those who were deracinated wanderers in foreign lands, or of those who were shadowy prisoners in their own home. The devil alone knows. I couldn't decide upon it that morning, nor can I do so now. I told Timo:

"Well, then . . . Yes, I think that's fair."

Georg started to say something, probably by way of protest, but contented himself with a wave of his hand. He took the die, made a fist around it, and punched the air.

"Timo, it's just as I said: you never went mad! You've been mad all your life!" He laughed raucously and told Eeva, "Kitty —roll your die!"

Eeva did so, and the matter was resolved in the first round. On that polished fireside table, Eeva rolled a five, Georg a three. In all likelihood, Georg was disappointed: the Governor General would not have denied his request, even if he would have had to pay the sum out of the separate trust fund the Governor General himself had established for the younger Georg's education. He could have justified this by pointing out that the family no longer had any expenses in regard to the boy's education, now that the emperor himself in his munificence, *et cetera* . . . Nevertheless, Georg did not show his disappointment but remained as jovial and cheerful as ever. His departure, however, immediately after dinner—first to Riga, then back to Germany—announced by him two hours later, while we were waiting for the food to be served, seemed to come sooner than he had originally planned.

The eleventh of February, 1828

Again, six weeks of journal fatigue: and once again, it must mean that nothing extraordinary has happened in the meantime. It seems that our life has gradually become quite mundane, even in the slightly curious form it has assumed.

It is a quiet, almost silent life. We hardly pay any visits, nor do we receive many. Only Carl Lilienfeldt from Uus-Poltsamaa, a not too distant relative of the Bocks, paid us a surprise visit after the New Year, in a very pleasant and friendly fashion, accompanied by his wife, Charlotte, and thirteen-year-old son, Carl Junior, thus entirely *comme il faut*, as they say. It made me almost wistful to see how delighted Timo was, granted that he was more so on Eeva's behalf than on his own. Delighted to see that not all of his relatives regarded his wife as one whose company was to be avoided at all times. I think this matters a great deal to Timo because he feels personally responsible for his family's attitude toward his spouse—never mind that this feeling has nothing to do with rational thought. Besides, it's been a long time since the *isolation* in which we live was due to the stigma of an unequal match—as it was at first (which is not to say that the stigma won't exist forever in some minds). A month ago, at Epiphany, when Eeva and I entered Poltsamaa Castle Church and took our seats in the section reserved for nobility, Mrs. Samson rose and walked out of the church, just as she had done ten years ago. Yet there was a great difference. Ten years ago, the entire pewful of gentry filed out at her heels: but now she could no longer tug her Reinhold out of his seat—he has been resting in the mausoleum of this churchyard for several years now—and all the other ladies and gentlemen stayed put. When we left the church after the service, all the gentlemen greeted Eeva with a bow, and five or six of the ladies acknowledged her with a nod; two or three even pressed her hand, in passing, and asked with a smile how young Georg was doing at Tsarskoye . . . No, these days people avoid us mainly because of Timo. Only during the first months, and only at private gatherings, their curiosity was greater than their fear—their fear of compromising themselves by associating with Timotheus von Bock, and their curiosity about whether he was truly mad.

As far as people beyond our immediate circle are concerned, I have noticed that the issue of his madness or sanity does not matter to them at all. They got used to the fact of his nine years' imprisonment a long time ago, and now they are getting used to the fact that he was released, nine months ago. Their thinking goes like this: obviously, that man wrote something ill-considered to the Czar, and it must have been quite a rowdy missive, in keeping with the notorious, fiery temper that he never could keep in check despite his education and generally punctilious demeanor. Just think who he decided to marry. Of course he wasn't *completely mad* at that time, but *as the years have gone by*, his madness has become real, sadly enough. Otherwise, the imperial authorities wouldn't have declared him mad a second time, even if he may not have been mad the first time around . . . No, no, if that's what has been decided at the highest levels, then it must of course be so . . .

Thus, there are very few who doubt his madness, and even fewer who are curious enough to travel to some godforsaken village to gape and poke at the criminal who has been sentenced to pine away there. Thank God for small mercies!

Eeva received the goateed Baron Lilienfeldt and his wife and son in a manner as friendly as Timo's, though more reserved. The Lilienfeldts made themselves at home and spent one night in the main building, the other under our roof. During their visit, even Monsieur La Trobe set foot in The Foundation for the first time in a long while and brought his Alwine to dinner with us. Even though I had heard him say that he didn't much care for Beethoven ("Well, he's powerful, but too crude most of the time"), after dinner he played us Beethoven's "Proximity of the Beloved"—*in memory*, he said, *of a great lover*. Over coffee, he told us, on good authority, no doubt, that Beethoven had set Goethe's words to this song on the occasion of his hopeless, though reciprocated, love for the same Josephine von Brunswick who later, in Estonia, became the mistress of Vääna Estate, Josephine von Stackelberg, a close relative of Madame La Trobe. Whereupon Timo said that great lovers were also the greatest rebels, and that he wanted to play some Beethoven for us in honor of a great rebel. And he played. Something stern and solemn, and I didn't care for it much. But when Timo later left the room, I heard Baron Lilienfeldt ask Madame La Trobe for the name of the piece Timo had played, and Monsieur La Trobe replied:

"But that was the *Missa Solemnis!*"

"And *how* was his performance of it, in your opinion?" asked Lilienfeldt.

"Magnificent!" Monsieur La Trobe whispered. "I can't imagine where he ever found the time to learn it so well!"

"Meaning . . . ?" Lilienfeldt leaned closer to Monsieur La Trobe, and I couldn't quite figure out what he wanted to ask, but La Trobe seemed to understand the question immediately:

"I mean that we should thank God for the fact that his musical talents were not—the quality upon which his release depended . . ."

A day later, in the morning, the Lilienfeldts left, and since then we have had no further visitors this year. Matters relating to the estate are taken care of in the main building with La Trobe, or in the steward's house, in old Timm's office. Not even Dr. Robst has set foot in The Foundation for many a week. He comes only when Eeva summons him to attend to Timo's headaches or sudden sweats. Otherwise, we hear only the sounds of the estate from afar, from beyond the snow-covered wild rose hedge and the stone wall of the orchard, and in the mornings we can see deer tracks in the snow under our windows.

Thursday, the twenty-second of February, 1828

Yesterday morning, Eeva set out for Tartu, in bitterly cold weather. To obtain some books for Timo, and to gather some news of the outside world. She asked me to remain here, as she was uneasy about the state of Timo's health.

Eeva said, "He is more nervous than usual lately."

I stayed at home. And I remembered: exactly six years ago, on

the twenty-second of February, a windy and snowy evening, Dean
Masing's servant suddenly appeared at Voisiku with a letter for
Eeva.

I happened to be on leave from Major Tenner's surveying detail
and Eeva ran upstairs to show me the letter. It was written in
French, in a hasty scrawl. Naturally, I don't remember it verbatim,
but its general drift was as follows:

Dear Madame,
Regrettably, I have not been fortunate enough to make
your acquaintance personally, but have heard an infinite
number of infinitely good things about you. And I believe that my name will inspire confidence in you. I shall
arrive in Tartu today, for a visit of four or five days. If
this does not cause insurmountable difficulties for you, it
would make me very happy if you could take the trouble to journey here and permit me to make your acquaintance and *converse with you*. I shall be staying in
Professor Moier's house, which you have visited before.

With my deepest respect,
yours,
W. Joukoffsky

We knew, of course, that Zhukovski was an old friend of Timo's,
although I didn't understand, and don't to this day, what Timo
and this poet could have in common. The one, an officer, integrity
personified in practically an ancient Roman manner; the other,
hailed in Tartu as "Russia's Ossian" . . . In any case, it was clear
to us that Monsieur Joukoffsky hadn't sent this note in order to
court Eeva.

She said, "He must have some news of Timo."

We drove sixty-eight versts through untrodden snow that day,
and at eight in the evening we arrived in that low-ceilinged building on Karlova Road, where, in the guest parlor with its snow-
covered windows, four years ago, in the midst of a large social
gathering, I had listened to Timo's strange remarks on Praxiteles
and Eeva and Jesus Christ, whose face was ground in the mud

every day in Livonia . . . This time there was no punch, no cigar smoke, no debate; but there was a gathering—Mrs. Moier introduced us to a dozen ladies and gentlemen, all seated in green armchairs and looking quite expectant. I remember meeting Professor Voyeikov, Mrs. Moier's angular brother-in-law, formerly of Tartu, and at that time at the University of St. Petersburg; I had been told (I can't remember by whom) that he wrote elegant love poems to his wife while alternately neglecting and terrorizing his family. Also present was the morose, dark-haired giant Weyhrauch, a former postal official turned songwriter, whose sentimental lyrics and lilting refrains were especially popular with the youth of Tartu. The rest were gentlemen from the university and their spouses. Mrs. Moier announced that she was so pleased to receive us in her home on this festive occasion—a reading by the poet Zhukovski, for his friends, from a unique and particularly important work: the poet's recent translation into Russian of Schiller's *Maid of Orléans*.

When Mrs. Moier brought the poet down from upstairs, it became apparent to Eeva and me that we were the only ones who had not met him before and had to be introduced. Zhukovski was a tall, very elegantly attired gentleman; his pale and exceedingly smooth forehead and bony face were framed by a shock of dark hair, lively eyebrows, and carefully trimmed side-whiskers. The expression in his large, ever so slightly Asiatic eyes alternated, in a startling fashion, between bright attentiveness and dim indifference. He took both of Eeva's hands in his own and gave her a long and unmistakably attentive look:

"*Madame . . . the wife of my dear unfortunate friend* . . . Please forgive me, I didn't expect you to arrive so soon—and tonight, I promised our friends—and I am certain that everyone in this house is *your* friend, as well—I promised to read something to them— as you have heard. And so, I beg you to honor me by joining my listeners. And *afterwards*"—he lowered his voice, spontaneously, it seemed, but not enough to keep the company from hearing what he said—"I would like to have a little talk with you . . ."

And so we became part of his audience that evening. I had, of course, read Schiller's *Maid of Orléans* in German. It was one of the first poetic works old Masing had given us to read and memorize, passage by passage. It was quite odd to hear it in *Russian*, especially since my command of Russian is rather weak. The Russian spoken among Tenner's surveyors had always been leavened with German, and I mostly used Russian only to address the soldiers handling our horses and doing the spadework. In spite of my later reading of Karamzin and Derzhavin, my knowledge of the language has remained far from perfect; but listening to the excerpts Zhukovski read, I understood that his translation was truly impressive. Some passages have remained in my memory for yet another reason: the poet surprised us by addressing his commentaries on it to us, or rather, to Eeva. Thus, when Dunois, in the second scene of the first act, relates to the King his father's conquests of both castles and beautiful ladies, and says, in Zhukovski's version,

В старых книгах
Случилосъ мне читатъ, что неразлучны
Любовъ и рьщарская доблестъ были . . .

—Zhukovski raised his eyes from his manuscript, looked straight at Eeva, and said:

"But as far as the translator of these lines is concerned—*I* haven't needed old books to become convinced of this. I have been fortunate enough to see how love and chivalrous virtues can go together in real life. Among my own friends. Yes, indeed, my dear lady . . ."

However, he did not proceed beyond this—not even among old friends—to elaborate his reference to the dear lady's husband, the criminal against the state. He was, after all, a courtier and a man of the world . . .

And when he read the passage in which—

I just went to our library and brought back the Russian-language edition of *The Maid of Orléans*. According to the inscription, Zhukovski sent it to Timo and Eeva the autumn before last, from Stuttgart. I reread the lines I wanted to recall. It is the scene in which the Maid turns to the Duke of Burgundy, act two, scene ten. In it, Joan speaks of herself:

Когда же то, что я сказала, свято ——
Кто мог внущитъ его мне кроме неба?
Кто мог сойти ко мне в мою долину,
Чтобы дуще неопытной открытъ
Великую властителей науку?
Я пред лицом монархов не бывала,
Язык мой чужд искусству слов . . . Но что же?
Теперъ тебя должна я убедитъ ——
И ум мой светел, зрю дела земные . . .

Again, Zhukovski looked at Eeva. He said:

"Dear madam—I remember that when I was translating these lines, shortly before Christmas, *you* appeared before my mind's eye with such remarkable vividness. Even though I have never seen you before tonight. But I have heard such wondrous things about your fight for your husband's cause. About your visits to people in our government, to Maria Feodorovna. And, poring over these lines, I thought: Every word the Maid of Orléans says here about herself, Mrs. Bock could also say of herself."

After the reading we took tea with the assembled company. I listened to the praise with which the ladies and gentlemen showered Zhukovski for his work; I also studied the poet and the Protassov sisters—whose surnames were now Voyeikov and Moier. I had heard that Zhukovski had been in love with the latter for most of his life, but was prevented by fate from ever expressing this love to her—the fateful and only recently revealed reason being that the mother of these two daughters of the Protassov estate, which adjoined his own childhood home, was his own half-sister . . . Zhukovski did, indeed, come from a rather extraordinary family. Even before meeting him in Tartu, I had heard that his father had been a Bunin, a landowner from Tula District, but his true mother had been a Turkish woman who had converted to Christianity . . . I remember listening to Mrs. Voyeikova's calm and wise remarks; watching Mrs. Moier's marvelously quiet presence, which reminded me of a fairy godmother; watching Vassili Andreyevich Zhukovski imbibe his tea between the two of them with a smile tinged with melancholy; looking at the husbands of those women, the noisy Russian bohemian Voyeikov, the jolly

Dutch-Baltic pedant Moier, and pondering, a little irritably perhaps, whether Eeva or I needed to feel concerned about *their* rather
peculiar tangle of problems, in addition to our own—immeas-
urably more serious, more meaningful, located on the watershed
between life and death—

After tea we returned to the parlor overlooking the river, and
the guests soon took their leave. Our hosts retired, and Eeva and
I remained alone with Zhukovski. Eeva asked Zhukovski to allow
me to attend their conversation, and after a moment's hesitation,
he agreed. He sat down next to Eeva, on a sofa upholstered in
green silk, and began:

"Madame, I don't think I need to tell you, and your brother,
that Timofey Yegorovich was . . . *is* . . . one of the people closest
to my heart. You see, I believe that each and every one of us is
—to a large extent—a product of his personal fate. And my fate
has molded me in such a way"—he seemed to be looking for the
right words, and I noticed that he was absentmindedly stroking
the back rest of the sofa on which Mrs. Moier had sat listening
to *The Maid of Orléans*—"in such a way that . . . *friendship* has
gained a—a very great significance for me, in the realm of human
emotions . . . And I must tell you—not in order to justify my
distancing myself from him in the present situation, but to let you
know the truth: I am not a supporter of Timofey Yegorovich's
ideas. As far as I know them, he was—no, he *is* a *revolutionary*. I
do not believe that well-defined and existing values should be
endangered in favor of uncertain future ones, certainly not by those
who have strayed a long way from God's truth. Well, he, of
course, was surprisingly *close* to God's truth in his ideas. And on
that level, we became friends. But what astounded me most was
how systematic he is in his thinking. And what I respect most of
all in him is his *absolute sense of honor*. Because of all of this, dear
madam, I have tried to do everything on his behalf that seemed
at all possible. I have even taken up his case with the emperor.
But I have to admit that I have achieved nothing. Talking about
him to the emperor, I ran into a frightening wall of ice, and I
understood that there must have been some horrible misunderstanding—Timo was, after all, one of the men closest to the emperor . . . Then it occurred to me that Timo himself had told me:

'My wife, my dear Kitty, supports me and shares all my opinions.' And I decided to seek you out, thinking that you might be able to explain things to me. Well, here we are, and I would like to ask you: Dear madam, what *was* the article that Timo sent to the emperor—*if indeed* he sent him anything at all? Or, then, what do you think is the cause of the emperor's special displeasure with him? You must understand: without knowing that, without even the *faintest idea* of that, I can no longer do anything for him . . . Which is not to say that I would succeed even if I gained full knowledge of the case—but is there any way in which you could help me, and him and yourself at the same time?"

Now that I know the contents of Timo's fiery papers, and am quite certain that Eeva, too, was familiar with them from the very beginning, Eeva's response at that time strikes me as much more interesting than it did at the time, in the Moiers' parlor. With an expression of melancholic regret, Eeva shook her head and said in a calm and clear voice:

"Dear sir, I thank you with all my heart for everything you have tried to do for Timo—but I cannot help you at all. Not you, nor Timo, nor myself."

"So you do not know anything about what he wrote to the emperor?"

"Regretfully, I don't."

"He didn't leave you with any clues at all? Not even when he was arrested? Not even a hint?"

"Well, he did say one thing—"

"What was that?"

"When I asked him to whom I should turn for mercy in his case, he told me: 'No use to appeal for it from anyone but the emperor. But I beg you: do not plead with him!' "

"Dear God!" Zhukovski exclaimed. "Then it appears that I have to beg forgiveness for having spoken on his behalf . . ."

"But you did that only out of the kindness of your own heart. No need to apologize for it," Eeva said. "And besides, he only told *me* not to address myself to the emperor. I can't be sure that he meant that *no one* should. Although it seems to me that he did . . ."

"But *why* did he say that?"

"I don't know."

(I know now, with almost complete certainty, that Eeva *did* know; and although she did not mistrust Zhukovski, she chose to give him a less than candid answer. By this time, she was far removed both from Timo's personal charm and from the persuasiveness of his mad logic, and all the blows directed at Timo must have cleared her head.)

"No, I don't know," Eeva said, "I can only guess. There are two possible reasons. Either he felt that an appeal to the emperor's clemency would be morally indefensible—"

"Morally indefensible?" Zhukovski's exclamation bespoke complete incomprehension.

"Or else he regarded it as simply futile."

"But *why?*"

"Perhaps because of the letter . . ."

"But you don't even know for certain that he wrote a letter?"

"No . . . I don't."

"And if he did, you have no inkling of what he said in it?"

"I don't."

"In that case, only God can help us—there really is nothing we can do."

February twenty-third, 1828

That was, of course, quite true. What could they have done for a man who, in his reckless memorandum, voiced opinions such as these—

(Eeva is not here. Timo has gone riding. I have locked the door and for the first time in a while taken out his papers and put them on my desk . . .) Yes, indeed, what could Eeva or even Zhukovski or anyone else have done to placate the Czar, after black-on-white statements such as these:

As far as His Majesty's ability to command respect is concerned, his latest visit to Riga provides a telling example. The Emperor arrived, heaped opprobrium on the Governor for the discomforts of his journey, spent the night in the Castle, put an entire division through its paces in the morning, issued an order of the day that made him the laughingstock of all of Europe, babbling equal amounts of nonsense to deserving men, highwaymen, idiots, and educated people alike, dined and opined over his steak that the new taxation system was quite senseless, took tea, exerted himself on the dance floor, got back into the carriage provided by his imbecilic quartermaster, killed a dozen post-horses, and wrote to Marquis Paulucci that he had found Livonia to be in excellent shape.

Those poor horses!

Or, further on:

. . . enquire in all the governments in Russia about how much the yeomen of the Crown have to sacrifice—in addition to their taxes—to the greed of bureaucrats! And see if fear and rage do not overwhelm you when you take a look at the state of those localities in which His Majesty has deigned to establish garrisons!

Oh, if only our Emperor, like the Egyptian pharaohs of yore, would have to answer to a tribunal for the dead, at which every maltreated subject had the right to voice his complaint before it was decided to provide a burial place for the sovereign—what would the decision be in your case, Alexander?

When I see you, Alexander, among all your sycophants and pimps, lording it over those whose misfortune you are, in front of the colonnade that must remind you of duties neglected, when I see you step onto your own balcony there in front of the church, while the drums roll—then it seems to me that I stand beside you like a threatening shadow, and I hear the thunderous voice of the Son of God:

"What art thou doing, poor wretch? Do not attempt to cover up thy crimes with hypocrisy. Behold these nauseous apparitions: all three of them were once crowned heads. This one, here, is Justinian, a coward and lecher who owed his whole empire and glory to Belisarius, the noblest of them all—and thanked him by putting out his eyes! This is Philip II of Spain, the thankless, who coveted the crown of his venerable father, poisoned his brother, the heroic

Don Juan, and killed his own son and wife, since all his treachery could not separate them from each other. Thousands and again thousands of his victims perished under the axe blades of his henchmen. And here we have Louis XIV, a slave of his own frivolity, who killed entire nations and robbed bare the most prosperous countries. He let his own brother, who had not done him the least harm, languish in a dungeon. He scattered the wealth of his people to the winds. He enslaved the nobility and was a bloodthirsty barbarian who disguised himself as a Christian. And thou hast seen their consequences!

"All three of these built temples for me and proclaimed my divinity in all directions, day and night. Do not follow their example, because they were like whited sepulchres, handsome to behold from the outside, but filled with abomination and decay.

"Do not act like the hypocrites who pray at streetcorners and blow their horn when they give alms, but rather be like unto the little children, for theirs is the Kingdom of Heaven . . ."

Hellfire and tarnation, I still find it impossible to read this calmly, or to stay calm while copying it into my journal . . . What a strange preacher, yet his sermons are more impressive than those of most clergymen. His vision of transformation into the Son of God is even stranger—is, in fact, rather ridiculous, but also shocking . . . His appeal to the emperor is childish to the point of lunacy—but in it he accomplishes what he is urging the emperor to do: to be like unto the little children . . . A fool, he brings tears to my eyes, and greatly arouses my curiosity.

February the twenty-third, late at night

Short of any better ideas, I resorted to the tried and true. I returned the papers to their hiding place, went down to the cellar, and lit a fire under the sauna stove.

Around one o'clock in the afternoon, Timo returned from his

ride. To avoid frostbite, he had had to rub his cheeks with snow. I told him that the sauna was ready, and after a moment's consideration, he joined me there.

We exchanged a few words (I don't remember about what) while taking off our clothes. Once we had taken our seats on the sauna bench, I wanted to start a conversation and pondered whether my approach should be direct or indirect—neither felt quite right to me. Indirection struck me as tainted with subterfuge—perhaps because of the recommendation I had just read: be like unto the little children . . . But the thought of a direct approach also had a strangely paralyzing effect on my tongue.

We sat on the burning hot aspen boards of the sauna, in the bluish light that seeped in through the tiny, partly snow-covered cellar window, and the longer the silence between us stretched, the harder it seemed to break. Timo sat facing me, his elbows on his knees, his temples between his knuckles, his chin nestled in the steel-gray hairs of his chest. Drops of sweat rolled down his sallow face, which was gradually turning pink in the heat, and fell, audibly, onto the bench: drip, drip, drip, drip. I thought: By the nineteenth drop, something must happen, or else. After the seventeenth drop, Timo, still looking down at the floor, said:

"Last time, you asked me what really happened to my memory, there in Schlüsselburg . . ."

(I am trying to record what he told me in the sauna as accurately as possible, as if he himself had been taking notes, so as not to intrude between him and his tale. I don't expect any physician of the mentally deranged to ever read these lines, but you never know . . .)

". . . I already told you . . . about the nervousness and insomnia that began to plague me. And about those, what should I call them, torrents of arguments and counterarguments that overwhelmed me and inflamed my brain with sleeplessness in the evenings . . . At first, they didn't bother me that much. I remembered that I had experienced something similar before, between military engagements in Bessarabia and Prussia and outside of Paris, when I had argued about the following day's plans of action at staff meetings and continued those arguments by myself later at night. But in the summer of '20, those bouts grew strenuous. As you may understand, the plans I was arguing about in my head didn't concern just any battle but always had to do with the main question

—so I was mostly arguing with the emperor himself. I quoted not only him, but also wise thinkers, the Prophets, the Gospels— partly to keep my memory active, as an act of my free will, but often, and with increasing frequency, in moments of a veritable deluge of thought, *against* my own will . . . In incredible torrents, and with a strange clarity, structures of thought I had learned from Lehrberg, from university lectures, from books, tumbled into my mind, until, all of a sudden, there were so many of them that I be- came frightened . . . Just imagine—argument upon argument, growing more dense, assuming a shape, as in geometry . . . Syllo- gisms become stairs . . . Theses rise like polished stone pillars, and from between them, Plato and Aristotle descend the stairs and start shouting at Schlegel and Kant . . . Their edifices of thought begin to merge and mirror each other . . . Suddenly, there is such an insane abundance of images and concepts that I feel like a drowning man in a raging torrent—raging in my head—and giving me a raging headache . . . Puns like that, you see, also come tumbling along, every moment—and I am madly trying to catch hold of some con- scious thought, in order to escape from the torrent . . . And then— in the autumn of '20, late at night, when these attacks had become very strong and I was often afraid of losing my mind—I suddenly felt that I had been able to latch onto something, by the grace of God, and I clung to it and tried to discover *what it was*—and then I noticed that it was this banging on the door and the shout: 'Silence! Silence! Silence, prisoner!'

"It took me a while to understand, and I was truly appalled when I did, that I had spoken everything that rushed through my mind *out loud* . . . Then it happened again . . . The first time, they didn't lay hands on me to shut me up, but later they became more severe, and when I came to, I found myself strapped in a strait- jacket. They had thrown cold water on me, my shirt was soaked, and my skin was black and blue. I was told that I had hurt myself by throwing myself on the floor and against the latrine . . . Well, I doubt that . . . And so forth . . ."

Here, it seemed to me that Timo was trying to bypass the loss of his teeth, and I interjected:

"Was that when you lost your teeth? While they were trying to subdue you?"

"Yes—" Timo said, and I thought I noticed a shudder run

through him. "Though I don't remember those times all that well
. . . The more rabid my arguments with the emperor became, the
harder they tried to subdue me. And there were times, apparently,
when my fury was, well, quite beyond the bounds of sanity . . .
Plutalov told me that I had smashed the stool to pieces against the
wall, that I had tried to batter down the door of my casemate.
And the louder I was, the more severely they dealt with me. The
other prisoners, as well as the guards, had to be kept from hearing
my rants against the Czar . . . Clearly, they didn't stop at much
to make me shut up. Plutalov may have told them to avoid unnecessary violence . . . But it was I, myself, who called forth their
violence—loudly applying Beccaria's standards to the emperor,
and declaring that he was a murderer. As soon as my head cleared
again, I understood how it had all come about, and, as you may
imagine, I was immediately gripped by a terrible fear of the next
attack . . . Because I was completely defenseless, during those
attacks—not only in a bodily sense, but also in terms of my
soul—completely naked—and in *such a place* . . . Well, I tried to
tell myself that it wouldn't happen again, but that didn't work at
all, it had rather the opposite effect—it made my fear stronger, so
that it sucked me into my own destruction . . . Then I tried to
make a rule for myself: because of them, I had to conduct my
thinking in foreign tongues. I remember training myself to think
in English and Polish and Latin and Estonian, and I did, to some
extent, succeed in using those languages even when I was in the
clutches of my, well, madness. And to a degree this saved me
from the rage of the officers of the guard. It only annoyed them
insofar as anyone speaking a foreign language annoys any Russian
noncommissioned officer. But in a foreign language, it was merely
a matter of *laesio optionis*, no longer *laesio majestatis*, you see. Because the content of my speech was no longer within their grasp.
At first. But I must not have been completely successful in avoid-
ing Russian and German. Besides, they found some guards who
understood foreign languages . . . So that, on one occasion, in the
autumn of '22—in any event, it was after the Czar's visit to the
casemate, and while Plutalov was on leave . . . On the shift of a
certain sergeant of the guard . . . of course I don't know his
name—we didn't exchange cards back there . . . I seem to re-

member that they did it on two separate occasions . . . The first
time was when I tried to break through the wall—all the while
holding forth, of course . . . And the second time was when I had
managed to make my way into the guards' room and started to
explain something to them . . . I remember that some of them
held my arms and legs down, and one of them smashed . . . About
eight of my teeth, that first time. The second time, a week later,
they no longer showed the least hesitation but were truly furious,
that's when I lost the rest . . . Everything but my molars. I think
they were using the key to the Secret House, a heavy chunk of
iron, about a foot long . . . I really didn't feel any *pain* when it
happened. Only later, when I got a fever and my mouth was one
big wound and I spent a long time lying on the floor, unable to
take nourishment . . . When Plutalov returned from his leave, I
sent for him. Of course he couldn't give me a new set of teeth,
but I wanted him to know of *what kind* of establishment he was
in charge . . . Of course it was childish. It wasn't news to him,
any more than it is news to any of them . . . My face had begun
to heal. He looked at me. I said: 'Greetings, General, sir . . .' and
smiled at him, parting my lips. He looked at my mouth for a
second, then looked away. As we all do, at times like that. We
look away. When things are only *too* clear. Then he told me he'd
been informed that I had, in the throes of my attacks of rage,
ground my teeth so hard that I had managed to break them . . .
He said that this was, undoubtedly, the best explanation. As we
always say in such situations: Isn't that the truth . . . ? And there
the matter rested. There it rests, thank God. Because it is the least
of my problems . . . Well, let's use these whisks, shall we?"

We did, and after hearing his tale, I did not muster the courage
to ask him any further questions. Hence, I did not find out what
other problems he meant.

Saturday, the twenty-fourth of February, 1828

But I found out soon enough. After a few casual words over
this morning's coffee (Timo rarely says more than that, these days,
while Käsper and Liiso are within earshot), he invited me to his

study. He closed a desk drawer that appeared full of manuscripts, pushed a meerschaum pipe over to my side of the desk, and lit his own. Then he said, without any preliminaries:

"You want to know my great problem? It is that Kitty thinks I am sane."

Not disingenuously, though still aware of what he had told me yesterday, I said, "But you *are* sane."

He blew a dense cloud of blue smoke into the air, then spoke into it, looking down at the bumpy oak floor:

"Just try coming down with the pox sometime, and have people hear about it. No matter how well you medicate and heal yourself, it won't improve your reputation. Sulphur and mercury won't do anything for your reputation. Well, that's the first point I wanted to make. Secondly"—his voice dropped very low—"I am the best judge of the state of my health."

"Well, then—what is the state of your health?"

Puffing smoke, he said, "You don't know—nobody does—what an effort it is for me. To be *normal*. To be calm. To be quiet. To drown those torrents of thoughts with sleeping draughts. So far, I have managed, more or less. For Kitty's sake. She believes that I am sane. At least *now*. And if there are times when I—well, let's just say when I deviate from that—she thinks it's playacting. Doing something I have to do, so they won't take me back there . . ."

"And there are times when you are, indeed, playacting . . ."

"Such as?"

"Well, the time when you pretended that that slippery Laming was Alexander . . ."

For a fleeting moment, Timo looked as if he was about to smile, but then he said, in dead earnest:

"Well, that's a damnably two-faced business . . . In the case of someone who is in my employ and then insinuates himself into my own house to spy on me—never mind it's on an emperor's —or three emperors'—orders, I feel released from all normal moral obligations . . . In my case, I can't free myself from—from the notion that it would be best to just perceive everything while understanding nothing—to just walk through it all, you know— *like a child* . . . Yes, well, I did hoodwink Laming a bit . . . Out of vanity. Because it was so easy to do! And because Kitty expected something like that from me. From the husband she considers sane, but who—in self-defense—can act the madman so convincingly . . . And here we are, back at my problem. It was, of course, Kitty who restored my so-called *sanity*. When, at last, they allowed her to see me at Petropavlovsk . . . Her arrival, her existence were the things that brought me back to the surface. I remember how the commandant, General Sukin, and that doctor, what was his name—Elkan—brought me out of the cell into some room into which the sun was shining, at the end of February—God, just a year ago—and there, in the sunlight . . . As weak as I was, I was still suspicious, ready for whatever tricks they wanted to play on me . . . That woman—the light was so dazzling that I couldn't look at her straight—that woman, it seemed to me, looked just like Kitty ought to look, except for her black hair . . . I hadn't seen Kitty for nine years, and this certainly wasn't the slip of a girl who had stood waving farewell on the steps of Voisiku . . . I thought: How like the powers that be, to attempt to trap me by means of a double . . .

"Sukin asked me, 'Well, don't you recognize your own wife?'

"And I said, 'With your permission, let me take a look . . .' And I took out of my pocket the blue beadwork pouch Kitty had made and pulled out the medallion with her miniature portrait. I don't know who painted it, but she had made the pouch and sent it to me in '20. It had taken five months for it to get into my hands. The gilded edge of the medallion had been forced open, they had made sure there was no letter behind the painting. So I took the portrait, and I looked at it, and I looked at *her* . . . and it seemed to me that I was rising up from the bottom of the sea, that all things were regaining their firm outlines, and all voices sounded clear. I went over to Kitty and put my arms around her. And she asked me, in a whisper—they had already been telling her all sorts of things—she asked me: '*My love, how are you?*'

"As I inhaled her scent—you have no idea how powerful the odors of the past and the future can be in the air of prison—I guessed at her struggle on my behalf, all nine years of it, and sensed the reality of *our son* . . . During those years, she had written me forty letters, and I had received two of them, and from those

I knew that we had a son . . . You know, at that moment I really *believed* I was well again. And I told her, in a whisper, and with a wink of complicity: '*I'm fine, quite recovered . . .*'

"Jakob—that was a year ago. And ever since, I haven't had the courage to tell her the truth. What's more, there have been times I really believed in my recovery. I have been aware of my responsibilities as a father, and I have gained an understanding of what Kitty's life has been like. I haven't had the *heart . . .* and . . . I've also been ashamed . . . I have told her that there had been times when my nerves went out of kilter, but that it was something that happened to anyone condemned to solitary confinement. This corresponded with her own intuition—that I had *acted* the madman in order to gain my freedom, that the physicians had looked the other way—and that Nicholas, too, had looked the other way, just to get rid of Alexander's stinking legacy . . . And that I'm keeping up that pretense just enough to remain safe. It goes without saying that Kitty wants me to be well, wishes for that with all her heart! But if it all turns out to be a cruel lie—Jakob, I want you to help me."

"How?"

"I want you to tell her, gradually . . ."

"To tell her what?"

"That I am not as sane as she believes. That I may be ill, after all. And when she has been prepared for it, I'll pull myself together and tell her the truth."

"What is that truth?"

"Well . . . that my recovery has been superficial . . . *That she is, in spite of everything, the wife of a madman.*"

Only now I noticed that I had left my chair and had been pacing back and forth between the stacks of books in the study; and that I did not know what to tell him. Finally, I said that this was a very important question, one that deserved a considered answer, and that I wanted time to think it over until the next day.

So—should I support him in his madness or in his sanity? Or should I just tell him: Leave me alone, deal with your problems as best you can!

I have been pondering this all day.

The latter alternative (well, put yourself in my position) would, of course, be the simplest. But I'm afraid it is impossible. Regrettably enough, their problems are to a very great extent my own . . . So, back to the first question: Should I support him in his madness or in his sanity?

That would seem to depend on whether he *is*, in fact, mad or sane. I can't tell—I don't even know what I *judge* him to be. Is it possible to recover from such a state, under such circumstances? I believe (while being aware of my deep ignorance, I still have to voice an opinion)—I believe that such a recovery may well be rare but not impossible.

Sunday, February twenty-fifth
three o'clock in the morning

I took his manuscript out again, put it next to my journal, and kept reading it until now, asking myself twice after every sentence: Was Czar Alexander right when he claimed that signs of madness were evident even then? I arrived at a strange conclusion: the conviction that everything Timo wrote was nothing but the truth, as it was known to many, if not to all. The only thing incorrect was what he did with it. Addressing it to the Czar had to be considered a crime—as were the actions of the Decembrists, three years ago. But it was not the act of a madman. As far as I know, no one accused the Decembrists of mental derangement: it is easy to declare one man a lunatic, but not hundreds.

In any case, now I know what I shall tell him later this morning.

Sunday, February twenty-fifth, in the evening

I did not have a chance to speak to Timo in private this morning. Eeva returned just before breakfast. She had reached Poltsamaa last night, but the snow-covered road had persuaded her to stay the night with the Wahls. Now she sat at the breakfast table, refreshed from (and by) her travels, pouring coffee for Timo and telling us the news from Tartu and the world. On the fourth, vacant, chair at our round table lay the stack of books she had brought back. I leafed through one of them (a slim volume, published last year in Hamburg, of some quirky, sentimental little poems, titled *Buch der Lieder*—suddenly I can't remember the author's name) while Eeva told us about Tartu. Mrs. Voyeikova had been taken ill, according to the doctors the malady was in her lungs, and she intended to travel to Switzerland or Italy for a cure in the spring. The doctors expected her to make a full recovery. Eeva added, to Timo: "You see how everybody is heading that way, to improve their health . . . ?" But Professor Moier (I thought of his bald pate, shiny as a pink bird's egg in a nest of reddish hair) had told her, sounding both amused and exasperated, that a certain Doctor von Baer, a former student of Moier's at Tartu and now a junior professor at Königsberg, had advanced the claim that human beings were descended from birds—basing the claim on his discovery of a human egg . . . To which I said, well, why not, maybe we *are*—and perhaps not only from birds, but from *nobility* as well—and I read them some verses I had chanced upon in that little book:

> Jetzo, da ich ausgewachsen,
> Viel gelesen, viel gereist,
> Schwillt mein Herz, und ganz von Herzen
> Glaub' ich an den Heil'gen Geist.
>
> Dieser tat die grössten Wunder,
> Und viel grössre tut er noch;
> Er zerbrach die Zwingherrnburgen,
> Und zerbrach des Knechtes Joch.
>
> Alte Todeswunden heilt er
> Und erneut das alte Recht:
> Alle Menschen, gleichgeboren,
> Sind ein adliches Geschlecht . . .

Eeva's return, her tales of the city, and finally these fine and daring verses put Timo, and I think all of us, in a curiously good mood. But I was still determined to give Timo his answer, and when we rose from the table, I said:

"Timo, would you like to help me shovel some snow?"

I didn't have to ask him twice—I had seen him before, attacking the drifts around the house. He kissed Eeva on the forehead and sent her off to the drawing room with the books. We put on our coats and in a couple of minutes were on our way out the front door of The Foundation, to wield our broad shovels and clear a path up to the orchard gate, to make the snow fly . . . When I had worked up a sweat and somehow managed to get a load of snow into one of my mittens, I leaned against the stone pillar of the orchard gate, shook the snow out of the mitten, and said:

"Timo, could you come over here . . . ?"

Timo came over, leaned on his shovel: "Well?"

I told him all the conclusions I had reached, in detail and with complete candor, because I believed that to be the only way I could convince him.

"Timo, there are two possibilities. Either you are ill, or you are well but afraid that you're still affected by your malady. I do not know which of the two is the case, and you don't know it either. That is the way things are with these conditions. One can only make assumptions. But if you assume that you are, after all, well and sane, that blesses you with obligations. Do you see? It obliges you to protect Eeva, and Jüri, and yourself. And Eeva's quandary is a mirror image of your own. The assumption that you are ill is bound to paralyze both of you. And so, my advice to you is: trust your sanity! Only in the case that you were profoundly ill, and refused any help from the medical profession, could that decision be harmful. There is no reason for you to avoid the physicians, they can reinforce your trust in your sanity. Dr. Faehlmann, for instance. I have talked to him. He considers you sane. And in every other respect, a belief in sanity is preferable, even if it should be the case that you are ill. Do you see—it's like Kant's argument for the existence of God—remember, in those notebooks of Lehrberg's? So, this is what I suggest: if you are well—let us work together to keep you that way. If you aren't—let us deceive the world, and ourselves, in hopes of improvement."

I had said my piece. I stopped, waited for my breathing to slow down. I heard the sparrows twitter in the snowy hedge and smelled the invigorating odor of horse manure and straw wafting across the snow-covered yard from the arched open doors of the stables;

and the morning coffee, and the exertion of shoveling, and those lines—"All men are created equal / In a single noble race"—made me tingle all over. I'm sure Timo was tingling, too. He said, quietly (and there was no need to say it any louder):

"All right, then. If it should ever seem to me that I can't go on, I'll let you know."

March sixteenth, 1828

I think I have already mentioned the Roika mirrorworks, also called "Katharina's Works" in these parts. It operates on Voisiku land, although at a distance of twenty versts from the manor, and is a rare enterprise. There are only a few of their kind in the Baltic provinces, and none too many in the whole empire.

These mirrorworks were first conceived by Major Lauw of Poltsamaa, a fellow considered half-mad who clearly must have been a man of singular talents. Some sixty years ago, as Hupel relates in his well-known *Chronicle*, he created a big stir in the district by starting up all kinds of unheard-of enterprises—copper smithies, porcelain factories, glassworks, apothecary's shops, print shops, and even newspapers in the people's tongue.

The mirrorworks' true beginnings at Voisiku, however, occurred at a slightly later date, after the notorious major had gone bankrupt and passed away. Eight years after his death, his idea was revived by another equally eccentric aristocrat who had heard about the plan from the locals: old Baron von Bock, Timo's father. With his father-in-law, Magistrate von Rautenfeldt of Riga, and the merchant Amelung the Elder from St. Petersburg, he had, at about the time when the French were topping their king, built the mirrorworks by Poltsamaa River, twenty versts from the manor. They had been named Katharina's Works in memory of von Rautenfeldt's daughter, Baron von Bock's wife, Timo's mother, who had died young. They built a grinding mill, a polishing mill, and about twenty dwellings for the local workers and for masters and mirror makers imported from Brunswick. A few versts farther away, in Meleski Forest, they built a new glassworks. The *manor* itself, by the way, has not had anything to do with these enterprises

for a long time: when Eeva and I arrived at Voisiku, even the land
they stood on no longer belonged to the estate but, in the modern
fashion, to the "Amelung Company." The old buildings still remain, next to the new two-story polishing mill, its lower story
built out of stone, the upper of stuccoed logs, under a tile roof
that is beginning to be overgrown with moss. The old polishing
mill, a wooden structure throughout, is two stories under a
thatched roof. From the ends of both buildings, large canopies
protrude over the river: their function is to shelter the waterwheels,
which are several fathoms in diameter. All summer long, the huge
wheels turn with a squelching sound; at the beginning of winter,
when the river freezes over, they are hoisted up above the ice.
The two mill buildings contain a total of ninety-six grinding and
polishing benches as well as many different kinds of stamp ham-
mers for the preparation of clay, plaster of Paris, and emery, more
than twenty all told. The inside walls of the buildings, stained red
by iron powder and gray by glass and emery dust, shine and glitter
in the sunshine of summer and the glow of the big brick furnaces
in the winter. By their grindstones, which are powered by the
waterwheels by means of a transmission shaft, stand the grinders
and polishers, plying their highly skilled trade in the midst of
clouds of red iron dust. Even the youngest of the mirror makers
are middle-aged men: from the days of Amelung the founder to
the present grandson, the works have hired only married men,
preferably with children, since such men are less prone to loiter
in the works tavern (although it, too, produces a tidy profit for
Mr. Amelung), less likely to chase after God knows what skirts,
and generally more apt to keep the peace and remain in the company's employ. To the left of the mill buildings stand the barns,
more flimsily constructed, thatched buildings containing crates of
unground glass brought from Melesk, sacks of plaster of Paris and
emery, and big clay demijohns of precious mercury. To the right,
by the edge of a stand of pines, is a row of dwellings, and there
is another row of them down by the river. These houses are of
varying types and ages; some of them have six or eight rooms
with a communal kitchen, in the manner of outbuildings for farmhands, and the ordinary laborers live in these. There are four
houses with two rooms each for the foremen, and a few more for
the masters or journeymen with three rooms and a kitchen and

even a small potato patch in the yard surrounded by a few scrawny apple trees and currant bushes.

Thus separated by rank, but also somewhat intermingled, live the locally hired laborers and bargemen of peasant stock, the German, Estonian, and Russian mirror grinders, and the polishers who hail from Brunswick or from the Livonian-German communities; the last-mentioned like to regard themselves as the elite, but in recent times they have had to admit some Estonians and Russians to their ranks.

Saturday, April the fourteenth, 1828

As I was returning home from the Roika works this morning, I saw this spring's first dandelions by the side of the bridge across Riivli Creek. On my journey, I pondered various facts about those works and other enterprises in our region.

These enterprises, owned by the likes of Lauw and von Bock and von Rautenfeldt and Amelung, have brought a great number of rather peculiar people to our remote corner of the world in the hinterland of northern Livonia. First of all, the gentlemen themselves. About Major Lauw I really don't know all that much, except that the initial success of his enterprises so went to his head that he refurbished his castle at Poltsamaa along princely standards and then proceeded to live in commensurate style until he was laid low by bankruptcy. All he left behind were enormous debts and, I've been told, an equally enormous collection of lewd French engravings. In spite of his bourgeois entrepreneurship, I imagine he was a powdered and bewigged gent of the last century. I know little more about the elder Baron von Bock, hardly anything about von Rautenfeldt the magistrate. Nevertheless, one thing strikes me: *in some respect*, these gentlemen were of a different cut from your average Livonian aristocrat—just as their enterprises differed from those of other estates. And the Amelungs, father, son, and grandson, were—and are—of an entirely new breed in these parts, the kind that harnesses people, some unskilled, some skilled, to work on machines—*and gains wealth in the process* (as the estate owners have always done, but mainly by having people till their fields), and then begins to play a part in society that until now belonged only to the aristocrats. If these people keep their wits about them, they may even supersede the old gentry.

There is an anecdote, common enough in the lore of Voisiku, that explains the means by which Amelung Senior, when he was still a young man, managed to obtain the works and machinery of Poltsamaa from old Major Lauw. Although the story was forged on the anvil of gossip, it strikes me as true enough in its general outline. It is said that Amelung found out about Lauw's shameless amorous escapades and used that knowledge to pressure the old man into selling the property to him for a song—by threatening to inform the major's wife about her husband's lechery. And since the major was entirely dependent on the dowry of his wealthy spouse . . .

Well, if I were writing a novel instead of just keeping a journal, there is no end to the intrigues I could construct out of material provided by a region no more than a league wide, and a time span of only a few generations.

In any case, the thousands of rubles these gentlemen have invested in land, buildings, and machinery, have attracted an entirely new kind of populace to the region, one that now outnumbers them by far: works managers and masters, bookkeepers and clerks, warehouse keepers, shopkeepers, artisans, and hundreds of laborers of at least three different nationalities . . . I parade them past my mind's eye: the first comers just common folk, but those that followed them, one after the other, almost identical, at least when seen in church or at their family tables on holidays, well-starched and self-important—and *in the performance of their tasks*, by their office desks and tables and grinding benches, so very very brisk and businesslike . . . And suddenly it occurred to me *where* Timo may have made the observations that led him to a startling thought I found in his memorandum. Speaking of the Russian empire, he writes as follows:

Unfortunately, we do not have a third estate. As a result of that lack, we keep sinking back into the mire, time and again, even after our greatest exertions [*here, he obviously refers to Russia's victory over Napoleon*]. But what prevents us from creating a third estate? Considering the sterling qualities of the Russian people, it should not take us more than twelve well-planned years to do so . . .

Impressions gathered here at home must have raised the question in Timo's mind—whether, in fact, under the pressure of German and Russian influence, a third estate *was not already being born* here in Livonia, out of the qualities—ill-defined so far—of the indigenous Estonian people? Being born, and perhaps already dividing again (as seems to have been the case in France) into an upper crust that rides around in carriages, enjoying its prosperity, and—down below—a populace engaged in heavy labor, sweating and coughing in the heat and glare of glass furnaces, in the dust of grinding benches, in the mercury vapors . . .

Good Lord, look at me, digressing on industrial enterprise and economics and so forth! No one will read these pages in my lifetime. No one will cart me off to a casemate for being excessively honest with myself, though such honesty may not be less rare a thing than inordinate candor toward the Czar . . . What am I really trying to avoid here? *Cherchez la femme!* Indeed, that is whence these digressions spring.

Well, no doubt I might find those houses of the Roika works settlement, the ones by the woods and by the river, interesting in themselves—but the truth of the matter is that I find them interesting because of my particular interest in one of them: the first house from the north, right by the river's edge. It has three rooms and white curtains and flower pots in the window, and in the yard, where the snow has just begun to melt, there are five or six young apple trees that promise to bear fruit this year for the first time. Anna Klaassen's house.

Thursday, April the nineteenth

The first time I noticed her was last year, not long before Christmas, during a service conducted by old Rücker at Kolga-Jaan Church. Even though I was there with Eeva and our parents, I couldn't help noticing her and the devout and receptive expression on her pale face as she sat listening to Rücker's boring drone;

and the enthusiasm with which her gaze almost took flight with the organ notes. After the service, I saw her again at the counter of the inn below the church. She opened her sheepskin coat, giving me an opportunity to notice her exceptionally large breasts under a dress made out of some fine light-brown fabric, took a purse out of a coat pocket and, with a guileless private smile, put a copper coin on the counter in payment for a bun and a bag of sweets.

The next time I saw her was three weeks later, at the house of Schwalbe, the bookkeeper at the Roika works, where I had dropped in a few times before for a cup of tea and a chat. Red-mustachioed Schwalbe, in his fifties, a half-German from somewhere near Pärnu, has practiced his profession in Riga, Courland, and St. Petersburg; he has seen the world and likes to philosophize, quite engagingly at times. According to gossip (and I find this hard to believe, considering his lowly station), he even belonged to a Freemasons' Lodge in Riga until Paulucci banned all lodges under the law concerning secret societies. His gray-haired wife seems quite a bit older than her husband, and even though she looks as if she had been designed with a ruler, she is a kind lady. I don't know which one of them distills the pleasantly bitter cherry liqueur they serve with their tea. But I did find out quite a few things about Anna that first time we talked at the Schwalbes' table—some from herself, and other things from Schwalbe, when she excused herself for a moment.

She told me that she had known who I was for quite some time. She is in her late twenties, the daughter of a cooper from Viljandi and his widow, Maali Vahteri. For seven or eight years, she was the wife of Peeter Klaassen, the assistant master at the mirror-works; in the spring of last year, her husband died after a prolonged bout with consumption. Now Anna looks after the children of the Malm family—Malm is the director of the works, and thanks to his wife's intervention, he has agreed to let her go on living in the assistant master's house for the time being.

Since this is an entirely private journal, I can be honest: I did not find Anna all that genial at first. I remember that I noticed, when she sat next to me and handed me the sugar bowl, her ash-blond hair, combed straight back from her forehead, her round, dark gray eyes, and her small pink mouth. I thought: She has a slightly mysterious smile. At the same time, there is something a bit fishlike about that little mouth . . . Her female charms seemed disproportionate to her otherwise slight body, and she was perhaps too aware of her feminine attractions . . . Yet she also appeared to regard with a kind of amused indifference those affairs of particular interest to the women (and even the ladies) of the community. Except for her wedding rings—she wore two of them, as widows do—she did not (nor does she now) wear any other jewelry. On topics of female conversation such as bustles, curlers, permanent pleats, and the like, over which even Mrs. Schwalbe sometimes waxes quite excited, she has simply nothing to say. The same applies when I and old Schwalbe discuss the observatory at Tartu, or Rosenplänter's newspaper; in fact, I can't really say *what* subject I ever heard her address, though I can easily recall her rather low, dark-timbred, and almost half-whispering voice.

In any case, I did find Anna *exciting*, from the very first moment. From that first time at the Schwalbes I remember sitting at a small mahogany table playing chess with the master of the house while the lady and Anna were setting the supper table in the next room. Then Anna came in and stood behind my back—I don't know why, she doesn't play chess, she wasn't even watching our game. Suddenly I sensed her delicate but powerful perfume of lilac blossoms in my nostrils and became physically aware of her proximity. My whole body sensed how close we were in our loneliness. In a shared hunger.

I allowed that feeling to roil inside me for a while, then turned my chair around and looked at her. I remember elbowing a couple of chess pieces to the floor, and while Schwalbe was picking them up, I looked straight at her:

"What is it?"

She replied with a long, silent, and unceremonious gaze—then said, with an almost imperceptible smile, as if she had read the word *hunger* in my thoughts of a moment ago:

"Come to supper . . ."

And so, we supped. And talked. About different kinds of mirrors, the importance of mirrors, the rising price of mirrors. Anna sat next to me, and I'm afraid it would have been only too easy for anyone observing the looks we exchanged to perceive a foregone conclusion.

It had been my intention to stay overnight at the Schwalbes and return to Voisiku in the morning. After supper, all four of us put on our felt boots and walked a quarter of a verst along the riverside path, past the inn and the little township, to escort Anna home— out of courtesy, and as a constitutional. Next to a couple of sheds and a well, protected by snowy hedges, her tiny cottage stood in the moonlight, its back to a stand of spruce, the front looking out over the frozen and snow-covered river. Anna asked us to come in for a moment and we sat in her parlor for half an hour. She offered us glasses of the Schwalbes' bitter cherry liqueur from a small bottle they had given her. I remember the damp tracks our felt boots left on the red rug, and I also remember that I must not have exchanged a single word with her. A week later, the Schwalbes invited me again. This time I told them right after my arrival that I intended to ride back to Voisiku that evening. We had tea, played chess, ate supper, escorted Anna home, and walked back to the Schwalbes'. I wished them a good night and saddled up. The Schwalbes tried to persuade me to stay, but I told them that I had to be at Poltsamaa first thing in the morning. They asked me if I wasn't worried about wolves, and I reassured them by showing them my pistol.

I rode a verst or so in the direction of Voisiku, then turned to the right, past the houses of the township behind their snow drifts; luckily, the moon was covered by dense clouds. Anna's light was still on. I knocked, and she did not call out, "Who's there?" but simply opened the door. She stood in the doorway holding a candle. I said, "Forgive me—but I think I left my mittens here?"

She said, "Oh, well, then. Wait here a moment, I'll bring a lantern, so you can put the horse in the shed, out of the cold."

And everything was surprisingly simple. There were moments when I thought it had been almost *too* simple.

Sunday, the sixth of May, 1828

Tomorrow morning I leave for Pärnu to find out about Captain Snyder. A week from now, Eeva will go to Tsarskoye Selo and bring Jüri home, so that the family will be together and ready if matters should progress to that stage.

Monday, the fourteenth of May, 1828

I had hardly arrived in Pärnu and entered the Rosenplänters' house when the pastor returned from town, closed the door of his study behind us, and told me what he had just learned at Jacke's store: a ship from Oporto had arrived in the harbor yesterday, and its captain had brought word from Captain Snyder that he was going to forsake the Baltic this spring in favor for some other, presumably more lucrative, voyage. He had, however, given his solemn promise: at the end of September he would be back in his berth in Pärnu harbor, "snug as a strawberry in a bear's arsehole." (I can't swear that those were his exact words, but Rosenplänter deemed this the most appropriate Estonian phrase.) Furthermore, Snyder had asked the Portuguese captain to *make this known to one and all who were interested in his arrival*—a statement I thought was rather superfluous in regard to my particular errand. For a moment I wondered whether I shouldn't approach that Portuguese captain instead of Snyder, but decided against it, and was glad I had not once I got a close view of the man at the counter of Parkman's tavern. Blue-chinned, he sported a brass earring and had the face of a pirate—compared to him, Snyder, with his copper-hued visage and blue eyes, looked like trustworthiness personified.

The following morning I went to the marketplace, obtained a seat in the mail-coach, and managed to get home just in time to tell Eeva the news before her planned departure. She won't go to Tsarskoye this spring. Under normal circumstances, students of the lyceum are not allowed to go home, not even for the summer holidays, and Eeva decided to save until September the excuse of *his father's suddenly deteriorated state of health*. But I did notice that her voice trembled a little when she said, "Well, no matter . . . As far as the money is concerned, we could have taken the risk, I think . . . Let's just hope things will work out in the fall . . ."

Timo listened to my Pärnu news without any visible sign of disappointment.

He said, "Well, since we've managed to get by this far, I'm sure we can manage until September. Or even longer."

And so, I'll be rumbling over to Pärnu again around St. Martin's Day. Maybe I'll have some new folk songs for Pastor Rosenplänter.

Friday, the eighth of June, 1828

I really should have brought my journal to the place where I spent the past week, trying to collect my thoughts: in Paluka Cottage at Kolga-Jaan Church, under my parents' roof. Had I done so, I could have recorded a few of my thoughts during that week in a very different atmosphere and state of mind.

My rather Spartan room here in The Foundation; these evening hours behind carefully closed doors; my perennial, although unnecessary but, by now, completely habitual, attempts to remove the journal from its hiding place as *quietly* as possible, even to turn its leaves without a sound; my glances at the window to make sure that the curtains are still properly drawn—I'm afraid that all this tends to infuse my writing with a kind of subterranean spirit. *There*, on the other hand . . . Well, I don't know.

I don't know whether I have related this at some previous time: my father managed to build a cottage for himself and my mother on land belonging to Rücker's deanery back in '14, when Eeva and I returned to Voisiku. It was, of course, Timo who arranged this for him, probably paying Dean Rücker a handsome sum for what had been a parcel of grazing land. For fifteen years Father has grown his four or five bushels on it, enough to put bread on the table; and in order to earn the butter on that bread, he has worked as a cobbler, much to the annoyance of the journeymen in Viljandi. In addition to her household chores, Mother has knitted socks and stockings for people at the deanery and in the township. Not that they really need to do these things: for the last ten years, Eeva has provided them with a couple of hundred rubles a year, which I consider enough not to have bothered to offer them any more out of my scant sergeant's pension. When I first offered to contribute, Eeva told me this wasn't necessary. Considering the difference in income between a lady of the manor and a retired sergeant, she was, of course, right . . .

Even before Timo's arrest, and naturally with Timo's permission, Eeva had asked the old folks to come and live at Voisiku. I remember clearly how Father pursed his mouth and told her that she should first find out for herself what it was like, living there . . . Perhaps, he said, she would manage to jump into an alien way of life without breaking her neck. Especially if that young master really held and carried her with the strength people claimed he did. And *if* (this he couldn't help saying with a note of deep regret in his voice)—*if* indeed she managed not to break her neck—although she had abandoned her Christian name and become a Katharina, to please the young master and in memory of the young master's mother—in any case, it was all very well and good for her, but he, an old man, and Mother likewise, were already too old, too ingrained in their native ways, to try to change themselves into gentlefolk . . .

After that speech, Eeva looked crestfallen, turned to her mother, and asked:

"Mother—do you, too, reject our invitation?"

And our mother replied, albeit looking down at the floor, their new floor in a house that was almost as good as those in the township, the dwelling to which they had already become accustomed:

"Yes, my dear, in this matter I am of exactly the same opinion as Father."

And there the matter rested. With all the more reason after Timo was taken away and Eeva had more than enough to do managing her own life. Father and Mother never visited the manor, even though they lived only a little over ten versts from it, but Eeva went to see them several times a year and always stayed with them for a day or two. I went with her, a few times—once immediately after Timo's arrest, and another time a few years later when I happened to be on leave from Tenner's surveyors.

I remember that first time. They had, of course, heard of Timo's arrest a week before. We had shared their repast, oat grits and soft bread, and were sitting at the low table in the cool, bluish-yellow dusk.

Father said, ". . . I had a premonition that nothing good would come of such a thing . . ."

Mother turned to me and said, "Jaagup, please make sure—that

she won't try too hard—that they won't make her try too hard
—now that she has to be the mistress of the manor . . ."

Father asked, "And you have no inkling why they arrested
him?"

Eeva shook her head. Then Father said, and there was such a
conflict in him between simple faith, a desire to console, and a
desire to scoff, that his voice turned hoarse with it:

"Well, I don't suppose they'll treat him all that badly there . . .
They're all gentlefolk, after all . . ."

And I remember how, three years later, in the autumn of 1821,
Eeva and I again sat in their parlor. I had been helping Father plow
the dean's stubble field. The hired hands had fallen prey to some
disease of the alimentary tract, and the dean had asked the old man
to plow the field for him. Father hadn't hesitated to accept the
task—I'm not sure whether he just wanted to please the dean or
if the old workhorse simply liked the idea of plowing a field larger
than his own. So there he was, laboring over the deanery field,
when Eeva and I arrived at Paluka. I changed into some of his old
work clothes, harnessed the old sorrel, and started plowing the
other side. It began to rain, but we defied the weather and kept
on working until nightfall to get the job finished—and finish it
we did. Now our coats, foot cloths, and felt boots hung steaming
in front of the stove. Mother had baked and served some hotcakes,
and Eeva refilled our old blue Poltsamaa cups with coffee.

I don't know what the old man had heard or thought about
Timo's situation in the meantime. He picked up his steaming coffee
cup, then set it down again, and said:

"They say they're keeping him in the dungeon of some fortress
. . . I don't know—is that true?"

Eeva nodded.

I said, "And the place where they're keeping him is so secret
that his own brother had to go to great lengths to find out where
he was."

Father asked, "Are you allowed to send him anything?"

Eeva said, probably to console herself and others, and perhaps
she did believe that the pearl-purse she had made had reached
Timo:

"Now and again, they let us . . ."

Father closed his eyes for a moment. Then he said, slowly:

"I've been thinking about this business, to the best of my un-tutored ability . . . It brings Golgotha to my mind. Either he is the worst of robbers—or the most righteous man. Which do you think?"

Eeva stared at him and said quietly but in a tone that broached no contradiction:

"He is the most righteous man!"

Mother sighed: "That may well be . . . But all it brings us is misfortune . . ."

"Whoa, there," Father said. "That's what Mary told Joseph, wasn't it . . ." He got up and went to the back room, then returned with a bundle under his arm. "I made a pair of boots for him . . . They're not parade boots, I wouldn't know how to make those. But for a dungeon . . . They're lined with sheepskin . . ."

Now I was spending a whole week at Paluka. I helped the old man with the sowing, made a new trough for the piglets, repaired the roof of the cottage, went out and hunted. And arrived at a foreseen but nevertheless painful conclusion: this wasn't "home," either.

In fifteen years, my parents have settled into their cottage, on their own patch of land, and they feel more comfortable with that than most local country folk would. Compared to them, an or-dinary Livonian peasant family has to depend far more on the estate owner's will and whim. With the passage of time, they have, of course, become quite used to their privileged state, one they had found troublesome at first (Timo insisted that their cot-tage have a proper chimney and wooden floors). But I remain a very odd bird in the eyes of the villagers of Vissuvere and Ta-ganurga. I accompanied my father on visits to a couple of those families, around Whitsuntide. A jug of special holiday ale was brought to the table and everyone seemed pleased to see Peeter from Paluka. The bony-faced old men and the women of their families had no trouble understanding that I was Peeter's son, Jakob. Nor did they have any trouble registering that I had served the crown for eight years. But the fact that I lived in the old *manor* at Voisiku, and was the brother-in-law of that reputed madman, Baron von Bock—that fact made me into such an odd visitor from another world that my skin crawled with the realization: my pres-ence made them go rigid, in almost the same way they would

have gone rigid if some strange *gentleman* had entered the room
. . . From time to time, to tell the truth, I feel the same thing
under my own parents' roof, though to a much lesser degree. The
feeling is somewhat similar to one I get when childhood memories,
grown indistinct and nearly forgotten, suddenly return with in-
creased vividness . . .

. . . One morning, I'm standing in the middle of the parlor
(which they have put at my disposal), combing my hair and glancing at the fifty-kopeck mirror hanging on the whitewashed log
wall. In this district, even country folk have mirrors in their
houses, and Eeva has given them this really handsome specimen.
Then I see my mother in the open doorway. She is looking at me.

"Well, Mama, what are you looking at?" I ask. "You think you
shook me by the hair enough, when I was little—?"

"Such talk! How often did I ever . . . ?"

"No, no, you certainly did—when you weren't stroking it . . .
Remember those ducks we had in the creek, close to the Kannuka
yard—"

"Sure . . . sure I do, you were six or seven . . . Well, that
deserved some chastisement, your running back and forth between
the yard and the house with your feet covered in duck droppings
. . . But, oh my—you said you were going to meet the gentlefolk
at Roika today—and your boots are still muddy . . . Let me clean
them—"

And I exclaim, "No, Mama—don't do it! First of all, I'm not
going to Roika. And secondly, I don't want you to! I clean my
own boots! Mama—don't . . ." All of a sudden, it seems incredibly
important to prevent my mother from cleaning my boots. I sense
in her readiness to clean her son's boots—the son whose hair she
used to pull—the measure of my estrangement from her, and its
blend of a little pride with a painful degree of shame. At the same
time, I worry (or, at least, I ask myself, in some lower compart-
ment of my brain) whether my refusal to let her clean them also
has the baser motive of my fear that she'll start spreading lard on
them instead of the Schreiber's Wax I've been using for a long
time now . . . And I feel miserable and disconnected. I *force* myself
to look at my old mother's perplexed and resigned face, its cheeks
like February apples, and I say:

"I'm not going to Roika. At least, not today . . ."

I clean my boots, and I don't go to Roika that day. But I know already that there isn't anywhere else for me to go—and that I do have to go *somewhere*, once Eeva and Timo make good their escape in September. After that, there will be nothing to keep me at Voisiku, quite apart from the fact that I don't think the Mann-teuffels would let me stay. Even if they did, I wouldn't want to —not even if they asked me, not even if Peter Mannteuffel came and *begged* me to stay . . . Because without Eeva and Timo I am a *stranger* there (how odd: I did write "and Timo" . . .). Without them, I would be worse than a stranger. And so I would be at Paluka—well, perhaps not to the same degree, but precisely for that reason, much more painfully aware of it.

Monday, the nineteenth of August, 1828

Upriver, seven or eight versts from the Roika works, lies a densely forested region to the west of the great Epra Swamp. The Amelungs have acquired this forest for the use of the glassworks at Melesk and the mirror factory, and they have hired a forester, not so much to discourage poachers as to make sure that the stewards of Voisiku and Soosaar don't steal firewood from it.

Off the Roika road, a hardly visible trail meanders through dense woods for a couple of versts in a southeasterly direction, ending close to the river on a sandy bluff, at the forester's cabin. This spring, I made the acquaintance of the present forester, Tiit of Näresaar, who went to fight Bonaparte in Prussia and returned minus one eye and plus one decoration on his chest. His remaining eye is sharp enough for the demands of his district, which lies on both sides of the river. To get over to the eastern side, Tiit has to take a boat across.

After having struck up a conversation with him once in the tavern at the Roika works, his lively stories enticed me to visit him at his cabin, to hear more and to sample his homebrew. The cabin is a primitive structure, its interior walls shiny and black from smoke. Fifty paces away, in among the dense reeds, is a small landing stage for his boat—and it was there that I thought of something . . .

Last spring, as the evenings and mornings were growing lighter, Anna had started warning me about gossip, particularly after her neighbor, Lotte Palter, a silver-plater's wife—also known as Scuttlebutt Lotte—had appeared at Anna's door twice while I was visiting . . . Of course, she could easily have suggested a trip to Dean Rücker, but she didn't. There were times when it seemed to me she not only was content with our clandestine affair but even took some kind of half-amused pleasure in its secretiveness . . . It even seemed to me that there was a kind of secret laughter bubbling under her intense whispers when she wrapped her surprisingly smooth arms around my neck (the curtains closed tight, the door locked, the candles snuffed, birds twittering at sunrise) and murmured, "Jakob, the days are getting longer . . . And people have noticed your visits . . . We have to think of something . . ."

I thought of something. My eagerness may have been due to an apprehension that if I didn't come up with a solution, there would soon be talk of marriage . . . From the Wahls' gardener at Poltsamaa, I bought a handsome green rowboat, covered at the stem and stern. In The Foundation's storage room, and in the arbor on the island in Voisiku Lake, I rummaged for fishing poles and fishhooks and collected the best. In the loft of the coach house I found a large piece of green sailcloth, and I chose the largest of three old hunting rifles that were part of The Foundation's inventory. Thus equipped, I spent much of last spring and this summer on the river.

I nailed four polished and curved willow saplings so as to arch over the bow of the boat and attached the sailcloth to them for a canopy. Tiit gave me a berth at his landing stage.

My usual pattern is to ride over from Voisiku to the forester's cabin, tether my horse in the spruce woods behind it, get into my boat, and drift downstream.

The river twists and turns in unpredictable ways between its reedy and overgrown banks all the way down to Päover Island. To the best of my ability, I have tried to memorize its branches and bluffs. After three or four versts, due to the dam at the mirrorworks, the river widens from several dozen cubits to almost two hundred cubits across.

I don't spend much time fishing. Now and again I'll catch a perch or a roach, especially when I expect to be spending the evening with Tiit and want to present him with something for a stew. I find even less use for the old blunderbuss. But *this* is what I do, at the times agreed upon: I row into an almost invisible inlet a few hundred steps above the northernmost house of the township, where Anna sits waiting for me in a green thicket of reeds, and lift her into my boat.

She is wearing a thin, light-blue summer gown with short puffed sleeves and a gossamer veil over her hair. She sits down next to me on the back thwart, a little concerned about rocking the boat. I put my arm on her waist and guide her forward under the canopy that protects us from the sun, and people's eyes. I start rowing.

"Lotte didn't catch you?"

She shakes her head, smiles.

There is something mysteriously familiar about her. Into her wide-eyed, smiling silence, it is possible to project the most profound or the most trivial thoughts. She stretches out a round, white arm and catches a yellow water lily floating past the side of the boat. Its serpentine stem rises out of the water and stretches behind us. At the *exact* moment when I think she'll tear the water lily off its stem, she lets it sink back into the water—

"Why?"

"Oh, it's so pretty there . . ."

In half an hour, rowing upstream—the current is not very strong here above the dam—I get to a place where the river narrows and I steer the boat into a creek bordered by reeds. Behind those reeds, there is nothing but forest, and behind that, the huge swamp of Epra. For versts around, not a house, not a berry picker. Above us, the ever-changing ceiling of the sky. We are surrounded by the quiet waters of the creek and the green curtain of reeds. Now and again, a perch jumps, or a mallard takes off, slapping the water. The reeds rustle. Some stalks bend in curious ways. As you get closer, a single reed among millions becomes astoundingly unique: with its long narrow leaves, its domelike top of hairy, brownish-violet spikelets, it is like a building, a flowering world of its own. It floats past our attentive faces as we sit there side by side, so close that it seems one needed only to take a tiny, inch-long step to find oneself reduced to one five-hundredth of one's previous size, a dweller in that quite different, gently swaying, separate world . . .

There are sandy stretches and grassy ridges by the river that are dry enough to let us stretch out and embrace. Most of the time, Anna gives herself to me in the boat. We are stark naked in the greening, swaying dawn or dusk—in a gently swaying, separate world . . . We know, or at least I do, that words cannot penetrate our solitudes, cannot bring us closer to one another—but we have discovered that our bodies can do that for us. The old sorrows of our solitude, and our ever-uncertain joy in our experience of release from them, make us eager for one another. I don't know what she thinks of me; I'd like to know but don't have the courage to ask. But I am now writing down *my thoughts about her*, in order to remember it later. Or, to be more precise: I am recording my feelings for her on our rowboat excursions on Poltsamaa River, in a certain green and gently swaying separate world, in the late summer of the year 1828.

Her ardor bothers me a little—it shows that she has had previous experiences, yet I like it very much when I believe that I am able to revive it in her, each time. The overabundance of her white flesh might seem a little ridiculous or even a little obscene—if she were to make any pretense of refinement. But she has no pretenses. She is simply who she is. Good or bad, clever or stupid—that I do not know, nor do I really care, as long as she attracts and welcomes me. After all, it is not my intention to—to what?—to found an ideal dynasty for an ideal state, such as the one Timo must still be dreaming about . . . And she is completely without affectation, insofar as I know anything about female nature. In any case, and in some strange way, she seems *familiar*.

And so, when I return to myself on one of these nuptial nights in the reeds, on a bag of straw on the bottom of a boat, and hear Anna's breath growing calmer, hear the quiet water-sounds of the creek on the other side of the thin boards, the rustle of reeds against the bow, when I run my fingers over Anna's burning cheeks and discover traces of tears on them, let my other hand sweep aside a stalk that leans into the boat in the darkness—I recall the real world by remembering a passage from Timo's memorandum to the Czar: ". . . *I have no need to seek for happiness outside my home* . . ." Well, I could amend that to *outside this boat*, this swaying separate world . . . "*And even though I have often experienced ingratitude and insults,*" Timo writes, "*I have, on the other hand, been rewarded by kindness and friendship in places where I did not expect them; and even if I should lose my faith in the human race*"—and it is entirely possible to find oneself in circumstances in which the possibility of such a loss of faith occurs to one, just as it did to me in the case of Iette and Laming—"*I would still find solace in each and every green leaf, in every butterfly* . . ." Then, of course, Timo goes on to say that he cannot, after all, restrict himself to happiness at home and the enjoyment of butterflies, art, and science—he must also consider *God and the fatherland* . . .

Here is a conclusion I have reached: leaving the question of God aside, I certainly won't lose any sleep over "the fatherland." I have seen what *total* devotion to it may entail. *Partial* devotion to it may imply treason, but a true and total devotion to the fatherland, such as Timo's, would be sheer madness. Or is there yet another alternative? Or are all possibilities in this world simply *alternatives?* Even in the "gently swaying separate world of the reeds at dusk"?

The twenty-first of August, 1828

I just reread my entry of the day before yesterday. Good Lord, never before have I written such absurd stuff. But for whose benefit should I bother to tear out these pages?

Monday, the third of September, 1828

Tomorrow I'll leave for Pärnu again to find out if Captain Snyder has returned. Eeva went to Tsarskoye at the beginning of last week.

Yesterday evening Anna and I went out on the river once more. The weather was cool, autumn must be here. After taking Anna ashore in the reeds near her house, I rowed over to Tiit's place and spent the night there. After we had enjoyed our fish stew and a drink of brandy (I had brought a small bottle from the estate distillery), he presented me with such an intriguing addendum to a story I already knew that it made me ask myself (whom else could I ask here!): Is it not—when all is said and done—the case, with regard to all the events of this world, that every visible occurrence is also, or perhaps *merely*, a hint of invisible connections, of some invisible world?

I had heard the story from Georg, at least ten years ago.

In the autumn of 1813, Timo and his regiment had been in Germany, under Barclay de Tolly's command. His regiment had not taken part in the famous Battle of Three Emperors at Leipzig, but after that battle, it had been his task to protect the town of Weimar against the French, who, in a dangerous mood of defeat, were retreating westward from Leipzig. Word of the great victory reached Weimar on the evening of the twentieth of October, and reports from reconnaissance indicated that the French retreat would bypass Weimar, on a northerly route. This seemed more than likely, since Leipzig lies a hundred versts to the northeast from Weimar.

Nevertheless, and considering the news of the terrible destruction of all of Saxony, the population of Weimar felt so relieved that the Duke arranged for a banquet to be given in the castle on the twenty-second. In addition to himself, the Duchess, and their court, the guests included all the councillors, Goethe among them, and one Lieutenant-Colonel Timotheus von Bock. As the commander of the allied forces of the town, Duke Karl August, in his formal banquet speech, thanked all the victors in general, and Mr. von Bock in particular—for the courageous spirit with which the presence of his regiment had imbued the town and the assembled guests, and for the good appetite that resulted from this feeling of security. Then table talk had proceeded in an appropriately dignified manner, and, across the ducal tableware, the old Parnassian Privy Councillor enjoyed a pleasant exchange of thoughts with the young, mustachioed lieutenant-colonel with the Greek profile who seemed to know his Kant as well as his Clausewitz . . . (During which conversation he may have thought, in passing, that in addition to such a comprehensive phenomenon as *world literature*, for which he had once wanted to make a claim—if only there had been enough time in this seething and chaotic world— there might also be another, perhaps even more comprehensive

phenomenon, which might be called *world culture* . . .) After ladies
of the ducal court had claimed his young partner's attention, old
Goethe called for a sheet of paper and writing implements. These
were brought to him on a silver salver, and he penned something,
then asked the Duke's permission to read aloud what he had
written:

AN HERRN OBRISTLEUTNANT VON BOCK

Von allen Dingen die gescheh'n,
Wenn ich es redlich sagen sollte,
So war's Kosaken hier zu sehn
Nicht eben was ich wünschen wollte.
Doch als die heilig grosse Fluth
Den Damm durchbrach, der uns beengte
Und Well' auf Welle uns bedrängte,
War dein Kosak uns lieb und gut.

During the enthusiastic applause of the ducal company, he had
signed his verses and handed them across the table to Timo.

Dessert had just been served when some messengers, pallid with
fright, rushed into the dining hall to inform the guests that a
division of Frenchmen had turned south from the main body of
the retreat and were about to enter the town of Weimar . . .

Timo immediately left the panic-stricken table, threw open a
window, and shouted down to the courtyard: "Saddle up!"

He charged downstairs, leapt over the balustrade of the terrace,
and bounded into the saddle. A sergeant and Timo's orderly were
already waiting for him, and the three of them pulled their sabers
and charged out of the castle yard, disappearing from the view of
observers at the back windows of the banquet hall. A moment
later, they appeared in the field of vision of those gathered by the
windows in the front, and at that instant, French cuirassiers, in
their purple uniforms, on dust-covered horses, began to clatter
into the square from all the streets leading into it.

Waving their sabers, Timo's trio charged past the first Frenchmen but soon ran into a group of at least a dozen cavalrymen.
They knocked a few out of their saddles, parried blows, dodged

bullets, and miraculously made their way through the melee. One of Timo's men must have been hit, because the watchers in the dining hall windows saw him slump onto the neck of his horse but hang on and disappear with the others into one of the streets leading from the square.

Georg had heard all this later from the chief forester of the Duke of Weimar, who had been among the banquet guests and had witnessed the events; half an hour later, Timo led his regiment back into town from its encampment on the other side of the Ilmi River and chased the French out of Weimar in a pitched battle, before they could do any damage beyond emptying the kitchens of a couple of inns and the wine cellars of a few taverns, paying for what they received with horrible grins.

And so, last night, I sat on the clay bench in front of Tiit's cabin, leaning against the log wall, a jug of ale and a bottle of brandy between us. We had dined on perch stew and whetted our whistles with Tiit's floury-tasting ale and my estate brandy. With some anxiety, I thought about my impending journey to Pärnu. It would really be a shame if I came back without any results, like the last time; on the other hand, I wasn't sure I relished the responsibility of setting things in motion if Captain Snyder was indeed there . . . There would be endless risks of discovery: we might be stopped on our way to Pärnu and asked for our destination. Even on the pier in Pärnu Harbor, a heavy hand could descend on one's shoulder. Some fast-sailing border guard vessel might intercept Snyder on the open sea, to dig the stowaways out of the flax (if, say, even one among Snyder's sailors was interested in a reward) . . . Tiit was sitting close to me, to my right, and we were looking out under the low eaves of the cabin at the moonlit river. Tiit's empty eye socket and the scar running across it from his forehead to halfway down his cheek showed black on his gray, stubbled face. I thought, well—I have lived through decades in which there have been so many killed and wounded, so many starved or frozen to death, so many who have lost arms and legs and eyes, that to survive those decades without a scratch is, of course, *fortunate*, but also a little *embarrassing* . . . and that is why I *must* take this risk to help Eeva and Timo—for my own peace of mind, and for their sake, of course . . . I asked:

"Tiit, where did you lose your eye?"

Tiit picked the brandy bottle off the bench and said:

"Well, it was over there in Germany. In the year thirteen, late October, I think. In a town called Weimar, after the French had been trounced in the Battle of the Three Emperors . . ."

I pretended to mull that over, then said:

"Wait a minute—that was when my brother-in-law was there too—or so I've heard?"

"That's right," Tiit said. "I was his orderly."

Which was, come to think of it, not all that surprising. On the contrary: when the commander of a regiment is the master of Voisiku Estate, his orderly would most likely be a man from a nearby village. And not just any man, but one who had from boyhood worked on the estate both as a servant and a stable boy, knew horses inside and out—a very necessary skill in a crack cavalry regiment—and also would know from just looking at the steam when his colonel's shaving water was the right temperature . . . Nevertheless, the reemergence of that old story here at a forester's cabin at Näresaar seemed to me like yet another demonstration of the fact that the world is really so much smaller than we think, and the probability of unlikely coincidences infinitely greater than it appears. My interest aroused by that premonition, I asked Tiit to tell me about it, and he, the shy, tangle-haired eccentric and, in his own modest way, independent spirit that he was, told me the tale in his almost reluctant manner:

"Let's see . . . We were quartered in these old German barracks by a little river. And one day, the colonel took our Sergeant Lvovich and myself into town, saying he had to go dine with the Duke there. So we rode to the castle—it was quite a bit nicer than what we've got at Voisiku, but not really all that, how should I put it . . . Anyways, the colonel told us to wait for him, and he was escorted inside. We watched the lords and ladies drive up in their carriages, and then we were escorted to the stables where we put feedbags on our horses. Never mind how scorched the fields may be all around, there's always oats in a Duke's stables . . . Then they gave us a bite to eat, German bread that tasted like sawdust, and a chunk of tough salt pork. But the ale was all right. So we sat there chatting with the Duke's stable boys, with me translating for Lvovich as best I could. Saying things like now we should go straight to Paris and string that Bonaparte up by his balls! The Germans felt the same way we did. Then, all of a sudden, a window flies open up above, and the colonel shouts down to us, "Saddle up!" So we go to it on the double, and people are shouting in the yard, saying the French are in town, and the colonel comes charging down, and we all jump into our saddles and ride away to raise the regiment and beat back the Frenchies. But as soon as we reach the square, there they *are* . . ."

He fell silent, and I asked:

"I've been told you knocked quite a few off their horses?"

"Well, the colonel led the way," Tiit said and took a long draft from the brandy bottle. "He led the way and knocked at least three of those fellows out of their saddles . . ."

I asked, "And was that when you were wounded?"

"That's right." Suddenly he turned to look at me with his right eye. It shone in the dark. "But it wasn't a Frenchman that got me."

"Say what?!"

"The colonel was swinging his saber, forward and back. And I was just two paces behind him, on his right."

"Dear God—are you saying that Timo struck you in the face with his saber?" I still don't know what suddenly caused me to feel so appalled by that.

"Yes, unfortunately. By mistake, of course."

"And—and what did he do?"

"Don't think he noticed."

"Well, I guess not, in a melee like that . . . But later?"

"Later he thought I'd been struck by a Frenchman."

"But when he found out about what really happened?" Suddenly, it seemed terribly important to hear what Timo had done after he had found out about this.

"*Well? What did he do when he found out?*"

"Well . . . Don't think he knows, to this day."

Apparently, Timo had helped Tiit to hang on and stay in the saddle while they galloped across the river and to the barracks. He had sent Tiit to the surgery and later recommended him to Barclay, and Barclay himself had given Tiit his medal for bravery. But Timo had never found out how Tiit lost his eye . . .

Looking out into the dark, Tiit said:

"Didn't see no reason to bother him with it . . ."

I asked, "But what about the others? What about Lvovich?"

Tiit said, "Well, he was the only other fellow there. But he had his hands full, so I don't think he saw what happened . . ."

"But you have told people about it?"

". . . No, I haven't."

"Why did you tell me, just now?"

Tiit shrugged.

"The devil knows why. Once in a while a fellow gets to talking, you know . . ."

Tonight, back in my own room, I pondered for a long while why Tiit had told me this old story. Perhaps, at long last, he wanted to correct a deep misunderstanding, explain it to at least one other person, to have it off his mind and out in the world. God alone knows. Obviously, the old incident was a bad omen for Timo, one that hung over him, across the years, like the shadow of a curse . . . He wanted to strike an enemy—and deprived his most trusted man of an eye. He wanted happiness for the person he loved most in this world—and made her unhappier than anyone else, near or far. He wanted to destroy the blindness and baseness and injustice rampant in our Russian Empire—in other words, the emperor—and destroyed himself . . .

Thursday, the thirteenth of September, 1828

Once again, it is time for a report on my journey to Pärnu.

I arrived there on the sixth. True, there were inns in town, but since Rosenplänter had always welcomed me, and since staying with him seemed least likely to arouse suspicion, I accepted, once again, his invitation to stay at his house.

This time, it seemed that God was favoring our project. Captain Snyder was already in Pärnu, having arrived a few days before me. While taking the air, I saw his handsome three-masted *Ameland* in the harbor; however, I did not approach the ship, thinking it better not to risk being noticed and remembered by anyone. On my very first evening at the Rosenplänters, Snyder came to tea, looking as sprightly as ever, and while the Pastor strolled in the garden communing with his conscience, and his wife was putting the children to bed up in their mansard rooms, the captain and I agreed on the necessary details.

One thousand rubles, in gold, to be paid to Snyder before departure. Another thousand in the first safe harbor. Departure, weather permitting, let us say Monday, the sixteenth, or Tuesday, the seventeenth, at the crack of dawn. Those were the earliest possible dates, but a slightly later one could be thought about.

Captain Snyder himself gave me the following hint: that the captain of the port guard took his evening meals at Ingerfeld's Restaurant. I must admit I had great misgivings about my final and decisive involvement in the affair, not only because of the personal risks I would run but also because I have a great deal of distaste for the kind of playacting it required. Nevertheless, on some street corner behind the Winter Harbor, I gave myself the necessary kick in the seat and strode quickly through the drizzle down the cobblestone street to that restaurant. As I entered, I saw the captain, a dark-haired, rawboned, deeply tanned man whose uniform collar looked soiled; he was slurping his soup at a table near the counter. I took the plunge, walked across the room to his table, and asked for permission to join him. He gave me a slightly surprised look, then nodded. So, there I was. I ordered a bottle of port—from the *Ameland*'s recent cargo—and two glasses. Then, just to put him and myself on equal footing, I introduced myself as Lieutenant ——tik, retired, of the Cartography Task Force, and filled both our glasses. I have to admit that once there was no looking back, I wanted to do as well as possible and was quite pleased with the success of my first moves.

I told him that my work as a cartographer (dealing mainly with sea charts!) had damaged my eyes and the doctors had recommended sea air and some kind of work that would require me to scan for distances. Then I asked him if there might be a position for me in his port guard—*one commensurate with my modest rank.* Or, if the captain did not have the authority to decide on that, would he put in a good word for me with his superiors? By this time, we had arrived at the main course, and I called for another bottle. Finally I said that making his acquaintance had been such a pleasure that I would be deeply offended if he didn't allow me to deal with the reckoning. He was a sensible man and did not want to offend me. He assured me he would keep my request in mind, and we agreed to meet again to dine at the same establishment. And so we did. After our second dinner, we went and had a few at Parkman's Tavern, and I stuffed a few rubles in his pocket for a round of drinks and beer for his men. When we parted, we were the best of friends. It seemed to me that I had succeeded in gaining his confidence, mainly by virtue of two things: first of all, I had demonstrated some expert knowledge of sea charts (something he was keenly interested in), and secondly, I had treated him, unstintingly, with the respect that a retired lieutenant must show a captain on active duty. The upshot was that Captain Glans gave me his solemn assurance that he would raise my matter with his friend, a general whose name I cannot recall. I told him I had to leave town for a week to set my affairs in order, but upon my return I would arrange a proper feast for him and his trusty guards. By this time, it was obvious that he regarded me as a goose that laid golden eggs—and I had every intention of keeping my promise . . .

But when I got back here yesterday and rushed into The Foundation to tell them quietly but with authority that they should hurry and collect their dearest possessions in a couple of inconspicuous valises—I found no one in Eeva's or Jüri's rooms, and Timo's door locked, as usual. No one responded to my knocking. Then Käsper appeared and told me that the lady of the house and the young master had not yet returned from the capital, and the master was out riding . . .

Timo returned around dinnertime and listened calmly to my urgent report—so calmly that I began to ask myself whether he was even interested in the escape I was planning for him. I noticed, however, that when I told him the ship was ready to depart at sunrise on the sixteenth of September, he closed his eyes and took a deep breath. Then he opened his eyes again and handed me a letter in Eeva's handwriting. He said, "Read this. Unfortunately, it won't be possible for us to do it this time."

Eeva wrote, from Tsarskoye, that she hoped her dear Timosha's health had not gotten any *worse* since she left: that would be very sad indeed, because their son Jüri would simply not be able to hasten to his bedside at this time, even though Eeva had managed to get a special permission for Jüri's visit from the friendly headmaster of the lyceum. It had been God's will to afflict Jüri, only yesterday, with a high fever and a serious throat infection, and,

due to the danger of contagion, the school's physician had quarantined the boy in his room. Even his mother had to observe great
precautions while attending to him.

And Eeva ended her letter—I remember it exactly:

So, dearest Timosha, in view of all this, the only course
of action open to me is to stay here with our son until
he recovers, as I hope he will, with all my heart. I love
both of you and pray for both of you.

Forever your
K.

Then Timo took ten golden imperials out of his desk drawer,
handed them to me, and asked me to convey them to Pastor
Rosenplänter, to be passed on to Captain Snyder with our regrets
and apologies. I objected and told him we should wait a little
longer—perhaps Eeva and Jüri would still manage to get back in
time. I told Timo it would be better to offer the money to Snyder
as an incentive to wait for us a little longer in Pärnu. But Timo
shook his head.

"They can't possibly get back here in time. The most important
thing is not our departure but Georg's recovery. Kitty's letter
makes me fear that his throat infection is of the kind called *angina
maligna sive gangraenosa*. If that's the case, he can use every prayer
Kitty can manage. And even if God hears those prayers, his recovery may take several months."

I suggested that we should at least wait a day or two for Eeva's
next letter. Then we would still have time to make a final decision.
Timo agreed.

The fifteenth of September, 1828

According to the letter we received today (it took six days to
get here), Jüri has been in bed for nine days with a swollen throat
and a high fever. Thus, he would not be able to return home
before the end of three weeks, at best—which means that I have

to set out for Pärnu again tomorrow, stay out of Captain Glans's sight, and take Timo's ten imperials to Rosenplänter or Captain Snyder, explaining the situation to them and expressing our hopes for next spring.

The twenty-third of October

A fortnight ago, Eeva returned from Tsarskoye, and I came back from Pärnu. Eeva still hasn't recovered from her grievous trials. She came home in a frightfully emaciated condition, and her face was ashen, even though her eyes shone—because, with God's help, Jüri is alive and convalescing well, unafflicted by hoarseness or paralysis or any of the other side effects that such throat ailments often cause. Last night, Eeva invited me to her room and told me:

"Do you know, Jakob, I've been thinking about everything—how our escape plan has failed, and how all the trouble you took and the risks you ran were in vain. It really makes me sad, especially for Timo's sake. But, on the other hand, if we hadn't held fast to our plan, I would not have gone to Tsarskoye. And that's where I see Providence at work—because I arrived on the very day Jüri was taken ill. If I hadn't been there, we would have heard about it only much later, or in a death notice! Because, in all modesty, I *strongly doubt* that he would still be among the living if I hadn't been there to nurse him."

Her answers to my questions had already given me a pretty good idea of what that had been like. On the third and fourth day, the boy had still been in the clutches of a violent fever and, according to the doctor, quite weak. The swelling and the abscesses in his throat had grown steadily worse. Then Eeva had sat at his bedside for five days and nights without a break, feeding him drops of bouillon and wine and painting the terrible lesions in his throat with medications the school physician had left outside the quarantined sickroom . . . At last, Jüri took a turn for the better.

Eeva picked up Jüri's small oval watercolor portrait from the mantelpiece. It had been painted while he still had long reddish-brown hair. She looked at it and said:

"I feel as if I have given birth to him all over again . . ."

I said, "And it shows. Now you must take a good, long rest. Instead of cleaning house—"

While we were talking, Eeva was pulling letters and other papers out of the drawers of her curly-grained writing desk and sorting them, crumpling some, throwing bundles of others into the fireplace. She seemed to have been busy this way for some time—the pile in the fireplace was quite large. She said:

"This, too, needs to be done. I was quite appalled when it occurred to me how many letters and things we would have left here, of a kind not intended for strangers' eyes—if we had forgotten to deal with them before running off in September!"

She took a candle and set fire to the stack of papers, but the weak, bluish flame only charred their edges and soon went out. Obviously, the chimney wasn't drawing, and the air in The Foundation was more humid than it seemed. I tried to light the papers again but only managed to fill the room with smoke. It was sleeting outside, and the papers simply wouldn't burn. Besides, my last attempt to light them may not have been all that energetic . . .

On the hearthstone stood a firewood basket made out of copper wire, with only a couple of logs in it. I took the logs out and said:

"Why don't I just take all this and burn it in my own fireplace? My chimney seems to be drawing just fine."

Eeva said, "All right, go ahead. Just make sure you don't leave anything lying around."

I filled the wire basket with papers and carried it to my room. Eeva didn't come with me, and I used this opportunity to (I don't know how to put this: Was I being a blackguard, or would anyone else have done the same? Yes, I think so, unless the person had been completely uninterested in our affairs)—to go through the papers before throwing them into the fire.

Most of them were of no interest, being ancient memoranda concerning affairs of the estate dating back to Klarfeldt's day—budget projections, notes on planting and harvesting, building repairs, and agricultural improvements, some even from Laming's tenure. However, there are a few letters, or drafts of letters, and a few other documents that seem so essential to the matters at hand that I shall store them in a certain place (certainly not *lying around*) in order to transcribe them into this book, and soon.

The second of November, 1828

My journal already contains entries more ridiculous than my dream of last night, so why hesitate to record it here, especially considering that for much of the day I've been unable to shake off the feeling that I am still in it?

Toward morning, I found myself rowing on the water. At first, it seemed to be a wide, but calm, body of water, perhaps even the open sea, and I was surprised, though certainly not perturbed, that I was able to stay afloat. At the very first moment, I had assumed that the vessel was my own green boat—but then I realized that it was merely a box-shaped basket, woven out of green rushes, of a kind I had never seen with my own eyes but had pictured since I was a child: it was a basket like the one in which the newborn Moses had been set afloat on the Nile. This woven boat in which I was rocking on the waters had been caulked with pitch, but rather more carelessly than those of ancient days, so that I was able to see the waves through holes in its sides. Yet I wasn't the least bit afraid, partly because the vessel seemed large enough. Suddenly it grew surprisingly large: it had three thwarts, and I was sitting on the foremost one, not really rowing—the boat moved along by itself, as if floating down a river. At first I couldn't see anyone sitting on the thwarts behind me, but when I took another look, I saw Iette sitting on the middle thwart. I looked again, and it was Anna. I wanted to say something to both of them but couldn't make out which one was sitting there. Then I realized that if I looked over my right shoulder, I saw Iette, if over my left, it was Anna—which meant that they were sitting there side by side, Iette on the right, Anna on the left. But then I was no longer able to turn to them, because I noticed that as we had moved from open waters into a reedy river, water began to seep into the boat. I wondered why that hadn't happened sooner,

the reed boat had been full of holes from the very beginning, but
when I wanted to say something about it to Iette and Anna (the
water had almost reached the thwarts) I looked back and saw: Iette
and Anna had their arms around one another, and each had raised
her forefinger in front of the other one's lips. I wanted to ask them
what they wanted to prevent each other from telling me—but then
I understood that they were telling me to remain silent. And I
understood why. The third thwart, behind them, was no longer
vacant. Now Czar Alexander was sitting on it in a white linen
suit, cleaning a pistol. At the same moment, I felt the boat sinking
under us. Apart from a dreamy shiver, I did not feel afraid, because
I knew that the emperor wasn't cleaning his pistol in order to
shoot *me*. Besides, we had reached a very dense stand of reeds,
hence the water could not be very deep. I saw that we were in
the same place, at the same inlet, where Anna and I had spent
time last summer. Then the boat disintegrated under and around
us, and I saw Czar Alexander, his white trousers completely
soaked, charge ashore in his sloshing spats and run up the bluff.
I saw how the grass his boots had crushed down rose up again,
and asked myself, in the dream: How can the tread of dead people
seen in dreams be so heavy that it crushes the grass they walk on?
After the Czar disappeared into the undergrowth, I turned to look
for Iette and Anna. Both were gone. I called their names, and
woke up at the sound of my own voice.

Wednesday, the fourteenth of November, 1828

Yesterday was Timo's fortieth birthday. Just as last year, we
had Eeva's plum torte with our morning coffee, but no peasants
appeared to congratulate Timo, as they had done last year. Monsieur La Trobe had already told me, two weeks ago, when we
happened to run into each other in front of the brewery building
and were striding across the freezing mud toward The Foundation:

"I heard that a delegation of peasants came to congratulate Mr.
von Bock on his birthday last year. And not too long ago I heard
that they were planning to do so again this year. But, you know,

Mr. Jakob—I let them know that it would be better, both for them and for Mr. Bock, if they refrained from that plan . . ."

I asked, perhaps to tease him a little, "But who would report such a trivial matter to the authorities—that's what you're worrying about, isn't it?"

And he said, with an odd gesture—passing his hand over his eyes as if trying to clear cobwebs off his face, "Surely you know that we're all being watched, by everybody . . . So, I hope you won't mind if I seem rather cautious. I have given the matter some thought . . ."

Tuesday, the fourth of December, 1828

Before I transcribe the letters I have mentioned, I should say a few words about the events of three years ago, when we had a change of Czars. I should do this because one of these letters, written by Eeva, was occasioned by that change, and another, from Georg, shows clearly how crucial the change was to our affairs.

Let others, destined either to write or to keep silent about it, write or keep their peace about how Czar Alexander died in the town of Taganrog in November 1825; how the Russians who first received word of that death considered Grand Duke Konstantin his successor; how it soon became apparent that his successor would be his younger brother Nicholas, and how, in St. Petersburg, as Nicholas was being sworn in, a few regiments of guards began to riot, and what horrors that led to—because what can I really claim to know about any of these things? All I may presume to know are perhaps a few curious details; true, such details can sometimes make grand events seem purely accidental . . . This is a tale I heard in the gentlemen's bar at Kiling's Tavern, on one of my journeys to Pärnu:

The news that Alexander had died in Taganrog had reached St. Petersburg. Grand Duke Nicholas must have realized that it had also reached his older brother Konstantin in Warsaw, where their younger brother Mikhail was visiting at the time. It fell to Mikhail

to travel to St. Petersburg to inform Nicholas how Konstantin
now felt about his former decision to renounce the crown. Was
he going to allow his younger brother Nicholas to become the
Czar? Nicholas was unable to muster the patience to wait for
Mikhail in St. Petersburg but went forth to meet him. They met
in Estonia, on St. Peter's Highway, at the Ninas post station by
the Peipsi River (one station farther toward Narva from where,
at Torma, Eeva and I had waited for Maria Feodorovna). From
there, they traveled back to the capital together, Nicholas with
Konstantin's letter of renunciation in his pocket, the crown practically on his head. They arrived in St. Petersburg on the morning
of the fourteenth of December. The riots would start in two hours.
Nicholas proceeded to the headquarters of the Army Engineering
Corps, whose honorary commander he was. As he stood on the
square, with the ranks of officers and soldiers on either side of
him, and began to exhort them to confirm his imperial powers,
some conspiratorial officer (of whom there were many in the various corps) pulled a pistol, took aim, and fired—the bullet went
into the ground when another man struck his arm at exactly the
right moment. I can only surmise what happened to the would-
be assassin. The man who deflected his aim (and this is why I
heard the story at Kiling's Tavern) was an Estonian noncommissioned officer, one Friedrich from the district of Saard. He had
been promoted to ensign on the spot, and for some reason, the
Czar had also appointed him the commander of the guard at
Ninas—apparently Czar Nicholas regarded it as the place where
his imperial reign had begun. When I heard this story, I thought:
That blow struck by Ensign Friedrich from Saard demonstrates
how accidental and arbitrary Nicholas's czardom really is. And
Russia's progression, under his rule, "from a dimly lit hall into a
dark cellar passage"—nothing but an accident. It was accidental,
too, that the Decembrists' uprising did not end quite differently,
and that their wild-eyed ideas did not win out—those same ideas
for which (yes, it is because of them that all this happened) Timo
was imprisoned all those years. And it was yet another accident
that exchanged Timo's incarceration at Schlüsselburg for detention
at Voisiku, his casemate now the size of a county . . .

As I understand it, the empire's prominent liberals regarded

Alexander's death as a loss to Russia, despite the oppression he had exercised in the last years of his reign. Surely, the intuition of those in the know proved correct, surely they were proven right who predicted that Russia would, after Alexander's death, descend from a dimly lit room above ground into a dark cellar passage— I can't recall who coined that phrase. But the situation of one or the other person or family may diverge from general conditions to such an extent that their hopes may rise at the very moment when they are finally dashed in the minds of others . . .

I remember well how cheerful Eeva looked one day when she came to my old room in the main building. It had to be early December of '25, during my winter leave from Major Tenner. Eeva put the new St. Petersburg newspaper on the coffee table in front of me. Before it touched the table top, I saw the black borders on the front page and instantly surmised the Czar's death. I read the official announcement, then said:

"Well, so we'll have a new Czar. And?"

I could feel the energy radiating from Eeva as she spoke:

"First of all, Timo hasn't forbidden me to appeal to a new Czar—"

"And secondly?"

"Secondly—the new Czar will be one of Alexander's brothers. He needn't be *as* offended by words someone once addressed to Alexander. That stands to reason, doesn't it? So there just might be a glimmer of hope . . ."

I have not read Eeva's first letter to Nicholas—there wasn't even a draft of it among the papers I was supposed to burn. But here is a copy, presumably an exact one, of Georg's plea to Nicholas —his first plea to Nicholas the Czar, written from Berlin and dated the thirtieth of July, 1826:

Sire,

Five years ago, when I first begged for Your Imperial Majesty's bountiful intercession with our late blessed Majesty, Emperor Alexander, I had occasion to regret a step that caused you, Sire, to respond negatively in the matter I had proposed, and which was the more hurtful to me inasmuch as it demonstrated, in all respects, your broad-mindedness, and if there was any consolation to be found in such a situation, it was only on the ground that had compelled me to act, which, in your eyes, Sire, and I do not doubt this at all, was a mitigating circumstance.

From that moment on, complete retirement became the fundamental rule of my conduct; while willing to wait for all the deliberations of your broad-minded predecessor, I gave the dolorous anguish that filled my heart orders to be silent, and tried to exercise patience and calm. Years passed without the fulfillment of the hope of seeing my brother free, a hope that the Venerable Late Emperor himself had given me not long after my brother's arrest . . .

Well, it was my original intention to copy the entire letter and postpone my comments to the end, but the temptation has proven too great . . . Georg's courtly phrases may seem gratuitous and truckling, but gradually their sly consistency becomes apparent. As far as Alexander's talk about Timo's impending release goes, the above quote indicates two alternatives: either Georg was bluffing, or Alexander was. If Alexander never told Georg anything like that, Georg is, in this letter, blatantly banking on the fact that Nicholas can no longer ask his late brother about the matter, but has to accept the statement as one made by an officer and a gentleman . . . If, on the other hand, Alexander did tell Georg that Timo would be released soon, that, too, could be taken as characteristic —an imperial subterfuge, based on sheer cowardice. I have been told that Alexander was considered notorious for baseless promises, assurances, hints—at least among those circles of gentlefolk whose syrupy nonsense I have absorbed in my years of listening.

. . . I was almost overwhelmed by the severity of my grief; I felt, more clearly than ever before, in how implacable a manner fate was divesting me of the faith that I still had in those illustrious words, but then my courage returned, in the most surprising circumstances. The great truth that Your Imperial Majesty deigned to express in one of your first manifestoes, that "foresight often uses evil means to bring forth good"—this truth, I told myself, will surely hold, even in the case of my unfortunate brother.

The investigation that Your Imperial Majesty has ordered in regard to the repugnant events that occurred immediately after your ascension must have reassured you, Sire, that my brother could never have had anything in common with such disrupters of the common peace; the mere thought, that he might be associated with them in the mind of the Sovereign, would surely send cold shivers down his back . . .

Clearly, Georg believes that Timo had nothing to do with the conspirators. The speed with which he hastens to state this to the Czar on his brother's behalf does him honor: on the thirteenth of July, the Decembrists' leaders were hanged on the ramparts of the Fortress of Peter and Paul, and on the thirtieth Georg writes to the Czar from Berlin:

. . . With the greatest satisfaction, I have noticed that the results of the investigation also support my own innermost conviction that the accused was unable to take part in any criminal plans . . .

It is, of course, obvious that Georg had no idea of the contents of the memorandum Timo had sent to the Czar. For he continues:

. . . I have not wavered in this conviction for one moment, for I know my brother from childhood, and my conviction has always lent me courage and does so to this day, combined with the certainty that the Blessed and Forever Unforgettable Late Emperor must already have realized, in his heavenly abode, to what an extent the assumption upon which his opinion of my brother was based has proven unreliable, after all . . .

Poor Georg, is all I can say . . . But the turn his letter takes, right here, is so unexpected and masterful that it raises my admiration for him:

> . . . Nevertheless, I am fully aware, Sire, how griev-
> ously my brother must have transgressed: it is highly rep-
> rehensible to break prescribed forms and to express less
> than complete respect for one's own Sovereign, even if
> this is done solely out of a burning desire, arising out of
> the nation's needs and a boundless devotion to the Sov-
> ereign, to proclaim the truth all the way to the steps of
> the throne . . .

Well, no, it is "poor Georg," after all! "Boundless devotion" to a sovereign—while proclaiming him a traitor and a clown?

> . . . never even stopping to consider whether one is en-
> dangering one's entire future by doing so. Such a step,
> even if it could be defended by the purity of intent to
> which I refer, must nevertheless be considered worthy
> of reprimand. But does Your Imperial Majesty's sense of
> justice truly place this guilt, my brother's blind fervor,
> on the same level as the guilt of treason against the fa-
> therland? Might not Your Imperial Majesty consider that
> my brother has already atoned for his thoughtless be-
> havior by giving up eight of the best years of his life,
> separated from all whom he loves? And may not I my-
> self, Sire, once more speak for him to the kindness that
> is one of your traits?
> Many remarks made by His Late Majesty Alexander,
> particularly the one you were so kind to pass on to me
> in Berlin, have led me to the belief that my unfortunate
> brother's sufferings have frequently been aggravated due
> to disturbances of his mind; not that this has ever been
> expressed quite so clearly, no doubt in order to spare
> my sensibilities. However, if my fears in this regard
> should prove justified, I beg Your Imperial Highness not
> to consider that as an impediment to the prisoner's re-

lease, because that state of affairs, frightful in itself, adds
to the hardships he has had to suffer until now, and ren-
ders quite impossible his recovery, which can be expected to occur only in the care of his family, in
peaceful surroundings created to provide a counter-
weight to the fury of his thoughts, and in the proximity
of loved ones, of which he has been deprived for so
long . . .

I have to admit that this is the most skillful and substantive passage
of his letter. What follows, strikes me as somehow embarrassing,
if not a trifle repulsive—but for the fact that Georg does seem to
aspire to the possibility of finally joining his brother in a truly
heroic manner:

I would ask Your Imperial Highness for permission to
deliver my petition in person, accompanying it with a
personal expression of my esteem and my sincere good
wishes for the Prosperity of Your Government, but a
pernicious affliction of my eyes that has troubled me for
a long time [*for several years, Georg had, indeed, suffered
from intermittent bouts with some kind of eye inflammation*]
compels me to stay close to the physicians who attend
to me. Thus, Sire, and to my great disappointment, I
cannot join your devoted servants and be present at the
solemn ceremony that will join us to Your Imperial
Highness by means of a new oath, and, as I have said,
cannot present this petition which concerns the wishes
dearest to my heart, but even find myself compelled to
use another's hand to convey it to paper.
    Sire, I beg you to receive this graciously, and to gra-
ciously return to a grief-stricken spouse her protector, to
a child orphaned before his birth, his father who has
never set eyes on him, and to a deeply grieving brother,
the most reliable friend he has ever had . . .

Damn the fellow! He does not know what Timo has written to
the Czar. But he knows his brother. He knows his ironclad up-

bringing, he knows his impetuous temper. His notions of what his brother's letter to the Czar must have been like *must* include an inkling of the possibilities! And yet, in his own letter to the Czar he calls his brother *the most reliable friend he has ever had* . . . What should one call that? Courage? Pride? Thoughtlessness? Loyalty?

May the day when these lines reach you, Sire, be a day graced in your soul by the sweet knowledge that you have returned peace to an entire family!

With the deepest respect, Sire,
Your Imperial Majesty's devoted subject,
Georges de Bock,
Colonel

Thursday, the sixth of December, 1828

And this is Eeva's letter to Nicholas, written on the twenty-third of January of last year:

Our Highly Esteemed Emperor,
Gracious and Benevolent Lord
Nikolai Pavlovich,

Monarch of all Russians, etc. etc. Once again, this unfortunate spouse, this deeply grieving mother of an underage son, most humbly presumes to approach Your Imperial Majesty's throne on her knees.

Eight years ago, my husband, Colonel Timofey von Bock, was taken from us, and we were not given any recourse that would have enabled us to learn anything about his fate: whether he is still among the living, or whether I am a widow, and my son a poor fatherless orphan . . .

That seems rather bold, to write as if she had no knowledge of Timo's fate . . . But, why not? No one had deigned to make an *official* reply to any of our desperate inquiries! All we knew we had found out piecemeal, from hearsay, and through bribes and madcap tricks! Gone for eight years—that was God's truth. And for six of those, no letter, not a single word. Why shouldn't Eeva write the way she does.

> Save me, save me, Your Imperial Majesty, let me at
> least have some news, should it prove impossible to sat-
> isfy my even more ardent and humble request to pardon
> my beloved husband and father of my child!

That "should it prove impossible" indicates, to me at least, that she knows everything—including the fact that a pardon is impossible (or has been so up to this time), and also why that is the case . . . For that reason, she ends her letter in the following manner:

> I address my prayers to Your Imperial Majesty's benev-
> olence: so many thousands enjoy the fatherly care of a
> kind Emperor, and I, too, dare to hope for a noble
> Monarch's solace for my grief. I pray, I beg for it with
> the deepest loyalty and humility.

Your Imperial Majesty's
most loyal servant,
K. v. Bock

In St. Petersburg, on the twenty-third of January, 1827

Still at Voisiku, the eleventh of December, 1828

As I drank my coffee this morning in the company of Eeva and Timo, I think I observed my sister more closely than is my habit, the above letter still fresh in my mind.

No feelings of embarrassment or repugnance are evoked in me

by that letter. In its lines, it is almost classical, of a concision worthy of the ancients. It feels surprisingly *right* in its abandonment of attempts to justify anything, and in addressing the recipient's *feelings* (never mind the fact that imperial feelings tend to be stern and petrified), it displays an exemplary feminine virtue . . .

Somewhere in this journal I have remarked that I do not love my sister. This morning I sat and studied her. For a while now, she has worn her hair loose, in an unaffected, domestic fashion; it is abundant, of a reddish chestnut color, set off by a plain grass-green gown with a small pin, a cameo in a gold setting. Her face, now that she has recovered from the hardship of nursing Jüri all those weeks, looks as fresh as if she had just stepped out of a warm bath. On her temples, her hair has those two startlingly white bands, like traces left by fate's icy fingers. I looked at her. She turns to somber Timo with a cheerful smile: "But of course, let's go riding together today, if you like . . ." She says to our aging Käsper, the faintest note of reproof in her voice: "The coffee-cosy is in the second drawer from the top, Käsper. Where it's always been . . ." Then she turns back to Timo: "Yesterday, I wrote a letter to Jüri. I'll read it to you when we get back, and I'd like you to add a couple of lines, you know he expects that . . ." And right after that, she says to me: "Jakob, if you go to Roika—to see the Schwalbes?—could you go to the works and see if they have a mirror that would fit in our dining room? Take the measurements—it should go on the wall between those doors."

And I am thinking: This is too harmonious, too unbroken—how could I *love* it? Even *respect* would seem inadequate—if it weren't all so natural at the same time . . .

After Timo left the table to go to his study, Eeva took a moment to study a cookbook in order to see what kind of sauce she would suggest for the veal Liiso was to prepare for dinner. I said to her:

"Eeva—those papers? I burned them . . . But I didn't think you expected me to do it with my eyes closed . . ."

She looked up from her sauce recipe.

I said, "The beginning of one letter stuck in my mind . . . One you wrote to Timo, in the summer of 1820 . . ."

"What was I writing about?"

"Oh, domestic things . . . You told Timo how loyal his brother

Georg was, and how that loyalty made him worry about you, too. And then you said, 'Your brother Karl stays away, and I prefer it that way, because I could not live in peace here at Voisiku if he were here . . .' How so? How would Karl have affected your life here?"

Eeva looked straight at me. Then she cast a glance to the left, at the door to the corridor through which Timo had passed a moment ago, then looked at me again and said:

"If you really want to know, I'll tell you. Tonight."

Now it is eleven o'clock, but she hasn't appeared here. All I really wanted to effect with my question was a little pinprick at her *perfection* . . .

I have only seen Timo's younger brother Karl (he is five years younger than Timo, three years younger than Georg) a couple of times. In the autumn of 1817, a few weeks after Eeva and Timo's wedding, he came to visit the newlyweds at Voisiku and stayed almost a week. During the years of Timo's absence I heard that he had visited once or twice while I was lugging Tenner's theodolites around the countryside. At one time there were rumors that Karl had joined a regiment in St. Petersburg, but it seems he hadn't; as far as I know, he dabbled in jurisprudence at the University of Tartu for a while, though he never acquired any official rank or degree. He is simply Mr. von Bock, or he could use the meaningless *Gerichtsassessor*, if a title were required for some reason. These days, he is said to be living in Germany, or elsewhere in Europe, relying, like Georg, on funds extracted from Voisiku, but is not close to Georg, and is even said to have separated from his wife. I remember him as a very handsome, swarthy young man, closer to Georg's frivolous type than to Timo's more solemn one. It seemed to me that Lehrberg's humanism had left some traces in him, even if he did not seem to live up to Lehrberg's ethical demands . . .

At half past eleven, Eeva knocked on my door. I shoved my journal into a drawer and asked her to come in. She sat down in my old wicker armchair.

"Well, my grand inquisitor, you don't miss much, do you? Sometimes you even notice things that don't exist . . . Are you saying that you never noticed that Karl—how should I put it— made advances to me?"

I had to admit that this was one thing I had, indeed, missed. I asked her how and when this had happened, and she told me—a little stiffly and flippantly, but she told me, nevertheless.

Karl had declared his love for Eeva on that very first visit in '17, when he came to stay with the newlyweds for a week. He had also proclaimed it to Timo, who had then told him to join the army and to stay away from Voisiku. Karl had left, for the army, or abroad, or wherever, but a year after Timo's arrest he had returned, looking genuinely downcast. He told Eeva that he had left his wife, and once again he declared his love and implored her . . . When Eeva explained to him that he should not expect anything from her, Karl told her that he had just realized it was indeed Eeva's—as he put it—*sacred austerity* that had driven him mad with love for her . . .

"Then he left and swore he would never return, and I was so relieved I wrote those words to Timo that you saw . . ."

I asked (perhaps, once again, goading her a little), "And has Karl left you in peace since that time?"

Eeva shook her head.

"In the spring of '26, he came back to Voisiku, that awful spring . . . Jüri had that bad case of scarlet fever . . . Then there was the trial of the Decembrists . . . And renewed rumors about Timo losing his mind . . . No, Karl did not come right out with it and say that those rumors were enough reason for me to get a divorce from Timo—but it seemed to me that that was what he was trying to tell me, almost against his will . . . He invited me to go abroad with him, to give my mind a rest, as he put it . . . He said all he expected from me was the sort of intimate friendship that was natural among kinfolk . . . And I was so overwrought with all my worries that I almost told him, all right, for God's sake, let me see some new faces, breathe another kind of air for a couple of weeks . . . But what I said to him was—and I don't know what made me so brazen, I suppose it was simply the state I was in— I told him that there was one thing he had to understand: if I were to go and 'give my mind a rest' with anybody, it would *not* be on terms of 'intimate friendship'—but that he, Timo's brother, just did not fit the bill . . ."

"What happened then?"

"Oh, he started spouting all kinds of things . . . In the end, I had to shut his mouth with my own hands . . ."

I looked at her and tried to picture that exact image, of her shutting his mouth with her own hands—but all I had the nerve to ask her was simply, "And then?"

"Then he explained that it was precisely because I was—oh, I don't know—because I was such an *unspoiled child of nature* that it was impossible for him to leave me alone . . ."

"But he has?"

"Yes. He went away, and a year later, Timo was released. Since then, no one has heard a thing from or about him."

Monday, the nineteenth of March, 1829

I'm amazed to see that date: I haven't had a chance to open this journal for more than three months . . .

This morning I rode to Poltsamaa. Anna had asked me to bring her some cardamom from Kärm's store when I came to Roika at Eastertime. She claimed that the Russian women of the township had taught her how to prepare some Easter delicacy.

After some warmer weather, it had turned cold again, and this morning the road was bone-hard after many weeks of thaw. I had already traveled a couple of versts in the direction of the Pilistver Highway, the snowy Nomaver Woods to my left, when I heard behind me the hoofbeats of another horse and then a shout.

"Hallo! Mr. Jakob!"

It was Monsieur La Trobe, our landlord, as it were. I reined in my bay and let Monsieur La Trobe catch up with me on his blue roan. Looking at his face and hearing his stertorous breathing I could tell that he had been tearing along, but now he slowed down to a more measured pace and said, still catching his breath:

". . . I see you're headed to Poltsamaa as well . . . I'm—on my way to bring back Dr. Robst . . . You never know . . . Though I myself . . . But when it is one's own child . . . It's our Pauline, she's eighteen months old . . . She's had a fever for a while now . . . I can't figure it out . . . And, yes: we're leaving Voisiku, in a week . . . One doesn't want to do that with an ailing child. It's still so cold . . . But—it's the Governor General's orders . . ."

This was news to me, and I saw immediately that it could bring about great changes at Voisiku. I tried to conceal my ignorance and surprise and asked him:

"Oh, you are moving? So soon?"

"You don't know?" Monsieur La Trobe grabbed the reins of my horse, and we stopped in the middle of the road. His eyes were earnest below his slightly shabby otter-fur hat.

"Just a moment. I can't tell this to Mr. von Bock, nor to his lady. But I want *someone* to know, and you are rather familiar with the matter. You see, after your brother-in-law refused my offer—to have him read through my reports and amend them as needed—no, no one can hear us here, except for these horses— you see, after that I simply *couldn't write those reports . . .*" He looked at me, expecting me to indicate that I believed him, but I didn't say a word. I don't really know why—in part, I suppose, simply to let him continue, but also out of a desire to let him stew a little, although I don't see why I felt he deserved that. He shouted, so loudly that the horses trembled and twitched their ears:

"Do you understand—I haven't written a single word for them!"

I remained silent but nodded, and that seemed to calm him down. He continued, quietly: "And thank God for that . . . But now we see the consequences. Mr. von Mannteuffel will arrive and take possession of the manor on St. George's Day."

I asked, "As the new leaseholder appointed by the guardianship board?"

"Exactly."

I said, "And also as the Governor General's new spy?"

Monsieur La Trobe let go of the reins, spread his arms in the air.

"Mr. Mettich—please! I did not want to say anything about *that* aspect of the matter . . ."

"Not even if no one can hear us except for our horses?"

Now he was standing in his stirrups, and his hands were still spread out against the snowy fields and copses—only now I noticed that he wasn't wearing gloves.

"No! Not even then," he said. "I speak only about what concerns myself, and remain silent about the rest, as a matter of principle. I certainly hope I won't ever again have anything to do with those gentlemen. We are moving first to Poltsamaa, but then I'll try to get to Tartu as soon as I can. Von Liphart has asked me to come there to instruct his string quartet. And then, you know—I have plans for

Tartu: I'll start a *big mixed choir there!* Just think of it: *a hundred voices* singing Handel's 'Hallelujah' between the vaulted walls of Jaan's Church . . . Let me tell you: if the angels in heaven sing any differently from that Handel, then I don't want to go to heaven! But now, excuse me—I am in a hurry, I must catch Dr. Robst before he starts out on his rounds. I shall see you before we move . . ."

April the ninth, 1829

A fortnight has passed since the La Trobes moved away, and I did not really get to see them before their move, except to bid farewell in front of the manor as their carriage stood waiting for them in the sleeting rain. Madame Alwine sat in the carriage with the children, looking paler than usual, the little girl in her lap, the boy next to her. Monsieur La Trobe stood by the open carriage door and shook my hand for a surprisingly long time; he didn't let go of it, but leaned forward and asked:

"Mr. Jakob—tell me, did I, while I was here—" his left hand described an arc that was meant to include all of Voisiku, but when it came to a halt, it clearly pointed in the direction of The Foundation behind its now skeletal wild rose bushes—"did I, in every respect, behave like what the English call a—*gentleman?* Tell me!"

For some reason, I hesitated for a moment before answering.

"Yes, Monsieur La Trobe, you did. No question of it."

Whereafter the sweet old fool kissed me on the left temple and bounded into the carriage. I haven't heard anything from them since. Von Mannteuffel isn't here yet, and I try not to think about his arrival. I thank God that I have pleasanter kinfolk—at least two.

This morning, Eeva gave me a letter that arrived recently from Georg. I copy it verbatim:

My Dear Brother and My Dear Brother's Wife!

When I returned from Livonia, our affairs in Berlin looked rather hopeless, but then a few surprisingly favorable events came to our aid, and we have, at last,

been able to establish ourselves in a respectable manner.
First and foremost this was possible thanks to our dear
brother-in-law Peter, who sent us my share of the value
of Voisiku, fifteen thousand rubles in silver. Here that
amounts to a little more than two thousand louis d'or.
So we have moved from Berlin to Switzerland, and
have rented a small chateau in the vicinity of Vevey. It
really is a tiny chateau, and if it were of more recent
vintage, it would hardly be called one; but since it dates
from the sixteenth century, it retains its grandiose desig-
nation in local parlance, and Teresa was even more
amused by that than was I . . . In reality, it is a stone
tower with a circular ground plan and four floors. Each
floor has an entrance hall and two or three larger or
smaller rooms. All the windows have a marvelous view
over the vineyards in the middle of which we live, and
of the mountains to the north; but all the south-facing
windows open onto the shimmering turquoise waters of
Lake Geneva, reflecting both the sky and the mountains.
From our gate, it is less than a quarter of a verst to its
shore. As one ascends from one floor to the next, the
views expand and become more magnificent. I can only
imagine how beneficial it would be for your nerves,
Timo, and how restful for Kitty, if you could be our
guests and—I go on fantasizing—stand in front of an
open window in the big room on the top floor, breathing in the breeze wafting across the lake from Ferney
and the south . . . We have a serious proposal for you:
address yourselves to the gracious Emperor and apply
for permission, for yourselves and, of course, little
Georg to visit us. Surely, where his subjects' health is
concerned, our present Emperor won't be stingier in regard to such a permission than his brother was, only a
few years ago, when he graciously permitted us, due to
our Agnes's weak lungs, to exchange the air of Russia
for the air of foreign climes . . . But if, contrary to expectation, you were to be denied permission to travel to
us, this would naturally cause chagrin to all concerned;

nevertheless, a thoughtful human being can find solace
in the midst of the sorest of tribulations, and so, I am
sure, you would, too—perhaps for example in the droll
manner one of the late General Plutalov's nephews (the
general told me this himself on one occasion) had employed when he had encountered difficulties in his attempt to clink glasses with his dear uncle. Ho-ho-ho-ho
—whoa! I don't know if you recall the anecdote, but I
remember telling it to you, or one of you, and we
laughed fit to bust . . . Well, then. Teresa and Agnes
send their sincerest regards with mine, and all of us believe that we shall soon see you with our own eyes and
touch you with our own hands.

> Your loving brother and brother-in-law,
> Georg

At Vevey, the twenty-sixth of March, 1829

In the afternoon, Eeva came to my room and asked me what I
thought of Georg's letter. I had already copied it into my journal,
and I gave it back to her, saying:

"I really can't forgive him his extravagance. Never mind his
dice game last Christmas—but with those fifteen thousand rubles,
which are the reason we now have to endure Mannteuffel, he rents
himself a *chateau* over there . . . What affectation! But I forgive
him his frivolous babble about praying to the Czar, although it
truly got my goat when I first read it. It is the suggestion of an
idiot, as he well knows. But then I suddenly understood: Georg
isn't being literal here, he's just pulling the wool over the censors'
eyes. He doesn't really believe for a moment that the Czar would
give you permission to travel abroad. He is, in fact, inciting
you—this is the message—to flee Russia in some equally precip-
itate manner as the one he himself once employed to gain entrance
to Schlüsselburg—remember?"

"Of course I do," Eeva said.

I asked her if she agreed with my interpretation of the letter,
and she said she agreed completely. Then I asked her why she was
quizzing me about it, and she said she had done so to gain cor-
roboration of her own thoughts. Then she said she thought I

should go to Pärnu again in June and arrange a meeting with Captain Snyder, after she had gone to Tsarskoye in May and brought Jüri home.

I said, "But, Eeva—it occurred to me in the autumn, when I was on that same errand—how will Timo be able to leave this place? If we're out of luck, they may have gendarmes on his trail from the very start . . ."

"But we won't be out of luck. And not in the spring," Eeva said. Then she moved closer, sat down on the corner of my desk and continued in a whisper. "On the guardianship board, La Trobe has been replaced by von Lilienfeldt from Uus-Poltsamaa. Who knows what he is really like, but he is a friend of Viljandi's *Ordnungsrichter*, Loringhoven." Eeva bent forward and said, in an even quieter voice, "I asked von Lilienfeldt for an introduction, and last week I went to see Loringhoven and discussed the matter with him, as best I could. I asked him whether he couldn't, in his capacity as an *Ordnungsrichter*, give Timo permission to travel to Harjumaa in the spring, for his health, and to visit relatives. In my company, as my responsibility . . ."

"What did Loringhoven say?"

"He—he smiled and squirmed in his chair and tried to be *chivalrous* . . . You see, he's so proud of his ancestry that he regards being the *Ordnungsrichter* at Viljandi as something of a joke . . ."

I asked her what blasted ancestry he was so proud of.

"Well, the ancestral Loringhoven was a Grand Master of the Livonian Knights. And they have always been regarded as the peers of kings."

I whistled and asked Eeva again what this descendant of kings had told her.

"He immediately took out the stipulations the Governor General had sent him, read them again in my presence, and noticed—well, I don't know whether he was speaking the truth or trying to be chivalrous, it's all the same to me—he noticed that if one so wished, the stipulations could be understood to say that an *Ordnungsrichter* may at his own discretion issue a permit for such a journey . . ."

"And so?"

"So I asked him to issue a permit for me . . . You know, I've noticed something: when I gather up all my strength and *will* someone to do something, they usually do it, as long as they are close by. And that's what happened."

"How?"

"I have the permit. I only need to fill in the date when we leave."

Now, this was quite an achievement. Still, I asked her, "And you'll go with him, and be *responsible* for him?"

Eeva bit her soft but stubborn-looking lower lip and nodded.

I asked, "But you gave your signature and your assurance that you'll be responsible, that you . . ."

Eeva slid off the corner of the desk—I knew that she did this so she'd be able to emphasize her words by stamping her foot, and the realization made me smile in spite of her words.

"Such a signature doesn't mean a thing to me! When it is given under *such* conditions . . ."

I said, "But to the Czar's way of thinking, it means . . ."

Eeva said, "Let it mean! He's only pretending to think. And so am I, until we get going. Then the pretense is over, and the game begins in earnest."

The twenty-ninth of April, 1829

The inevitable has happened. Last week, in spite of terrible road conditions, the Mannteuffels arrived here with two enormous pack trains—and that wasn't even the whole family. Already there seem to be more than enough of them: Peter, as stodgy, blue-chinned, and crew-cut as ever, who has already managed to stick his peevish nose into everything. His Elsy, the same old catarrh-ridden busybody, but really not such a bad sort. Fifteen-year-old Claire, shaped like a baker's wife, who tries to overcome her embarrassment about her obesity by chattering constantly, in a boring, but sometimes quite intelligent, fashion. Emma, a dark-haired eleven-year-old dumpling. Ten-year-old Max and six-year-old Alex, two freckled and rather noisy little monkeys. Mannteuffel also has three older sons from his first marriage, Gerhard, Otto, and Karl, all of them over twenty and busy elsewhere, the first two as officers of the crown, the last one as a student at the

University of Tartu. We'll have the honor and pleasure of receiving Karl this summer—at what is now his father's hereditary estate . . .

The third of May, 1829

The inevitable has happened . . . This morning, the three of us were celebrating the Sabbath by sitting in The Foundation's drawing room, and Timo was playing the piano, when Peter walked in with a most accommodating expression on his face. Well, as accommodating as is possible given a mouth too small and twisted for the massive chin, and a pair of lugubrious, deep-set eyes.

Timo acknowledged his salutation rather absentmindedly, but Eeva offered him a seat. After he had settled on our squeaky sofa, he uttered a few polite phrases in his deep and somehow plaintive voice. Then he said:

"My dear friends—I'd like us to lay our cards on the table. Mutually, and in every matter. Timo—I've heard that you are writing something. Of course I won't tell you that you can't do that. Go on, write, if that's all you want to do. But I want to read what you are writing."

All three of us looked at him with unconcealed astonishment. Timo must have been the first to understand, for his voice, to my ears, sounded choked with indignation:

"How am I supposed to take that . . . ?"

"I meant just what I said," Peter replied. "As I told you, I want us to lay our cards on the table." (This is an expression I have heard Peter use frequently during his first week here at Voisiku —just as I've heard Elsy, behind his back, insisting that Peter is a vastly honorable man.) "Yes, cards on the table. So, Timo, you should know—and all of you should know: I am writing reports on you to the Governor General. Twice a month. I note how you are doing, what you are saying, with what you are busying yourself. How could I report that you are *writing* without stating *what* it is you're writing?"

"And why not?" Timo asked. "No one who knows you would suspect you of a passionate interest in the written word. Besides, aren't you breaking your own stipulations? By announcing to us that you've been obliged to write reports on me? Isn't my surveillance supposed to be secret?"

Peter tilted his head to the right, made his jaw jut even farther:

"Listen, von Bock, you ought to understand one thing, even if your understanding may be impaired. A von Mannteuffel is not a spy. Nor does he go by the book, in blind obedience. What use would secret surveillance be?"

"But openly declared surveillance *is* useful?" Timo said.

"Well, it *might* be. Particularly if you have enough sense to stop wasting paper—because you know that it arouses suspicions against you, and that it is being observed."

"So you want to read what I have written? You think you'll enjoy it?"

"I don't know whether I will or not," Peter said, "but then, I'm not that keen on enjoyment, anyway. I have to go and examine a huge tract of fields to see whether Timm made sure the manure was spread properly. So—*give me the key to your desk.*"

Timo set his elbows on the armrests of his chair and tapped his fingertips as if miming the itsy bitsy spider. He said, in a quiet, completely unemotional voice:

"Not to you, not voluntarily."

I saw Eeva blanch and compress her lips, but before she had time to say anything, Peter went on, more promptly and compliantly than I would have expected:

"I see. Well, I'm not going to force you. I'll take your no for a no." He smiled acidly and changed the subject:

"Do you remember how offended you were when I had you move here from the main building? And now you're doing so well here—the place is bone dry. And outside those windows— I can just imagine how fragrant it will be in here, come spring, when everything is in flower. Lovely, really. If *we* could all squeeze in here, I'd take this place at the drop of a hat, and let you go back to the main building. There, all the inside walls on the orchard side are dripping with moisture."

Timo asked, "Well, weren't they dripping back at Harm, too?"

Peter said, without guile, "Much less so than here."

"Then I'd like to recommend that you move back to Harm," Timo said, in a tone almost devoid of irony. "It would be better for you, and for all of us."

Peter looked at Eeva and me as if pleading for help. He almost smiled but kept his serious mien, spread out his palms, and sighed in our direction:

"What can you say to a madman?"

Then he got up, nodded his goodbyes, and left. I asked Timo if he was going to protect his papers from Peter somehow, and Timo replied, curtly, "We'll see . . ." For a moment I had thought of telling him about the hiding place I had made for my own papers. Then I realized that this would have been *too great* a revelation about myself. I doubt, however, that Peter has given up his designs on Timo's papers.

The fourth of May, 1829

Late in the evening, Timo knocked on my door, asked me to come over to their rooms for a moment, then said:

"You've acted as a mediator before—remember that time with Georg and me? Please, render that service to my wife and me."

In the dining room, Eeva sat behind the table knitting a stocking, and I noticed that her face was far stonier than I had seen it in recent times. Between the half-empty teacups on the table was a silver platter covered with a white napkin, and on it an arrangement of slices of golden-yellow raisin cake.

I said, "Look at that, you baked a nice cake"—for it didn't look like one of Liiso's. I had never seen her serve anything like it.

"I didn't bake it," Eeva said. "That's exactly why Timo thought it was necessary to ask you—"

As it turned out, these were slices of a cake that Elsy had baked in the main building. A little while ago, Elsy had brought them over to The Foundation and set the platter on the dining room table while Timo and Eeva were taking their Sunday evening stroll along the fields behind the orchard, pondering and worrying about

Peter's remarks that morning. When they returned, Käsper had showed them Elsy's cake and had also conveyed her message to them: that the cake had been made according to their mother's— Elsy and Timo's sainted mother's—raisin-cake recipe . . . Timo said to me:

"I noticed how Eeva's brow clouded over when she heard that. I asked her why it disturbed her that my sister had brought us some cake, and when she didn't reply, I told her to be completely frank with me. But it seems one can't even ask one's nearest and dearest for that—because . . . Please, Kitty, tell Jakob what you said to me."

Eeva looked up from her knitting. I thought I detected the faintest trace of an embarrassed smile on her face, but her eyes were painfully serious.

"I said that I did not think it was appropriate for us to accept Elsy's cake. Because I'm certain that Elsy knew about Peter's visit to us this morning, and she brought us the cake as *her good deed.* At least that was part of the reason, and if we accept it, she'll think that we have agreed to what Peter suggested this morning."

"That's what you said," Timo nodded. "And I said that Elsy is my sister, after all. That she is *eine geborene von Bock.* And just because she is—regrettably—married to Peter, one cannot assume that she approves everything Peter does . . ."

At which point, Eeva said, "And then I asked Timo if he didn't know from experience how greatly conjoined a wife is to her husband in his actions! And I said that I mightn't be splitting hairs quite so fine in this case if he himself had not taught me to be attentive in matters like these . . ."

I looked at them. I felt very uncomfortable and indecisive. (I suspect that this new situation may create truly discouraging tensions.)

I asked, "And what do you think I should be able to tell you?"

Timo paced back and forth behind Eeva's chair.

He said, "Please, tell us what we should do. As far as I can see, Kitty is right, up to a point. But surely we can't send the cake back to Elsy—how would we do it? Who would take it there? One of the servants? Or I? Or Kitty? In each and every case, it would be an unwarranted insult to Elsy. It would end our familial relations as brother and sister. Maybe I *have* to sever that bond.

Maybe even soon. But we don't have to do it *tonight* . . . And I don't want Kitty to take the cake back—because then Elsy would see *her* as the evil spirit that comes between sister and brother . . . So . . ."—he turned to me—"what should we do?"

I said I didn't know, and added that I thought they would now have to be extremely tolerant, because they would otherwise have to deal with ridiculous family conflicts—and extremely watchful, because Peter might otherwise really do them some harm. How they would manage to combine those two, tolerance and watchfulness, I really couldn't tell them. Then I went back to my room and lay between my slightly damp sheets, feeling distressed and perplexed until I fell asleep.

At today's breakfast table, Timo and Eeva looked rather more cheerful, thank God, and Eeva told me that last night, ten minutes after I had left, Claire had come to see them. She regards herself as sufficiently grown-up not to have to go to bed at the same time "as the children," and she had come to chat with her uncle and her uncle's wife. She hadn't noticed their slightly odd expressions, but she certainly noticed the raisin cake. She had clapped her hands and exclaimed that half of that "terribly terribly tasty cake" had mysteriously disappeared from their coffee table in the main building—and now she discovers it here! She asked if she might have a slice. Eeva said to me, "You know, she is one of those young girls who weep because they're overweight yet keep stuffing themselves, so I really didn't want to let her have a slice—but what I said was: 'Have all four slices—on the condition that you tell your mother that it was you who ate them!' And Claire promised that she would confess her sin to her mother on the first suitable occasion, then went ahead and ate the lot . . ."

Nevertheless, I'm still haunted by dark premonitions.

The ninth of May, 1829

It didn't take very long for those premonitions to prove true. We received a taste of what lay ahead of us, how we were going to be treated in the future. (How naïve of me to write that we received that "taste" today, considering that these things have been quite clear to me for many weeks—God, years . . .)

This morning, Eeva journeyed to Viljandi to replenish our home pharmacy from Schoeler's stores. Eeva mentioned that Timo was once again suffering from his rash, and that she also had to take medicines to a few needy villagers. Timo himself went out riding around eleven o'clock; he would be back by four, as was his habit, in time to get ready for dinner.

He had hardly cantered across our mill bridge and disappeared in the alder grove when there was a knock on my door. Since I hadn't locked it, I shouted, "Come in!" and Peter Mannteuffel entered.

Some instinctive perversity kept me from rising to greet him. I stayed put in my wicker armchair. I can't remember whether he said anything by way of greeting, but his tone was clearly peremptory:

"Jakob—come with me!"

Feeling all the more comfortable in my seat, I waved nonchalantly at the other wicker chair.

"Hold on, Mr. Peter. *Where* do you want me to go with you?"

Still on his feet, he explained:

"As you must know, *I* am now the officer of the law on this estate. Well, then. Here I have the key to your brother-in-law's desk. A skeleton key, it's called. It works. I shall now go and look through his papers. In his absence. Only to keep him from trying to prevent me. And I will admit it to him, of course. So he can protest as much as he wants—later. I don't think he will, because he knows that it is futile to make a fuss, for someone in his legal situation."

"But why do you want me to go with you?"

"Well, to have you as my witness, in case your sister starts protesting. She, too, has been appointed her husband's guardian, to some extent—although I consider that a rather risky choice on the authorities' part. But it is the case, and she might start spouting all kinds of female nonsense—the wife of a man who has been declared insane!—accusing me of God knows what infractions of the law. And there are those who might, well, perhaps not believe her, but at least listen to her. She is Mrs. von Bock, isn't she? No one asks her where she was born. In some circles you can even find fools who will regard her scandalously humble birth as a point in her favor. And so, I want you to witness my visit to their quarters. You can follow me and ask me for an explanation. So, please come, right away."

Surprising myself, I took the time to consider whether Mannteuffel's behavior was that of a pure-bred cynic or that of a simple and straightforward Baltic nobleman. Then I realized that the question I really needed to answer was quite different . . .

I said, "So you have a key for his desk. But I happen to know that the door to his study will also be locked."

"We have a complete set of keys for The Foundation, over there in the main building," Peter said, imperturbably. He took a key out of the pocket of his blue smoking jacket. "Here it is: number five."

I had to say something to him.

I said, "Listen—Mr. Mannteuffel . . ." and I wanted to continue: "Listen, do as you please! But *I* won't take part in it. I won't! And I urge you not to break into his study, because I think it would be an act of utmost disrespect, an outrage!"

But I did not speak those words. I told myself that they would have no effect on him. As I knew him, he would go ahead and do exactly what he had decided to do. But—perhaps I could manage to conceal something, if I did go with him after all? Not likely . . . But at least I'd see *what* he did there—if, say, he removed some of Timo's papers . . . God knows—at least I'd be able to testify about what took place . . .

I said, "Well, all right, then. I'll go with you . . ." Now, it seemed to me that this sounded too different from what I would have liked to say, and as we were leaving my room, I added: "But I still urge you to *abandon* the idea . . ." As I said that, I slowed down a bit, but he kept moving along at such clip that I had to hurry to keep up with him as we traversed the dining room. As we entered the corridor on the far side of the dining room, I said, pointedly (perhaps even more pointedly than I had intended, because he had forced me to run after him):

"And the only reason I'm coming with you is to be able to testify against you, if need be."

Mannteuffel stopped and turned to me, so that we were suddenly standing very close, face to face, in the half-dark corridor. I thought: Well, that got me off the hook—and I also thought: Well, now he won't let me see what he's doing there . . . *and I won't see what papers Timo has there* . . .

He was, however, a more self-assured man than I had thought. He glared at me for a moment, then grunted, by way of some kind of vague affirmation. He turned again, took five strides, and unlocked the door to Timo's study: *"Bitte schön."*

Once in the room, he made a show of ignoring me. With deliberate carelessness, he sat down on Timo's chair, produced his skeleton key, opened the drawers and pulled them out.

Two of the six drawers contained a haphazard collection of stuff: a pair of spurs, one of them broken, an old tobacco pouch made out of a pig's bladder, a rusty pistol, a few cartridge shells, a couple of bronze spoons, a belt, a few buckles without belts, two low candlesticks, a few simple tinderboxes obviously made by the blacksmith at Voisiku, a couple of bundles of untrimmed goose quills, a few knives for trimming them, and half a box of sleigh bells. One drawer contained almost a quarter of a ream of paper, one was full of books, and two had stacks of manuscript pages in them.

Mannteuffel didn't waste time studying the miscellaneous items. He put his thumb on the edge of the quarter-ream and turned a few sheets until he was satisfied that nothing had been written on them. The books he took out, one by one, stacking them on the table. I counted twenty-seven volumes of different sizes. He opened the first volume, glanced at the title page, and returned the book to the drawer. He repeated the procedure with the second, the third, the fourth, the fifth volume . . . I thought I detected a degree of uncertainty in his ponderous gestures. I stood a couple of steps away from him and let my eyes roam across the sofa and the chairs and the smoking table with Timo's pipes, and over the big globe that reminded me of Eeva's dramatic "confrontation," with Paulucci, then over the bookcases with their five hundred–odd volumes—the books Timo hadn't considered worth locking up . . . I stepped a little closer and looked over Mannteuffel's shoulder at the ninth volume he had picked from the pile. It was a cookbook, in French. The next one was also a French cookbook, as was the one after that. Followed by cookbooks in German, French, Polish, English, and Estonian. There were two in Estonian, dating from 1781 and 1816, if memory serves . . .

I asked, "Cookbooks? *All of them?*"

"All of them," Mannteuffel said. "I've always said that he is mad." Suddenly he turned and squinted at me. "Or do you believe he isn't?"

I looked him in the eye and said, without the least pang of conscience:

"Well, of course he is—two emperors have said so, and so have you."

He looked at me for a moment, snorted, and turned to the manuscript drawers. He leafed through and sorted the handwritten pages for more than two hours. I'm sure that he would have taken at least one more hour, if I hadn't been there, or perhaps three times as long. From the very first pages I glanced at, I knew I could have told him exactly what they were: Timo's school notes from Lehrberg's classes in the years 1794 to 1800. They were the same pages I had studied in Masing's house and later returned to Voisiku. Only at the bottom of the lower manuscript drawer, beneath the last batch of school books, after the final installment of Laplace's astronomical mechanics, Mannteuffel found the only page in those drawers that was something else, that was of a later date, and thus perhaps corresponded to his notion of the kind of writing he was looking for.

He pulled out that final page and took a long time perusing it. Then he grunted:

"See what you make of this."

I looked. I'll try to reproduce what I read as exactly as possible. It may not be exactly right, because it is impossible to recall this kind of stuff verbatim:

My Most Highly Revered and Most Illustrious Sire,
Field Marshal Burkhard Christoforovich!

After it has come to my notice that Neptun Votano-
vich Perunski has been appointed the new Head Procur-

ator of the Holy Synod, I beg Your Illustriousness to
make certain that my letter with its enclosed proposals
of utmost importance to the State is brought to the attention of the appropriate authorities without delay.

The most spherical virtue of my most trusted friend,
Ivan Diabolovich, is his unique ability to inseminate the
likes of Thucydides with organ music. But Vassili Nikolayevich buys and sells the bathwater of the muses with
money that hardly smells at all. And if Your Illustriousness should happen to require an Imperial Head Mediator of Respectability to be appointed to a commensurate,
undoubtedly most lucrative, post, it would be quite
gauche to forget our dear uncle, Pyotr Pavlovich! For
who would deserve our esteem more than our so very
dear kinsmen! And give my cordial regards to your
nephew, the Captain of the Guards, whom I last met in
Nicaragua, or was it at Vitebsk, and who, alas, has been
dead for only thirty years and hence is such a novice to
this basic human activity that it may be difficult for
Your Illustriousness to establish contact with him in order to convey to him these regards of mine,

>   despite the fact that I am, forever,
>   the most suspect servant
>   of the enemies of Your Illustriousness,
>   Timothy Shock

"Well, what is this?" Mannteuffel (Mr. Pyotr Pavlovich Mannteuffel) asked me through clenched teeth.

I told him I had no idea.

"But who is this Field Marshal Burkhard Christoforovich?"

I said, "Münnich, I suppose."

"How long has it been since Münnich died?"

"Oh, about seventy years."

Mr. Peter did not ask me who I thought "our dear uncle
Pyotr Pavlovich" was. He had another, emphatically voiced question:

"But what the hell do you think all this means?"

Once again, I told him I had no idea. With a shrug and a har-rumph, he forgave me my peasant's simplemindedness. He put Timo's fantastic letter back on the bottom of the drawer and stacked Lehrberg's lessons on top of it in neat piles. He closed the drawers carefully and locked them. As he was locking the study door behind us, he told me:

"Well, you can tell them or not, as you please. Only—if you keep quiet about this, it may not . . ."

I said, "Don't worry, I'll tell them."

He harrumphed again and gave me a long stare. At the dining room door we parted ways, and I came back to my room to try to figure out what happened.

I'll tell Eeva as soon as possible about this examination of Timo's desk drawers. I'll tell Eeva first, as soon as she returns from Vil-jandi, because I can't predict how the news might affect Timo. Let Eeva decide if she wants to tell Timo about it or not. The main thing is something else. The main thing is that Peter's out-rageous search for Timo's papers is an incontrovertible fact. Timo must have hidden his real writings of recent times somewhere else, and Peter knows that they exist. Even if I shouldn't happen to be present at his further investigations, I know that he will go on with them. The main thing is this new oppressive regime, not only in regard to Timo's papers, but to Timo himself, to Eeva, all of us . . . So, there is that. Then there is, without a doubt, the fact that Peter may ask himself—and considering his dismally skeptical cast of mind, he'll ask himself sooner rather than later— whether his mad brother-in-law does not have an accomplice in his lowly born wife's brother? Perhaps his mad (or half-mad, or all too sane) brother-in-law is deceiving him and storing his sus-picious papers in his wife's brother's room? Peter has all the keys to The Foundation, I witnessed that myself . . . The next time I go to see Anna—five minutes after my departure—he'll detach key number six from his bunch and come to my door with such an imperturbable, gentlemanly mien that it'll be obvious he doesn't care whether anyone sees him or not—and he'll unlock the door, and enter the room, as tirelessly curious as ever . . . And then, only a half-inch thick board of pine above the connecting door will separate him from this journal of mine . . .

I have to decide if it is possible for me to stay in this house—if I want to preserve my journal. Or if it is possible to stay even if I decide to burn it. In that case, I have to decide what to do with the manuscript of Timo's memorandum to the Czar. It seems to me I do not have the right to burn it—never mind what he himself would do if I gave it back to him.

I know what I'll do: saddle up and ride away. And stay away until tomorrow night. In an hour, Timo will return from his ride, but Eeva won't be back from Viljandi until noon tomorrow. I don't want to see Timo before I have had the opportunity to tell Eeva about Peter's investigations. Yes, I'll saddle up and ride away, with this journal and Timo's manuscript in my saddlebag . . . No, I won't go to Anna's place. I need a quiet spot to think things over. Tiit's cabin at Näresaar. I'll hide the papers in a dry place in the loft of his cowshed, which is where I'll also stretch out, use my arm for a pillow, watch the cobwebs tremble as the breeze blows through the eaves, listen to the murmur of the forest, and try to figure out what will become of us all.

The thirteenth of May, 1829

Well, it has all been decided, and I want to give a quick summary of the sequence of events.

Just as I had written on the ninth, I rode off to Tiit's place in the woods. I could tell from a distance, seeing the rake handle leaning against the door, that he was not at home, but I didn't let that deter me. I put my horse in the shed, took the oilcloth bag full of papers to the loft and pushed it under the roof-straw behind the fourth rafter from the right. I climbed down again and stood in the middle of the yard, looking at the rickety shed from which Tiit had taken his nag and the old cow out to pasture, so that the only noise to be heard from between the half-closed doors was the snorting of my bay. I looked at the empty doghouse: Tiit must have taken Klähv along on his rounds in the woods. I looked at the trails Tiit had trodden between shed and doghouse and cabin door on the pale-green, still sparse grass of the yard, and back at the cabin door, where the rake handle leaning against the door proclaimed: Don't enter if you are a stranger . . . I wasn't a stranger here, and yet . . .

I stood there in Tiit's yard, on that cool and bright day in May, one of those when it seems like every grass stalk and pine needle is about to reveal its secrets, not that this will change anything . . . I stood there, still burdened by my worries and at the same time completely free of some other burden, and at the same time, I felt so damnably *lonely* . . . I raised my eyes and looked at my boat which lay upside down on the shore: last week, I had caulked it and given it a fresh coat of paint. I ran over to it, wrestled it right side up and into the water, grabbed the oars from the bank, jumped in, and started rowing downriver. Only after a verst or so it occurred to me that my horse would have conveyed me to my destination in half the time.

I tied my boat to Anna's landing stage and walked in. I wrapped my arms around her, kissed her dumbfounded, half-open mouth, and sensed that my eagerness to speak washed out all the question marks around my words:

"Anna . . . *Some things have happened that helped me . . . fanned the fire, as it were . . . come to a decision that has been bubbling in me for a long while . . . Anna—before God, you have been my wife for almost a year now . . . Please be my wife in the world's eyes, as well . . ."*

Then I proceeded to enumerate all the good reasons for our getting married. In hindsight, it seems to me that she didn't really need such a long list. I told her: "I've decided to leave Voisiku. You told me, just a couple of weeks ago, that you must vacate this house by the beginning of this summer. Last week I heard that the widow of the former steward at the estate of Lilienfeldt of Uus-Poltsamaa is selling her house—in Poltsamaa township, a quarter of a verst down from the castle, close to the left bank of the river, a brick house built in old Fick's time . . . It's an old pile, to be sure, but it has a pretty garden by the river, and four spacious rooms, and a kitchen with an open flue to the roof—I've been there, I know the place, and if the two of us spruce it up a little, it will be just grand . . ." Then I made my way to Schwalbe's office at the mirrorworks and asked him for the loan of a horse and cart. An hour later I was back at Anna's house. In the meantime, Anna had put on her new light-brown dress and draped a dark-brown cape around her shoulders. Never before had I seen her ash-hued hair look as lovely in the sunshine as it did then, with her next to me in the yellow mirrorworks cart, as we drove to ask old Rücker to post the banns for us.

In the cart, she took my arm and said, "But how much does that house in Poltsamaa cost?"

I told her what I had heard. "The asking price is seven hundred rubles. But for ready cash, we can have it for five hundred."

"And how much cash can you put on the table?" Anna asked.

I examined my thoughts for a moment, feeling that I had to decide on a question of far-reaching consequence. Then I realized that it was already decided: the question of candor toward my wife. I knew that there were *certain* matters (concerning not so much myself as others) I did not want to reveal to her—matters concerning my sister and brother-in-law that I sometimes find difficult to reveal even in this journal. Thus, I felt I ought to be all the more candid with her in matters of my own trivial finances.

I said, "I have three hundred, and I think that my sister—"

I must have slowed down at that point, because Anna interrupted me before I could finish saying that I thought my sister would lend me the rest.

"But wouldn't you rather accept it from your wife?"

It turned out that Anna had inherited from her late husband more than four hundred rubles and saved them for a rainy day— and I remember thinking, as we drove past Türg, in the cool breeze, with forest shadows and sunlight flickering past: She's not a virgin—of course, how could I complain about that when I was ready to overlook it even for Iette? But the fact that she is also far from poor—that was a genuine surprise, for I had not considered that aspect at all in making my decision . . .

That afternoon, a beaming Rücker posted our banns, and I told him that we were in a great hurry just now and did not have time to visit my parents that day to tell them about it—so, would he please not tell them before we had a chance to do so ourselves? But when we had gone about a verst on our way back in the light evening dusk and caught a glimpse of Paluka's roof on the right

side of the road, behind the deanery field and a copse, then saw
it begin to disappear behind the treetops, I turned off the road and
drove into my parents' yard. It was my intention to make a brief
stop, introduce Anna to them, and then continue our drive back.
But Mama just happened to have the coffee pot on the hob, and
so our quick visit turned into an hour around the table. After I
had told them that this was, well, er, the woman who was going
to make sure that they'd get a daughter-in-law, after all, everybody
became quite taciturn—the old folks out of sheer astonishment,
for they had not heard a word about any candidate for the
daughter-in-law's position until that moment, and I myself because, well, I don't know—and the situation seemed a little comical
and embarrassing. Just then, and surprisingly, Anna was the one
who kept the conversation going very properly until Mama had
poured the coffee and Papa had brought out the rowanberry spirits.
By the time we got back to Anna's, it was dark, and I stayed the
night. Early the next morning we drove to Poltsamaa in the
mirror-works cart. I stopped at Näresaar to retrieve my papers
and slide them into my overcoat pocket when Anna wasn't looking. Tiit had been privy to our liaison for a while, and now he
brought out his bottle of home brew to celebrate the occasion. To
humor him, we took little sips—we wanted to be quite sober and
ready for some tough bargaining with Mrs. Kolts.

As it turned out, there was no need to bargain. We made a quick
inspection of the old and slightly run-down brick house, and in
our frivolous enthusiasm found no serious fault with it. Old Mrs.
Kolts was in the middle of her move to her sister's house in
Viljandi, and her belongings were strewn about in piles and half-
packed willow baskets in the middle of the room. When she heard
our offer, she did not shake her puff-ball head but immediately
accepted it: five hundred rubles cash the following Monday, at
Redlich the notary's office, and on that same day, the house would
be ready for us to move in. After that, we drove to Tiit's, and
Anna took the cart back to the township while I saddled my bay
and rode—well, home, since I still had to call Voisiku home.

Back at The Foundation, I returned this journal and the other
papers to their hiding place, hung up my overcoat, and asked Eeva
to come to my room, where I told her everything that had hap-

pened to me during the last two days. Everything, though I may have reordered things a bit—as if it mattered. First, I told her that I had decided to get married and to move to Poltsamaa. I said I assumed that she had no objections to that—since it was obvious that I could no longer help her or her husband in any way. Then I told her that Peter had, a few days ago, snooped around in Timo's papers, and that he possessed a set of keys to every room in The Foundation. *That* news caused Eeva to look at me in surprise and dismay. I said that Peter hadn't found or removed anything, at least not at that time, and that I knew this because I was with him, at his request . . . Then I told her I would attend to the matter of their escape at the beginning of June to the best of my ability, just as we had agreed.

Eeva heard me out, then said, even more calmly than I had expected:

"I don't need to tell you that it has always been a great help to have you here . . . But I have to learn how to manage by myself—and I did manage all the years you were with your surveyors. I can't ask you to sacrifice your life to Timo and me . . . You and Anna have truly been patient—and as far as I am concerned, I'd be pleased if you brought her here to Voisiku, but I understand . . . So you bought the Kolts house? Well, if there's ever a time when I really need you here, that really isn't so far away . . . And since you promise to help us in our attempt this summer—God be with you . . ."

Eeva said that there was no reason for me to keep Peter's intrusion from Timo—that I should, in fact, tell him; he would be amused.

I asked her why she thought he'd be amused, and she said:

"Well, you must have realized when you were there: those cookbooks and sleigh bells and God knows what else in the drawers—he'd planted that stuff especially to confound his dear brother-in-law . . . As for our escape—I want to write Jüri soon, so that he can take my letter to the headmaster and ask for a leave of absence due to his father's grave illness. We have already agreed that that's what he'll do, but I haven't told him a word about our escape plan. He's still a child . . . So, God willing, if Captain Snyder shows up and you manage to arrange things, you'll soon be free of our problems, at last . . ."

The twentieth of May, 1829, late at night

This is my first time with my journal in our house at
Poltsamaa—I am writing on the old kitchen table Mrs. Kolts left
here, in the light of a candle on a broken plate, the window covered
with an old flour sack.

Three days ago we went to the notary. I counted out the bank
notes from Anna's and my own savings and left with the sealed
deed in my pocket. Now Anna is at Roika, gathering her belongings, and I have spent a couple of days getting the house ready.
I have a new hiding place for my papers, under a floorboard in
the small room I intend to use as a study. Even here, it does not
seem advisable to keep such papers in too obvious a place, even
though Peter does not have keys to this house, and even though
I doubt they'll send any Lamings to snoop on me.

This afternoon, I whitewashed the walls of our large room
(which Anna refers to as our drawing room—ho-ho!). I would
like to get as much work done on the house as possible before I
go to Pärnu, so that Anna can move in before I go to play games
with the gentlemen at the port. If, God forbid, Timo and Eeva
should be discovered and apprehended, I might also be arrested,
for conspiring to assist in the escape of a person under political
surveillance. If something like that should happen to me, I would
like to think that they won't chase my wife out of our house, once
she has moved into it.

I was just standing there, on old sacks with which I had covered
the floor, spreading gluey whitewash over the brick walls of the
big room, when Eeva appeared out of nowhere—and I could tell
from her expression that something must have happened.

"Jakob—are you alone here?"

I nodded, and Eeva said, "Once again, our escape plan is out
of the question."

"But why? Captain Snyder promised—"

"It's not Snyder," Eeva said. "It's Peter. I was going to prepare
him for our journey. A couple of days ago I told him that Timo
and I would like to visit the Radigs at Harjumaa some time in

June. I said we would do this only if I could obtain permission from the Governor General or the *Ordnungsrichter*. I also showed him Mr. von Radig's invitation, which I had arranged to be sent to me a long time ago. Peter read it and said—and you can imagine his whiny voice: 'First of all, you won't get permission. And secondly, even if you did, I don't have time to laze about there in June.' I said: 'But Peter, there's no need for *you* to waste your precious time with us. I'll be there to watch over Timo.' But he just jutted his stony chin at me and said: 'Without me—not a step.' And when I told this to Timo, he said that it's hopeless as long as Peter lives here and acts as our guardian . . ."

I asked her what she thought we should do now, and she said:

"Well, we can't try to do it this summer. I haven't written to Jüri. But I think I'll be able to come up with something for the autumn—I talked to Timo about it, and he seems to agree in principle, although he wants to think it over. You see, what I want to do is to get rid of Peter for a while, in September . . ."

"How do you think you'll manage that?"

Eeva picked at the bristles of my paint brush. She said:

"Well—as you know, Peter is a truly repulsive and secretive character. But he has one weakness: he is completely henpecked by his Elsy, even though he likes to act the tyrant even with her. So, we have to use Elsy: we have to initiate her into our secret! I have been studying her, and I think it's possible. She won't betray us to her husband. Ever since she was a child, Elsy has been strongly attached to Timo—he is her beloved and adored brother . . . I have noticed how deeply perturbed she is about Peter's tyrannical behavior toward him. If Timo manages to get away, Elsy will be relieved on two counts: she'll no longer suffer for Timo's sake, nor will she feel ashamed for Peter . . ."

"And how do you see the specifics of all this?"

Eeva spoke in a near-whisper, and I realized that she had given her plan a great deal of thought:

"Let us say that in August—no sooner—and after Peter has once again behaved outrageously toward Timo, and Elsy feels mortified about it—we tell Elsy about our plan. *We tell her that we have made all the arrangements for our escape, and that her life will be free of all the pressures our presence has caused. She only has to help* us a little! Us, and herself. And, in the final analysis, her dear Peter, as well . . . If she agrees—and she has to agree, or she isn't *eine geborene von Bock*—she will, I expect, invent some pretext to go to, let's say, Tallinn around the middle of August. To visit relatives., And then, at the beginning of September, she'll send word to Peter: Peter must come to her! He must come because she has been taken very ill! Then Peter will undoubtedly jump into the saddle and hasten to his wife's side. It won't matter how skilled or how inept she'll be at feigning illness—but, let me tell you: a woman can be really clever in such matters, she can manage to deceive even the wisest doctors for a while, simulating faintness or bleeding or whatever—so that even in the worst case we'll have at least a week to make good our escape. And that'll be more than enough . . ."

Old Mrs. Kolts had planted a couple of beds of potatoes in the northern corner of our garden, although it doesn't seem like she was particularly interested in them; many of the people in these parts still regard the tubers more as a gift from the Devil than from God. She had let me have half a binful of potatoes in the cellar for fifty kopecks. I had put a couple of them into the hot ashes on the hearth; I had also brought a loaf of bread from Voisiku. That morning I had caught a couple of perch and roach at the reedy riverfront of our plot, and a fish stew was simmering in a clay bowl next to the potatoes. I invited Eeva to share my humble peasant repast. We set the bowl with the stew, the bread, and a bag of salt on a low bench and sat down next to it on the hearthstone, Eeva in her elegant pink and brown crepe-de-chine dress flaring around her ankles, I in my rough shirt and trousers stained by lime and paint, both our lips and fingers sticky from the baked potatoes. I glanced at my sister, spat some perch bones into the glowing ashes, and thought: *What a wildcat* . . . I said:

"All right, then. If you need me in the autumn, send word. And on Saturday—that's a week from today—please bring Timo, if he cares to, and come around six or seven o'clock to taste your brother's wedding ale. If all goes well, we'll also have a big wedding cake. It seems we won't be able to do without all that foolishness after all . . ."

Around four, Eeva left in the high-wheeled buggy from the

estate stables, driving it herself, just as she had on the way over, and I worked on the house until dark. I almost forgot: as she was about to leave, reins in hand, Eeva told me that I would not have to go to Pärnu on their behalf. Somehow, she'd manage to get word to Captain Snyder about the postponement of the trip, with some recompense for his troubles.

The twenty-second, at six o'clock in the morning

I have to write this down before I forget the details.

It started somewhere in the grayish darkness: I heard someone *calling* and started out in the direction of the sound. My legs felt as if my knees had been tied together, and it was very difficult to proceed, but I *had to* press on. Then, I was struck on the chest and shoulders and face—it didn't hurt much, but it felt as if I had been struck with heavy black fly-swatters made out of leather, and these were always pulled out of reach as soon as I tried to grab them. My inability to reach them made me feel curiously helpless and discouraged, and I gave up trying to get hold of them. Another reason I gave up was that they also kept slapping (not really the right word, there was no sound) my hands, nailing them down, as it were, so that even when I managed to pull my hands free, they were paralyzed by the effort. Now and again those soundless slaps hit my face, which made it hard to breathe. I recall that they covered my eyes for the duration of three or four heartbeats and I thought: Never mind. There's so little light here anyway, I'm not really missing anything . . .

I kept going toward the calling voice, even though it was getting harder and harder to do so, and I understood (a little surprised at the fact that it didn't surprise me more) *what* my tormentors were: they were Timo's *equibs*. I also knew that I was struggling toward the call in order to explain to the caller that he was mistaken—because it wasn't *me* that he wanted. I could hear, clearly—well, not all that clearly in the normal sense of that word, but undeniably, nevertheless—that loud, reverberating whisper somewhere ahead of me:

"Timothée! . . . Timothée! . . ."

My only reason for staggering on was to explain that I wasn't he, that I didn't have anything to do with any of that . . . And even though everything was oppressively strange (as it often is in dreams), I was really puzzled only by one thing: that I had to, all of a sudden, struggle with these equibs. Never before had I had anything to do with them, they had never belonged to me, I had never seen them with my own eyes, and even now I couldn't see what they looked like because it was so dark. But I knew without a doubt that that's what they were. And I knew that the salty taste I noticed on the skin around my mouth was due to their clawing my face with tiny little barbs, and that my face was bleeding . . . All of a sudden I was released from the tunnel of oppression and found myself in my childhood village of Tömbi, in the yard of Kannuka . . . There is a pile of freshly peeled pine bark in the yard, with my father's knife sticking out of it. Next to the well, on the lawn, rises a cross, made out of two dazzlingly white tree trunks, one and a half fathoms tall and a fathom wide . . . At the foot of the cross stands Iette, drying her eyes with a white handkerchief. Anna is there, too, conversing calmly with Monsieur La Trobe and Tiit of Näresaar. Monsieur La Trobe is holding a carpenter's hammer, and Tiit has four long forged nails in his hand. Timo detaches himself from the group and comes over to me, puts his hands on my shoulders and says, with a tremor in his voice:

"Jakob—this is truly noble of you—well done—coming here to be crucified in my stead . . ."

He turns to Mr. Laming, who has suddenly appeared, and tells him:

"Your Majesty—let us have the ladder—so that we have something to stand on. Then do your duty."

I see how Laming leans a frame with three crossbars against the big cross. Then he comes over to Timo and me, takes hold of our arms and starts walking us toward the cross. Good God—I don't know what to do . . . If I were sure that they want to crucify me—if I were sure, I'd push Timo aside and scream: *What madness is this?* But I don't dare to scream or protest—because it may be Timo, after all, who is to be crucified . . . And if that is the case, I don't know whether I should *offer* to be crucified instead of him? Because Timo seems to believe that that is what I am doing, and Iette and Anna are both watching. Apart from the terrible pain and the slow death it entails, crucifixion is, after all, a matter of honor . . . I don't know what I should do. And my indecision becomes such a tight knot inside me that I feel I'll suffocate in their hands long before we reach the cross—

And so, I woke up, sweaty and gasping for breath, and stared uncomprehendingly at the old beams, the freshly whitewashed walls, and the cross shapes of the window frames outlined against the first ashen glow of dawn—before I understood that I was in my own new old house at Poltsamaa, on the floor of our future bedroom, on a bed of straw . . .

At Poltsamaa, Monday, the twenty-ninth of May, 1829

On Saturday morning, Anna and I went to old Rücker's vestry for our marriage ceremony. Privately, I had already told him (and I assume he knew it already) that Anna and I could have had offspring a long time ago, had we wanted any, and thus it would not be necessary for him to waste his breath on the kind of advice that is commonly dispensed to newlyweds. Rücker was also wise enough to refrain from chastising us for incontinent premarital fornication. But after forty years as a clergyman he was, in any event, so set in his ways that he ran on for about twice as long as was necessary.

During the week, we had gathered what worldly goods we had. I really didn't own anything except for clothes, books, and the desk that had come from the attic of the main building at Voisiku. Before I left, I asked Mr. Mannteuffel about the desk; spitefully, he asked for four rubles, which I paid him on the spot, just as spitefully. Anna, of course, had more possessions, for her late husband apparently hadn't spent a kopeck on drink or other frivolities but had invested his earnings in furniture. The two wagons borrowed from the Roika works were loaded down with it: a small sofa, a couple of chairs and an étagère for the living room, a table, benches, and a sideboard for the dining room, a double bed and a dresser for the bedroom, two or three chests, household utensils and washtubs and wooden flasks. With all that in place, and a few wall hangings and runners placed here and there by Anna's skillful hands, the old house has received a new lease on life. And on Saturday, when we returned from Rücker's, our guests were waiting for us, at our so-called wedding reception.

I really don't understand why I wrote "so-called"—after all, in addition to mere peasants, the party included not only artisans and burghers, but, something unheard-of, even *born members of the aristocracy*—not just one, but two! Maybe that was why it seemed a little strange . . . Eeva had obtained a permit for Timo from the *Ordnungsrichter*—to appease Peter, who kept insisting that the stipulations allowed Timo to travel only within the boundaries of the *county*. Which meant that it was quite in order for him to ride twenty-five versts from the manor in a south-southeasterly direction, but no more than five versts to the northeast. When Timo and Eeva presented him with the permit for Poltsamaa, he had once again expressed his stupid obstinacy by saying: "You can't go there without me—but I haven't been invited." And Timo had said to him: "No one invites prison warders to a wedding . . . Well, one has to endure the hardships imposed upon one, by one's chosen vocation . . . I'm afraid you'll have to come uninvited." To which Peter had replied: "I wouldn't dream of showing myself there, making a fool of myself with a madman in tow!"

Then, however, Elsy had intervened on Timo's behalf. She had shouted that she, Elsy, was Mannteuffel enough to qualify as Timo's appointed companion, whether she had been invited or not, and that Peter would have to accept that. And Elsy's otherwise calm gray eyes had become so bright, and her otherwise quiet, catarrhal voice so loud, that Peter had to give her his grumbling permission.

It was, indeed, a remarkable Saturday night gathering, this motley crowd of relatives, family, and friends—from the erstwhile imperial aide-de-camp, colonel, and madman, and his buxom sister, and my own no less impressive sister, to the bushy-whiskered Mr. Malm of Roika, whom Anna had insisted on inviting, and the Schwalbes, and many other men from the works with their wives, all the way to my mother-in-law, an artisan's widow, and my own parents, cottagers at the deanery.

I met my mother-in-law for the first time that Saturday. She lives by herself on the outskirts of Viljandi, and Anna does not seem to feel very close to her. Unlike her opulent and languid daughter, the cooper's widow is a lean and surprisingly energetic old woman. The wedding ale and a couple of glasses of wine soon went to her head, and she kept trying to explain to me that I had, in fact, married a far greater beauty than I even knew. I did, of course, refrain from telling her that Anna and I had cohabited for almost eighteen months and that I was quite familiar with her pulchritude, from stem to stern.

I had told Tiit of Näresaar to join us on Saturday night, promising him that I had no intention of telling Timo about the unfortunate business with his eye. But Tiit had told me right away: "Dear friend, you don't want an old crow like me at your nice wedding. Whenever you feel like spending some time on the river, with her or without, don't you dare row past my cabin. But a wedding—no thanks, old chap."

So Tiit didn't show up, but who did, quite unexpectedly (it hadn't even occurred to me to ask him to come all the way from Tartu), was Monsieur La Trobe. He had come to Poltsamaa on business, and the Wahls had told him about our wedding. Somewhere on the way he had cut an enormous bunch of pink lilac branches, and now he presented these to Anna with a bow that bespoke a man of the world. Then he sat at our table until the wee hours, babbling about the problems he'd encountered in the musical circles of Tartu and saying that if he couldn't fulfill his ambitions for the improvement of those circles, he would emigrate to America, where, he claimed, his brother was a terrifically famous architect and builder of bridges. Long before sunrise, he walked down to the river to greet the new day, a tankard of ale in his hand, then stumbled on a tussock and soaked his trousers up to his knees. He also made a speech, using both German and Estonian and taking his own sweet time. It was hard for me to be annoyed with him, although he spent much more time praising the groom's sister, Eeva, than the bride and groom themselves, waxing so eloquent that I'll write some of it down just because it was so ridiculous: *eine vom Himmel gegebene Erscheinung, eine Dame, die überall geboren werden kann, wo Gott will . . . Eine ganz ausserordentliche Frau . . .* An extra-ordinary—an extrah-oohrdinary woman! If the people among whom she was born, if that people were more conscious of its own history than it was, it would praise her as a heroine of sensitivity and wisdom . . . And so forth. It seems ridiculous even to write it down.

Eeva listened to Monsieur La Trobe's high-flown speech with a pained expression. I knew the reason for that, and the reason for the slightly ironical curl of her lips. A short while ago she had told me the following: that there had, indeed, been a time when Monsieur La Trobe proclaimed that those members of the aristocracy who didn't respect Mrs. von Bock were jackasses. This was when the lady was the new bride of a friend of the Czar's, walking on the Czar's friend's arm in the gardens of Voisiku. Later (while I was lugging a sextant and copying maps for Tenner, with little time to keep up with events at Voisiku), when Mrs. von Bock had been awarded the crown of thorns of the wife of a criminal against the state, Monsieur La Trobe had taken care to give the impression that he had nothing to do with the lady. At some gatherings, he had gone so far as to claim that he did not know Eeva at all . . .

Well, yes—but if we consider how Peter denied Our Savior thrice before the cock crowed twice—the same Peter whom the Savior had called the rock upon which Christ's congregation was to be established . . . ? Upon La Trobe, the Czar had not been able to establish even the surveillance of Voisiku Estate . . . So, what could one expect of La Trobe?

(Generally speaking, is it fair to say that one really can't expect much from this one or that one? Or should one, nevertheless, demand more? It seems to me *both* attitudes are correct, but I can't for the life of me explain why that may be. Profound thought is not my forte . . .)

Treacherous Peter later atoned for his betrayal by a martyr's death in the city of Rome; Monsieur La Trobe was let off rather more lightly at Poltsamaa, and on Sunday afternoon he left for Tartu in good order.

By the way, Monsieur La Trobe had not left Timo out of his speech: he said that it was a great honor for all of us to be seated in this dear humble abode, at this dear humble table, in the company of a man who has been closer to the brightest stars of his own day than any of us can imagine, and that he, the speaker, was particularly fortunate and honored to take this opportunity to wish Mr. von Bock the happiest of recoveries in the care of his charming wife.

This was, in fact, the first time since Timo's release that I had had an opportunity to observe him in the company of a couple of dozen people, most of whom were strangers to him. He certainly seemed to behave in a completely normal fashion, although I sensed his irritation at being kept on a leash. Smiling, he introduced Elsy to the company as his wardress and teased her several times (but always in a humorous and cordial manner) about her role as the uninvited wedding guest. He even managed to make an adroit pun in Estonian, with the assistance of myself and another person—I don't know if it was accidental or premeditated. He asked me: *"Wie heisst eigentlich 'Brüderlichkeit' auf Estnisch?"* I said: *"Vendlus."* He asked: *"Aber 'Schwesterlichkeit'?"* Someone said: *"Es dürfte dann wohl 'oelus' sein . . ."* And Timo asked: *"Aber wie heisst 'oelus' auf Deutsch?"* Disingenuously, Mrs. Schwalbe, who really hadn't been following our conversation, chimed in: *"Bosheit."* Whereupon Timo patted Elsy's cheek and exclaimed: *"Siehst du, da hast du's, mein Schwesterchen!"*

After my parents had retired to the back room, I saw Timo go in there and put his hands on their shoulders.

He said, "Those boots Kitty sent to me—you made them, didn't you, Father?"

The old man mumbled, "Well, I don't know if the ones you got were of my making . . . But I did make some for you . . . at least three pair, those years . . ."

Then he asked Mother, "And the shearlings whose skin they were lined with—you raised them, didn't you?"

And Mother said, "Well, yes, I did . . . It was no trouble at all . . ."

Timo said, "I haven't had a chance to thank you for them. They were my favorite boots, in the wintertime. *There*, there are times when a man can feel so low—I know *I* did—that his heart sinks all the way down into his boots . . . But when I wore *those* boots, my heart warmed up so much in them that it rose back up into my chest."

Toward morning, in my so-called study that had been converted into a smoking room, Mr. Schwalbe, who had imbibed a little more than was his habit, began to ask Timo what it had really been like *there*. Into the silence that followed that question, Timo said:

"You know, I made a medical observation there: a man's memory and his teeth are curiously connected. And so, if you lose your teeth in a certain way, you don't retain much of a memory, either."

In the course of that whole evening and half the night, I heard Timo utter only one sentence one might consider a little strange. Or maybe not? Mr. Malm of the mirrorworks asked him:

"Mr. von Bock, according to some rumors, you were seen in Germany—Berlin and elsewhere—around 1820 . . ."

Timo said, with a smile, "Yes, I've heard those rumors, too . . . They came about because some people mistook my brother Georg for me."

"Oh, was that it," Mr. Malm said, sounding a little disappointed. "So you really spent all those years in Russia . . . ?"

Timo stared at the first glimmer of dawn in the window.

". . . I don't know what country it was. Maybe it wasn't Russia . . . In any case, the sky was so low that it was really hard to stand straight . . ."

We couldn't offer our guests sleeping quarters, and so the last ones departed in the small hours. Timo had returned home with Elsy but Eeva stayed to help Anna and her mother clean up the place after the celebration. I walked down to the river and sat down on a bunch of old willow roots in the completely impenetrable, cottony morning mist. As opaque as that mist was, I could clearly see that a chapter of my life had come to an end and a new chapter was about to begin. I wasn't able to pursue that thought any further and contented myself with listening to the rush of the water over the castle dam a quarter of a verst away and staring at the completely immobile raft of mist that surrounded me. Tired and a little befuddled with ale as I was, I felt curiously agitated. Then I realized why that was: the curious contrast between the audible motion of the water and the visible immobility of the mist made the world, as I observed it from behind the moat of my weariness, seem both confidence-inspiring and dangerous . . . And then, I remember, I imagined that I saw reflected on the motionless wall of mist, over by some dry cattails from last year, Anna's bright breasts and hips in the morning light . . . I got up and headed back to the house. The house itself was invisible behind the mist and the bright white tops of apple trees. I thought: those breasts and hips, now so familiar, are waiting for me in that still so unfamiliar house. It seemed like a good thing, a relief—and yet I felt a little ashamed . . .

Sunday, the thirty-first of July, 1829
No longer at Voisiku
but at Poltsamaa

Anna went to church this morning, and I stayed home, claiming I had a headache, because I wanted to write down a few things after a hiatus of three months.

Eeva came here the day before yesterday. She brought the necessary funds and we talked things over. I'll be going to Pärnu this week. I'll try to find lodgings in a suitably isolated location, an apartment or, even better, a small house. I'll move into it around the middle of August, for—we hope—no longer than a month. I have to come up with a credible story for Anna. As for the inhabitants of Pärnu, I'll tell them that my physician has recommended sea bathing, or at least sea air. I'll renew my acquaintance with Captain Glans. Then, my sister, her husband, and their son will come to visit me for a few days in mid-September, a few days after the arrival of Captain Snyder's *Ameland*. If I manage to arrange everything and God is on our side, our plan is bound to succeed. Eeva has initiated Elsy into our secret, and Elsy is ready and willing to engage in whatever subterfuge is necessary on behalf of her brother. She will go to Tallinn at the end of August and persuade Peter to come there in mid-September. Eeva mentioned that she had received a letter from Jüri. It appears that he has been transferred, by imperial order, from the lyceum at Tsarskoye to the Naval Academy in St. Petersburg. I asked Eeva how she felt about it, and she said that as far as she knew, the Academy was an institution in which boys were educated in a stricter and purely military fashion.

Eeva said, "And the fact that he was singled out, once again, by that imperial order—God, he's only ten years old—that makes me a little apprehensive and doubtful about his future . . ."

Now to another matter, one that preoccupies me despite its absurdity.

Earlier on, I described my dream about the reed-boat, with Czar Alexander and Iette and Anna in it, and its subsequent foundering.

This summer, I have seen that dream again, several times. On the last occasion, I looked back over my right shoulder and saw Anna, and when I looked over my left shoulder, it was Iette. Then, when I turned all the way around to see which one of them it really was, there was, indeed, only one of them, but I still couldn't make out *which one* . . .

The dream must have set my thoughts in motion even in regard to the real and present state of affairs. Last Sunday morning, I woke up at my accustomed time, and as far as I recall, not from that particular dream. I woke up in our bedroom, next to Anna. The small wall clock, with the two small snub-beaked robins on either side of its face, told me it was seven o'clock. The window facing the river was open, and the morning looked mild and cloudy. I raised myself onto my elbow and looked at Anna. Her otherwise smoothly combed hair was spread out on her pillow and showed its true abundance. I looked at it with pleasure. Her breast visible above the neckline of her nightgown, her whole body under that gown and a thin summer coverlet was even ampler than it appeared when she was fully clothed. I found it easy to overlook this as I recalled how we had, a few hours ago in the dark of the night, striven for the joys of the flesh and finally achieved them, panting with exertion and joy—and that was when it suddenly struck me *whom* I had been thinking about at that moment, under cover of night and silence . . . Not about her, but about Iette! Or about Anna only to the extent that she is, in some incomprehensible way, *like* Iette . . . Only because she truly resembles Iette, in some mysterious way. Even though she is ten years older and very differently formed. Even though Iette is still only a child compared to Anna . . . Nevertheless, their clearly defined, plumlike lips are similar, as is the curve of their eyebrows. Their clear gray eyes have the same rounded shape, and the outer corners of those eyes are a little lower than the ones next to their noses. Their voices, dark and gentle, are curiously similar, and both of them have the same habit of holding you very tight in emotional moments, going rigid and not moving at all . . .

Last week, I suddenly understood that it was mainly because of that marvelous and initially unnoticed similarity that I was attracted to Anna a year and a half ago. And due to their accidental similarity, I have always, and especially in our most intimate moments, always replaced Anna with the unfortunate and tearful child I rejected but still desire . . .

Why with her? is, inevitably, a nonsensical question, since one could only answer it by saying: Because she was so lovely. And that is an even more meaningless word than many others. Why I have been deceiving Anna in this way—why I have chosen her, from the very beginning, if not truly consciously, to be the one whom I would deceive?—that is a question I may try to answer at some time, at least to myself.

Otherwise, I do not regard the fact that my marriage is, as it were, founded on a deception as intrinsically tragic. A great proportion, perhaps the *greatest* proportion of relationships between men and women are either entirely or at least occasionally based on similar deceptions. I could, of course, declare myself such a grand egotist that I am bound to suffer because *my* marriage is of the more common and trivial and not of the rarer and nobler kind—but I thank God that I am too old for such convulsions of idealism, either in my thinking about the family (when I consider my own case) or about the state (when I think about Timo's dreams). As for the deeper reasons for my choice of Anna—perhaps it came about because I knew that I had hurt Iette terribly when I rejected her on account of her father. From my point of view, it was inevitable. But from hers, it must have been an incomprehensible—well, perhaps comprehensible, but an undeserved —act of cruelty . . . And so, perhaps, I have simply tried to atone, while not being too clear about it myself until now, to somehow rectify the injustice done to Iette, in the eyes of someone, I don't even know *whose*—by . . .

Oh, hang it all, I can't believe that my story is quite as complicated (and noble) as that. Some time ago, I read a book I got from Wahl on the theories of some Viennese doctor, and I tend to think that the *animal magnetism* of those women has, in some fateful way, attracted my—

Tuesday, the second of August, 1829

Anna returned home much sooner on Sunday than I had expected. But I can see that there is no need for me to add anything to the last couple of pages. And I won't erase them, either; that would be adding insult to injury.

I have told Anna that I received a letter from Major Tenner and that I have to travel to Tallinn to assist him with the completion of certain projects. I am leaving tomorrow—for Pärnu, of course. Ill-advised as it may be, I have decided to take this journal with me. If I leave it here, I'll be imagining the whole time that as soon as Anna sets foot in my study she'll see straight through the floorboards, over there below the window . . . If I leave only Timo's memorandum, no such magical attraction will be exerted. Is that what they mean by a "subterranean sun"?

In Pärnu, Thursday, the eleventh of August

I have found a house that is perfectly suited to our purpose. It is the summer villa of the local merchant, Zwiebelberg, five hundred paces south of the center of town, behind overgrown bastions among stretches of sand and grass, and so close to the harbor that I can see the masts of ships above the shrubbery. It is only two hundred paces down to the water.

The house itself is in rather poor shape and has only three small rooms and a small, glassed-in verandah. But there is a coach house and a stable in the yard, so carriages and horses can be hidden from sight. Best of all, if one approaches the house from the Riga Highway and turns onto a road that runs northwest through the meadows, one can get there without entering the town at all.

Pärnu, the fourteenth of August, '29

Yesterday I dropped into Ingerfeld's Restaurant at lunchtime, and sure enough, Captain Glans was there. His enthusiasm about our reunion was encouraging. The front of his blue uniform bears even more stains than it did a year ago—not a bad sign. We ate and drank some red rotgut. I wanted to order genuine port, but they were out of it, since the *Ameland* isn't due for another couple of weeks. The captain and I took up where we left off a year ago. That is all I can do here at present. I shall return to Poltsamaa for a week.

Poltsamaa, the twentieth of August '29

Anna is visiting her mother in Viljandi. When I left, we agreed that she would go there for a week or two.

Yesterday morning, Eeva stopped here on her way to St. Petersburg to bring Jüri home. May God grant that the boy is well and gets permission to go with her.

Eeva also brought me a case made out of pinewood that contained, she told me, all kinds of papers Timo had asked me to keep for him. Timo had said that he did not want to take them abroad, that he didn't want to burn them quite yet either, and that he was afraid to keep them in The Foundation any longer because of Peter's snooping.

When Eeva gave me the case, it was locked. It was a plain, undecorated, dark-brown box. I wasn't given a key, and I didn't ask for one. With Eeva there, I didn't want to move my desk and raise the secret floorboard, so I simply put it in my desk drawer. After we had talked a while longer, I escorted Eeva to her carriage by the gate. As I returned to my study and took the case out in order to conceal it in my hiding place, I noticed the edge of a piece of paper protruding slightly from between the case and its lid. I tried to push it in with my thumbnail, but that didn't work. I tried to raise the lid a little bit more, but that didn't work, either. My desk drawer was still open, and I contemplated the pipe cleaners and miniature tools I kept in it. I picked a small screwdriver and tried to widen the gap between lid and box enough to be able to push that page back in. God knows I hardly used any force— but the lid suddenly gave and the case flew open! The latch had detached itself from its pins, and now it stuck out of the lock in the lid, like a single tooth.

At this point, I found it impossible to restrain myself from taking a peek at the contents. Besides, what I found was so much like what I expected that I felt almost clairvoyant.

I read some hundred and fifty pages quickly but nevertheless carefully. Quickly because the material was of a kind that did not invite contemplation, yet carefully because it seemed to demand attention . . .

I can't copy it all here, but I will copy the first few pages, in order to study them later.

Timo's manuscript begins in mid-sentence:

1.

through whom Zebaoth is understandably the chief prosector of both the upper and also the lower seas and the wealth of dead cabinet members, both financial and moral, to be distributed among these lively sheep according to the midst of the drum roll. Last night with the aid of two violin strings and three witches' whips a certain red-headed Moor clarified Ivan Ivanovich, the Apostle Lucas, and myself more efficiently than the thickest fog. Thus, our first fundamental question is this: Republic or monarchy. Because the distance from the southernmost tip of Yucatán to Maria Theresa's beard is three and a half octaves. So

that there was until recently more room for the employ
of global imperial music than there was incense

2.
for the living or bread for the dead. Which clearly demonstrates that the sum of an angel's wingspan fits remarkably well, although some think not at all, into Fraunhofer's
tube, and that we are languishing in the ashes of the coals
of Babylon. Besides, preference for a republic over a monarchy or vice versa carries weight in only one case. But
the scent of flowers and the kindness of headsman's servants releases the one who has been taken down from the
cross under cover of darkness does not in the least resemble
the highest powers of Macedon, furthermore the honorable
Moises Nilovich goes on to claim that the light shall not
come but due to the darkness what drives Satan mad. In
reality neither Jason nor Theseus has ever employed wagon
wheels in order to turn that cheek to his enemy

3.
only expects to have his ears boxed. Because even though
the flight of birds need be no more telling than the entrails
of sacrificial beasts, in at least one case the boots must be
dyed green. That is when we are able to liberate ourselves
to the point where we may ask: first, is it or is it not possible
to reduce the vices of monarchy to a tolerable level by
means of a conscious choice of a type of monarchy and
the person who is the monarch. Never mind that certain
noble ladies are in the habit of offering some of their guests
a fish sandwich along with secret poisons. And never mind
that the foundation of the art of composition, as Count L.
tried to demonstrate upon at least one occasion, consists
in pulling the note-darts out of the skin of the board, so
that the music emanating from the wounds may be explained as for instance a

4.
paean to the devil, because in actual fact the wounds are
entirely silent. There is also no doubt that gunpowder is

in one sense a problem for the manufacturers of bird catchers' glue and in another sense for hunting dogs. Secondly: can a republic survive adverse conditions—the only kind in which it can come into being—without resorting to dictatorship and thus acquiescing to its transformation into tyranny and thus killing itself. For the circle belongs to the nature of nature—just consider: the pupil, the tree stump, the wave produced by a stone falling into water, the rainbow, the sun, the jellyfish, the imperial court, the thrush. But what distinguishes Neptune's trident from Elijah's carriage is of course the pretty bright yellow

At this time, I can't quite decide what is going on here, but I have noticed one thing: the fact that on every page, the sentence between the second and third period seems to make sense, and that those sentences, when read together, seem to form a coherent and sensible text. Given time and opportunity—should this manuscript stay in my possession for any length of time—I'll try to ascertain if this is so.

Poltsamaa, the thirtieth of August, '29

Today I received the agreed-upon letter from Eeva in St. Petersburg. It was mailed on the twenty-fifth and it says that the weather there is turning really beautiful. This tells me that she and Jüri have set out on their journey home, on that date. Tomorrow, I'll ride over to Voisiku to see how things are progressing there: whether they have arrived, and whether Peter has left for Tallinn. If everything is as it should be, I'll proceed to Pärnu. The von Bocks will have to make their way to Pärnu on their own, and I'm sure they'll manage—under Eeva's supervision, and with Juhan as their coachman.

Poltsamaa, the first of September

Praise the Lord: everything is as it should be.

True, Eeva and Jüri aren't back yet, but I don't doubt that they will be here soon. The main thing is that Claire told me yesterday, looking so downcast that it was hard for me not to tell her the truth, that her mother had been stricken with a sudden illness in Tallinn. The day before yesterday, her father had received a very upsetting letter from a Dr. Frese. (It would be amusing to know what Elsy did to cause physicians to write letters about her! Ho-ho.) And yesterday morning, Papa Peter had dashed off to Tallinn. *Quod erat probandum*, as the saying goes. Thus, the biggest obstacle to the von Bocks' flight has been removed, thanks to Eeva's wonderfully feminine and straightforward idea . . .

Pärnu, the seventeenth of September, '29

I have been here since the fourth. The *Ameland* arrived on the sixth, took a couple of days to unship its cargo and replace it, the following week, with one of flax. Now the new cargo has been stowed in the hold with a hiding place and provisions for three persons inside it. The three are expected here tomorrow afternoon. We won't waste a minute: as soon as they are in this house, I'll go to town and set up a feast for Captain Glans at Ingerfeld's, to keep him from inspecting his guards during the night. The three men, one of them a noncommissioned officer, who will be on active guard duty will also receive a hamper containing choice morsels and a few bottles to prevent their resentment from keeping them awake. At half-past midnight I'll leave the captain at Ingerfeld's (by then, he'll be drunk as a lord), return here, and wake up Juhan. I'm sure my friends won't need waking. We'll divide up their baggage to be carried by the three grown men, and I'll guide them quickly and quietly to an empty, half-ruined building behind the Winter Harbor, where men sent by Captain Snyder will receive them and take them to the ship.

The eighteenth of September, at eight o'clock in the evening

They have arrived.

Juhan has taken care of the horses and the carriage, and I have sent him off to sleep in the stable loft. We'll need him tonight to help with the baggage. After repacking their eight valises into seven, Eeva has stretched out for half an hour's rest on a straw pallet, and when she gets up again, she will consolidate those seven into six, because that is all they can take (plus a couple of light bundles to be carried by Eeva and Jüri) if we are to manage it in one go.

Timo is sitting in the yard under a rowan tree next to the glass verandah. I can see him from my window.

I tell Jüri to stay awake, too. Now it is time for me to go.

The nineteenth of September, in the afternoon

Well. They're gone.

I shall do my best to give a detailed description of last night's events.

They arrived here last night, around seven o'clock. Understand-ably, all of us were under a certain strain. When Eeva began to repack the valises, Jüri asked her:

"Mother, where are we going now?"

Eeva said, "I've told you—to Saaremaa. To visit the Bux-hoevdens. They are really good people, relatives of ours."

"But why are we traveling in secret if Father has the emperor's permission?" Jüri asked. He was setting up the chessboard for a game with me—the same pieces I had given him two years ago.

"We have to do it in secret," Eeva said, "because these petty officials here at Pärnu may not believe that our permit is genuine, and it could take many days, maybe even a week, before they let us go."

I let Jüri win in twenty moves, not to be delayed by the game. He might have beat me with his thirtieth move—he plays a surprisingly good game for a ten-year-old. Altogether, he has grown up to be quite an independent little thinker. I wonder—is it because he has absorbed his lyceum education with particular energy, or because he has resisted that education with particular vigor?

As I noted before, Eeva took a rest between her packing chores, and in spite of the wind and rain, Timo sat outside on a bench under a rowan tree and looked out to sea, although there wasn't much to be seen in the dark. The gray grass in the yard and a stand of marram grass on the far side of the gate waved in the wind. Timo had picked a fistful of rowanberries off the tree— they looked almost black in the twilight—and was chewing them one by one, his head leaned back in a curious way. It occurred to me that those berries surely were especially tart, this year.

At half past nine, I pulled on my sailcloth coat and walked to Ingerfeld's, where I could tell from Captain Glans's open collar and glazed eyes that he was already quite inebriated. In a private chamber behind the dining room, we enjoyed a three-course dinner—meatball soup, Tallinn schnitzel with anchovies and lemon, and a plum fool—accompanied by copious draughts of ale, clear vodka, and port wine from the *Ameland*. I told the captain some scabrous barrack-room stories that made him crow and cackle, and otherwise kept him on a tight rein, constantly reminding him of that recommendation to the general in Riga. It was all my treat, of course, and I kept the drinks coming. By half past eleven, the captain was completely befuddled, and I led him to rest on the sofa in our private chamber, turned the hands of his pocket watch back by three hours, and hid his boots in the tiled stove in the hallway.

Through wind, rain, and pitch darkness I plodded down the street to the end of the pier and looked into the window of the port guards' sentry hut. The hamper I had sent from Ingerfeld's had contained three bottles of vodka and six flagons of ale—the boy had delivered them with the captain's compliments, and the guards had not been loath to obey such orders. The light of a storm lantern on the small table shone on three men stretched out on their benches. I opened the door a crack in order to reach in to extinguish the lantern but changed my mind when it occurred to me that a dark sentry hut might attract more attention. I closed the door again. I could see the light from the *Ameland*'s rear cabin twinkle by the same pier, a hundred paces away in the direction of the river.

It took me fifteen minutes to get back to the Zwiebelberg villa. Jüri was asleep on a straw pallet on the floor. Eeva and Timo were sitting on their valises. The room was lit by a candle on the rickety table, and Eeva had found a pot and some firewood and had made tea. The cups from her *sac-voyage* were steaming on the table.

I said, *"It's time."*

Eeva said, "Right. Just a moment. I'll put the cups away and wake up Jüri. You go and wake up Juhan."

Timo rose to his feet and raised his clasped hands up to the level of his neckerchief.

He said, "Wait—dear friends—I am truly mortified—that I wasn't able to gain some clarity about this sooner . . ."

Eeva, too, had stood up and was busy pouring out the tea leaves and wiping the cups with a white cloth. After Timo's words, I saw my sister turn toward him with a curiously frightened, almost frozen expression, and part her lips to say something.

Timo said, "But, thank God—I have reached a decision." He raised his eyes and looked at Eeva and me:

"I cannot go."

Eeva sat back down on her valise and closed her eyes. For a moment, nothing was heard but the wind blowing outside. Then something cracked inside the white cloth in Eeva's hands. She was staring at the wall. She dropped the broken handle of the teacup on the table. Timo paid no attention. He stepped forward between the table and the valises.

I said, "Timo—you are—truly—mad . . ."

He glanced at me and said, not really in reply to my words:

"Yes. I am so very sorry. Kitty has been planning this for two years. And so have you. And I let you do it. *Out of weakness . . .*"

His voice was strained and flat but quite feverish at the same time:

". . . I don't know if you can understand . . . When you realize that you're standing in a hail of grapeshot—of course you want to escape from it . . . And if your wife and child . . . are close by . . . in mortal danger . . . and want to help you get away . . . and you *yourself* ought to help them get away from where they are *because* of you . . . but you are in a *battle* . . . then it can happen that the pros and cons of the situation . . . are so evenly matched . . . that you get paralyzed . . . you can't decide . . . you just push the most categorical imperative out of your mind—which is that *one must never flee from a battle!* Kitty, surely you remember—I once sent you a letter expressing that thought. And both of you must remember what Pahlen said, that time—"

I shouted: "I remember exactly what Pahlen said! He said that he would accept your flight, without hesitation, if you were in a situation similar to his. Then you weren't. But now you are, and yours is a hundred times worse! And you're not alone! Your wife is wasting away by your side! Your son is being carved into a pillar for that order of things you were trying to break—"

Timo interrupted me: "But Pahlen said something else, too—remember: he said that only those go into exile who wish for revenge . . ."

I asked, and I know I did so not only to spur him into action but also out of sheer grief, anger, and disappointment:

"Don't you feel that it is about time for you to—avenge yourself?"

He brushed my thought aside with a sweep of his right hand:

"Jakob—remember—Pahlen said: who wants something more important, he stays at home—"

I shouted: "Oh damn it all to hell—it's no use arguing with a madman like you! . . . Who is *so* blind that he gives up our entire endeavor at a moment like this . . . Tell me, what are the *more important* things you want to achieve as a prisoner of Voisiku? You fool!"

Timo grabbed his neckerchief with both hands, so hard that his fingertips turned white.

"Jakob—don't you understand—Kitty, at least, ought to understand—*this is my battle*—against the Czar, against the empire—and I'm waging it with what we have . . . I thank God for giving me the strength to decide. For making me understand. What could I do abroad? I don't have the funds to publish anything. And even if I managed to raise them, my words wouldn't reach this land. And even if they did, there would be too many who would regard them as the words of a traitor! No, no—if I had to go anywhere, it wouldn't be Switzerland. Rather somewhere there"—he pointed at the darkness behind the windows—"somewhere beyond Irkutsk, where others have already gone . . . But for me, the only right place to be is the place where I am being forced to remain! *To stay there*—like an iron nail in the body of the empire . . ."

"Fool!" I said, once again, out of the depths of my heart. Of course I understood that it made no sense to argue with him after he had made this senseless decision. Perhaps I was going to say: For God's sake—this is worse than madness! Five times I've had to travel to Pärnu—but never mind . . . People have risked prison and horrible punishments . . . In order to establish a bridgehead, reaching out all the way to Tallinn and St. Petersburg . . . And now you'll have to pay Snyder for his risk and trouble, at least five hundred rubles, for nothing . . . I want you to know that as far as I'm concerned, you can go wherever the devil takes you, and do what ever you want—I won't waste my time on you anymore! But I said none of that—because all three of us turned toward Jüri's pallet on the floor between the windows. The boy was sitting up now, the golden buttons on his black marine guard's jacket glittering in the candlelight.

He shouted: "Father! Are they trying to get us to flee the country? I understand it now! But we won't do it, will we? We won't, we won't! It would be against the emperor's orders, wouldn't it? It would be shameful . . ."

Eeva shouted: "Jüri—for God's sake, be quiet!"

I said, without believing that my words would change Timo's mind—really just out of spite—well, no, out of a feeling of disappointment and betrayal:

"There, Timo—do you hear how they've taught your son to think? 'Against the emperor's orders' . . . 'shame' . . ."

Eeva said, "Jakob, try to be a little more generous . . ." She went to Timo and put her hands on his shoulders. She said, "I respect your decision. Because I do, well, I *almost* do understand your motives . . . It *is* a pity that you reached this decision so late . . . What took you so long?"

Timo took Eeva's hands in his own. Now there was an almost merry note of relief in his voice.

"You know . . . I have been thinking about it as hard as I possibly could. But just now, during the past hour, out there—I remembered, besides Pahlen's arguments, I remembered his Valencia oranges, his story about them, how he suspected he'd stayed where he was out of love for his own oranges—they were supposed to be the most northern in all of Europe—and the curiously tart taste of those oranges . . . I don't know if you've noticed how powerful taste sensations can sometimes be . . . At that very moment I remembered their taste—I had a handful of rowanberries I'd picked off the tree, and, without thinking, I put some in my mouth—and all of a sudden that same faintly sweet and incredibly tart taste filled my mouth, my whole body—the same taste—but it was the particular taste of these berries, and much stronger, of much greater bitterness . . ."

He pulled a cluster of rowanberries out of his pocket and held it in front of her face. "See—here it is . . ." He put his hand on Eeva's neck and pressed his face against hers, squashing the orange berry cluster between their lips. He said, "And I understood: let them do with me whatever they want—*because of these berries*, I can't go anywhere . . ."

Well, that was that. At midnight I went to a certain empty building and gave the boatswain of the *Ameland* five hundred rubles in gold as recompense to Captain Snyder for the risk and trouble taken, and asked the boatswain to tell the captain that we would no longer require his services. And since I was already out and about in the rain, I walked back to Ingerfeld's, knocked quietly, and slunk in through the open back door—I had spent enough money there not to feel out of place doing that. Captain Glans didn't look like he had moved since I left him. I reset his watch to the right time and brought his boots back from the hallway stove and set them under his resting place.

At the crack of dawn, the Bock family and their belongings set out for Voisiku again, and I don't know whether to laugh, spit, or cry.

Poltsamaa, the eighteenth of March, 1830

This year's quiet and very snowy winter should be drawing to an end by now, but when I look at the height of the snowdrifts it doesn't seem that way. I haven't heard anything from or about Voisiku all winter. A week after I returned from Pärnu, Eeva came by and said Timo wanted his manuscript case back. Thus I didn't have a chance to study that manuscript more, though I'm still pretty sure my conjecture about it is right.

But I didn't open this journal, after a hiatus of half a year, to discuss Voisiku matters; rather, to record what Anna told me last night. At the moment, she is at the steward's house, enjoying a Saturday afternoon around the Wahls' coffee table. Lately, we have been favored guests there, and I am beginning to find their invitations to coffee and cards a little tedious; but it seems Anna still enjoys them.

Last night, Anna told me that she believes we are expecting a child.

Still here at Poltsamaa, the twelfth of November, '30

I have decided to visit Voisiku tomorrow, to see how they are getting on there. Anna reminded me that the thirteenth is Timo's birthday. I've heard that he has turned completely gray this past year. He is only forty-three. During his nine years in the casemate, only his temples and his mustache turned salt-and-pepper.

Here in our house, the past year has been one of toil and trouble. When I returned from Pärnu last autumn, our cash reserves had dwindled to exactly six rubles. True, our larder and cellar were not entirely empty, but our little piece of land had not been cultivated properly, due to the move in the spring and my adventures in the fall; thus, we had no grain at all. Above our bedroom, the tile roof was falling apart. I couldn't afford to buy new tiles, so I spent a week repairing the roof with clay, and managed to make it more or less watertight. Eeva sent us three poods of flour from Voisiku (Anna had told her about our meager supplies); and with that, and a quarter of a bushel of cabbages and apples, we managed to survive. I also caught the odd fish in the river. And then I invented a profession for myself.

I had heard that Major Tenner had gone to Riga to attend to cartographic tasks there over the winter. With our remaining rubles in my purse, I made the journey of two hundred and twenty versts and sought him out. He wrote an affidavit and asked for, and received, a recommendation for me from old Count Mellin; then he took me to the office of the Russian government of Livonia, presented a few surveys of his own as *my* work (well, to some extent, they were), and obtained for me an official surveyor's certificate with all the requisite signatures and seals. According to a Russian law passed in 1806, it does not entitle me to work for the state, but no one has ever paid any attention to that in Livonia, and the certificate is certainly valid for local commissions. Be that as it may, word of my new profession was out before I had time to advertise it: I had hardly returned from Riga when Mr. Schwalbe sent word from Roika offering work. This consisted of a survey and mapping of the mirrorworks' timber stands on the far side of the river, and of their newly purchased forests at Valgamaa. Work on this commission could, of course, only begin in the spring. Through Mr. Schwalbe I asked Mr. Amelung for an advance that would enable me to buy food for the winter and to rent the surveying equipment I would require. I knew that old Winter, the long-since retired surveyor of the city of Tartu, had kept all his instruments, such as a good theodolite, surveyor's chains, pennant poles (rather rusty), and even a Wagner's planimeter. Well, he wouldn't rent them out to me, but he was willing to sell them. After extended bargaining, we agreed that I would pay only forty rubles down, another forty in the autumn. On the remainder of my advance, Anna and I survived through the winter, and as soon as the ground was dry, I went to work. Even though that work didn't put all that much money in my pocket, I was suddenly swamped with commissions and almost didn't have time to do the necessary grafting on our apple trees and to turn over our vegetable beds. In the lighter tasks of gardening and house maintenance, Anna was, I must admit, a strong and skillful helper—I say "lighter tasks" because the announcement she had made in March turned out to be true. In early autumn, while I was working for the younger Wahls, surveying the boundaries of their estates, Kaave and Pajus, Anna asked her mother to come and stay here. Now, I suppose, she has only a week or two to go.

Hence, I'll be going to Voisiku by myself, on a horse borrowed from Mr. Wahl, and even so, those five versts will prove an ordeal because of the incredibly muddy roads.

The fifteenth of November, 1830, late at night

Now I have to repeat that ancient saying: The Lord gives, and the Lord takes away. Or, rather: The Lord took what he hadn't given. But let me try to take events in their proper order.

I left Anna in good health, busy making applesauce from the last of this year's apples, with her mother helping her attend to the fire and stir the big copper cauldron. I had collected the horse from Wahl's steward, who had orders to let me have a mount whenever I needed one, and in the afternoon I rode off to Voisiku.

God, yes, even in the mild candlelight, Timo looked much grayer than he had the previous autumn. But Eeva seemed completely unchanged, and altogether they made the impression of people who had made their peace with the world.

The only other birthday guests were Elsy and Claire. At the coffee table, and later at supper, I did not ask whether details of our escapade of last year had somehow reached Peter's ears, nor whether this had caused problems, or of what kind. But after supper, when Claire had gone back to the main building, Elsy broached the subject herself.

When Elsy returned from Tallinn with Peter, having barely recovered from her imaginary illness and still feeling quite weak, and ran into Timo in the Voisiku yard (Eeva was on her way to St. Petersburg with Jüri), she had been hard put to conceal her amazement from Peter. She had, of course, been the last person to reveal anything, but somehow, from stable boy to stable hand, from stable hand to the steward's kitchen maid, and from her to the steward himself, and then from old Timm, in the form of mild, somewhat muddled but nevertheless servile mumblings, word had reached Peter's ears that Mr. Bock and his wife had undertaken a journey somewhere while he, Peter, was away . . . It would have been impossible, no doubt, to conceal that journey from everyone. Then again, none of us had worried about covering our tracks, since there was to be no return . . . A week after his return, Peter had summoned Juhan the coachman to come and see him. Juhan had sworn complete allegiance to Timo a long time ago, and the summons made him fear the worst—on the way back, Eeva had told him not to breathe a word about their journey. Juhan had hastened to The Foundation to get advice on how to act in front of Mr. Peter if the latter decided to cross-examine him. Timo gave him twenty rubles and a letter of recommendation and sent him off to old Masing at Äksi, out of Peter's reach. Given his position as master of the estate, and his sense of civic duty, Peter might have ordered Juhan strapped to the bench to have the truth flogged out of him, and Timo had said that he'd rather have Peter try to do that to *him* . . .

(Once again, I have to ask: How did a Baltic nobleman turn out this way? But I know him too well to ask that question. Rather, one should ask: How did a mere mortal turn out his way . . . ?)

After Juhan's disappearance, Peter came to The Foundation, seated himself in his customary sprawling manner on their old drawing room sofa, and asked:

"Tell me where you went!"

Eeva had positioned herself in front of him, arms akimbo in a rather unladylike manner, and told him, with a most ladylike smile:

"Dear kinsman—we shall not submit to your interrogations. Please know that today, and in days to come."

Then Peter had begun to berate them (as Eeva told me: "You know, in that completely idiotic way of his that makes him sound like an old codger dispensing words of wisdom") with: "My dear friends, you must understand, I have to note in my report that you went somewhere while I was away. I know you did. But I can't say that in the report if I don't know *where* you went!"

Timo had said, "Why not? Just write: 'When I asked Mr. Bock about it, he explained that they had taken their carriage thirteen times around the county, naturally remaining at all points exactly *within* the county boundaries. Unfortunately, Mr. Bock cannot recall if they did so clockwise or counterclockwise.' "

Peter shouted: "Stop that nonsense! You were gone for four days!"

Timo replied: "Before the Lord, a thousand years is but the blink of an eye."

Peter roared: "Stop playing the fool!"

And Timo replied: "What do you mean, *playing?* Watch out, Peter—you're casting doubt on the words of two emperors."

Juhan didn't return, Peter wasn't able to find out more, and it seems that he simply omitted the rumor of the Bocks' mysterious excursion from his report. It was obvious that he did not suspect it to have been an escape attempt—and if he did, he kept that to himself, because one thing was certain: if suspicion of an escape attempt had reached the Governor General's, and hence the emperor's, ears, drastic changes would have been made in the conditions of Timo's life, changes that probably would have affected the surveillance mechanism itself and removed the chairman of the guardianship board himself from the premises. But no such changes had occurred.

As it was obvious that Timo and Eeva had no secrets from Elsy, I asked Timo:

"And is Mr. Peter still as interested in your literary endeavors?"

Timo said, "Of course he is. Every so often, he uses his privilege as a kinsman to come and peruse my cookbooks."

I asked, "But he has not had an opportunity to read anything *else?*"

I don't know if Timo heard my question or not, but he did not give an audible reply. However, I thought I noticed a minute shake of the head.

It was late, and Eeva had told the servants to light a fire in the fireplace of my old bedroom and make up a bed for me there. I was on the verge of sleep when there was a knock on the door.

"Mr. Jakob! Mr. Jakob! Please, get up! People have come for you, your wife is—"

It was Käsper's cautious old man's voice, interrupted by a stranger:

"Dr. Robst has asked you to come. Even though it is late. He is there. The birth has begun. And it looks like—it may—you see—"

It took me only a minute or two to get dressed. It goes without saying that I was frightened. Somehow, my dark premonitions were so strong that I might have been disappointed if they had proved groundless. I ran to the stable, led the horse into the yard. Dr. Robst's servant rode with me. The horses had to find their way around deep mud puddles in the pitch-dark night. As we turned from the estate drive onto the highway, my clumsy steed took the turn so tight that an invisible tree branch struck my hat off my head. I was not about to stop to look for it in the mud and the dark—this was an emergency. I rode on, bare-headed, thinking, quite lucidly as I recall: It doesn't matter whether I look for it or not, it doesn't matter whether I find it or not—the very fact that my hat was struck off my head at the very beginning of such a journey home means that Death is waiting for me there . . .

When I arrived at the house, it was all over.

Anna was in a swoon, having lost a great deal of blood, and no one had told her anything yet. My mother-in-law's face was bloated with drink and damp with tears. On the kitchen table stood an empty bottle of last year's hard cider. On a bench on the stone floor in the hallway behind the kitchen, lit by a candle, lay the one who had wanted to be born but had changed his mind at the last moment: a small, yellow and purple bump under a white sheet. My son who had not wanted to be my son. Dr. Robst showed him to me. Then, in the kitchen, he asked me to pour water over his hands as he washed them in the stone basin. He told me that the heartbeat had been clearly audible, but egress from the mother's body had taken much longer and had been much harder than anticipated, and by the time they had managed to bring him out, he had been strangled by his own navel cord . . .

I know that this is a false assumption—but I also know that I'll never be rid of it: if I had not, on that thirteenth day of November which was not to be my son's birthday but certainly was

Timo's—if I had not, on that day, gone to celebrate Timo's birth-day, but had stayed at home—if I had been present at the birth of my own son (and it cannot be regarded as a premature birth, even though it happened on Timo's birthday)—perhaps things would have turned out differently . . .

And I have thought: Should I understand Dr. Robst's words that he had, with his own ears, heard that child's heartbeat as a con-solation (as Dr. Robst himself tried to imply in his own sentimental way), or should I take them as proof of a great tragedy . . . ? What I mean is, this was not some long-dead fetus that had to be removed from its mother to be buried in the ground, this had been a living child . . .

And I have also thought: Was my abandonment of Iette truly such a grave betrayal that it shall be avenged upon my children unto the third and fourth generation—that my son, even before entering this world, hanged himself like Judas Iscariot . . . ?

The twenty-first of November, '30

I buried him the next day, with just my mother-in-law present, in a small wooden coffin I nailed together out of smooth pieces of board, in a hard sleeting rain, next to the stone wall at the far end of the cemetery. Without any religious rites, of course, but in consecrated ground nevertheless.

Today, Anna insisted on coming with me to visit his grave. True, it's only a few hundred paces from our house, but it was still a great effort for her, not much longer than a week after it all happened. Nevertheless, her physical recovery surprised me less than her spiritual, how should I put it—*equilibrium*. The ominous side of our misfortune does not seem to oppress her at all . . .

I did not speak to her about Iette, of course not, nor about my fears of Old Testament–style retribution. But I did tell her about my sense that the loss of our child might have had some inex-plicable connection with Timo's fate. Had he not hurried to be born on the same day as Timo . . . and perhaps that was why he was not born at all. I told her this as we returned from the cemetery in the falling snow. She had to sit down to rest once more on a stone by the side of the road, only fifty paces from our house. But after we had walked through the gate into the yard and into the house, and after she had thrown herself on the bed, she called for me. I sat down on the edge of the bed, and she took my hand and stroked it, and I thought: I should really be consoling *her* . . . She pulled me close and said:

"Jakob, you mustn't think that way. This misfortune has befallen too many others before us . . . There is no point in looking for any hidden meanings. We should only pray to God and hope for better luck in the future . . . And if you still love me, as you have loved me until now—"

I felt how her self-deception made me shiver. But when I looked at her face, close up, I saw that she had, in the last days, become surprisingly free of the pained and estranged expression she had before giving birth . . . Her strange, weary freshness was more visible now, and more attractive, and—dear God—even more like herself and like *Iette* than before . . . And I knew, even as she was lying there, still wrapped in bloodied sheets, that we shall try again, be it in defiance of God or by His grace . . .

The twenty-sixth of December, '30

Eeva visited us this afternoon, and I want to write down a few bits of the news she told us, to make sure I'll remember them.

Timo's refusal to pursue our carefully prepared escape plan has made Elsy believe that Timo is truly a little deranged. Well, I don't think that Elsy would believe that so readily if her own role in the tale of Timo's escape had not been so prominent . . . The greater the help we offer, the blinder we find the person who refuses it. I know this from myself, because my contribution to the preparations for that escape was, indeed, the greatest—and I was also the first one to proclaim that Timo was blind to refuse . . .

Eeva also told us that now that Marquis Paulucci has resigned from the Czar's service and moved away from Russia, and Mr. von Pahlen has been appointed Governor General of the Baltic provinces, Timo has given the family his permission to prepare, should they want to do so, a petition to the Governor General on his behalf. Timo regards Pahlen as a man of honor, at least compared to Paulucci. Now Elsy has written such a letter of petition, and even Peter has signed it, at her demand. While nurturing her newfound belief in Timo's illness, or at least her doubt in his complete sanity, she has also made it her mission to make it possible for him to travel abroad, but only in accordance with the law and the permission of the Most Highest. She feels that if this can be accomplished, Timo ought to accept it. I can well understand Elsy's efforts, in view of the strained relations between her brother and her husband, but I also think (and Eeva agrees with me) that one cannot be at all certain of compliance on Timo's part . . . They have, in any case, written to Pahlen, saying, in effect, that their brother's and kinsman's mental deviance is of such a mild and harmless kind, and includes such moments of utmost lucidity, that, given continued and effective treatment, one might expect his complete recovery. However, since his circumstances are too straitened to make it possible to import physicians from Tallinn or Tartu to the distant dwelling place to which he has been restricted, the petitioners ask for permission on his behalf to spend a specified time in Tallinn or Tartu, preferably Tartu, where the university can provide some highly qualified physicians. In the same letter, they have also begged for gracious indulgence for another request they soon intend to make, in order to fulfill their natural and sacred family obligation, the request that Timo be granted permission to travel, in the company of relatives who will be responsible for him, to seek a complete cure in Germany—in Cöthen, for instance, under the famous Dr. Hahnemann's homeopathic care. As the entire civilized world knows, Dr. Hahnemann's trillionation cures have produced the most splendid results in the treatment of precisely those kinds of ailments with which Mr. Bock is afflicted . . .

After we had eaten our modest supper on this second day of Christmas, and after Eeva had driven away in her sleigh and Anna had gone to sleep, I decided to end the day by taking Timo's memorandum from its hiding place for the first time in a long while. By the way, not too long ago I obtained a couple of notebooks of exactly the same appearance as this journal to use for notes on survey tasks in progress, and also to protect the journal—to make it appear like an ordinary volume among several others, should someone notice it for some unforeseen reason. I have also thought of Timo's manuscript and acquired sheets of similar size and thickness for cartographic notes and sketches: now those piled-up, graying, and curling sheets look commonplace on my desk and in its vicinity. Thus, Timo's manuscript would attract no particular attention even if I should happen to leave it out . . .

And so, I placed Timo's memorandum in front of me; Eeva's mention of Elsy's doubts about his sanity tempted me to peruse it again.

I have to say: if I ignore a few ruminations that speak of too narrow a perspective—that of a Baltic aristocrat—I find myself enthralled and drawn, once again, into a strange and paradoxical circle: *those* thoughts that would seem to be the most obvious indications of his madness are also the clearest evidence of his penetrating vision and merciless sense of justice . . .

. . . How many people are there who can say with an untroubled conscience: "This was my intention, and this is how I have realized it"? If, among millions, one can be found who has genius as well as the energy required to remain honorable—then he is destined for exile . . .

. . . *Order* is the foundation of every society, and I respect it always, but it is wrong to imagine that there is no connection between order and truth . . .

. . . It is human nature to deny love to those who restrict our rights, all the more so when those rights are restricted in a biased and brutal manner . . .

. . . If it is one's intention to demolish a building beyond repair, one must hire new builders every month and give them exactly the same instructions . . .

. . . What certainty can there ever be in an absolute monarchy . . . ?

. . . Every nation goes through a period of bestiality and barbarity before it reaches civilization. And this, in turn, due to vicious human nature, degenerates into a new kind of barbarity. But a nation enlightened by the Kremlin fire is no longer the same that Buhren, the human dog of

Courland, tormented for a decade. Fateful surprises await those who believe it is. Just as in the lives of individuals, so there are moments in the lives of nations that suddenly transform their entire beings . . .

. . . As far as the arts and sciences are concerned, Russia deserves genuine respect. Who understands Derzhavin, Dmitriyev, Krylov, Zhukovski, Barjushkov, and Karamzin, who appreciates Ozerov, who has seen Minin and Pozharski and the works of Tolstoi, Yegorov, or Utkin, who has heard Bortnyanski's Mass, who has seen on stage Suserin, Branski, Semyonov, Danilov, will be more ready to acknowledge these glorious names if he is also familiar with the world of classics. To your ears, gentlemen, those names are unknown. But does that diminish their worth? Was it Goethe's and Schiller's fault that they were hardly known in Paris—until Madame de Staël informed the French that people knew how to read and write on the far side of the Rhine?

. . . Of what do Paulucci's merits consist? Is it that he sends his reports to the Emperor and the Emperor pays him a salary and hence notices his existence? Or is it his treacherous eagerness to erase his shame? If so—what meaning do faith and honor have? That he is loath to sacrifice his precious days to us was amply demonstrated in 1812. It is also very unlikely that he has depleted his own financial resources, especially considering that one of our countrymen, out of the goodness of his heart, released him from debtors' prison in Vienna, and he has now been able, as we know from a reliable source, to invest impressive sums in Italy, gained from his high salary and additional income as a field marshal. Why do we merely call him *Erlaucht*? Why not go ahead and address him as Your Majesty?

. . . In June 1816, I conveyed, through official channels, an official memorandum to the Emperor. It included authentic proof for the statements made in it. Last year, the director of the Petitions Office claimed, in conversation with me, that he had been unable to obtain an audience with the Emperor for almost a year. During that time, the Emperor has not missed a single parade.

The official order to investigate the barbaric appropriation of the Patkuls' family estate has been ignored for more than thirteen years.

What epithet does such management of affairs deserve?

. . . Let us never blame our rulers! They are nothing but what we ourselves make of them. When we spoil them in the cradle by groveling on the ground in front of them, how can we demand later that our well-being should be important to them?

. . . To tell the truth, we have noticed, ever since the founding of the Holy Alliance, that our press describes the Sovereign's rights as entirely God-given. Yet we who believe in God's omnipotence also regard as God-given the plague, the hyena, the scorpion, the louse, and the Beys of Algeria—and consider that rulers would do well to leave it up to coming generations to decide what they really were: instruments of God's mercy or tools of His anger . . .

Could a madman have written these things?

Can a normal person throw such things in his emperor's face?

But what if the emperor has made that normal person swear an oath to tell him the truth, always?

If the emperor has deprived the normal person of his normal freedom to tell lies?

Would only a madman let such things fall into his emperor's hands?

Sunday, the twenty-fifth of October, 1831

At ten o'clock this morning, Anna gave birth to a healthy girl-child.

Dr. Robst will be going to Germany next week, but he was still here to receive our daughter. Mother and child are well, thank

God. Anna, the doctor, and I noted that if there was any significance to the fact that the child was born during this autumn's
first big snowstorm—that she's sure to become a tomboy, say,
or that she'll suffer terribly from the cold all her life—any such
negative omen should be completely canceled by her being born
to the sound of our church bells calling the faithful to wor-
ship . . . Around noon, we drank to that happy augury, Anna
with a glassful of cider, the doctor and I with cherry liqueur.

Anna and I have decided to name the girl Eeva, a name that
befits gentlefolk and commoners alike. And Anna said just what
I had been thinking—that it would also remind us of my important
sister who is no longer referred to by that name anywhere except
in familiar usage in our house (and that of her parents).

The twenty-ninth of October

Yesterday morning, our parish clerk, Mets, christened Eeva
here in our dining room. We had asked Mrs. von Wahl and, of
course, Mrs. von Bock to be her godmothers; to balance things
out, and a little defiantly, I had also asked Tiit's golden-haired Juul
to be the third godmother. I don't think I have noted in this journal
that Tiit—the old one-eyed rascal—found himself a clever young
wife in Roika township last year.

Tomorrow, I have to go to Viljandi: once again, the shadow
of death is cast over a birth in our family. Anna has received word
that her mother is gravely ill. Anna can't travel with the child yet,
nor can she leave it at home, and she has asked me to go to Viljandi
in her stead.

I have to admit that my mother-in-law is a stranger to me, even
though we have met often enough for that not to be so. Last year,
and the year before last, she visited us several times, until she
became ill last autumn and said she could no longer visit us. Perhaps she hadn't felt welcome enough under our roof. I don't know
what has given me the impression—occasional remarks—a few
odd giggles and glances—the empty cider bottle?—that there is
something, I don't even know how to put it, something myste-

rious and *knowing* about her. And I would prefer Anna's mother not to be that kind of woman.

I have already asked Wahl for a horse and sleigh, and I'll take a shotgun along, in case I should run into wolves.

The eleventh of January, '32

The Christmas holidays and the New Year are already behind us. So is Twelfth Night, but I haven't noticed the days getting any longer yet.

We are submerged in the snowless darkness of this winter—and I feel as if I were sinking into something else, as well. Not in worries about money—I have been taking care of that by daily labors at my drawing board, inspired and goaded along by little Eeva's whining next door. *Sinking* isn't really the right word. I feel like someone who has caused something he would like to forget, something he condemns but cannot rid himself of. I feel that way even though I haven't done anything of the kind. Nevertheless—my mother-in-law has lain in her grave since the fourth of December, last year, but she left me with a tale I still carry with me, and that is what I can't get rid of, can't deposit anywhere but on these miserable pages.

At the end of October I drove to Viljandi to visit Maali, Anna's mother. I found her in her hovel, an outbuilding belonging to Rinne, the flax merchant, on a street leading down to the lake. Her room was pitiful, furnished with a broken chair with a woven backrest, a rough table that didn't look like it had been wiped clean for a long time, a chest of drawers, a sagging bed, a couple of pots and kettles on the cold stove. The chest of drawers was made of mahogany. Rinne's maid had been bringing her something to eat whenever she found the time, putting the food on a low stool next to the bed.

Maali never had much meat on her bones, at least not during the couple of years I had known her. But now she looked paper-thin. Once again, she was a little intoxicated, and this made her sharp cheekbones glow in that emaciated face. A half-empty bottle of cheap berry wine was jammed between the headboard of the bed and the wall. She looked at me, did not recognize me at first. Then she blinked her bloodshot eyes and said:

"It helps this pain in my side, you know . . . when I take a little drink . . ."

I explained to her why Anna couldn't come and asked her what I could do for her. She wanted me to fetch the pastor of Jaan Church.

I said, "All right, but I'll get a doctor to see you first."

Dr. Meyer of Viljandi, a local blacksmith's son, still young but learned, on first-name terms with Aesculapius, had visited us a couple of times at Voisiku. He recognized me and followed me immediately to Maali's hovel. After he examined her and told her that a few swigs from her bottle wouldn't do her any harm, I went out into the yard with him to pay him his fee and to ask his opinion on my mother-in-law's condition.

"You said she wanted to see a clergyman," Dr. Meyer said. "Well, you should have one come here."

I asked, "*Today?*" Even when one doesn't know a person all that well, these matters are always a little frightening.

"Today or tomorrow—makes no difference," Dr. Meyer said. "So why not grant her wish today."

I asked, "But what . . . ?"

Almost irritably, Dr. Meyer said, "My dear man—we can both see that she's on her deathbed. *What* is she dying of? I don't know. Nobody does. What use are a few Latin phrases in this case—or any other, for that matter? Her time's running out, that's all."

I went back in and told Maali that I was going to see the pastor. She probably guessed that I had asked the doctor about her condition, but she didn't ask me.

I went to the pastor's office and was told that Pastor Carlblom had gone to Riga for some meeting. When I came back, sat down on the stool next to Maali's bed, and told her this news, she closed her eyes for a moment, then looked at me, took my hand—hers was burning hot, and I let her hold mine—and said, almost in a whisper:

"Well, Jakob . . . then I'll tell it to you, now . . . And it may be better this way . . . Because what I want to tell you, is my shame . . . but your pride . . . And after I've told you, I won't have to feel too ashamed about it, either . . . You see, that Aadam of mine, the cooper—you never met him—all I can say about him, even on my deathbed . . . is that he was a brutal . . . and stupid man. You had to tell him everything twice, and when he finally understood something, he mostly just got angry, never mind what it was . . . So when Pastor Schröder, who was then the pastor at Jaan Church, married us . . . it was only because there was nothing else I could do . . . You see—I was more than two months pregnant . . . Well, you may imagine—me, the maid at the parsonage—and now this . . ."

She paused to draw breath. I didn't ask her anything. Only when she reached for her bottle and wanted me to help her take a drink did I realize that I had overcome my slight revulsion and let her hold my hand. She went on, and even in her almost toneless speech I could still hear pleasure and satisfaction in the turn things had taken:

"Well, now you must think that it was the pastor . . . No, no, it wasn't him. But it was no angel from heaven, either . . . You see, they were doing a great many repairs on the parsonage that spring, and Schröder hired this master builder to supervise them. He was young, handsome, and very knowledgeable. He was staying in the guest room on the garden side, and from the moment he set eyes on me, he started courting me. And I, of course, just looked at the floor, but as soon as he turned his back, I couldn't get my eyes off him . . ."

I listened and noticed, with mixed feelings of repugnance and pity and the joy of forgiveness, how Maali, who otherwise looked genuinely like she was approaching death's door, grew brighter as she remembered:

"It didn't take him long to get me into his room . . . He had arranged it so nicely, with pictures and pipes on the wall, and flowers on the table . . . a room like a cigar box . . . And when I resisted at first, he promised me heaven and earth . . . and then I didn't resist any more—may God forgive me . . . So, you see, it isn't Aadam, but that gentleman who is really your father-in-law . . ."

As she was speaking, she was still holding my hand tight, but it seemed to me that this was not so much due to the difficulty of her confession as to her sense that I had now become an accomplice to her secret. I didn't mind; I had decided to be fair and conciliatory.

"Maali," I said, "you know that I cannot give you absolution for your sins, the way a clergyman could. But I do believe that . . . that the Lord is telling you: 'Because of what you did, you have suffered enough' (I really wasn't so sure of this . . .) 'yes, you've suffered enough—so come to my peace now . . .' But you said that your story would make me proud . . . Well, if your Aadam was a rough and stupid man—"

I saw how Maali's lips tightened and her sharp chin twitched, in a prideful nod. I continued:

"—and if that young man was a decent fellow—but I don't know how decent he really was—if he abandoned you like that—"

Maali said, "He gave Pastor Schröder thirty rubles to give to me when he left—and that mahogany chest of drawers . . . Over the years, I've had to sell everything I inherited from Aadam . . . but I'll leave this to Anna . . ."

I won't deny that I was a little touched by this.

I said, "Well, then, if he was a kind and honest man—then I do feel good about it, for Anna's and our child's sake . . ."

Maali whispered, "Yes . . . He was a dear man . . . You know him, too . . . It's that same Mr. Laming . . . he was later the steward at Voisiku for many years . . ."

I felt stupefied and spellbound. For a moment, I didn't say anything. I had heard very clearly what Maali had said but asked her, nevertheless:

"Maali—are you sure you're not delirious . . . ?"

She had sunk into the hollow of her mattress. Her forehead was sweaty, and strands of her gray hair stuck out from under her cap. She gave me a reproachful look as she whispered:

"Why? Don't you believe me . . . ? After all, I was the prettiest girl in the parsonage . . . And I'm telling you this so it'll go a little easier with me . . . when I meet my Maker . . ."

I asked her if Anna knew about this. She shook her head.

"I did want to tell her before I died . . ."

I left a kopeck with Rinne's maid, told her to stop in tonight to see how Maali was, and then went back to the Valuoja Inn. I wanted to make sure that my horse was taken care of and wanted to spend a night where no one knew me. I sat down at a table in the tavern, feeling as if someone had pushed my face up against an invisible wall. I ate a couple of slices of ham and downed a considerable amount of spirits, but to no avail—I did not become the least bit inebriated. My thoughts were painfully lucid, and I felt that they would always remain thus, like the thoughts of a convict facing a life sentence . . .

I did, of course, pull myself together the next morning to go to her. Even though it was true that I had only decided to be fair and conciliatory *before* she made her confession, I knew that it wouldn't do to seem even mutely accusatory in the presence of a dying person. Still, I found it hard to reconcile myself to her after that conversation . . . I remember being quite pleased, that morning, because she was hardly able to speak, and her gaze was so dim that I did not find it particularly difficult to avoid her eyes. And I remember feeling deeply ashamed. There was a moment when I had the urge to call for help—it was so overwhelmingly impossible to understand myself and this dying old woman. And since I did not know how to perform the sacred comedy of forgiveness for her . . . If she had appeared repentant, I suppose I could have managed. I would have been able to suppress my revulsion, to take her hand, tell her: *Mother*—the way a reconciled son-in-law ought to say at such a moment—*Mother, of course I'll tell Anna everything you told me, and may it be your consolation that she and I will take pride in it . . .* But my dying mother-in-law's pride in her sin, and her nonsensical notion that I, too, ought to take pride in it, completely paralyzed my intention to practice self-denial . . .

I promised to come back in the afternoon and walked into town, where I wanted to look for a pair of good fur-lined house slippers for Anna. Our kitchen had a stone floor, and last year Anna had often complained that her feet became ice-cold as soon as she stepped away from the heat of the stove. I spent quite a long time in the establishments of three or four bootmakers and in two general stores. As I was walking back, around four o'clock, to the

Valuoja Inn, with Anna's new slippers and other parcels, I ran into
Rinne's maid who was coming from that direction. She had just
left word for me at the inn that Maali had died at three o'clock
that afternoon.

I sent a message by post to Anna at Poltsamaa. Anna left tiny
Eeva for a few days in the care of the Wahls' housekeeper who
had an infant of a couple of months herself, and arrived in Viljandi
in time for her mother's funeral. Pastor Carlblom had returned
from Riga, and we gave Maali a proper burial at the Jaan Church
cemetery. I recall that Anna, who is always easily moved to tears,
wept when she and some matron of the neighborhood dressed
Maali in a white skirt and black blouse from her chest of drawers,
and she also wept when we threw frozen clods of earth on Maali's
coffin at the cemetery. It seemed to me, however, that Anna was
not grieving as much as I had expected. She did want to take that
mahogany chest of drawers back home, and it took me a long
time to convince her that everything else Maali had left would
easily fit into a couple of bundles we could carry in our small
borrowed sleigh, whereas we would have to rent a bigger sleigh
if we wanted to take the chest as well—while Binder, the cabinet
maker, would give us thirty rubles cash for it, right here in
Viljandi!

As it turned out, Binder only paid me eighteen rubles for it,
but I told Anna I had sold it for thirty. As we were on our journey
home on the day after Maali's funeral—the day was cloudy, and
most of the way we had to face cold, driving snow—I asked, not
turning my gaze from the frost-covered hindquarters of the horse:

"Anna, do you remember your father at all?"

Anna had covered her face with a woolen scarf wrapped around
her winter hat. She pushed the scarf away from her mouth and
said:

"Of course I do. I was ten years old when he died."

I closed my eyes for a moment so that I wouldn't have reason
to feel guilty about spying on her expression.

I asked, "How did your father and mother get along, as far as
you can remember?"

Anna pondered that a moment. "I don't know . . . Not too
well, I don't think."

"*Why not*—do you think?" I asked—and couldn't resist turning my head and looking at her, probably with a strange intense expression on my face. But she replied, divinely calm as ever:

"As a cooper, my father was a good and hard worker. But he drank, the way such men often do. And Mother couldn't stand that, back then."

That was all we said on that subject. I could see that what Maali had told me on her deathbed was true: Anna knew nothing about her real father.

The nineteenth of February, 1832

Once in a while, I manage to make it clear to myself that it is simply ridiculous to speak of some fateful twist in my life. Dear God—you call that a *twist?*

True enough, my wife's real father is not the one registered by the authorities, some long-dead cooper of peasant stock from the town of Viljandi, a drunkard and a clod, as he would no doubt be described by those who happen to remember him. No, he is a German-born Livonian gentleman. Or half a gentleman. One of those busybodies of indeterminate education and profession and tenuous means, most of them climbers and pedants, of whom there are hundreds in our cities, towns, and villages. Civil servants, shop clerks, scriveners, officials, master builders, stewards. Well, in any case, one of those slightly better-born types. Whom I should really thank for my wife's sense of order and eye for color . . . And that this *half-gentleman* may have performed a certain task assigned to him by the authorities, in regard to a nobleman who had been declared insane, and whose thinking was, indeed, completely beyond the pale (although no one has ever seen any black-on-white proof of that!)—a certain imperial task—twenty or thirty years after the gent in question had abandoned my mother-in-law and her unborn daughter—well, dear God—what does my wife have to do with any of that!

On the other hand, there are times when I see, with absolute clarity, the fateful and idiotic twist of fate that has affected my life.

I loved Iette. I won't conceal that anymore, at least not on these pages. And I love her still. Four years ago, I sent her away because of her father . . . Now, if I told someone this, he might say to me: Well, that meant you didn't love her enough . . . To which I would answer: Surely great love does not mean complete blindness? It does not, to my mind, and it is, in any case, the deepest love I have ever felt. It is so great that every time I think about it, something still rejoices and comes alive inside me, and then subsides with a kind of sweet pain. I know: the thorn is still in my flesh . . . I rejected Iette because I did not want to have anything to do with her father—Laming, a government spy. Then I felt guilty for leaving my sister and brother-in-law at the mercy of Laming's successors—fleeing . . . Fleeing into the arms of another woman because she reminded me, somehow, of my love. And now it turns out, in a perfectly fiendish way, that this other woman is also a child of that same informer . . .

I hear little Eeva crying in her sleep, behind the wall—I hear her once in a while as I sit here working on my drawings at night. It is one o'clock, and I have been writing in this journal again after a long hiatus. I hear her creaky little voice and think what I have thought so many times before—and every time I have felt as if an iron band had wound itself around my forehead: that little bumblebee, in whom I recognize Anna and myself on alternate days, is my child . . . Yet, at the same time, she is—I have to force my hand to write this—she is, my own child is also the grandchild of Laming, the government informer. My daughter who was to take pride in my noble sister's name, does, there's no denying it, also bear this other secret name—and I have seen my sister, when she mentions it, curl her lips in fear and revulsion, as if she had put a cranberry in her mouth and discovered that it was a wood louse . . .

The twenty-second of February, 1832

In the light of day, no silly notions disturb my peace of mind. I sit in front of the maps of the Lilienfeldt estate, spread out on my table just as grandiosely white, and decorated here and there with a little black, as the surrounding landscape I see through my window. Or I work outside—digging ditches into the snowdrifts, which thaw in the daytime and freeze again at night, to hasten the snowmelt into the river, since the stretch between the garden and the riverbank tends to get waterlogged in the spring. Or else I keep our two greedy wood stoves burning, or go to the shed and repair spade handles and pruning saws, anticipating the needs of our belated spring. Or I help Anna carry buckets of laundry water out of the kitchen, help her hang up diapers and other laundry to dry on a string between the walls of our fourth room, which is otherwise empty in the winter . . .

In the daytime, I am too busy to indulge in thoughts of discontent. But late at night, after I have been reading Friedrich Schlosser's *History of the Eighteenth Century* to the point of fatigue and complete wakefulness, and sit here listening to the wind howl in the chimney and rattle branches in the yard as if uncertain whether it wants winter to stay or spring to come, it quite often seems like something is happening to me that resembles what Timo once told me about . . . My thoughts—and they aren't so much images as *questions* in my mind—start running wild . . . And that is when I ask myself what has happened to the great ferment Timo wrote about fifteen years ago, which was to stretch from the shores of Peru to the faraway walls of China . . . ? It seems to me that it has not abated at all during these fifteen years, no matter how eagerly everybody is trying to cover it up with dirt and snow and ashes. Just think about what has been going on in Poland this year and last: first of all, they deposed the Grand Duke and Viceroy—an unheard-of thing! Then Czartoryski formed a government of Poles, whereafter General Diebitsch, at the head of two hundred thousand men, was despatched to restore order . . . Our newspapers give us only a pale reflection of what has really happened there . . . But I have read straightforward reports about the deaths of both Grand Duke Konstantin and General Diebitsch, between battles, in last year's horrible cholera epidemic. There is no shortage of strong generals in our empire: Diebitsch's successor, General Paskevich, even more energetic, has vanquished and expelled from Warsaw—so the papers tell—those hordes of rebels and criminals with the greatest of ease, thanks to help from the true sons of the Polish people . . . Only that brazen French *Constitutionnel*, they say, reported that for many days after that battle the Vistula ran red—the red of—which?—sunset or sunrise? And now, they say, order has been restored in Poland, and military tribunals and gravediggers are very busy indeed . . . And yet, and yet, I often ask myself in those quiet evening hours—won't a new era begin here, too, at last?

Eeva, I mean Kitty, visited us last week. Apparently, nothing much has changed at Voisiku. With Georg's help, Mannteuffel has hired a Swiss-born French teacher for his children who has now been there for several months, instructing Peter and Elsy's young boys. It seems that she likes to visit The Foundation to chat with its inhabitants, and so far the Mannteuffels have not frowned upon that. This young lady, who hails from the same town of Vevey near which Georg still lives in his rented chateau, has told them Switzerland is teeming with Polish refugees. Georg and his Teresa have had to shelter four, sometimes five of them at a time in their stone tower. From Switzerland, these refugees slowly drift on to Paris—to prepare, with French assistance, another and more successful Polish rebellion . . .

So, won't conditions change at last, in Poland as well as Russia, with a different breed of men taking charge? Different from our Pauluccis, Pahlens, Mannteuffels, Lamings, or—in the best case? —La Trobes? Or perhaps men like those who have been working in the mines somewhere beyond Irkutsk, in shackles, for the past six years . . . ? And if that should happen, would it not be possible (on a few evenings like this, with the wind soughing and the candleflame flickering, I have tormented myself with such fantasies) that my officially insane brother-in-law would be declared the most honored forerunner of the nation's noblest men? And wouldn't my clever sister be raised up next to him, to receive her share of glory? Because I am certain that she knows her husband's utopian dreams—she may even have shared them, to a certain extent . . . And might it not happen, some evening like this, ten or twenty years from now, that my own daughter, the same one I can now hear being rocked in her cradle by her mother, will come to me and ask: "Papa—tell me, why do people fall silent and look away when I tell them that my grandfather was Mr.

Laming . . . ?" And won't that hurt like my thumb, which I've cut on a hidden nail while holding on hard to the armrest of my chair, at this desk . . . just now?

No, it won't. Because no one will ever know.

Oh, Lord—are we not completely defenseless when our only defense is the ignorance of the world?

The sixth of March, '32

▦ Eeva—Kitty, brought us word of a death: Dean Masing passed away at Äksi after several days of severe chest pains, on the third of March. The day after tomorrow, his body will be taken from Äksi to Tartu, and Eeva thinks that we should go both to Äksi for the funeral service and on to Tartu for the burial.

I must say that I find Eeva's punctiliousness in the observance of so-called good manners a little bothersome. I would prefer to observe them less, and have always done so, at least when no one else has interfered in my decisions. Yet there is something imperious and enviable about Eeva's politesse. Well, we may feel differently, since she has, in the course of all these years, become a true noblewoman . . .

So be it, I won't argue with her, especially considering that old Masing was not only our mentor for so many years, but also a true foster father.

Eeva had one other piece of news: she had heard that Iette Laming, around Christmastime, had become the wife of the assistant chief of police at Vonnu. Well—if that's how it has to be, may it be that way.

The thirteenth of March, 1832

▦ We arrived at the Äksi parsonage early on the morning of the tenth.

Eeva and I looked at all the spaces and objects in that unchanged house where we lived for almost five years. During the fifteen years that we had not seen the place, everything had dwindled and faded. I whispered this to Eeva as we tried to make our way through the crowd to express our condolences to the widow. Eeva whispered back: "It's the same with people, isn't it? The only difference is—you'll see what I mean—that people become the same again as soon as they open their mouths . . ."

We found the widow in the drawing room, surrounded by mourners, and I studied her closely. She first came here as the Italian-born governess of the dean's children . . . Many is the time I have heard this mentioned with a certain awe, but I understand (who better than me?) how unfair and silly it would be to mull over that erstwhile master-servant relationship. I would say that this woman was almost too good for old Masing! Not least when you consider that she was thirty years younger than her late husband.

Now she was past forty, and she looked more grief-stricken than I had expected. She squeezed our hands and whispered a few polite words to us before going on to make some arrangement or another. The dean's four daughters from his first marriage were all present—three old maids and Mrs. Schultz with her lawyer husband. The daughters, our former study mates, shook our hands as if we were relatives they had not seen for a long time but remembered fondly. When we began to tell each other the stories of our lives, the conversation became so lively, even though it was conducted in near-whispers, that other mourners began to cast long glances in our direction. But little Rosalie, the dean's nine-year-old daughter whom we met here for the first time, her face blotchy with tears, was inconsolable: she turned away in the middle of her curtsey and went behind a large rubber plant to go on crying there.

We had not expected to see so many mourners who were less familiar to us: the local estate owners and their wives, and almost all the clergymen and parish clerks of the northern Tartu district, also accompanied by their spouses. A group of university professors had arrived from Tartu, led by old Jäsche—it seemed odd that they had not, in spite of this winter's snow-poor and badly frozen highways, contented themselves with waiting for the dean's mortal remains in Tartu, but had come to pay their respects here. There were also all kinds of younger folk from Tartu, respectable gentlemen of the cloth, perhaps councilors of the consistory, and a few students from the College of Theology who distinguished themselves by their more tattered and bold-faced appearance. Gray-coated local schoolmasters and churchwardens hovered in the far corners of the drawing room.

In charge of the funeral ceremony at the church was the Palamus congregation's Pastor Kolbe, whose wife was a close relative of Masing's. Eeva and I went to the church at nine in the morning. About a hundred local folk had already gathered there, and candles were burning on the altar and around the open coffin, by which four churchwardens stood at attention as a guard of honor. We went up to pay our last respects to the old man. Never mind what they say about him, he was without question our second great benefactor—perhaps, come to think of it, the first, because what he and his home gave me, and Eeva to an even greater extent, during those four years (the rudiments of knowledge, the seeds of a critical worldview—and, I believe, the fundamentals of self-respect, not to mention the fundamentals of all kinds of skills, including the draftsmanship that I now use to earn my family's daily bread)—all that has been more essential for Eeva's and my own development as human beings than any other inheritance. Which is not to say that I find the matters Timo opened up for us later to be less important: they gave me the opportunity—and the temptation—to continue my education after Masing's school on my own, and to discover—now that my eyes had been opened a little—a progression of further and ever more discouraging problems . . . They forced Eeva to confront the new world that had been imposed on her, and obliged her to take her own indomitable measure of that world . . . And so, one might ask: In his role as our first benefactor, has Timo not really proven to be our—how should I put it—our perverse Mephistopheles . . . ?

For the last time, we looked at the dean, there amidst his candles. His nose looked even more pointy than usual, and one of the corners of his thin-lipped and sardonic mouth was just as mischievous, the other just as stern as at the time when (I had such a vivid memory of that as we stood there) he told us, at breakfast twenty years ago (and perhaps that wasn't the only time), that now the Estonian people at last, and thanks to him, had their own comprehensible and expressive literary language—but that the common people weren't aware of it yet . . .

We had an hour to kill before the service. Slowly, Eeva and I walked along the road back to the deanery. The snow by the sides of the road had been decorated with spruce branches. The distance back to the house was only a hundred paces. As soon as we entered, I understood immediately that *something* must have happened in the meantime.

All the doors to the dining room, the library, and the dean's study were open, but the rooms themselves were empty. Everybody had congregated in the drawing room. Eeva and I gave each other quizzical looks and walked down the hall to the drawing room. The black-clad mourners looked frightened, disturbed, upset, disbelieving; in their midst stood Mrs. Masing, very pale, and an apoplectic Professor Jäsche. Jäsche was speaking, and the widow seemed to be trying to calm him down.

Jäsche shouted: "*Herrschaften!* Do you understand? It has disappeared. *Disappeared!* And we must find it immediately!"

Anton—the Masings' only son-in-law, Anton von Schultz—who seemed to have a penchant for frivolous remarks (probably because he felt that the family did not show him sufficient respect), quipped back:

"Is the professor saying that one of us has stolen it?"

Jäsche shouted in an almost falsetto voice:

"*Donnerwetter!* I'm saying that it has disappeared, and that we must find it!"

Mrs. Masing exclaimed, wringing her hands:

"Oh, Lord, please let's not stoop to vulgarities . . ."

I asked someone next to me what had happened, but before he had time to give me an answer, Professor Jäsche made his explanatory speech:

"Ladies and gentlemen, I see that you do not know what has happened. You see, in this case"—Professor Jäsche raised a black box, a span and a half long, up to face level and turned it right and left—"in this case, the dean kept the fruit of his labors for the last eighteen years—the manuscript of his great Estonian–German dictionary. It is a practically complete work, a monumental work. Nine hundred and sixty printed pages. There has never been anything like it. It is four times larger than Hupel's dictionary, and it was going to be published next year. On Tuesday, the dean told me that he would very much like to complete his three score and ten, just in order to see its printed form with his own eyes. And he believed that the revenue from it would free his family from all financial care . . ."

At this point in his speech, the church bells began to toll. The service was about to begin. Jäsche went on:

"That same day, Tuesday, the dean asked me to bring the boxed manuscript to his sickbed. On Thursday morning, after he had passed away, Mrs. Masing took it to his study and placed it on his desk. This morning, it was still there—"

Someone shouted: "And you're holding it now—"

Jäsche almost roared: "But it is *empty!*"

He raised the lid and showed us the empty interior of the box. The crowd of mourners stared at it in silence. The church bells tolled. Jäsche said:

"This morning, the manuscript was still in this box. Which means that it was removed at some point during the last hour—"

Anton shouted: "There's a thief among us!"

Mrs. Masing said, in a quiet voice:

"My dear Jäsche—I beg you—I have cried enough—"

Jäsche interrupted her:

"Dear madam, I understand: you are ready to sacrifice your own and your family's well-being in order to avoid a scandal. But I tell you, in the name of scholarship—that is impossible! A bad jest is a bad jest, but theft is theft. You must post a guard to make sure that no one leaves. You must send someone to fetch the police!"

Anton quipped: "Let's split up into two groups and take turns checking each other's pockets and purses!"

Mrs. Masing took the professor's hand:

"Dear friend, I am now going to my husband's funeral service. And I invite all of you who loved and respected him to come with me." She turned to Jäsche: "Tell me, what else can I do?"

Jäsche shrugged. "As you wish." He turned and looked directly at the crowd. "I shall leave this box here on this table, and I expect the manuscript to be in it when we return from church. Whoever took it must understand: no one else could possibly publish it under his own name for at least fifty years—because no one but Masing is capable of such a work."

We went to the church, but I truly cannot remember a word of what Kolbe said in his eulogy. When we came back to the deanery, the box was, of course, still empty. Only when this became apparent did I realize that I *had* been half-hoping that whoever had taken it would have put it back. Because I understood, or was at least able to make an educated guess, what its disappearance would mean for the development of our native tongue.

In the cortege of twenty-odd sleighs, we followed Masing's coffin to Tartu. That same afternoon, the dean was buried in the cemetery of Jaan Church, in the family mausoleum of his first father-in-law, Alderman Ehlertz. A number of valedictory speeches were made in the sleeting rain outside the chapel. Once again, in his speech, Professor Jäsche brought up the disappearance of the manuscript. He told us that a few entries of the dictionary had already been set up in proof—one of them for the word *gardener*, another for the word *death*. And even though death had now claimed the esteemed colleague, his indefatigable horticultural labors in the overgrown weedy garden of our national tongue would be to our great benefit—had not some, in the best case, childishly stupid, or perhaps even *criminal* hand deprived us of the most valuable seed collection . . . Jäsche exhorted the culprit to come to his senses, even if only *post facto*, and to bring or send the manuscript back to the family, or to the university or the consistory. The culprit could not expect any benefit from its possession during his lifetime, since it would be impossible to publish under any other name but that of our late esteemed friend. Any attempt to do so would immediately reveal the sparrow that claimed its beeping was the song of a canary . . .

The mourners stood around the speaker in the rain, and the accusations, just and unjust, rained down upon their bare heads mingling with the wet snow, even upon the hundred or so people from Tartu who had come to the cemetery and couldn't possibly have had anything to do with the matter; and little Mrs. Masing was pursing her still pretty lips and imploring Jäsche with her perplexed doe-eyes behind her mourning veil, but refrained from trying to stop his harangue.

As we returned from the cemetery, I heard that Judge Himmelstjerna had promised to place an announcement in the *Dörptsche Zeitung* urging the person who had taken the manuscript to return it without delay . . . And as we were getting into our sleighs by the cemetery gate, I heard Mrs. Masing say to her stepdaughter's husband, Schultz (whom she generally disliked, so that this must have been an effort on her part): "Anton, you know Judge Himmelstjerna—could you dissuade him from his idea to put an announcement in the paper? Just think what a terrible shadow it would cast over our circle, over us all . . . Oh, dear God . . ."

It was dark when we got back to Äksi, and we stayed the night at Mrs. Masing's home. The consistory has decided that Kolbe can serve Äksi as well as his own Palamus congregation for the time being, and thus Mrs. Masing and her daughter will be able to remain in the deanery.

The guests at our late supper included Kolbe and his wife and a few local people who had been there in the morning, but even though Jäsche had stayed in Tartu, the seeds he had sowed were germinating in my mind. Inevitably, the case of the missing manuscript came up again, and I said:

"Madame Cara—forgive me, but I think you really should have followed Professor Jäsche's advice this morning. You could have posted a few persons by the doors and windows to make sure that no one left, and then called the police."

Cara showed her Mediterranean temper:

"The police? And what would a policeman have done—*if* he had managed to appear at all? Searched our persons? Yes, I would have liked to see him try that on our pastor and on the master of our estate!"

I said, "He would have searched the *suspects* . . ."

Mrs. Masing shouted: "But I don't want there to be any suspects in our company!"

I held my ground: "And yet, there they *were* . . ."

Mrs. Masing shouted with an intensity no Estonian or German could have credibly managed:

"*Yes?* He *still* wouldn't have found anything! They never find anything in these situations! And Anton would have said what he did say, anyway—"

I realized that I was, after all, a guest, and that I had gone too far. I decided not to ask what Anton had said, as it might be something Cara would not care to repeat, but then Kolbe did it for me:

"Pray tell, what did Mr. Anton say?"

Now that the question had been asked by a venerable and incontestably benevolent person, Cara did not object but even seemed relieved to get it off her chest:

"Anton said to me, 'Cara, it's obvious that that manuscript never existed.' Imagine! He grinned into his fox-fur collar and said, 'Obviously, the old man was just bluffing all those eighteen years. What a great deceiver!' And then he repeated, as if I didn't understand German: 'Do you understand: *il grandissimo bluffo!*' He said that I would, however, have to go on with the pretense, to garner more sympathy and interest . . . What a *porco* he is! Forgive me . . ."

Kolbe shook his round gray head indignantly:

"That kind of talk is terrible, of course. Personally, I never saw the dean's completed manuscript. But I have, with my own eyes, seen the mountainous stacks of drafts and linguistic material . . ."

Cara shouted: "I got so angry with Anton that I almost fainted. But as we were seated in our respective sleighs, I whispered to him: 'Anton—now I know! It was you who took it—out of spite, because you think Otto and I never respected you enough!' And Anton started screaming at me—well, he couldn't really scream with all the other mourners around us—he *hissed* at me that I had lost my mind. That just made me laugh, and I gave the horse a touch of the whip and left him spluttering. But now I'm afraid that he won't honor my request to ask Himmelstjerna to give up that idea of an announcement in the newspaper . . . Dear Lord, I don't want any rumors to spread . . ."

I would have liked to say: Dear madam, they are spreading already! But I held my peace.

At our request, we were given the same tiny partitioned rooms we had once inhabited in that house, and the rooms aroused so many memories from almost twenty years ago that we kept reminiscing until midnight, talking through the thin partition.

"Jakob, do you remember how Cara—then she was still our

nanny—would come to wake us up at six? Remember how she made us sing together:

> *Frère Jacques, Soeur Cathérine!*
> *Sonnez les matines! Sonnez les matines!*

Timo had already told them that he was going to call me Katharina . . .”

“Do you remember, Eeva, how the dean would come and drag us out of here for our violin lessons?”

“Of course I do . . . And he made his own daughters practice the violin every single day.”

“Eeva—do you still have that violin? It was Timo who gave it to you, wasn’t it? But I’ve never heard you perform anything on it.”

On the other side of the partition, Eeva said:

“I’ve had to *perform* so many other things—”

She left her words hanging in the dark, and I asked her:

“You mean—the part of a woman married to a friend of the Czar—and then later, the part of a woman married to a man regarded as a criminal who had threatened the Czar’s life?”

Eeva said, almost in a whisper:

“. . . Right . . . And I have tried to be the wife of a great thinker, and the wife of a dangerous madman . . . So there really wasn’t much left for the violin . . . I don’t really remember anything except for the *sostenuto* old Masing taught me . . .”

In the morning, we began our journey home. After we had turned toward Puurmann and were driving through the forest, where there was enough snow on the frozen road so that the sleigh no longer swayed and rattled, I said:

“But I really don’t understand Mrs. Masing’s fear of damage being done to the family’s reputation, or some such . . . As things stand now, if the manuscript isn’t found, *that* will always be seen as Mrs. Masing’s fault, *to some extent.* Even though it is unlikely that it would have been found even if Mrs. Masing had tried to take some measures. But for the sake of scholarship, as Jäsche said—or simply for truth’s sake—she *ought* to have done some-

thing to discover the culprit! Instead of . . ." I didn't want to heap
too much opprobrium on poor Mrs. Masing.

For a while, we listened to the steady hoofbeats of our sleigh
horse. Then Eeva said:

". . . There's many a thing that ought to have been done . . .
God knows whom Mrs. Masing may suspect of the crime. Maybe
she really believes it was Anton, or maybe someone else. There's
no way for us to know . . . And so, as far as I can see, she had
the right to do what she thought best."

On the night of the old dean's funeral, in our old partitioned
room, I had felt close to my sister again. But it had been a false
impression, brought on by our memories. In reality, fate has detached her from me, changed her, trained her to think differently
. . . In reality, she truly is a *lady*.

The eighteenth of February, 1836

I see that four years have passed since my last entry. An eternity,
one might say.

If such long periods elapse between entries in a journal, can it
still be called a journal? One might also ask: If periods between
events, occasions that rise above the gray stream of time, become
that long—can a life still be called a life?

Today I took this book out from under the floorboard and blew
the dust and dirt off its covers. Not in order to record my own
story of the last four years—what would I have to write about?
We have led the most quotidian of lives in this old brick house
by the riverside. Anna has been a good wife to me, and I have
tried to be an impeccable husband. Especially during the first year
after Maali's death, I often found myself showing my love for her
in small ways, favors, expressions of tenderness—which, when I
became conscious of them myself, suddenly struck me as embarrassing. For instance . . . ?

The spring after Maali's death, in mid-June as I recall, Anna
casually mentioned to me one Sunday morning that it was her
father's birthday.

I didn't ask her how old her father would have been, because that would have forced me to pretend to be thinking about a very different person from the one who immediately came to my mind . . . I got up quickly—we had finished our coffee—hugged Anna tight, and kissed her right there in the middle of the room, with gusto and for a long while (also preventing her from saying anything else about her father), then hurried outside. In the shed, I turned my old boat onto its keel, found the old willow frames, nailed them to the sides of the boat, covered them with the green sailcloth, dragged the boat to the river, and invited Anna for a ride . . . Having fed Eeva and put her to bed for her nap, Anna accepted, and I rowed upstream in the direction of Liigrisaar. The wind was cool, and I wrapped my coat around Anna's shoulders—and she asked me (and not only then) *if something was wrong with me—since I was so nice to her, all of a sudden?*

When I thought about those occasions, I realized that the reason for my spells of tenderness was not that anything was wrong with me, but that I felt there was something wrong with *her*—and my loving behavior was an attempt to correct that flaw in her, and in our lives . . .

Well, well; I have learned to regard all that with a touch of humor, and our lives have been most peaceful and ordinary. Our finances remain precarious. My initial flood of commissions soon petered out, and we have mainly relied on the river and our little plot. Thanks to them, we haven't gone hungry, though our wardrobes are showing signs of wear, even though Anna keeps them clean and mended.

Eeva will soon celebrate her fifth birthday. She is a wonderful little snub-nosed thing who has her mothers bright eyes, and during our playtimes, I have taught her half the letters of the alphabet . . . She is still our only child. I don't know why, because we haven't taken any precautions, and I don't think it is because I have sometimes thought, at the decisive moment: Is Mr. Laming going to receive another grandchild? No, I learned to smile at such thoughts, a long time ago. And, as I have already said: I didn't retrieve this old journal in order to write about myself, but because I want to discuss an event in my sister and brother-in-law's life at Voisiku: the visit of our young Navy Cadet, Georg von Bock, Junior.

Anna—

The twenty-second of February

Last night, Anna came to see what was keeping me up so late.

To resume: last week, Jüri visited his parents at Voisiku. Eeva had notified me of this, in a note: Jüri tells me he is getting a few days' leave to visit us. We're expecting him on Thursday. If you want to see your nephew, come and have lunch with us on Thursday.

Eeva knew, of course, that the boy had always impressed me with his brightness and that I was interested in his progress. A budding officer of half-peasant stock is a phenomenon rare enough to be considered interesting—*sadly* interesting, I would have said after our last encounter in Pärnu and his surprising words to his father on the night of our ill-fated escape attempt. But, who knows, more detached observers might say, he probably said exactly what was to be expected of him.

On Thursday morning, just as I was looking at my watch and thinking I'd have to set out for Voisiku in a few hours, who should jump out of his saddle by our gate but this stripling of a naval cadet in a pea coat with gold buttons and calf-length boots . . . Yes—he arrived at Voisiku a day early, and this morning he had already visited the Wahls and the Lilienfeldts at Old and New Poltsamaa, and here he was, entering the house of his Uncle Jakob and his wife.

Jüri is almost eighteen now. I had a chance to study him in broad daylight. He has, of course, changed greatly since our last meeting at Pärnu. At his age, six or seven years bring about a complete transformation. Yet there was quite a bit that was familiar about him. He is a tad shorter than his father, he has his mother's gray-green eyes, his father's relentless gaze. He is slim but looks strong. He has Eeva's chestnut curls, and his wispy reddish mustache is carefully trimmed.

His conversation with us was temperate and precise. He treated Anna with impeccable courtesy and called me Uncle without the least hesitation. He told us, laconically and modestly, about his cruises on the training ships of his unit—until now, in accordance with regulations, only as far as Porkkala, Gotland, and Riga. But in March they would sail the Black Sea, setting out from Niko-layev, and next year, past Copenhagen to the North Sea. The year after that would come a voyage past Gibralter to the Mediterra-nean.

I said, "Well, well . . . and what is life like at the Naval Academy in St. Petersburg?"

"It's a normal cadet's life."

"You have a lot of studying to do?"

"Yes, a lot."

"Well—are you courting any girls yet?"

He smiled pleasantly, showing his fine white teeth, and shook his head:

"I've decided to postpone that until I get my lieutenant's epaulets."

"I see . . . And have you been thinking—about how high you'll set your sights? How high do you want to fly?"

He smiled again, this time with a modest twitch of his downy mustache:

"First Lord of the Admiralty. Of course."

I asked (remembering a previous conversation, late at night, on his ninth birthday, before he left for Tsarskoye):

"But how do you stand in relation to the Czar . . . ?"

"How do you think?"

(He now uses the formal you with me—which may only be natural: he was only a child when he used the more familiar thou, and now he is—well, in many respects more grown-up than many of us will ever be.)

I said, "What I meant was how you feel about him. Are you his friend? Or not? It's bound to be a rather complicated question, considering your father's history."

He looked at me calmly, then said, not too quickly but with sufficient ease to make me realize that he had given the question careful consideration and formulated his answer a long time ago:

"I don't regard it as complicated. If Czar Alexander were still alive, I might have some trouble with it. But to feel resentful toward Czar Nicholas—that wouldn't just be rebellious. That would be *ingratitude*."

Dear God, I admit my thoughts have also run in that direction —but when I hear it from this boy's lips, I feel there is something wrong . . . Then I have a brainstorm. We are sitting in the dining room. Anna is busy in the kitchen, she won't disturb us. It is a wild thought . . . But why shouldn't the boy know the truth? What right does he have to just skim over his own fate and the fate of his country? What right does he have to be so confidently and naïvely innocent?! Why shouldn't the truth soak all the way into him, like vinegar . . . ?

I ask, "Jüri—do you know the *reason* for what happened to your father?"

He says, "It was some petition—or so I've heard. No one knows exactly."

And I say, surprising myself, and no doubt inconsiderately— heaven knows if this is necessary at all—and yet, and yet, I do want to attach this boy to his father . . . I want to make good (and hope the result isn't the opposite) what I neglected nine years ago when he was leaving for Tsarskoye.

"Jüri—*I know* the reason."

He looks at me with unconcealed youthful curiosity.

"So—would you like to know?"

"God Almighty! Of course!"

"But first you have to give me your word of honor as an officer that you will keep this to yourself, no matter what happens."

He ponders this for a moment. An officer's word of honor is serious business.

"I give you my word."

"Wait here a moment."

I don't want to reveal the hiding place of my papers to him. I go to my study, raise the floorboard, pull out Timo's manuscript. I blow the dust and dirt off it and put it on my desk. Then I call for Jüri to come to the study.

"Here. Sit down at the desk. Read. I found it in the manor house, in a place where your father must have hidden it before he was arrested. In the course of the nine years he was imprisoned, which impaired his memory, he lost track of it. He suffers from blank stretches in his memory. He told me so himself. In any case, I can't give it back to him now. It might throw his mind off balance. And I haven't offered it to your mother, either. So I think you should have it, except that you won't be able to take it and keep it now. But you must read it, and give it some thought . . ."

(In hindsight, it seems to me that I was, perhaps, jealous of the Czar—because of that boy's loyal peace of mind. Or something of that sort . . .)

He doesn't say a word. He is reading. I sit down on the other side of the desk and watch his face.

He reads the accompanying letter and puts it aside. Well, now he has a hint. Now he understands. Now he concentrates. I see his eyes focus more sharply. I hear the scratchy sound of a steel brush Anna is using in the kitchen. I hear some horse (probably that of the Lilienfeldt steward) thumping past our gate, pulling a sleigh. I see the color rise in Jüri's cheeks—as he reads about the duty to deny one's own father and mother, if the fatherland demands it . . . I can sense how the verve of Timo's introductory sentences is tickling his own budding wings . . . He reads surprisingly fast. He must, indeed, have lightning-quick powers of comprehension . . . Then I observe that his enthusiasm wanes, he is almost struggling with boredom by the time he gets to page six or seven and has to wade through the précis of Russian history, then looks livelier again when he comes across surprising and touching concrete details—and how he, on page thirty-one (I am reading the thoroughly familiar text with him, albeit upside down), swallows and grows tense . . .

> Have you never heard of Speranski, Beck, and certain other professors? Not to mention the thousands that have been killed by our so-called tribunals . . . ? Then, suddenly, there appears the redeemed Emperor, the leader of the Holy Alliance, the superior of all Bible study groups, who reminisces about Christ's sufferings and hands his own Empire over to pious sycophants and adventurers—and who has such an enormous collection of toys that we are

ready to sacrifice our last drop of blood for them; who turns all our noblemen into clowns and corporals; who issues the order to transform all our peasant hovels into Greek temples by a certain date; and now tells us to keep only those kinds of horses that will eat oats when there is a shortage of straw; who bans all books by banning all home education and forces us to send our children to be schooled by his own hypocrites or caned by his own corporals . . . There appears the Emperor who without a blush proceeds to proclaim the Pharisee spirit, in the company of a prostitute—

I see how beads of perspiration cover Jüri's forehead. His earlobes are glowing as if he'd had both his ears boxed. But his face is frighteningly pale. His hands tremble as he carefully stacks the pages he has read on top of the rest. Under the reddish down, his upper lip twitches in a curious fashion. He stares at the desk and says:

"Uncle Jakob—I can't read it . . ."

I ask—and I won't deny it was with a bit of malice, because I remember only too clearly my own feelings when I first confronted this fateful manuscript—I ask him:

"Well—do you think that what your father wrote there is a lie?"

He is silent.

I ask, "Or does it seem to you that it may have been true in its *own* time, but that after eighteen years it no longer is the truth?"

He doesn't say anything. I can tell that he is on the verge of tears. Oh, dear God, he's just a seventeen-year-old boy. A child. A poor child, cast among strangers and strange opinions—he deserves my sympathy. And he has it . . . But at that moment, he overcomes his lapse of weakness. He sits up straight in his chair and says in a curiously chilly tone (but perhaps I don't hear it right and it is nothing more than modesty):

"I don't know the answer to that. But I do know one thing. I don't want to make excuses for my father. Already, I have read too much of this. I suspect that if I go on reading, I shall have to condemn him. And I don't want to do that . . ."

As he sits there on the other side of the desk, he takes out a neatly folded white percale handkerchief and wipes his brow. He has regained his equilibrium. I tell myself that I should take more of an interest in him personally, so I ask him:

"How were your visits to the neighbors?"

"Oh, well . . ." He accepts this new turn of our conversation with obvious relief, almost with gratitude, and rather too easily. "You know—our neighbors have some curious prejudices against us. Mother told me about that, and I did notice it today. When I visited with old Mrs. Lilienfeldt. I'll be home for a week, so I'll pay a few more visits. I'll see the Samsons in Lustivere. I'll do my best to dispel those prejudices."

"I see . . . How do you go about it?"

"I just have these conversations with the ladies and gentlemen. I let them become convinced that a certain von Bock is the perfect naval cadet. I tell them that the emperor thinks so, too."

"He does?"

"Yes, sir."

"How do you know that?"

"A month ago, he visited our school, in the company of the Crown Prince. He talked to the cadets. The Crown Prince and I are the same age. The emperor said, 'Aha . . . Georgi Timofeyevich von Bock?' Then he asked the Crown Prince, right there in front of everybody, 'Tell me, Alexander Nikolayevich—does that name mean anything to you?' The Crown Prince nodded, and the emperor said, 'And now, just look. Now he is the academy's youngest and most correct naval cadet.' "

I asked Jüri, "Did you tell that, too, to the local gentryfolk you visited?"

Jüri said, "And why shouldn't I tell them? Of course I'm no judge of my own correctness. But the emperor's mention of my youth—why not? When all those people claim that the emperor declared my father insane—even though they have no proof of it? When, on the other hand, the emperor says in front of a hundred witnesses that I am the academy's youngest naval cadet—and that is true! I want to restore the honor of the name von Bock. Don't you see?"

I said I did. But when he looked at his watch and asked me to come with him so that I wouldn't be late for our meal, I said:

"You know—I was going to come in order to see you and talk to you . . . Now I have seen you and had a chat with you . . . So, I'll come and dine with you next Thursday, before you leave."

The twenty-fifth of February, 1836

Yesterday I went to Voisiku for Jüri's farewell dinner. I hadn't been there for a whole year, and got the impression you always get after such prolonged absences: that the furnishings are somehow more faded and smaller than you recalled, and people's faces and outlines seem a little mistier than last time but almost return to their remembered state as soon as you start talking to them.

The table was laid. Jüri's dark-green, iron-banded sea chest stood by the drawing room door, but he himself was nowhere to be seen. I asked for him, and Timo said:

"He is over at Elsy's and Peter's, saying goodbye—"

Something about Timo's voice prompted me to take a close look at him. I thought: Well, it's only natural that the boy takes his leave from his aunt and her husband, since they won't come to our table in The Foundation . . . Timo and I stood by the fireplace and looked into each other's eyes. He said nothing more, simply patted my shoulder, and his look before he turned toward the window and began to fill his pipe said only one thing: *Yes. That's the way it is. And it could be no other way. Don't be the least bit surprised . . .*

While Jüri had talked to Peter and Elsy in the main building, the young Mannteuffels, Max and Alex, big adolescents of fifteen and thirteen, had been waiting for him in order to escort their impressive navy cousin back to The Foundation. Claire and Emma were already waiting for him here, twittering in unison about how well-bred and manly Jüri was. Eighteen-year-old Emma sighed, half in jest and half in earnest: "What a pity that he's our cousin! If he weren't, I'd fall in love with him in the blink of an eye . . ."

After half an hour, Jüri arrived, accompanied by the Mannteuffel boys. As they entered the vestibule, I heard him say: "Now let's get all that snow off our boots!" after which they stamped their feet on the doormat for a whole minute before entering, Jüri looking as cheerful and dapper as ever. He greeted me politely, then continued his conversation with the boys, about the frigates *Pamyat Azova* and *Maria* and about his voyage across the Finnish Archipelago to Gotland and the storm they had run into south of Ahvenanmaa . . . The boys listened with bated breath, and I noticed that even Max, who is only two years younger than Jüri, is still a child compared to him. At table, Jüri acted the well-bred adult gentleman, picking up Emma's dropped handkerchief in a flash and complimenting Claire on her lovely hair. Claire's corpulence neither fazed him nor made him break out in ill-suppressed giggles, which, as I recall, was the way it had once affected young master Lilienfeldt.

Eeva was the life and soul of the occasion. She helped Liiso serve and asked Jüri many kinds of questions (a week hadn't been long enough to exhaust them all): had he packed the fresh set of underwear and the three pairs of home-knit wool stockings? And was the cutter *Lebed*, the one on which Jüri was to serve on the Black Sea, a big ship? And was military action anticipated on the Abkhazian expedition?

The meal was quite simple, it consisted of gruel and braised beef with a sharp horseradish sauce. But for dessert, Eeva brought out the plum torte she had made, the one she otherwise made only on family birthdays. I noticed that Timo shook his head at the offer of a slice and lit his pipe. His face looked as gray as the smoke surrounding it. He sat at the table without saying a word, almost fading into the darkening February afternoon and his own smoke cloud but for the flashes from his uncommonly bright eyes when he looked at the rest of us.

Then we all stood by the drawing room door and said goodbye to Jüri. Eeva's face was wet with tears (the only time I have ever seen that), but the farewell hug she gave him was brief. Timo's parting words to his son I remember well. Timo took Jüri's elbow as they walked outside, and when they had reached the steps, Jüri turned to his father and stood before him in the snow. Timo looked him up and down, then said: "*Na—geh. Und werde, wer du wirst.*" And patted him on the shoulder, just as he had patted me when I first arrived, and with exactly the same look: *Yes. That's the way it is. And it could be no other way. Don't be the least bit surprised . . .*

Jüri jumped into the sleigh, and they were off. I followed Timo back to the drawing room. Eeva had gone to the dining room with the Mannteuffel children. A thought flashed through my mind: is it Timo's taciturn nature or the frightening aspect of his reputation as a madman that makes even close and more or less well-disposed persons avoid him a little . . . ? He sat down next to the fireplace and stared at the fire. I sat down next to him in an old armchair. Timo picked the pipe he had been smoking after dinner out of an ashtray on the fireside table. He sucked on it for a moment, and it was still going. He took it out of his mouth and blew a long stream of smoke into the air. Then, quite calmly, without raising his elbow off the armrest of his chair, but nevertheless so suddenly that it startled me—he threw the pipe into the fire. I asked:

"What's the matter?"

He turned to me as if he had only just noticed me. He said, calmly but with exaggerated precision:

"Nothing. No pipe, no son."

The second of March

Of course I did not repeat Timo's words to Eeva. I had no desire whatsoever to make her feel worse than she already did after Jüri's thoughtless remark that he would probably receive his baptism of fire in an engagement with Abkhazian rebels . . . But in the evening (I stayed the night at Voisiku, in my old back room, heated and ready for me), Eeva came to inquire about my life with Anna and our daughter. Casually, I asked her how things had gone between Jüri and his father and mother during this week, and in general. And that was when she blurted it all out, in, I thought, quite uncharacteristic fashion:

"Jakob—you can't imagine how I am always torn between those two . . . I understand both of them, Timo and Jüri. I can see that they are both in the right! But I also see that they can't both be right at the same time . . ."

I said, "Listen—I don't quite understand what you're saying

here." I had a pretty good idea, of course, but I wanted my sister to tell me how matters really stood. And she did, candidly and with, I should say, admirable clarity for a woman:

"I'm referring to their completely different ways of pursuing perfection. To Timo's 'iron nail' ideal—the one in the empire's body—you remember, what he talked about at Pärnu? And Jüri's ideal to serve the empire as an officer . . . Timo believes that unless he sticks to his ideal, the name von Bock will disappear from the lists of honorable names. And Jüri believes that unless he accomplishes his, that name will not be returned to those lists . . . And I am caught between them, you see: as Timo's wife, I must understand and share his ideals, and as Jüri's mother, I ought to support him in his—"

I asked her, "But what about you? What do you yourself . . . ?"

"Oh God . . ." She pressed her fingertips to her temples the way she does when she feels agitated. "I myself—" She got up from the squeaky wicker chair and paced back and forth between the door and the blue tile stove. I looked at her—her small, still fresh and glowing face, and her chestnut hair, her straight indigo-blue woolen gown and the perennial pink cameo—and thought: She is thirty-six, and even though she has lived a noblewoman's life, her life has been harder in many ways than that of a peasant woman—yet she is such a rare orchid that when you look at her with eyes that can remember her as a girl, you still have to agree with those frivolous gentlemen of yore: she is dazzlingly beautiful . . . And it doesn't surprise me at all that her brother-in-law Karl, the only skirt-chaser among the Bock brothers, tried to seduce her.

"I myself . . ." my sister said, "I have been thinking. If I could get away from here . . . anywhere, on my own little plot of land . . . so the villagers wouldn't think I was living off the labor of others—and Timo would be with me, and be the way he is on his bright days . . . And if Jüri were at the University of Tartu, studying medicine . . . And I would have my own cow in the shed, and could give my mother and my aunt at Tömbi a little money each year, and bring them a fatted calf, without having to ask anyone for it . . . Oh, I've been thinking that Anna and you —you are really so lucky—"

I exclaimed, "But, in God's name—why don't you just—" I left my question hanging because I realized that it was naïve, but Eeva answered it nevertheless.

"As if you didn't know . . . *They* would never make me Timo's guardian. That would require the Czar's permission, so there's no point in asking. And if we have to live under the supervision of strangers—even at Timo's childhood home—we're just cottagers here . . ."

Then I asked her my old question, one more time:

"Eeva—tell me—in your opinion—is Timo mad?"

Eeva stopped in front of me. She was looking at me, but I think that what she tried to see, and did see, was Timo's face, Timo's thousands, tens of thousands of faces, impenetrable, somber, unpredictable, ironic, childishly open, as she had studied them over the years with melancholic care . . . She said:

"As you know, his ways of thinking about things have always been different from those of others . . . Dr. Elkan told me that once, when he had come to examine Timo, he had asked Timo how much two times two was. Timo had answered: 'To a newborn, infinity; to a dying man, as much as he wants; to an emperor, nothing.' Then Dr. Elkan had said: 'So it isn't *four?*' And Timo said: 'Yes, it is—to God, but no one ever asks Him.' So, you see . . . Of course his nerves are in worse shape than we can imagine. But *mad*"—Eeva shook her head—"mad he is not." Now she looked straight into my eyes. "But, well—this is, of course, just the self-deception and self-consolation of the unfortunate wife of a poor madman . . ."

The sixth of April

This morning old Käsper rode over from Voisiku, on incredibly broken-up roads, to bring word from Eeva. She had to travel to Tartu on some essential errand—could I come to Voisiku tomorrow, or the day after at the latest, and would I be willing to stay there for five days, or perhaps even a week, to keep Timo company and set her mind at rest? Apparently, Timo has been more nervous and tense than otherwise in recent times.

I told Käsper to tell Eeva that I would come. When I told Anna, she decided that she didn't want to stay here alone with the child for a whole week—so she'd take little Eeva and go with me. I was pleased. It will make my stay easier, as well. I'll borrow a horse and sleigh from Wahl's steward. A sleigh with high runners will get us there without any trouble. Since I'll have a whole week there, I'll also bring my old journal—to visit its old hiding place . . .

The thirteenth of April, 1836

It is my duty to record what has happened as precisely as I am able.

Anna, little Eeva, and I arrived at The Foundation around noon on the nineteenth. Eeva gave us my old room. We dined together. Timo struck me as rather more genial than he normally was, not somber at all. He told me he had been shooting his pistols that morning in the park. He also said that his barometric observations predicted a dry summer, but that certain local influences were causing disturbances in the functioning of the barometer. I couldn't follow him there and told him so.

He explained: "Yesterday morning my dear brother-in-law left for Adavere, and for every mile that he put between himself and here, the mercury rose a degree and a half!"

Eeva and the coachman left after we had eaten. She said that the journey to Tartu and back might take her a week or perhaps even a day or two longer. I asked what business took her there. She said she was going to see a physician. As I was carrying her trunk to the sleigh, I asked her what was ailing her. She said: "Woman's problems."

After she had left, I decided to get a couple of books from Timo's library. His door was locked, as always, and I knocked on it as we had agreed at the dinner table. After calling out, "Yes! Just a moment!" he kept me waiting for a couple of minutes. He came to the door and let me in. There were no papers on his desk, but the goose quill next to the ink stand was sharp and wet with ink. It takes one to know one, I thought and almost grinned but managed to suppress the urge.

Little Eeva played on the carpet in our room with Jüri's old tin soldiers which big Eeva had given her to play with before her departure. Anna sat knitting a stocking for the child, and we decided that when my sister came back from Tartu, we would ask her for a sack of flour to take home. In the evening, I played chess with Timo. He sacrificed his rook, as usual, and after an audacious game beat me on the sixtieth move. He seemed truly on top of things.

On the morning of the tenth, we had a heavy rain and sleet storm, and Käsper complained to me that the shingle roof above the foyer was rotten and leaked, so that the walls were damp and the wallpaper cockled. After the rain stopped, and after we had had breakfast, Timo went to the park for target practice, and I went to the steward's house to find someone to repair the roof. In old Timm's office, a few day laborers, strangers to me, sat waiting for their instructions. They got up as I entered to ask for the steward, but before they could answer, some other man and old Timm appeared from the back room—as always, Timm's belly hung over his belt and the cold pipe with its bent stem dangled from the corner of his mouth. I started talking to him about the roof, then noticed that the man who had entered with him nodded his square, stubble-haired head toward me by way of greeting. I recognized him. It was Mr. Laming. He looked quite respectable in his dark blue homespun coat with large gray and brown bone buttons. From a distance, it looked like a pea coat. He held a dog-fur hat in one hand, and he was shod in high boots of Russian leather. His face wore the same watchful expression and noncommittal smile as in the old days when I used to see him in the main building of the estate . . .

I delayed my response to his greeting for a moment but couldn't very well ignore it. I had, after all, had dealings with him for quite a number of years. And I was the younger man. It may also have occurred to me that if I didn't acknowledge his greeting, tomorrow's gossip among the working folk at Voisiku would be that Jakob Mättik, that half-a-gentleman, had become completely benighted by arrogance . . . I returned his greeting, and once I had done that, I felt that I might as well say something to him—and also ask him a question . . . Without giving it any further thought, I asked him (in hindsight, in a slightly awkward manner):

"Well, well, Mr. Laming—where are you living these days?"

(I didn't want to ask him: What are you doing these days?) "And how is Iette doing?" (That, of course, was what I really wanted to know.)

Mr. Laming replied, in his familiar, quiet, and slightly rusty voice:

"I'm living in Riga, Mr. Jakob. Yes. But Iette—last month, she made me a grandfather, *for the second time . . .*"

That gave me a start. I didn't let it show but looked into his eyes and thought for a fleeting moment that this bristle-haired devil of a peasant was in league not only with Benckendorff but also with Satan, and *knew* everything, and was mocking me: *Four and a half years ago, you made me a grandfather for the first time, and now Iette has done it for the second . . .* Only then I realized that he was referring to Iette's second child. To get over that sudden hallucination, I said:

"And what brings you here to Voisiku?"

Laming turned surprisingly voluble in his explanation:

"Oh, you see, the heirs of an old creditor of mine have started accusing me, back in Riga, that I didn't pay off a debt of a hundred and fifty rubles to him—to the grain merchant Hacke, if you remember him, by the Powder Tower. I knew that I had a receipt he gave me but wasn't able to find it—and then I remembered that I had left it here, among the papers of the estate. But now it appears that those old papers are in the custody of Mr. Mannteuffel, and he has just gone away for a couple of days. So the steward, Timm here, is going to put me up, and I'll wait for Mr. Mannteuffel's return . . ."

None of this was of any interest to me. I grunted:

"Give Iette my regards—whenever," and left the steward's office.

The day passed without any notable events. Truly, even considering all that *has* happened, it still seems to me that nothing notable occurred. Except, perhaps, for one thing:

After dinner, Timo and I sat down by the fireplace and lit our pipes, and I thought—why not admit my curiosity, for once? I asked him, casually:

"So, are you writing anything these days?"

I thought: Maybe I'll find out what he is writing. Is it that

strange manuscript that was once concealed under my floor, or is
it something else? What are the questions he ponders, what plans
does he have for his work—if any . . .

He said: "Yes, I am. As long as they'll let me."

"Who do you mean?"

I am quite certain that I heard exactly what he said:

"My equibs. And the *enquibs.*"

Then he got up, rather abruptly, I thought, and left the drawing
room with a wave of his hand. For a moment I thought that he
meant for me to follow him. I waited and listened, but he didn't
call for me. I finished my pipe and went to my room.

He did not come to supper but had something to eat in his
room. Toward evening, the wind started blowing harder, and the
trees in the park rustled all night. I woke up several times and
listened to that sound while Anna got up and tucked little Eeva
in again on the sofa. The child slept fitfully in this place that was
strange to her.

On the morning of the eleventh, we had a full-fledged early
spring storm. Timo did not come to breakfast, but I ran into him
in the corridor after we had left the table. It must have been half
past nine. He came out of his room carrying the pistol case and
locked the door behind him. I said:

"Good morning. You really think you can hit anything in this
wind?"

He said, "Well, I'll try, I'll try. Imagine, Peter hasn't returned
yet—but the barometer has dropped six degrees! I can't see why!"

I asked, "How do you practice, these days? You still use that
crossbar and the pine cones?"

He said, on his way through the front door, "Same old set-up.
But now from fifty paces."

I went back to our rooms, and Anna and I talked about this and
that. I made little Eeva recite the alphabet. Once in a while, we
heard someone banging nails into shingles on the roof above the
foyer—the workman had arrived today. Now and again we could
also hear, through the gusty wind and the soughing of the trees,
the report of a pistol. Timo was firing at an average of once every
third minute, but we probably didn't hear all the reports because
of the wind, and I didn't note when the firing stopped.

At around half past eleven, there was a knock on the door and Liiso stuck her head in:

"Mr. Jakob—I don't know—Mr. Timo came in a while ago and asked me to bring breakfast to his room. But now he isn't opening the door—"

I said, "Well, why don't you try again in fifteen minutes." I know that I, myself, am quite capable of forgetting, in the midst of some task or train of thought, that I just asked someone to bring me breakfast . . . And when it is brought to me, I act as if I didn't even notice.

Liiso said, "It's just that . . . I thought I heard—"

"What?"

". . . I don't know . . . It was when I started out from the kitchen . . . And it sounded like a shot, or something . . ."

I went to Timo's door, knocked, rattled the door handle, shouted. There was no reply. I peered into the keyhole and saw that the door was locked from the inside. Liiso returned with the breakfast tray. I told her to stay by the door and keep knocking on it while I ran to the kitchen and called old Käsper. He emerged from the room behind the kitchen, and I told him to go to Timo's door to see if he could help Liiso—I couldn't imagine how, but I was in a hurry and ran out into the yard and around the house. The snow had melted off the strip of dead grass between the walls of the house and the wild rose bushes. The gray grass blades rustled in the wind. When I got to Timo's window, it seemed to me that I noticed—or perhaps only *guessed at*—two or three bootprints in the dead grass, from which the blades were just straightening up again—but it was like something seen before, in a dreaming or half-wakeful state . . .

I grabbed the window ledge, got a foothold on the foundation, and looked into the room. Timo was stretched out on the floor. He lay on his left side, and a chair obscured my view of his head.

I ran back into the house and told Käsper, "Run over to the steward and fetch Mihkel the blacksmith!"

It took Mihkel about ten minutes to get there. I told Liiso to stop knocking, and we just stood in front of the door and waited. Anna came and asked us what had happened, and I told her, in a few words, what I had seen through the window. Then Mihkel and his apprentice arrived, and it took them only a couple of minutes to pick the lock. I told the men to stay put and went in with Anna and Käsper.

Timo was dead. There was a puddle of blood on the rug next to his head. It wasn't very large, perhaps the size of a palm. His forehead and the area around his right eye were peppered with buckshot. Anna cried, "Oh God!" and retreated behind the desk. The open pistol case lay on the desk with three pistols in it. The fourth Kuchenreiter lay next to Timo on the rug. I picked it up and looked at it: it had been fired. I returned it to its place on the rug. One of the desk drawers was open, and on the bottom lay a few dozen cartridges Timo had probably loaded himself, some with bullets, some with shot. Käsper wanted to move his master's body to the sofa. I told him not to touch it. I bent down once more to look at Timo.

Anna asked me, from the other side of the desk, "What did you find?"

I said, "Nothing."

We left the room and I locked the door. Anna asked, "Dear God—how did that happen? Was it an accident—or did he—?"

I went to Timm and told him that since he was now the representative of the legal authorities at the estate, he would have to take the necessary steps. Timm said he did not want to have anything to do with the matter. I said that in that case I would keep the key to Mr. Bock's room. He said, "Yes, for God's sake, keep it!" Then, however, he gave orders to saddle a horse and sent a man to Poltsamaa with a scrawled three-line note to summon the district judge and a doctor. Even under the best of circumstances, they would not arrive until later in the afternoon.

I went to The Foundation and told Anna a judge and a doctor had been sent for, but in the child's presence we weren't free to talk about what had happened. I told Anna that I wanted to step outside for a moment. Anna followed me into the corridor and asked me, in a whisper, what I thought about Timo's death. I told her that I didn't have an opinion now, and if I would have one later, it wouldn't matter anyway. Or something to that effect.

I went into the park. My head was buzzing with a multitude of questions, and the rustling of the trees in the high wind kept interfering with my thoughts. Where the snow had melted I could see Timo's tracks of that morning, and I followed them to his shooting range. In the trampled snow I found a couple of burnt but now wet pieces of cartridge paper that had stuck to the snow and hadn't been blown away by the wind. This was, obviously, where Timo had stood while cleaning and reloading his pistols.

Fifty paces away, there was the crossbar nailed to a tree, with its holes drilled for the pine cone targets. There were no cones in the holes, but in the snow and the dead grass I saw bits of exploded cones and five that were still intact except for fresh bullet holes. On the crossbar, there was not a single shot-pellet or mark left by a pellet.

I walked back to the house. One of my questions had become more urgent: *Why were there shot pellets in Timo's head, when he had used only bullets at target practice?*

At lunch, we could no longer keep quiet about what had happened because Käsper and Liiso wanted to talk about it. Liiso didn't really say anything when she brought the soup bowl from the kitchen and set it on the sideboard, but she was having a difficult time suppressing her sobs. Käsper, on the other hand, couldn't control himself as he served us bowls of cabbage soup and plates of salt mutton:

"Mr. Timo was ten years old . . . A ten-year-old boy, he was, when old Baron Georg took me on as a house servant . . . And now . . . God help us all . . . Such a thing . . ." Tears ran down his stubbled cheeks and dripped onto our plates. I had to tell little Eeva:

"Listen, we haven't told you yet—but Uncle Timo died this morning . . ."

"How?" Eeva asked, matter-of-factly and as if registering only mild surprise, the way children do when you tell them such news.

I said, "It was an accident. He was loading his pistol."

There. I was the first one to say it.

The fourteenth of April, in the small hours

I just looked at my watch and saw that tomorrow had become today.

On the eleventh, around six in the evening, District Judge Krüdener and his clerk and Dr. Norden arrived, accompanied by Mr. Mannteuffel and Elsy. Mannteuffel had been on his way back from Adavere and had heard the news at Poltsamaa. Thus, I should have phrased it differently: Mr. Mannteuffel arrived with the judge and the doctor, Elsy and the clerk bringing up the rear . . . Because from that moment on, Mannteuffel was completely in charge. Who knows if that made a difference . . .

I told them briefly what had happened and unlocked Timo's door. Even before entering the room, to his audience of Käsper, Liiso, Elsy, and the officials, Mannteuffel said in a loud voice:

"An extremely regrettable *accident!* He was, even with all his quiet eccentricities, such an *extremely* sympathetic man . . ."

We entered the room. For a moment, we stood around the body in silence. Then Elsy burst into loud tears, and Mr. Mannteuffel asked Käsper to escort the lady from the room. Käsper did as he was told, but Elsy apparently didn't require his services, because he reappeared in just a couple of minutes. After a quick examination, the doctor gave permission to lift Timo onto the sofa. Käsper and I did so. The doctor examined the body more closely, and Judge Krüdener scrutinized the pistols. None of the three in the case was loaded. The clerk sat down at Timo's desk and started taking notes based on Mr. Mannteuffel's conversation with the judge and the doctor, Mannteuffel dictating choice passages to him. The clerk also asked the servants to clarify some things.

There was only one point on which Mr. Mannteuffel and the judge disagreed. Mannteuffel stated categorically: "Suicide is out of the question!" I don't quite know why he was so absolutely certain. He said: "Anyone who knew the colonel can testify to that."

To tell the truth, I share that opinion, to the extent that there can be any certainty in such cases. Yet I don't believe that Mr. Mannteuffel had really known his brother-in-law at all. Even I didn't know him well. So it must be said that Mannteuffel knew him to a considerably lesser degree.

The judge said, "But we cannot completely deny the possibility that it was suicide."

Mr. Mannteuffel asked me, "Jakob, do you think that's possible?"

I said, "As far as I can see, this is not a question of possibility, but rather one of probability. I don't think it is impossible that he killed himself—but it is improbable."

After which Mr. Mannteuffel and Judge Krüdener turned to face each other and proclaimed in unison: "There, you see!" Their manifestation of our perennial human desire for dispute and interpretation almost made me smile in spite of the sadness of the occasion. As I have said, the clerk's record consists mostly of what Mr. Mannteuffel dictated to him, with, however, an interpolation by the judge:

> Ritter Timofey von Bock, a retired Colonel, afflicted for many years with mental debility, resident in the Livonian district of Viljandi, at Voisiku Estate, was killed between ten and eleven A.M. on the eleventh of April, 1836, by a pistol discharged in his hand. Due to the absence of witnesses, it cannot be said with absolute certainty whether this was an accident or suicide, even though, in view of the Colonel's personality, the latter possibility appears entirely unlikely . . .

Dr. Norden, who seemed to fancy himself as an expert on hunting, informed us that the pellets that caused the colonel's death by penetrating his eye and perhaps even his cranium, were number three or four shot, but, he added, he couldn't tell us with any certainty whether they had been manufactured at Goslar or at Magdeburg. The shot had been fired at very close range, and there was really only one significant wound, in addition to the superficial damage done by several stray pellets.

After the doctor had finished, the very young, downy-mustached clerk, whose name I don't remember, looked up through his oval eyeglasses, opened his small mouth, and said:

"But, gentlemen—if Mr. Bock had just been at *target practice* and intended to go back to *target practice*—why did he suddenly load his pistol with shot?"

Mr. Mannteuffel said, "My dear young friend—surely we mustn't think you have a sparrow's memory! Five minutes ago you wrote in your own hand: '*Timofey von Bock, afflicted for many years with mental debility!*' Did you not? Well?"

The clerk blushed so that his ears turned red and nodded his confused assent.

The judge asked, "But how do we explain, then, how Baron von Bock had access to pistols?"

Mr. Mannteuffel said to the clerk, "For the record: Bock had acquired the pistols in a manner unknown, taking advantage of the absence of his spouse, who always took care to hide them from him."

The clerk wrote that down. I didn't feel the least compulsion to say that it was a lie. Eeva had never hidden the pistols from him. If she had had any reason to consider Timo's possession of them a danger, she would not have "taken care to hide them from him" but would simply have thrown them away, destroyed them, or given them to someone—they would not have remained in the house.

Then the judge ordered Timo's desk drawers opened (they weren't locked), and those that contained papers were emptied into a gray bag brought by the clerk. In the meantime, Mannteuffel had told Liiso to bring some candles into the study. The judge melted wax in a candle flame and sealed the bag. I believe that the bag contained only occasional papers, not a single manuscript. I know that the one I had kept in its case under my floor six years ago was not among the papers that went into the bag. The judge did not proceed to look for any other papers, and thus his search was far more perfunctory than the one conducted by Paulucci eighteen years ago. Well, back then it had been a matter of the Czar's personal orders. And a *living* enemy of the state . . .

The gentlemen conferred and decided to place the body in the old ice cellar behind the main building while waiting for replies to reports that would be sent to Viljandi, Riga, and St. Petersburg. A long table was brought from the front room, divested of its flower pots, and the body was lifted onto it. Only three pallbearers could be found, Käsper and two night watchmen, and so I grabbed a corner of the table, thinking:

No one would join a guard of honor for my brother-in-law. There won't even be any churchwardens like there were at old Masing's funeral service. Of course Eeva would be there. Eeva would be ready to follow him right into the grave, if need be.

And, surely, Jüri would be willing, he'd stand guard, white gloves and all, to fulfill his obligation. Georg, if he could come, would join them out of defiance if nothing else, and sister Elsy would, of course, be there and shed a few tears. But they didn't really matter. *From outside the family*, there would be only Käsper, weeping into his stubbly beard. Of the peasants—none, especially since that warning La Trobe had given them. Maybe one—Tiit of Näresaar, the man who had lost his eye to Timo's saber . . . I thought: Let this, my assistance in carrying him out of his study, be my contribution to his guard of honor—in recompense for his role, intentional or not, as the Mephistopheles who helped me become a human being—to the extent that I have become one . . .

The gentlemen remained in the study to sign the record. We carried Timo down the corridor and through the dining and drawing rooms. Liiso ran from the dining room to her maid's room behind the kitchen and intercepted us, sobbing, as we turned into the entrance hall. She was holding a pillow. She whispered: "Wait . . ." We set the table down, and Liiso raised Timo's head to put the pillow under it. I said: "But, Liiso, you'll get blood on it—" She gave me a withering, tearful look from under her gray bangs that had slipped out from her bonnet, and gently placed her master's head on the pillow.

When we arrived at the door of the ice cellar, we realized that we had forgotten to bring candles. Only after some had been procured were we able to go in and make room for the bier among the storage shelves. When we were done, Käsper knelt down by Timo's head, between some empty barrels, and said a long silent prayer. I didn't want to leave while he was praying, so I stood beside him until he was done. When the five of us emerged from the cellar, we saw that someone had spread spruce branches on the snow in front of it.

I returned to The Foundation with Liiso and Käsper. Mr. Mannteuffel and the officials had completed their task and left—and the door to Timo's study was locked. Anna had come to find me there and had seen the gentlemen leave. She had also noticed that Mr. Mannteuffel used his own key to lock the study door. That didn't surprise me—I had known all along that he had a key. But the key, Timo's own, which I had pocketed after we picked the lock, and which I had later used to open the door for Mr.

Mannteuffel—it was still in my pocket . . . Mannteuffel had used his own key, like the master of the house he now was, and had obviously forgotten that I had another. It's also possible that he remembered and didn't care.

Be that as it may, that key burned in my pocket until the following morning. I couldn't do anything at night because my moving around the house with a candle might have attracted attention. Around six in the morning, when it was light enough, I dressed without rousing Anna and Eeva, went to Timo's study, unlocked the door and locked it again behind me.

The room looked unchanged. No one had done anything about the blood stain on the rug. I stopped in the middle of the room and closed my eyes. There was some notion in the back of my brain, something that had to do with this room, with my visits to it, and with what had happened here. After a moment, I realized what it was.

The curtains that stretched across the wall that had two windows separated by an expanse of about one fathom had been drawn, so that they now covered that expanse entirely. I went over and pulled them apart. Timo's short double-barreled duck gun hung on the wall between the windows. I took it down. The right-hand barrel was loaded with a shotgun cartridge. The left-hand barrel was empty.

I proceeded to examine the windows. The double-glazed one to the left had been carefully insulated for the winter. The cracks had been covered with strips of felt, and gray paper had been glued down over these. Dry reindeer moss had been spread between the double window frames. The uninsulated window to the right was the one that Timo opened several times a day to air out the study. I pulled the handle on the inside window frame, and the window opened. I pushed the outer window. It did not open. I pushed harder, and it flew open—the frame was slightly swollen with humidity, but it had not been latched.

Now it is half past six, and Anna and the child are still asleep next door. We can't go home until Eeva returns.

Well. I have tried to consider every aspect of the matter. I realize that not a single one of the things I have noticed proves anything, but it seems to me that all those things together *oblige me* to form a hypothesis, or perhaps more than one.

I'll write down the one that presently seems the most plausible to me.

From Peter's regular reports, or from some other source, Mr. Benckendorff's office under the Governor General found out that Timo *was writing something*. The office decided to discover what it was. It doesn't take too much thought to realize that this was inevitable: as long as the authorities did not believe that Timo had turned into a complete idiot, the nature of his earlier writings was enough to arouse interest in his present ones. Once that curiosity had been aroused, the office had to find a person who would be able to satisfy it. I would imagine that Peter was the first candidate, since he had already been asked to report on Timo and had complied with the request. Thus, there was no reason not to ask him to procure Timo's manuscripts or a review of their contents. In all likelihood, Peter promised to do, or at least to try to do, this, and he did probably give it a try. I tend to believe that the investigation of Timo's desk he asked me to witness was conducted on his own initiative, *before* he had received any orders. In any case, Timo both obfuscated and protected his writings. I remember the time, four or five years ago, when I asked Timo whether Peter was still interested in his writings, and Timo gave an affirmative answer. At the same time, he let me know that Peter had not been able to *see* those writings.

So—what were the interior mechanics of these events?

Peter got excited by the official suggestion that he should try to find Timo's secret manuscripts. When he didn't succeed, he felt that it would be demeaning to report that he was unable to outwit a man who had been declared mentally incompetent. He decided to put a "nobler" cast on the matter and reported: "I have asked Mr. Bock to show me his writings. Mr. Bock refuses to do so. It is, of course, impossible for me to use force against my own brother-in-law. It is even more impossible for me, as a Mannteuffel and a nobleman, to try to steal his manuscripts from him."

Nevertheless, it is possible that Peter maintained his efforts to find Timo's papers—but, it seems, in vain. Perhaps Benckendorff's office lost interest for a while, but sooner or later that interest revived, and the office decided to find someone else to act on their behalf. There were no likely candidates in Timo's immediate vicinity. (Dear God—if I am right about this, even *I* must have been on their list of people to be considered . . . And thank God they

decided I was unsuitable . . .) But they did find a suitable person.
(They always find a more or less suitable person.) A man who
had served the authorities faithfully and for a long time, if not
always in the most accomplished manner. A man, besides, who
was intimately familiar with Voisiku—who had, in fact, lived in
The Foundation: Mr. Laming.

Mr. Laming came to Voisiku. The former steward had no trouble inventing a pretext for his visit. Did Mr. Mannteuffel know
about his arrival and his assignment? I will assume that he didn't,
and I will assume that his and Elsy's journey to Adavere wasn't
undertaken merely to provide him with a castiron alibi in the event
something happened.

As it turned out, Mr. Laming arrived at a perfect time: Eeva
had gone to Tartu. However, Timo spent a great deal of time in
the house during those days. On the tenth, he left the house for
target practice. Mr. Laming was forced to make a decision: if Timo
went out again for the same purpose on the following day, Laming
had to use that opportunity. On the eleventh, he waited until Timo
went to the park, then entered his study, either with a copy of
the key or by picking the lock. He began to search the room. His
hopes weren't high, but the room was quite familiar to him, since
it had been his bedroom during his days here as a steward. He
had a skeleton key that would enable him to open the desk drawers.
He estimated that he had about two hours: that was how long
Timo usually practiced.

For some reason, Timo interrupted his target practice after half
an hour. He came back to the house, unlocked the study door,
went in, and locked the door again behind him, as was his custom.
He put the pistol case on the desk and opened it in order to clean,
and presumably also to reload, his Kuchenreiters. He took the first
pistol out of the case.

At that time, Laming was—let us say, squatting behind the fire
guard of the tile stove. He had managed to shut the desk drawers
and to erase the most visible signs of his presence. But then Timo's
gaze found him. And recognized him.

What could have happened next? I don't think that Timo would
have decided to kill Laming. In fact, I'm sure he wouldn't have.
But when I recall Timo's playacting that time when Laming was
impersonating Alexander at the shooting range, I think he may

have *pretended* that he'd decided to kill Laming, and with particular pleasure now that he had caught him snooping in his study.

So, Timo said—let's see: "A-ha—Mr. Laming . . ." or, "A-ha—my lord Alexander—now I'll sentence you to death for snooping around here! There will be no appeals! No pardon! And the sentence will be carried out on the spot!" Calmly, he started cleaning his pistol . . . I have noticed that Mr. Laming's nerves are stronger than one might assume; yet they may not have been all that strong. It seems that he had undertaken his mission unarmed—the self-confidence of unimaginative types can be rather inflated. And so, Laming began negotiations for his release. No need to attempt to recreate them. Within a minute or two, Laming realized that his position was weak, probably even fatal. Let's say that Timo told him all arguments were vain. Then the pistol was clean, and Timo opened the desk drawer that contained the cartridges. Laming had been standing between the stove and the right-hand window. Just as he was about to lose his nerve, he remembered something. Timo was looking at the drawer. Laming reached out and took down Timo's duck gun. Maybe he fired immediately. Maybe Timo tried to wrestle the gun away from him and there was a struggle.

The shot attracted the servants' attention and made it impossible for Laming to escape through the door, which was locked from the inside, with Timo's key in the lock. Laming returned the gun to its nail. He looked around. The only way out was through the window that opened onto the shrubbery behind the house. I don't know if Laming found any manuscripts or not, but I suspect he did. I think he had already found them by the time Timo arrived, and he took them along when he made his exit through the window—including, perhaps, the case I had once hidden, with the manuscript I had read.

Oh, Lord—maybe that isn't what happened, at all . . . Maybe I am completely mistaken. There are many questionable spots in my reconstruction. Perhaps my greatest mistake is to drag Laming into the hypothesis. Perhaps Timo's death wasn't caused by his —what did he call them—enquibs? Why did he return from the park after only half an hour? Did a swarm of his equibs attack him and drive him inside? Those equibs that grew out of the wet, dead oak leaves that the gale blew into his face? God, I don't even know where I get my image of them, is it my own invention or did

Timo once tell me about them—black, formless, winged shapes with claws . . . ? Perhaps they pursued him into the house, and it was for *them* that he loaded his pistol with shot? And when they started beating him about his eyes in order to blind him, perhaps he forgot that he would also kill himself if he fired at them. But perhaps he wasn't forgetting anything, never mind Peter's talk about suicide being out of the question: perhaps he remembered, at that moment, something—or everything—with such painful clarity that he *wanted* to hit that pain . . . ? Perhaps he wanted to hit what I saw on his face six weeks ago, after Jüri had left, when he threw his pipe into the fire: "No pipe, no son . . ."

All my ideas about this may be wrong, but I know that I am right about one thing: I know that even if I could prove with absolute certainty that Timo was murdered by Laming, this would not change anything at all. Timo would remain dead, Laming would go free. No matter how complete the evidence against him, he would go free, because he is one of Benckendorff's men.

That is enough reason for me to keep these observations to myself. I also refrain from any action due to another reason, one that seems even more compelling to me. While I believe it is possible that Laming committed this murder, in a more or less premeditated manner, I do not want to be the one to prove it. I don't want to prove that my wife is a murderer's daughter, and my own child the grandchild of a murderer.

Of course, the truth should be established for the sake of history, for the sake of *truth* itself . . . Well, yes, I do remember what I wrote in this journal four years ago when I condemned Mrs. Masing's fears regarding her family's reputation. (The manuscript of Masing's dictionary is still lost.) As soon as a similar thing happens to oneself, it is an *entirely* different matter . . . Anyway: history is history, truth is truth—but a person must have the right to a little ignorance for peace of mind!

At Poltsamaa, the twenty-third of April, '36

Eeva returned from Tartu on the eighteenth. She had stopped at Poltsamaa and knew what had happened. I did not have to explain much to her.

When I gave her the key to the ice cellar, she had a curious look of concentration that made her appear both petrified and radiant. She asked me not to come with her, she wanted to be alone with Timo's body. She was there for almost two hours. When she came back, it was already a little too dark for me to see her face clearly, and when we sat down in the drawing room, she allowed only two candles to be lit. I never could tell if she had shed any tears.

Three days ago, on the twentieth, we finally received permission from Riga to bury Timo. We laid him to rest in the southeastern corner of Kundrusaar Cemetery, next to all the other long-forgotten Bocks—strange in a way, considering *how different* he was from them.

We had been granted permission to bury him in consecrated land, but no speeches were to be made at his grave, and after the hymn, a prayer, and the funeral rites, Pastor Rücker did not have the courage to say a single personal word.

The authorities had also prescribed the time of the burial: eight o'clock at night. Thus, it was already quite dark when we stood by the grave—Rücker, Eeva, Elsy, Käsper, Liiso, Anna, little Eeva, and myself. And, of course Peter and four peasants whom Peter had ordered to lower the coffin into the grave and then to cover it. No one from the village was present. A few peasant children had stopped to peer over the low stone wall of the cemetery.

When we got back to Poltsamaa, late at night, and Anna and little Eeva had gone to sleep, I pulled Timo's memorandum out for the first time in many years and looked through it again. I read, with particular care, the closing paragraphs that followed the draft constitution:

These are the proposals I present to you, before God, to the best of my understanding.

I am completely aware that the enormity of these proposals and the dangers inherent in their realization are repellent to the majority, and that I am destroying myself for a sacrifice many might consider a matter of ridicule.

However, I am not used to paying attention to danger in the pursuit of duty. It is all the same to me what methods may be employed to deprive me of my life's happiness. I do not address myself only to Livonia, I address myself to all of Russia, and it will understand me.

Should, God forbid, some dangerous sparks arise from these well-meaning thoughts, do not fear that the end of the world is at hand.

When all is said and done, humanity's power, for better or worse, is infinitely hollow, and no matter what efforts it may make, whatever extremes it may resort to, it will not make our dear old planet deviate a hairsbreadth from its eternal course. Whether great or small—in the torrent of time, we all disappear and are transformed into the dust that knows neither terror nor joy.

No principles in this world are more enduring than these: Love, Truth, God.

The twenty-fifth of April

Yesterday, Eeva moved from Voisiku to our house here at Poltsamaa. We gave her our fourth, more or less vacant, room, and distributed her possessions in various other parts of the house. It is her intention to purchase a small house in the township in the near future—so she won't get in our way, nor we in hers, as she put it.

The twenty-sixth of May, 1837

Last autumn, Eeva moved into the house she had found in the township. It is a small wooden house with three rooms, right next to the millrace, and whenever I visit there I think that the endless sound of rushing water would make it hard for me to live there. Eeva claims that it helps her stay in harmony with the world. We have not visited Eeva very often, but last night I received a special invitation from her.

Mr. Karl von Bock had arrived at Voisiku and had sent word to Eeva that he would like to pay his respects to his brother's widow. Eeva thought it proper for her brother to be present during Karl's visit.

I had not seen him for many years. He told the coachman to wait by the gate and charged through Eeva's low front door bearing a large bouquet of daffodils. He kissed Eeva's hand and shook mine in a friendly fashion. At the age of forty-six, with his gray mustache and grizzled hair, he looked much more like his older brother than he had fifteen or twenty years ago. And he certainly hadn't lost the Bock family's straightforward nature—in no way embarrassed by my presence, he made this little speech:

"Dear Madame Katharina—a year has passed since events that were tragic for both of us. Our feelings for the living have their rightful place beside our feelings for the deceased. You have known my feelings for you for"—he counted on the fingers of his left hand—"you have known them for twenty years. I beg you to allow me to offer myself as a willing and devoted substitute for my brother."

Eeva turned him down, and she did it calmly and clearly and with sympathy. I don't remember her exact words, but I know that even though they weren't as smooth and prepared as Karl's proposal, they could not be gainsaid. The broad outlines of her response were as follows: In her mind, Karl would always remain only a shadow of his brother. In time, he would find this insufferable, no matter how deeply he respected Timo's memory. And Karl's hopes—that he might eventually rise out of Timo's shadow and become his substitute in Eeva's mind and heart—were, regrettably, vain hopes.

Karl shouted, "But why don't you give yourself time to think it over . . ."

Eeva said, "Karl, it would be irresponsible of me to let you go on hoping."

Then Karl said, in an unexpectedly sincere, kind, and both sad and embarrassed manner, ". . . Well, then, dear Eeva—I accept that . . . I understand you . . . That's all I can say, I do understand you . . . I can't very well start praising my bad fortune . . . So . . . what can I say . . . ? I have to get over this . . ."

In his embarrassment, he tried to light a cigar, then realized the impropriety of that and put the case back in his pocket. Then he had an idea. He had arrived at Voisiku in the morning but had not yet had time to visit the cemetery. He suggested that the three of us visit Timo's grave. Eeva agreed, and we went.

In the carriage, Karl made small talk. He told us about his solitary life in Germany, about his journey to Livonia, and about his plan to visit St. Petersburg for a while. He told us how, one evening, the three of them, Timo and Georg and he (when he was seven or eight years old), had impersonated the devil to *Hofmeister* Lehrberg in order to frighten him, and how Lehrberg had afterwards given them a series of lectures against superstition. But after we had reached the cemetery, which lies only a verst or a verst and a half from Voisiku, and had stood by Timo's grave, and sat on the bench, which Eeva had installed there for her weekly visits to water the flowers and just sit there, Karl pulled himself together and returned to the fray once more. He said:

"Eeva—please believe me—I would never dare to bring up my proposal again—and certainly not here—if I did not *sense* how gladly Timo might approve of it, over there in the Great Beyond—because you wouldn't be left so hopelessly alone—because the one who stands beside you would be a soul so close to Timo himself . . . Of course I know that my brother was a very special person, and I am just an ordinary von Bock . . . But, believe me—"

Eeva resisted him gently. I didn't listen to their conversation but stared at the grave mound in front of us and pondered, with a kind of teasing clarity: how interesting it would be to know what my brother-in-law's grave will look like in a hundred years—will it still bear this cast-iron cross on a marble plinth the size of a coachman's seat? No, that will have rusted away by then . . . Or will there be an honest-to-goodness memorial on this site? Or just brush and the weeds of forgetfulness?

I returned to Eeva's and Karl's exchanges only when Karl asked, with an intensity bordering on irritation:

"But Eeva—the decades ahead of you—what purpose will there be—to your lonely life?"

Eeva picked at a twig of the thornbush growing next to her

bench. Its flowers were hardly budding but its shiny green young leaves had already come out. Eeva said:

"Timo wanted to be an iron nail in the body of the empire . . . Now and again, he needed strong words—and proved his right to use them . . . I've been thinking: Perhaps I, too, might wish that I were—do you know what they call this bush in Estonian? It is 'the slave's whip'—*Sklavenrute*. So—I would like to be a slave's whip in the empire's bosom—as long as I live . . ."

In Tallinn, at the Hotel London,
room number 11,
the fourteenth of June, 1859

So, it's been twenty-two years . . .

And I really don't have anything to say about them. What have they been? A quiet, uneventful, pointless life. Working as a surveyor, earning my bread, even managing to put something aside for a rainy day. And now that rainy day has come . . .

Anna died five years ago, in the autumn, in our garden at Poltsamaa. She stretched out her hand to pick an apple off the tree, sank to the ground, and was gone. Little Eeva is in the sixth year of her marriage to Dr. Pürkson in Tartu. They don't have any children as yet. Big Eeva listens to the sound of the river by the millrace and waters the flowers on Timo's grave.

Soon I will be seventy years old. My health has been poor this last year. My gall bladder, or whatever it may be, is causing me a great deal of discomfort. I don't want to write about that, but it is the reason I am writing.

I have been in Tallinn for a week. The day after tomorrow, I'll take the steamboat to Stettin, and from there I'll travel to Karlsbad, via Berlin. Perhaps it will help. I have one large valise and a gripsack. Yesterday, I sent little Eeva my will, according to which she'll inherit our house at Poltsamaa.

It took me a long time to decide what to do with Timo's memorandum to the Czar. I couldn't give it to Eeva, because it seemed to me that once I had gained possession of that manuscript, I should have given it to Eeva either immediately or at least right after Timo died. I also felt that my keeping the manuscript from her has been a kind of *transgression* against Eeva—one I did not want to confess to her. At the last moment, I overcame my reluctance. As I was saying goodbye to Eeva, or after I had already said goodbye, I stood there for a moment in the hallway of her little Poltsamaa house, the endless sound of rushing water coming through the thin wall . . . I reached under my cape and pulled out the gray sheaf of paper and handed it to her, mumbling:

". . . Eeva—I found these once, in the main building at Voisiku . . . I've kept them all these years—in a crack in the wall, under the floor . . ." (God, yes—even as we confess our crimes we want to emphasize our virtues.) "I know that you, Eeva, will take better care of these than anyone else . . ."

It has taken me until now to decide what to do with my journal.

It would have made no sense to give it to Eeva. I was aware that besides those personal affairs that don't even seem important to myself anymore, everything contained between these covers exists in a more complete form in Eeva's own mind and memory. She has no need to add my view of things to her own. What I'm trying to say is: her understanding of them, even though it may be more personal and narrow in some ways, is nevertheless the more profound one.

I understood ages ago that it would be as wrong to carry this journal abroad as it would have been to take Timo's manuscript with me. If these notes really have any value, they have it here only.

Until this day, I was in a quandary about the fate of this book. I seriously considered burning it in the hotel fireplace if nothing better occurred to me before my departure. But today I found a solution—or rather, it found me.

Today, a navy lieutenant sought me out here at the hotel and brought word from *Jüri*, saying that Jüri had received my letter to him at Kronstadt and that he will visit me tomorrow morning at ten. Three days ago, his flagship arrived in the Navy Harbor at Tallinn. When he comes, I'll give the journal to Jüri. To Rear-Admiral Georg von Bock. However limited the truth presented in my book may be—my dear nephew should have a taste of the vinegar of truth. After all, he has turned forty and may not be as averse to that taste as he once was.

And I conclude—and no one can keep me from concluding:

If Jüri destroys my journal, there is no hope for the world.

If he keeps it, there is hope for the world.

It is a very good thing that I won't know what he'll do.

It gives me a chance to hope even when there may be no hope.

AFTERWORD

SOME READERS WHO SAW the preceding pages in manuscript form expressed the opinion that it might be helpful to include an afterword to guide the reader and shed some light on the question *to what extent* this tale consists of invention, and to what extent it is historical fact.

I realized, only too late, that this was a good suggestion—too late to ask an academic historian to provide an afterword. Such a scholar would have been the only appropriate choice for the task; however, a historian's scholarly sense of responsibility tends to be proportional to the measured pace of his research.

Thus, pressure of time is the main reason why I now attempt to write this afterword myself, yet there is another reason: I was, after all, the first reader of Jakob Mättik's journal, and in reading it I found myself confronted with the same questions concerning the boundary between fact and fancy, to which an afterword should provide answers. In my involvement with the journal, I managed to gain insight into a number of these, and now I feel that it is, indeed, my responsibility to present what I have found to other readers.

I must confess that my stance toward the boundary between fact and fancy in this journal remained rather uncertain in the midst of the chaotic welter of questions, stubborn enigmas, and unexpected answers that the journal provided. There were times when it seemed to me that Jakob Mättik was enticing me into a house of mirrors to dazzle me, the credulous fairgoer, with an array of reflections that wedded well-known facts to ambiguous phantoms. It also struck me that if one were to raise the question of truth and falsehood with regard to this journal, the only way to do that would be to ask: Is there anything at all in the manuscript that cannot be corroborated by, or is clearly contrary to, documentary evidence?

Then it seemed to me that such a procedure would inevitably produce a subjective result, since it would, finally, involve a total or near-total replacement of the boundary between fact and fancy with the boundary that existed between what I was able to verify and that which I had not been able to verify.

A procedure that on its surface would seem to be the opposite —i.e., to simply provide a catalogue of the most essential points I have been able to verify—is actually just as subjective, but in the end it was the one I found preferable. Perhaps for the sole reason that it seemed more reliable with regard to Jakob Mättik.

That being so:

The subjects discussed in Jakob Mättik's journal did exist. The Livonia ruled by Alexander I and Nicholas II, Marquis Paulucci and Count von Pahlen, did exist. The estate at Voisiku exists to this day, although it has been renovated out of recognition. Timotheus von Bock existed. There is even an entry for him in the *Soviet-Estonian Encyclopedia*. Eeva-Kitty-Katharina existed as well, and probably very much in the form in which she appears in the journal. Estonian literature has dealt with her on a few occasions, beginning with Martin Lipp's article in *Estonian Literature* of 1909, and, at least with regard to Eeva, that article did not reveal what Gustav Suits, in another context, has called Martin Lipp's "tendency to blather." By all accounts, Eeva-Kitty-Katharina was identical with the Eeva who, according to the church records at Paistu, was born on the eighth of September, 1799, the daughter of Holstre's coachman, Peeter, and his wife, Anna.

Even Dr. Robst is a historical figure. Seen through Jakob Mättik's eyes, he looks a little different from the figure he cuts in Sophie von Tieck's novel, *Evremont*, in which he also appears as a character. Nevertheless, with the reader's permission, I would choose to regard his brief portrait in the present book, if not more credible, at least more expressive than the one in Frau von Tieck's.

The Moiers' house in Tartu is factual, as were the persons frequenting it and the subjects debated within its walls. I became completely convinced of this during my attempts to verify Jakob Mättik's journal. The small suburban house at the corner of Kalev and Suola streets stood there until the autumn of 1944 (by which time it was quite close to the center of town). Thirty years later, I discovered that it had been this very house, the Moiers' house, in which I lived during my university days. I also realized that my former study chamber was that smoking room facing the garden and the river, and thus its low door lintel then still retained a touch of Timotheus von Bock's fawn-colored hair.

Timo's journey to Riga (journal entry of the sixth of June, 1827) did, it seems, actually take place. Surprisingly enough, an essential part of Timo's conversation with Count von Pahlen has even been documented. This has been pointed out in a small monograph on Bock by the Leningrad historian A. V. Predtechenski, published in Tallinn twenty-five years ago by the Estonian Academy of Arts and Sciences.

Even Timo's "equibs" are documented in one of his letters.

I have not been able to verify Dr. Faehlmann's visit to Voisiku. It is known, however, that Professor Erdmann often sent out his favorite student (i.e., Faehlmann) to visit patients when he was disinclined or unable to travel himself. To doubt the journal's veracity in regard to this incident would be to assume that Jakob Mättik had a prescient notion of its cultural-historical significance.

The details of Timo's arrest, as described in the journal, I have not been able to find anywhere else. Nevertheless, the one detail that strikes one as disproportionate, the Governor General's having supervised that arrest in person, is indeed true and compels one to reevaluate the dimensions and the particular gravity the affair had in its day.

Monsieur La Trobe, as well, is a historical figure who corresponds in all aspects to his description here—although his name was not familiar to anyone at the Estonian Soviet Republic's Theater and Music Museum in 1976.

The family tradition of Timo's oath to the Czar to always tell him the truth is also mentioned by Theodor Bernhardi in his own *Memoirs of Youth*. The Czar's letter to Paulucci was published sixty years after it had been written.

Contrary to any logical expectation, even the grand piano the Czar had installed in Timo's casemate proves to have been factual. This is documented by several reports sent by General Plutalov to Prince Volkonsky. It is also discussed by M. N. Gernet in his book *The History of the Czars' Dungeons*, vol. 1, Moscow, 1960, page 257. Thus it is, even here, necessary to expand one's imagination while exercising one's powers of logic.

The mysterious sixty thousand rubles have been documented in the papers of Voisiku Estate, preserved in the Central Historical Archives of the Estonian Soviet Republic. One may or may not credit Georg von Bock's explanation of the matter. Timo's relationship with Marina Naryshkina is also discussed, in a slightly different light, in an article published in *Russkaya Starina*.

About Timo's brother-in-law, Peter Mannteuffel, it must be said that he, too, existed in a most fateful way; but note that he was, indeed, Peter *Zoege* von Mannteuffel, not to be confused with another Peter Mannteuffel who was the Count of Ravila and whom Estonian literary history honors as the author of *Pastime* and *The Days of Villem Naavi's Life*.

Finally: the text of Timo's memorandum does exist, in a form that corresponds closely to Jakob Mättik's quotes from it, in all its incredible, incontrovertible, and fatal candor. The copy now to be found in a Moscow archive seems to be the original sent by him to the Czar.

I have not found any evidence outside the pages of the journal for the claim that Timo called Alexander I "Tartuffe" to his face, but the text of the "Memorandum" indicates that Timo was capable of doing so in writing.

Eeva's journey to Torma to see Maria Feodorovna is fact. Pastor Asverus's widow *was* present in the waiting room at Torma, and she was accompanied by the ten-year-old son of her daughter, a snub-nosed stripling with protuberant brown eyes. Fifty years later, that boy committed his memory of Eeva's visit to paper, in Dr. Bertram's (i.e., Georg Schultz-Bertram's) volume *Wagien, Baltische Studien und Erinnerungen*, Dorpat (Tartu), 1868, pp. 49 ff.

Georg von Bock's exploit, his visit to Schlüsselburg, receives its verification from an unexpected quarter: a letter from O. W. Masing to Superintendent Sonntag in Riga.

Eeva's written agreement to take responsibility for Timo's debt is preserved in Tartu at the Central Historical Archives among the Voisiku papers.

I have not succeeded in finding any outside documentation for Eeva's meeting with Zhukovski in Tartu, but it is known that Zhukovski visited Tartu at the indicated time and gave his friends a reading from his translation of *The Maid of Orléans*.

At first sight, "Plutalov," the name of the general who was the governor of Schlüsselburg, looks like a heavy-handed touch of irony on Jakob Mättik's part—since its translated meaning would be something like thief, swindler, or shyster. Perhaps in part because of his official task, the general's character was apparently much closer to the impression given by such a name than to the almost chivalrous figure in Georg von Bock's description. However, a selection of documents bearing the general's own signature prove that the ironist was not Jakob Mättik, but history itself: the name of the commandant of Schlüsselburg was, indeed, Plutalov. How extravagant history can be in its sense of irony (in forms that would be considered unforgivably exaggerated were they to appear in works of literature but must be seen as happy accidents when they are produced by history) may be observed in certain small but flintily undeniable facts—such as the one that during this same period, the Governor of Petropavlovsk Fortress was a General Sukin (i.e., General "Bitch").

Goethe's occasional poem to Timo can be found in all comprehensive editions of his works. W. von Bock has written about Timo's tragic saber stroke that injured one of his own soldiers. It would seem boorish to doubt that the recipient of that stroke turned out to be Tiit of Näresaar.

The letters of Georg von Bock and Eeva to Nicholas I, drafts of which Jakob Mättik copied into his journal, have survived and

can be found among the documents concerning Timo's imprisonment, in which can also be found many letters and fragments
that do not appear in the journal and serve, in one way or another,
as corollary material to the journal's narrative. One of these, a
letter written by Timo, was pointed out to me by Dr. Juhan Kahk,
who had found it in the archives of the Bergs of Sangaste Estate.
It is dated the fifth of September, 1817, and concerns Timo's
marriage. Its opening lines are worth quoting here:

Gracious Aunt,

My respectful thanks for the reception you have given
Eeva in your home; she will leave there today, because
tonight, on an anniversary that I regard as important,
she shall receive my ring. In a few brief hours, she will
no longer be a peasant girl but, irrevocably, my bride.
She must leave Uus-Poltsamaa because it would be un-
reasonable to demand that you should suddenly greet as
your equal the same creature whom you have till now
regarded as so much inferior to yourself. Of course you
will ask what I propose to do with her in the future,
since I readily admit that my marriage will neither make
me your equal nor your inferior? Well, what would you
say, Dear Aunt, if we [she and I] were to proceed a little
ahead [of all others]?!

To return to the documentary material presented in the journal:
it may be necessary to warn the reader of the danger inherent in
the remarkably exact presentation of this material. It may engender
greater confidence in the journal than such an ultimately subjective
piece of writing truly deserves.

Monsieur La Trobe's conflict with the authorities ("And I hope
I'll never have anything to do with those gentlemen again") is also
discussed in an article dealing with his biography, which appeared
in issue number 58 of *Baltische Monatshefte*, but it is fully explained
only in Jakob Mättik's journal.

Timo's letter to His Illustriousness, Burkhard Christoforovich,
as well as some of his subsequent papers, perhaps become a little
more credible when we recall Dr. Schultz-Bertram's words, from

his aforementioned book: "I have had in my possession some letters of his [i.e., Timotheus Bock's] in which whimsy and lofty strokes of genius so alternate with incomprehensible sentences that the reader is tempted to regard his insanity as a charade."

The well-known and mysterious tale of the disappearance of the manuscript of O. W. Masing's great Estonian–German dictionary is sadly corroborated by Jakob Mättik's journal, which does not cast any new light on it. The announcement in the *Dörptsche Zeitung* did appear, with its appeal to the possessor of the manuscript to redeem himself by returning that wonderful storehouse of language. We have waited in vain, and with diminishing hopes, these one hundred and fifty years.

Most of the details of Timo's death can be verified in numerous official sources that have been preserved and prove the journal to be sufficiently accurate. Nevertheless, not even the journal provides a satisfactory explanation for the mysterious pellet cartridge, although Jakob Mättik does stress the enigmatic nature of the event, and even goes some distance toward explaining it. Again, one may choose to believe or disbelieve his hypothesis.

Georg von Bock (the younger), the Jüri of the journal, did not become First Lord of the Imperial Russian Admiralty, but he did achieve the rank of rear-admiral. What's more, he became the nautical mentor of the Grand Dukes, and the confidant of Grand Duke Vladimir Nikolayevich. Yet he seems to have respected the memory of his father. Outside the pages of the journal, one piece of evidence of this is an article published in Moscow in 1859: it is N. P. Lyzhin's essay "On Zhukovski's Familiarity with the Views of the Romantic School"—as far as we know, the only piece of writing published during the reign of the Czars in which extensive mention is made of Timotheus von Bock. It is a very interesting text and seems almost schizophrenic, in that the author seems to pursue two very different goals: on one hand, there is the superficial intention, respectful of censorship, to discuss Zhukovski, on the other, the hidden intention to tell the reader as much about Bock as possible. In many matters concerning Bock, this article is the only extant source—for the sole reason that Jüri put at the author's disposal some papers of his father's which he had preserved with filial piety.

Jüri's wife, Anna Dmitriyevna Ignatyeva, was the daughter of a major-general who owned an estate in the government of Samara. They were married in 1847 and had at least one daughter and two sons.

In June, 1876, Jüri accompanied Grand Duke Vladimir, as his chamberlain, on a journey to Schwerin in Germany to visit the family of the Grand Duke of Mecklenburg-Schwerin—Vladimir's wife was the Grand Duke's daughter. At Schwerin Castle, Jüri died suddenly on the twelfth of June, 1876, according to the local newspapers from an embolism in his lungs.

And, finally: Eeva had gone to her final rest long before Jüri's demise. She died at Poltsamaa on the third of May, 1862, of the Old Calendar, at the age of sixty-two, and was buried on the seventh by the Orthodox priest Simeon Popov in the Lutheran cemetery at Voisiku next to her husband.

★   ★   ★

Some perceptive readers of Jakob Mättik's journal have also expressed the opinion that its author appears to be a rather mediocre soul. It seems to me that no matter how low an estimate the journal, in all its old-fashionedness, may now receive as a literary work, seen against the background of the thirties or even fifties of the nineteenth century, its fate should be a little more favorable—and by extension, likewise the fate of its writer, if indeed there is some kind of measurable reciprocity at work between books and their writers. As far as the journal as a collection of facts is concerned, J. M.'s disillusioned self-image only enhances its reliability.

★   ★   ★

The book's translation into Finnish gave me the opportunity to add yet another footnote. In Stockholm in October, 1979, Mrs. Margarethe Weckman, *née* von Bock, presented me with copies of the large genealogical work *Bockiana*. From these notes, made in 1935 at the Uue-Pernu Manor in Estonia, it becomes apparent that according to family tradition, Timo's grandmother, Helene von Schultze (born in Moscow on the twelfth of August, 1722; died at Voisiku on the fourteenth of August, 1783), was the daughter of the imperial lady-in-waiting Sophie von Fick and Czar Peter the Great. What this means is that Timo was in all likelihood aware of the fact that he was a great-grandson of Peter the Great.

Unfortunately, Jakob Mättik seems not to have been aware of this. Had he known it, there can be no doubt in my mind that he would have derived Timo's tendency to go to extremes (e.g., his curiously independent attitude toward Czar Alexander) not only from the originality of Timo's cast of mind but also from the self-esteem Timo gained from the knowledge that he, Timo, was a more direct descendant of, and in any case a whole generation closer to, the greatest representative of the Romanov family than his kinsman, Alexander.

NOTES

38 *"Madame—ich muss gestehen . . ."* (German)   "Madame—I have to admit: rarely do rumors prove so entirely accurate as the rumor that you are an extraordinary enchantress!"

38 *"Mais voilà—quels . . ."* (French)   "Now, then—what are your problems?"

45 **Curonus** (Latin)   Courlander.

50 **"Eher werde ich . . ."** (German)   "I'd rather say my prayers in a cowshed! At least you know where you are, there!"

55 *"Gardez!"* (French)   "Check!"

56 **Ahnung und Gegenwart** (German)   *Premonition and Presence.*

57 *"ce plat aventurier italien . . ."* (French)   "This insignificant Italian adventurer, perjurer, whose every decoration is a reminder of some dirty deed."

59 *"je dois vous prier de parler . . ."* (French)   "I must ask you to speak a comprehensible language."

62 *"Timothée, mon ami"* (French)   "Timotheus, my friend."

77 **the name defined the man**   See the discussion of Plutalov's name in the Afterword.

77 »Режим, уважаемая госпожа, конечно тот, который они своими престплениями заслужили.« (Russian)   "The regime, dear lady, is of course the one they have earned with their crimes."

84 **"Ich bin Frau Katharina . . ."** (German)   "I am Mrs. Katharina von Bock from Voisiku."

103 *eine stattliche Figur* (German)   A handsome figure.

103 **Hofmeister** (German)   Tutor.

104 **geborene** (German)   Born; *née.*

109 *friherrar* (Swedish)   barons

124 **"Holà-là—Monsieur le Comte . . ."** (French)   "Ooh-la-la—Count . . . Whence this honor?"

151 **"Son Altesse Impériale . . ."** (French)   "Her Imperial Highness has the pleasure of asking . . ."

152 **"Und Sie sind mir also . . ."** (German)   "And, you, dear sir, are the second marvelous specimen . . ."

155 **even their name. . .**   *"Bock"* in German means "ram," also "stubborn."

171   В старыхъ книгахъ
                       Случилосъ мне читатъ, что неразлучны
                       Любовъ и рьщарская доблестъ были . . .

                       If I read the old books right, love
                       Always goes with noble deeds of chivalry . . .

172   Когда же то, что я сказала, свято ——
Кто мог внущитъ его мне кроме неба?
Кто мог сойти ко мне в мою долину,
Чтобъı дуще неопытной открытъ
Великую властителей науку?

But if what I tell you is good, where else
But from on high could I receive it?
Who would have come to a poor girl
In a pasture to initiate her in the affairs
Of kings? I have never stood before
Great princes, I do not know
How to make speeches. But now
That I must persuade you, now
I have the skill to understand greatness,
Now the destinies of lands and kings
Are crystal clear to my childish eyes
And I speak thunderbolts.

180   *laesio optionis* (Latin)   A crime committed without understanding.
180   *laesio majestatis* (Latin)   A crime against the Crown, lèse-majesté.
186   *Jetzo, da ich ausgewachsen . . .*

Now, grown up, I've read and traveled
Through the world from cliff to coast,
And my heart puts all its faith now
Firmly in the Holy Ghost—

He who wrought the greatest wonders
With still greater yet to be,
Smashed the citadels of despots
And the yoke of slavery—

Healed the mortal wounds of ages,
Put the rights of old in place:
All men are created equal
In a single noble race.

(Heinrich Heine, translated by Hal Draper, in *The Complete Poems of
Heinrich Heine*, Oxford University Press, Oxford, 1982)
192   *Cherchez la femme!* (French)   Look for the woman! (I.e., there is a
woman behind everything.)
208   *An Herrn Obristleutnant von Bock . . .*

Of all the things that may happen,
If I am to be honest,
To see Cossacks here
Wasn't exactly what I'd hoped for.
But when the tremendous flood
Broke through the dam that protected us
And beat upon us, wave on wave,
Your Cossack was a welcome sight.

215   *angina maligna sive gangraenosa* (Latin)   A malign condition of pain or gangrene.

230   *Gerichtsassessor* (German)   Junior barrister.

237   *Ordnungsrichter* (German)   Town judge.

263   *eine vom Himmel gegebene . . .* (German)   An apparition given to us by Heaven, a noble woman who, God willing, can be born anywhere . . . An entirely exceptional woman.

264   *"Wie heisst eigentlich 'Brüderlichkeit' . . . "* (German)   The exchange is based on a mistaken derivation for the Estonian word for "sister-hood": the correct form, *oelikkus*, is derived from the root "sister," whereas the root for *oelus* is *oel*—"bad," or "evil." Thus, the conversation goes: "What is the Estonian word for brotherhood?" I said: *"Vendlus."* He asked: "And sisterhood?" Someone said: "Well, I suppose it would have to be *oelus* . . ." And Timo asked: "But what is *oelus* in German?" Disingenuously, Mrs. Schwalbe, who really hadn't been following our conversation, chimed in: "Evil." Whereupon Timo patted Elsy's cheek and exclaimed: "There you are, that's it—my dear sister!"

274   *Quod erat probandum* (Latin)   Which was to be proved.

277   *sac-voyage* (French)   Traveling bag.

291   *Erlaucht* (German)   Illustrious, noble.

307   *"Herrschaften!"* (German)   "Ladies and gentlemen!"

307   *"Donnerwetter!"* (German)   "Damn (or blast) it!" (Literally: thunderstorm.)

311   *il grandissimo bluffo* (Italian)   The greatest swindler.

311   *porco* (Italian)   Swine.

322   *"Na—geh. Und werde . . ."* (German)   "Well—go. And become what you will become."